ANARCHY ON THE STREETS OF LOS ANGELES

In a flash Christina wondered if they just wanted her bike. Should she drop it and run? But on foot she would be completely powerless.

The gap between her and her pursuers was down to three or four seconds and closing. A sob slipped from her lips. There was no escape.

Unless . . .

No time to analyze the risk.

Two cars ahead she saw the telltale dampness on the ground. She prayed the bacteria were still eating, still dumping their flammable waste. While moving, she lifted a foot from the pedal and reached for the kickstand. The metal stake popped into place. She steered the bike as close as she could to the side of the car. The men were almost upon her, shouting and lunging for her backpack. She allowed the bike to tilt slightly. The kickstand scraped along the ground. The bike wobbled but kept going. She turned sharply around the front of the car, encouraging the men to cut close around the fender.

The hydrogen flame she'd ignited was invisible but devastatingly hot. She never knew whether it caught one or both of the men. She pedaled away from the screams and didn't look back.

PETROPLAGUE

AMY ROGERS

PETROPLAGUE is a work of fiction. Characters and events are products of the author's imagination although much of the science content is based on fact.

First edition October 2011
Second edition July 2013

ISBN: 978-1-940419-00-8 (paperback)
ISBN: 978-1-4670-3826-3 (hardcover)
ISBN: 146703827X (ebook)
ASIN: B00ARDB8R4 (Audiobook)

Library of Congress Control Number: 2011917108

Science Educators: a PETROPLAGUE study guide is available. Visit http://ScienceThrillers.com or http://AmyRogers.com for details.

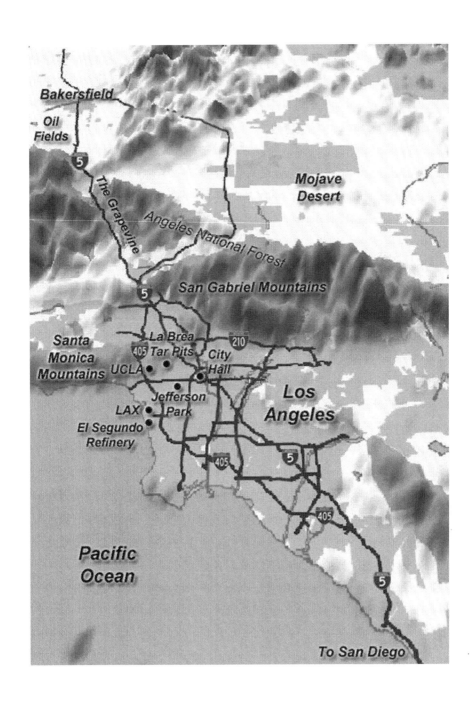

CHAPTER 1

Being tall helped Neil reach inside the Dumpster. The stench of warm, rotting garbage and the buzzing of flies didn't faze him. From experience he knew that this particular trash container, situated behind an AM/PM convenience store, was a reliable source of still-sealed, barely-expired sandwiches and burritos. On a good night, he could find dinner without even having to climb in.

His fingers touched a polyethylene food package and he fished out a previously-frozen Hot Pocket, then a Lean Cuisine chicken and rice entrée.

Disgusting. Not only in Los Angeles, but from sea to shining sea: rampant consumption, egregious waste.

A rasping sound came from behind the Dumpster and a filthy, bent-over man appeared. One of thousands who camped in dry canals and under freeways in L.A., the homeless wretch exhaled intoxicating fumes, his hungry eyes fixed on Neil's catch. Neil looked with pity on the man's mental and physical brokenness. This, too, America had thrown away. He handed the Hot Pocket to the man, who offered a toothless smile and staggered away.

Dumpster diving is un-American.

Neil strolled out of the dark alley, as young, strong, and sane as the transient was not. He was neither homeless nor destitute. Dumpster diving was his moral choice.

He sat on a bench at a bus stop, eating and enjoying the dry warmth of a July night in Southern California. He knew only ten miles away, on the coast, the weather was quite different. At that very moment, a chilly, damp marine layer probably covered his father's house.

How appropriate.

He checked his watch. Quarter to two. Axel should be here in fifteen minutes.

A girl in a red miniskirt and four-inch stilettos swayed her hips down the sidewalk, parading in the glare of the streetlights. An LAPD cruiser drove by and she scurried to the shadows like a cockroach.

He adjusted the Chico State hoodie he was wearing to make the letters more clearly visible. In this part of L.A., high school dropouts far outnumbered university graduates. A bit of shabby collegiate apparel from a town five hundred miles away was an easy way to identify himself to Axel.

They'd never met and knew little about each other. That's how the organization worked.

He found himself staring at the girl. She looked sixteen going on thirty. Though he was probably six years older than she was, she made him feel immature. He wondered what Pops would say if he brought home a girl like that. Dear old dad was a useful barometer of subversiveness; the paterfamilias thought flip-flops were an assault on decency, and he was proportionately outraged by most anything else. When Neil pierced his nose, the old man shrieked. When he dreadlocked his long, sandy-brown hair, the old man made threats. When he dropped out of college, the old man kicked him out of the house and cut him off. Neil found it all very satisfying. He never saw his father anymore.

Now he tested himself against bigger foes.

A silver Chevy Malibu pulled up to the curb. He smoothed the front of his sweatshirt. The girl in the miniskirt glided forward. He intercepted her before she reached the car door.

"I saw him first," she said.

"He's not here for you," Neil said.

The passenger window opened and Neil leaned in. The driver was a heavy-set, middle-aged man with a beard that nearly covered the scar in front of his right ear.

"Ready, Chico?" the driver said.

"Ready."

He stepped over a trickle of urine dribbling down the gutter toward a storm drain and climbed into the car with Axel.

His accomplice was older than he expected—probably in his fifties, at least as old as Pops. All the radicals Neil knew were youths. It made sense; Axel was probably a skilled freelancer, not a dedicated militant. For Neil, direct action was a passion; for Axel, it might be just a job.

"You got the address?" Axel said as the girl turned her back to them and they drove away.

"I got it but it wasn't easy. You wouldn't believe how many derelict gas stations there are in Jefferson Park."

"You sure you got the right one? If I have to do this twice, it's gonna cost you."

"I'll know when we get there. There won't be any mistake."

He spoke with false authority and glanced at the black duffel bag in the back seat.

"The detonator's up here," Axel said, patting a satchel on the armrest. "I always keep 'em separate until the end."

Neil swallowed and withdrew his arm into his lap. The wind slapped his face as the Chevy accelerated up an on-ramp, awakening his senses, heightening his anticipation. At night, a car could actually reach full speed on an L.A. freeway. They covered the mile and a half to the exit in less than two minutes.

In this part of the city, there was none of the famed Hollywood glamour. They drove down a street lined with thrift shops, space available signs, and billboards demanding to know if you'd been injured in an automobile accident. A paper McDonald's bag and cup lay squashed in front of a payday loan outlet, ketchup squirted like blood on the sidewalk. They traveled about ten blocks without speaking. The scenery didn't improve.

"Up ahead, on the left," he said.

Rush Limbaugh once suggested that environmental wackos were to blame for the Deepwater Horizon explosion in the Gulf of Mexico. Neil chuckled. The hypocritical old windbag had cried wolf. No sensible person would listen if he made such an accusation again.

Even if this time, he was right.

Axel made a U-turn and parked under a burned-out streetlight half a block from the abandoned gas station. While Axel gathered his gear, Neil stepped out of the car and scanned the area for witnesses. The block was empty.

He walked onto the disused property and wished Pops could see him now.

Vandals and thieves had stripped the CaliPetro station of everything valuable. All the windows were smashed. Gashes in the walls marked where the copper wiring had been ripped out. But he wasn't interested in the old building. Instead, he focused on the pavement behind the graffiti-covered gas pumps.

"Ain't much left," Axel said as he joined Neil in the shadows. "Don't look like you need my talents to finish it off."

"The target is the underground storage tank, not the building."

They walked past overgrown oleander shrubs that ringed the station, stepping on a carpet of pink flower petals.

Axel stopped. "You hear something?"

Neil listened. Soft rustling and babbling sounds were coming from behind a rusty propane tank. He crept closer to see who—or what—was hidden there.

A dirty sleeping bag and a shopping cart told him all he needed to know.

"It's some homeless nut job," he said. "Probably schizo. Don't worry about it."

He turned on a flashlight and skipped the beam across the pavement until it landed on a vented hole cover about eight inches in diameter.

"There it is," he said and padded to the spot. Axel handed him a tool and held the light while Neil pried open the cover and peered into the hole.

"Jackpot," he said.

"This is the one?"

"Absolutely. I can see the electronics. Digital readout, probably a pressure monitor."

Axel returned the flashlight to Neil and rummaged through his duffle bag. The crazy guy behind the propane tank cursed and muttered nonsense about green cars and the circus. Neil ignored him. He felt giddy. This was his biggest operation yet for Earth Jihad. If it succeeded, they might make him a Cell Leader.

"Package is ready for delivery," Axel said. He held up a homemade, tube-shaped explosive device.

"Dude, are you sure that's going to work?" Neil said. The pipe bomb was smaller than he imagined.

"Nah, it'll never work. Why don't you fix it," Axel said and pretended to toss the device at him.

He fell for the ruse and ducked. The bomb maker laughed at him.

"Don't worry, this baby'll mess things up. Plus there's gas down there. After we're done there won't be anything left."

"Good. We want to teach them a lesson they won't forget."

Cautiously, Axel slid his device into the hole and set the timer on the detonator. Neil replaced the cover.

"Five minutes," Axel said.

They sprinted for the car and sped off into the night.

*   *   *

The homeless man living behind the propane tank cursed the strange men for invading his territory. When they were gone, he cursed them for leaving. He crawled into his sleeping bag, cursing everything and nothing.

His eyes had only just closed when an explosion jolted him awake. The earth trembled and the metal disk that covered the underground storage tank was blown high into the air. It fell and clattered on the concrete. Blue flames shot like a geyser from the hole in the pavement, casting heat and a hellish light. The homeless man screamed and cast aside his sleeping bag as if it were on fire. For once, the discordant voices in his head spoke in unison. He ran away tearing his hair, looking every bit like the madman he was.

CHAPTER 2

Stinking black tar squeezed Christina's legs and held them fast. If she sank much deeper, it would be impossible to pull them out. Thick and hot, the asphalt bubbled and oozed around her, embracing the athletic young woman in the same murderous grip that had claimed the lives of countless creatures over tens of thousands of years.

Coffee-colored bones littered the pit where Christina stood, macabre proof of the tar's tenacity. The bones were all that remained of extinct animals that were trapped in the goo and died of dehydration millennia ago. The tar preserved their remains, just as it would Christina's if she didn't escape. She wondered how long her one-liter water bottle would keep her alive.

Until lunchtime, she thought, cheerily taking a swig.

"Chrissy! Is that your phone?" a female voice shouted from a nearby equipment shed.

Christina listened and could just make out the tinny notes of the ring tone she'd assigned to her cousin River.

"It's my cousin again. Can you turn it off for me?"

"Doesn't she know you're here?"

"She knows," Christina said. *But the world revolves around River, so what difference does it make if I'm knee-deep in hydrocarbon muck?*

"I'll take care of it. Is it the red button?"

"Yes, thanks, Linda."

"Be down in a sec."

Christina González tightened the ponytail which secured her glossy, shoulder-length black hair away from her face. She stood in a hole fourteen feet below the grassy lawn of Hancock Park. Down here she was shaded from L.A.'s midday summer sun, but Excavation Pit 91 was still hot. The air temperature on Wilshire Boulevard that day was at least eighty-five degrees and the tar itself was warm, radiating primal heat it had carried to the surface from its origin deep inside the earth.

Just another Saturday at Rancho La Brea, she thought. This morning before leaving the apartment, River had told her again what a geek she was. River maintained that a twenty-six-year-old Latina should spend her free time volunteering for socially responsible causes, not mucking around in asphalt seeps.

"Make change for the future, Chrissy. Don't waste time on the past," River had said.

But Christina was a scientist (at least in training), and she knew that understanding the past was crucial to predicting the future. Studying the environment and ecosystem of Los Angeles forty thousand years ago was actually quite relevant to contemporary models of climate change. True, her Saturday hobby was a bit geeky, but it was also challenging and fun and important.

Not to mention really messy.

"Ready for some help?" Linda asked as she emerged from the shed wearing asphalt-encrusted boots.

"As always," Christina said to the more experienced volunteer who was her mentor at the La Brea Tar Pits.

That famous name amused Christina, who spoke fluent Spanish and knew it literally meant "The Tar Tar Pits." But a slightly out of kilter name seemed appropriate for this place. Incongruously located in the crowded and affluent Miracle Mile district of downtown Los Angeles, La Brea was an untamed piece of Earth's ancient past. Amidst civilization and luxury, it represented the savagery of raw nature. The first time she descended into Pit 91 she felt the urge to cross herself; she was entering an apocalyptic scene. The pit, with its sulfurous fumes and blackened bones, was grotesque and disturbing like a Hieronymus Bosch painting hanging on the walls of the sleek Los Angeles County Museum of Art, which stood only a few hundred yards away.

A few tourists were gathered on the observation platform above Pit 91 to watch the excavation. They stared as Linda awkwardly climbed down a ladder into the pit, whose rectangular walls were shored up by filthy, tar-stained wooden boards. The bottom of the pit was partially covered by a plywood floor. The open part of the pit floor, where Christina stood in a puddle of gently simmering asphalt, was divided into three-square-foot sections by a grid of metal wires suspended over the tar like clotheslines. About a dozen five-gallon buckets, stained black with tar, stood nearby.

Linda joined her at the grid section where the dig was active. Over the course of about two weeks, volunteers would excavate only this one square, to a depth of six inches. Christina knew the tourists would be disappointed by the tedious pace of real-time fossil hunting.

"They're hoping you'll pull out an entire mastodon skeleton while they watch," Linda said softly.

"Right, with my magic dental pick," Christina said, waving one of the small tools that she used for the work.

Linda waved to the onlookers and cleared her throat to deliver her standard educational speech.

"Welcome to Pit 91. Currently, this is the only ongoing excavation at La Brea. The fossils found in these tar seeps over the past hundred years include many extinct species of Ice Age mammals that you might recognize: sabertoothed cats, dire wolves, mammoths and mastodons. While these big finds are real trophies, less charismatic life forms—like plants, seeds, and insects—are equally important to science. That's why instead of using a back hoe to dig up big chunks of asphalt, the volunteer paleontologists at La Brea use these small chisels and toothbrushes to find evidence of even the tiniest living things."

As usual, the visitors' attention quickly strayed. A toddler broke free from his mother and she left the platform, chasing after him. The remaining visitors pointed at things and talked among themselves. Then one of them asked, "Have you got any dinosaurs?"

Christina saw Linda roll her eyes ever so slightly as she answered this question for the umpteenth time.

"There aren't any dinosaur bones in the La Brea tar seeps. Dinosaurs became extinct sixty-five million years before the record here begins."

The man muttered something and moved on. The others on the platform looked down at the women as if they were animals in a zoo exhibit; they waited for them to growl or pounce or eat. Linda abandoned the natural history lesson and joined Christina at the dig.

"Let's get to it," Linda said. "I'm feeling lucky today."

But before Christina dipped a small trowel into the tar, she was interrupted by what sounded like the world's largest belch.

"What was that?"

Linda frowned. "Sounded like a gas bubble, but it was too big."

The sound repeated, a deep, resonant belch followed by a higher-pitched tinkling sound, like rain. A group of teenagers dashed onto the observation platform. They giggled and tittered with excitement.

"What's going on?" Christina shouted up to the crowd.

A middle-aged gentleman who looked like a high school teacher answered.

"The pool is spitting tar."

"What?"

Christina and Linda exchanged an incredulous look.

"That's impossible," Linda said.

"It happened," the man replied, "and I'll tell you, it's freaking us out."

"I have got to see this," Christina said.

The women abandoned their voluntary task and climbed out of the pit. In the shed, they quickly removed their boots and gloves, and dressed in street clothes. Christina noticed an asphalt smudge on her arm but ignored it for now. There wasn't any point in cleaning up as she expected to return to the pit to work for another hour or two.

"You hear anything?" Linda asked.

"No. I hope we didn't miss it."

Christina sprinted effortlessly up the path toward the Lake Pit, her legs well-toned from running and cycling. Aside from the

Page Museum, which displayed La Brea's unparalleled Ice Age fossil collection, Lake Pit was Hancock Park's main attraction: an enormous pool of bubbling tar that sat just a few yards off busy Wilshire Boulevard. She noticed a pattern of black droplets on the grass between the asphalt lake and the paved path that curled around it.

Wow, the lake did splatter pretty far.

"Have you ever seen this before?" she asked Linda.

"No, and I've been volunteering here for twelve years. We sometimes see fresh tar seeps in the grass. They come and go. But I've never seen the Lake Pit splash all the way up here."

The summer Saturday crowd at La Brea had dispersed when the lake acted up, but the more curious souls were again gathering at the ten-foot-tall wrought-iron fence that surrounded the lake. Christina approached cautiously, listening for unusual noises, and ready to run if necessary. At first, Lake Pit looked the same as always: black, sinister, and boiling with a rainbow-hued scum of oil floating on top. The life-sized statue of a female Columbian mammoth was frozen in a dramatized struggle to escape the murderous lake while a distressed baby and a daddy mammoth looked on from solid ground. The traffic on Wilshire Boulevard flowed past, oblivious.

"The pit looks normal now," Linda said.

Christina studied the lake with an analytical eye. The rate and size of bubbles popping at the surface seemed close to average, maybe a little more vigorous than usual, but she saw nothing like the size of the bubble that must have caused the spill. She stepped closer.

Contrary to what many visitors thought, the tar pits at La Brea were *not* boiling. In the summer, the tar was warm but not hot. The bubbles that continuously disturbed the surface of the Lake Pit were not filled with water vapor, like a pot of soup cooking on a stove. Instead, the bubbling was caused by rising gases produced by oil-eating bacteria. The bacteria lived underground in the Salt Lake Oil Field, a petroleum reservoir deep in the sedimentary rock upon which Los Angeles sits. Various components of the crude oil in the field escaped to the surface around Rancho La Brea through natural fissures in the rock. The accompanying gases floated to the top of the asphalt and burst into the atmosphere as bubbles in the "boiling" tar.

Christina had been waiting for a chance to tell some school kids on a field trip that the bubbles were bacteria farts. Today, she was puzzled by the magnitude of the fart required to expel asphalt fifteen feet from the edge of the tar seep. If the bubble had risen in the middle of the lake, then the droplets had flown even further.

"Chrissy—" Linda said, putting her hand on Christina's arm.

She followed Linda's anxious gaze to a distant corner of Lake Pit. A smooth, colorful dome was rising in the tar like an oily balloon. It was the largest gas bubble she'd ever seen at La Brea, and when it burst it sprinkled the onlookers on that side of the lake with tar. A girl shrieked and the people scattered, but before any of them had traveled more than a few steps, a second bubble appeared.

In what seemed like slow motion, this bubble grew wider and wider until she thought the surface tension couldn't possibly hold it together a millisecond longer. Then the bubble exploded. The sound reminded her of an ocean wave plunging into a blowhole—a low-pitched, almost musical blast followed immediately by the slopping sound of erupting liquid.

This time, the tar didn't sprinkle the crowd. It rained down in a torrent, a momentary geyser of sticky asphalt that washed over a few unlucky visitors and coated them like victims of a mishap at a molasses factory.

"Dear God!" Christina said, and instinctively dashed into the melee to help.

About a dozen people dripping with tar fled toward the shelter of the Page Museum, leaving black footprints on the path. Christina approached a group of three drenched individuals who seemed rooted to the spot. She guessed they were a family, two adults with a child. They each were covered with tar on one side. The child was wearing a baseball cap which mercifully had shielded his face from the worst of it; she could see he was a boy. His parents' faces, however, were completely tarred. Their eyes were closed, and they were gasping for breath through open mouths, lips black, arms extended and hands turned upward in a gesture of helpless supplication.

She had to get them away from the pit in case the blast was repeated.

"Hurry, this way," she said, grasping an outstretched hand from each blind adult and towing them to safety. "Come on," she encouraged the boy, who followed.

Zombie-like, they stumbled away from the pit until Christina felt they were out of danger. The adults gagged and moaned. The tar was choking them. Seeing no alternative, Christina swallowed her modesty and removed her shirt. She used the cotton tee to wipe tar from the eyes and nose of the one who appeared to be mom. Linda, who was now at her side, hesitated a moment, then pulled off her shirt and did the same for dad.

The boy tugged at a clean corner of his mother's shorts and pleaded over and over, "Mama? Mama?"

As the woman recovered her vision and began to breathe normally, she dropped to her knees to examine her son. The man, too, shook off his catalepsy and turned anxiously to his family.

Meanwhile, sirens wailed at the park's front entrance on Wilshire, and emergency workers poured into Hancock Park.

"Are you okay?" Christina asked the woman, handing her the ruined shirt. The woman nodded vigorously but didn't speak. She spat out a discolored glob of saliva and rubbed her son's hands with the soiled fabric.

A pair of EMS workers jostled Christina and Linda aside and took over care of the tarred family. Now standing uselessly on the fringe of the excitement, Christina crossed her arms to cover her partial nakedness. Her determined efforts to exercise and stay fit kept the natural curviness of her contours in check, but she didn't relish putting her body on display.

"Didn't expect to do a striptease today," Linda said. "I think there are some old undershirts in the Pit 91 shed."

"Let's get out of here," Christina said.

They returned to the shed, staying far away from the Lake Pit. Christina poured some solvent on a towel to clean the tar off her skin. Linda found the undershirts—dirty, worn cast-offs donated for use as rags. They smelled foul, but Christina had little choice and put one on.

"Not exactly red carpet wear, but I suppose it does the job," Linda said, using a small mirror to check her face for tar droplets.

"What does it mean?" Christina asked. The adrenaline rush was over, and her scientific mind was taking control.

"It means I won't see you next weekend," Linda said. "I'm sure they'll close La Brea until someone can explain what happened."

They stepped out of the shed and for a moment watched the activity and flashing lights over by Lake Pit and the museum. Christina tried to make sense of the exceptional event.

So much gas erupting from the pit, she thought. Why?

One of her Ph.D. research projects at UCLA had to do with the petroleum geology of the Los Angeles basin, so she knew quite a bit about asphalt seeps and underground crude oil. But nothing in her experience or knowledge could explain such a large deviation from the normal pattern of gas flow at Rancho La Brea.

"I'll ask my P.I. about it," she said.

"You have your own private eye?" Linda asked in confusion.

"No, no, not that kind of P.I. My principal investigator. That's what we graduate students call our boss. He might know if there's been some seismic activity or something to explain this."

Then she sniffed the air.

"Do you smell anything, Linda?"

"This disgusting shirt. But other than that, just the usual. A whiff of rotten eggs."

"Hydrogen sulfide gas," Christina said. "There's always some of it around here. But it doesn't seem any stronger than usual, even after those big bubbles."

"No, it doesn't," Linda agreed.

Christina closed her eyes and focused on her sense of smell. She sniffed again, trying to sort out the odors of sweat, solvent, tar, and hydrogen sulfide.

"I think I smell something else, something I've never noticed before at La Brea. But my nose may be playing tricks on me. Can you smell it, Linda?"

Linda sniffed, wrinkling her face in concentration. A few seconds passed.

"It's really faint, but it sort of smells like vinegar."

Christina gave a satisfied smile. "That's what I think, too."

"Is it important?"

She shrugged. "I don't know. But I'm a scientist. It's my job to make observations."

Chapter 3

On her way to the parking lot behind the Page Museum, Christina checked her cell phone and was surprised to see five text messages and a bunch of voicemails, all but one from her cousin. The back side of Hancock Park was still fairly quiet, so with a weary sigh, she sat down on a bench in the shade to catch up on the news River obviously was eager to share, whether Christina wanted to hear it or not. River was like that. She was so passionate about everything she did it never occurred to her that others might not share her enthusiasm. As River's roommate, relative, and childhood friend, Christina was often on the receiving end of River's zeal.

The first message was sent at 9:06 AM.

"U SHD B HERE 2 PRAY"

Oh, that was rich, coming from River who hadn't been to Mass since Christmas two years ago. Christina, a graduate of the University of Notre Dame, made it to church most Sundays. She tried to recall what River's cause *du jour* was and why it involved praying.

Then she remembered something about a teenage girl, an eighteen-year-old grape picker who died of heat exhaustion on a vineyard in the Central Valley. River was at a United Farm Workers march protesting the girl's death and the working conditions of undocumented farm laborers. The march was to begin with a memorial service downtown at the Cathedral of Our Lady of the Angels. She recalled with irony that River had to ask her where the Cathedral was.

10:13 AM.

"C TV WE R ON TEMPLE"

The march went up Temple Street. There must've been live news coverage. Busy day for the camera crews, she thought as she watched a van from KCAL local CBS news unloading right now in the parking lot at La Brea. She tapped to the next message.

10:51 AM.

"RITA MORENO SPEECH"

I'm sure that made River's day. The only thing River liked better than politically correct activism was activism involving celebrities—precisely the same combination that turned Christina off. She felt big names and publicity stunts didn't change the world; the small actions of a million unrecognized individuals did. Maybe that's why she favored the quiet, anonymous labor at Pit 91 over the grandstanding, media-pleasing stuff River got involved in.

12:17 PM

"MICKEY CHAIN ME 2 DEPT OF AG"

Good Lord, Mickey was there, too? Mickey was River's slacker boyfriend, and he was full of brilliant ideas like chaining yourself to a federal building. He'd probably like to chain himself to River's bed, but Christina (as the only one with a steady income) drew the line at letting him officially move in to their apartment. The two of them—Mickey and River—didn't have enough common sense to fill a thimble. Not that Mickey probably knew what a thimble was.

12:44 PM

"COPS"

Lovely. I'm so sorry I missed the party.

That was the last text message. Police, other emergency workers, and media were now arriving at Hancock Park in force, filling the parking spaces in the back lot that had been vacated by fleeing visitors. Christina was pretty sure in a few minutes she'd be asked to leave, but she took a moment to listen to her voicemails first. It was a good thing she did.

"Chrissy, Mickey and I need you to pick us up at the Central Community Police Station. It's at—" she heard some shuffling and discussion in the background, "—two fifty-one east sixth street, right downtown, you know? Okay, call me back."

River's voice was disgustingly cheerful. Obviously she got arrested. Probably thinks that makes her a hero, Christina thought. I should leave her there, let her see how heroic a night in jail is.

A whole series of irritating voice messages from her cousin followed.

"Okay, we're still here, I need you to call me."

"Chrissy, what are you doing? Why aren't you answering your phone? Call me."

"Hel—LOOO! Chrissy! Mickey and I got arrested. Don't worry, it's cool. But you have to pick us up. Sometime this year would be nice."

Cripes.

The only good thing about River having a scrape with the law was it justified Christina's decision not to move into her own place. Her cousin clearly needed a chaperone, and she had adopted the role, unbidden. Reluctantly she called back.

It took three rings for River to answer, and Christina could hear she'd interrupted her in mid-laugh. *What is wrong with that girl?*

"Hi Chrissy! What took you so long?"

"What did you do, River?" Christina said in her most parental tone, annoyed to the breaking point by her cousin's attitude.

"Oooo, the march got *so* intense! You should've been there, Chrissy. Mickey and I—"

"Skip it, I don't really want to know. You said you need a ride?"

"Yeah. You have the car this weekend, right?"

"I have it, but I don't know if I have enough fuel to get downtown and back to the apartment."

"I asked. It's only seven miles from here to West L.A."

Christina preferred to let River deal with the situation on her own, but she wasn't going to make up an excuse to avoid her duty. She did a quick calculation of how much driving she'd already done since getting the car from Dr. Chen yesterday. If River was right about the mileage, the experimental biodiesel car should be fine to make the trip.

She made an exasperated sigh into the phone, which didn't seem to bother River in the least, and said, "All right, I'm on my way."

"Thanks, Chrissy. Mickey'll be so psyched to ride in the X-car."

That sounds like Mickey, she thought as she hung up. Never mind that I just got arrested, what matters is I'm going for a ride in an eco-trendy vehicle.

The X-car, as she and her friends called it, was guaranteed not to be mistaken for an ordinary automobile. The fluorescent green Mini Cooper was wrapped in gaudy pronouncements declaring it was an "experimental biodiesel car"; that it was affiliated with UCLA; that it ran on "*E. coli* isobutanol" and was sponsored by "Bactofuels, Inc."

A uniformed police officer approached the bench. Christina put away her phone.

"Excuse me, miss, for your safety you'll have to leave," he said. "The park is now closed to the public."

He escorted her to the parking lot and paused to give her curious vehicle a once-over. With her modest stature, Christina slipped easily into the somewhat cramped driver's seat. As she started the X-car, she reflected that it was going to be interesting to hear what Dr. Chen had to say about the gas anomaly at the asphalt seep.

I wonder if there's a connection to our energy harvesting project, she thought, then dismissed the idea as fanciful. Their test site was several miles from here. It couldn't be related to the incident at Rancho La Brea.

Chapter 4

Waiting on the sidewalk in her "7 For All Mankind" designer jeans (purchased second-hand because it was "the right thing to do for the planet"), River had more in common with Eva Perón than Cesar Chávez. Despite her misadventures, her lipstick was fresh and her hair was arranged in flattering arcs around her slender, high-boned cheeks. Christina, who more or less wore a tar-flecked rag, fumed that her jailbird cousin looked and smelled better than she did. The two protesters climbed into the X-car. Mickey took the front seat.

"I can't believe how pissy they got about my name," River said with righteous indignation. "I can't be the first woman they've booked with a hyphenated name. Weber-Diaz, I said. How do you spell it? they said. Are you married, what's your maiden name, they wanted to know. They just couldn't handle that I'm single and have two last names. Well, I informed them that my parents had a relationship of equals, and their equality extended to the naming of offspring."

"I'm so glad I wasn't there," Christina mumbled.

"It was awesome," Mickey said. "Way better than digging up old dirt."

Christina stubbornly decided not to tell them what happened at the tar pits today.

"You're coming to the apartment with us?" she asked Mickey.

"Yeah—if it's okay with you."

"Sure," she sighed. "I suppose you can stay for dinner if you want. I went to Costco on Wednesday, bought too much as usual. You can help us eat through the excess."

"Thanks, Chrissy. You're the best."

Laying it on a little thick there, Mickey, but it worked. A little appreciation was nice; Mickey enjoyed the benefits of her grocery shopping and organized household management. Unfortunately, it made her feel like his mother. How could she be only a year older than River, but a generation more aged?

"Are you going to tell your parents?" Christina asked River.

"No, they're in Thailand or something working on a film. Anyway, they'd understand. You know my mom got arrested and stuff during the Vietnam War."

"Right," Christina said. She'd heard all about her aunt's free-wheeling past from her own mother. The older women's differences often strained their sisterly love. Her mom stayed at home in suburban St. Louis, a life both physically and metaphorically far removed from River's mom's world in the entertainment business of L.A.

Funny how River and I kind of have the same relationship.

Christina gingerly merged onto the westbound Santa Monica Freeway. The X-car lacked the powerful acceleration of most other cars on the road, but its eye-catching visibility usually prompted other drivers to make room for her.

"Your research project is down that way, isn't it?" Mickey asked, gesturing south as they passed the Normandie Avenue exit.

"The energy harvesting project is, yes," she replied, surprised that he remembered.

"You've gotta tell me about it again."

"I thought you and your eco friends didn't approve."

Mickey fidgeted in the cramped passenger seat. "Well, they—I mean, we—don't, but it's still kind of interesting. What's the deal with that again?"

River hummed a tune and leaned forward to check her makeup in the rear-view mirror. Christina ignored her and gave Mickey the low-tech summary. Her Ph.D. thesis project had been the center of her life for four years, and she was always eager to discuss it.

"The project is about getting energy from non-conventional oil fields. You see, the places on earth where oil is found aren't all the same. The best oil fields, like those in Saudi Arabia, contain light crude oil, a liquid that's relatively easy and cheap to pump out of the ground. The less-desirable oil fields have heavy crude, which is thick and syrupy. That makes it way more expensive to extract."

"And causes more harm to the environment," River added.

So she's listening.

"I suppose. Unfortunately the biggest petroleum deposits in the Western Hemisphere contain heavy crude, trapped in what we call tar sands. For example, the Athabasca tar sands of Alberta, Canada, and the Orinoco field in Venezuela. The purpose of Dr. Chen's project is to find a way to harvest the energy from these tar sands without actually digging up the oil."

"That sounds like a green idea," Mickey said in a confused tone.

She had to laugh as she explained to him why he was opposed to her research.

"If it works, our technology will allow oil companies to extract hydrocarbons from non-conventional oil fields that currently aren't in production. Your eco friends are worried that opening all those new fields to development will add to global warming."

"Oh yeah, that's right," Mickey said as if in answer to some internal debate.

"Even though the technology could free us from our dependence on despotic petrostates."

Mickey didn't respond, possibly because he was trying to digest the word "despotic."

"Oil from the Middle East," she clarified.

Mickey tapped his foot, a sure sign that he was puzzling over something.

"But how does it work? How can you get the energy without getting the oil?"

"By using bacteria."

"Huh?"

"Dr. Chen and I took some naturally-occurring bacteria that eat petroleum, and we modified their DNA to make them experts at breaking down oil into methane."

"Otherwise known as natural gas," River interjected as she flipped the rear-view mirror back into position.

"That's right," Christina said. "Our bacteria convert the complex hydrocarbons of heavy crude oil into the simplest hydrocarbon of all: CH_4. The stuff we burn in our stove at the apartment. Methane."

"Why?"

"Because methane is a gas. It's much easier to harvest than extra heavy crude."

River yawned. "So you don't have to pump the thick stuff out of the tar sands."

Christina glanced toward the back seat, surprised that her cousin was still engaged in the conversation.

"Exactly. Dr. Chen's goal is to introduce our genetically-engineered bacteria into a tar sand. While deep underground, the bacteria will convert the oil into natural gas, which we'll capture or pump out. That way, we can access the energy of the tar sand without extracting the tar itself."

"And you're testing this now?" Mickey asked.

Christina was flattered by Mickey's unusual interest in the subject.

"Yes, on a very small scale, at an abandoned gas station in Jefferson Park. We put simulated tar sand in an underground fuel storage tank and added microbes. Now we're monitoring methane production."

"That's nice, Chrissy," River interrupted. "Did I tell you what happened at the police station when I asked to go to the bathroom?" And with that, she launched into a monologue about her personal experiences with injustice and police brutality.

They arrived at the apartment and the three of them spilled out of the car. Mickey lovingly stroked the roof of the charismatic vehicle.

"Want me to wash it before you have to return it to your boss?" he asked. "There's these little black dots on it."

Poor guy is totally conflicted, Christina thought. He loves cars, but wants to save the planet.

"That'd be great, Mickey," she said, "but I should warn you, those dots are asphalt. It's going to take more than soapy water to get them off."

"Thanks for the ride, Chrissy," River said. "You've gotta come with us next time. You could use a little excitement in your life." She paused, really looking at Christina for the first time since she got in the car.

"What's with your shirt?"

CHAPTER 5

When Alethea Papadakis nearly stepped in a puddle of drain cleaner in the alley behind her house, she'd had enough.

For seven decades Alethea had lived in this part of central Los Angeles. She'd watched her street's long, slow decline, and at her age, she had no ambition of seeing it reversed. A year ago, the dilapidated two-story townhome next door went into foreclosure. It stood empty for months. She imagined a nice young family moving in and fixing up the place. But a nice family didn't move in. The bank sold the building for a song to a real estate speculator from another state. The house was now occupied by an indiscernible number of anonymous residents who were so secretive that every window in the house was covered, day and night. Instead of improving, the property continued to decay, blighting the neighborhood and Alethea's hopes.

She was resigned to ignore the newcomers, leaving them alone if they left her alone. But they—or at least their activities—were hard to ignore. Strangers came and went from the house at all hours of the night. People smoked outside and left piles of cigarette butts on the ground. And the smells—strange, chemical odors that at times reminded her of nail polish remover, at other times, of cat urine—emanated from the house strongly enough that once in a while she had to close her windows.

To all of this, she was willing to turn a blind eye, but a spilled bottle of drain cleaner could injure or kill the stray cats she fed a bowl of kibbles to every day. She was a tough woman who could tolerate a great deal herself, but she couldn't allow those people to hurt her kitties.

So she called the police.

Alethea reported the suspicious activities she'd observed. As she spoke, the bits of information formed an unmistakable pattern of illegality that she had refused to acknowledge until now. The dispatcher promised a squad car would investigate. Fearful that one of the cats would stick its nose in the poison while she waited for the police, Alethea took a bucket and filled it with water at the tap on the side of her house. She hauled the bucket into the alley to wash away the caustic liquid, and grimaced at the stink in the air.

What are they up to now, she wondered. The odor seemed familiar, yet it was different from any of the smells she'd noticed coming from the house before.

She poured the water into the drain cleaner, diluting and spreading it. One bucket obviously wasn't going to be enough. She cursed the faceless hooligans next door for making an old woman carry gallons of water like a mule in the midday heat. She trudged back to the tap, winded from the exertion. As she waited for the bucket to fill, she heard a shout from behind the curtained windows of the troublesome property.

The explosion followed less than a second later. It blew out every wall on the first floor of the flimsy wood-frame structure. Whether from the force of the blast, the heat of the fire, or the crush of rocketing debris, Alethea Papadakis died instantly.

* * *

Los Angeles Police Department officer Javier Gomez was waiting on a red light not far from the Papadakis residence when he heard the explosion. His partner in the passenger seat, who'd survived two tours of duty in Iraq with the Army Reserve, ducked for cover in about a millisecond. Gomez lacked such a highly developed self-preservation reflex. For a moment he stared dumbly at the fireball and smoke that billowed from a residential street just a few blocks ahead.

"Jesus, that's where the call came from," he said, turning on the cruiser's siren and lights and speeding through the intersection.

As far as a block away from the epicenter of the blast, the pavement was strewn with a bizarre collection of laboratory-style paraphernalia. Gomez had to steer his car around bottles, funnels, plastic tubing, and propane tanks as well as ordinary construction materials from the shattered building. Some of the debris was burning. By the time he pulled up near the blaze, area residents and passersby were gathering on the street. Gomez leaped out of the car while his partner radioed for fire and ambulance support.

At least three buildings were in flames; the one in the center was completely engulfed. Something flung upward from the fire was tangled and burning in the fronds of a tall, smooth-trunked palm tree, making it look like a giant torch. The air was filled with smoke, dust, and the acrid odor of scorched chemicals. Gomez and his partner looked in vain for Mrs. Papadakis or any other injured survivors needing rescue. He saw no one, and the fires were too fierce for him to try to enter one of the burning houses. He concentrated on clearing the area for the emergency workers whose sirens he could hear approaching.

Within eight minutes, firefighters were battling the blazes. Within twelve minutes, Gomez's superior, Police Lieutenant Jerry Branson, was on the scene.

Branson, a trim and muscular officer with a severe bearing, wandered around the edge of the chaos searching the ground. He bent down to pick something up, and cornered Gomez.

"You were the first man on the scene, correct?" Branson asked.

"Yes, sir. We were responding to a call at this location and only missed the explosion by maybe a minute," Gomez replied.

"Fucking tweaker lab," Branson said, holding a miraculously unscathed package of over-the-counter pseudoephedrine, one of the main ingredients for cooking crystal meth. "Took out their own sorry asses and half the neighborhood with them. Blast probably sprayed toxic chemicals over a quarter mile."

Gomez glanced uneasily at the growing crowd of onlookers who carelessly stood gawking at the disaster like it was on TV. "Sir, if that's the case . . ."

Branson nodded.

"Get those people out of here," he barked at any officers within hearing range. "I'll call in a hazmat team."

*   *   *

The firefighters extinguished the blazes before dark. Lieutenant Branson helped set up emergency spotlights in the last glimmer of the late sunset. Even with the fires out, he knew it was going to be a long night.

The hazmat crew finished its survey and declared the area safe. Branson approached the wreckage for a preliminary look around. Contorted beams and collapsed walls cast spooky shadows under the glare of the spotlights. The air smelled of smoke.

He studied the pattern of destruction. The building in the center of the wreckage was completely demolished; the blackened remains of its second story had collapsed onto the ground floor. He guessed the explosion originated there. The property to the right side was still standing, but just barely. They wouldn't need a wrecking ball to bring it down; one puff from the Big Bad Wolf ought to do it.

The citizen who'd called LAPD that morning owned the house to the left. Sadly, Branson turned and watched a team of workers in disposable white suits extract some charred human remains from the debris.

Too bad she didn't call yesterday.

A firefighter wearing a captain's insignia approached. Office Gomez was with him.

"Can I have a word with you, Lieutenant?" the fireman said. "Gomez here tells me LAPD thinks this was a meth lab accident."

Branson snorted. "Is there traffic on the four-oh-five? Of course it was."

"That may not be the whole story."

"Did ya miss the broken glassware and Bunsen burners?" Branson said.

"No, I agree there was a meth lab here. But it was a pretty big blast for a small-scale operation."

"Maybe they were scaling up, had a stock of sodium or ammonia sitting around."

"Yeah," the Captain said, rubbing his chin. "But look at the old lady's house."

"You mean what's left of it."

"The blast came from the east side of the structure. With a single source explosion, the debris should be thrown in a radial pattern away from the source."

"I guess," Branson agreed, shoving a fragment of broken ductwork with his foot.

"But we see pieces of the lady's east wall in the debris of the drug house."

"Where?" Branson said, surprised.

The firefighter pointed. Branson looked at the rubble.

"I'll be damned. What do you make of that?"

"Officer Gomez has a suggestion."

Branson turned to his subordinate with an expectant look.

"I heard two explosions," Gomez said. "Almost at the same time, but I'm pretty sure they were separate."

"A second blast, originating in the lady's house, could explain the debris pattern," the Captain said.

"Are you suggesting grandma had a little hobby of her own?" Branson said, snickering. "Maybe she called LAPD to shut down the competition?"

The firefighter ignored his sarcasm. "I'm just giving you a head's up that the Fire Department's report might raise some questions that can't be answered by blaming a simple crank dealer. Keep that in mind while you do your investigation."

"I'll keep it in mind," Branson said, walking away. He had a headache from breathing chemical fumes all afternoon, and it was irritating to think he might have to use his brain on this one.

CHAPTER 6

An olive-skinned, chiseled hunk of a guy pointed and said something to his buddy when Christina parked the X-car in its reserved spot on the UCLA campus. She didn't bother to flirt because she knew his attention was on the car, not her. As far as she could tell, guys in L.A. weren't interested in a brainy, cosmetic-free woman with a propensity to gain weight even if she had smooth, clear skin, a delicate nose, and arresting eyes. Her one weekend a month with sexy wheels—any motorized wheels, for that matter—was over. Mickey had cleaned off the tar, so other than an empty fuel tank, the X-car was returning to Dr. Chen in tip-top shape.

Summer school wasn't in session, so even though it was a Monday morning, the sunny campus was rather empty. The majority of patrons buying their morning coffee at the outdoor Court of Sciences plaza were graduate students, who worked year-round. Christina purchased her favorite caffeinated beverage, a fountain-fresh cup of cola, said good-bye to the sunshine and climbed the stairs to her research lab. Signs advertising the UCLA-CaliPetro Bioenergy Institute greeted her when she reached her floor.

When CaliPetro first negotiated with UCLA for this collaboration, leftish students, faculty, and members of the public organized protests against corporate corruption of university science. But as state support for the UC system withered, the university had to choose between shutting down the lab and accepting money from the energy conglomerate. Christina benefited from the university's decision. CaliPetro's involvement—both financial and technical—made her work possible.

She strolled down the hall and was surprised to find the door to her lab was unlocked; usually she was the first person to arrive on Mondays. The collection of oversized "DO NOT DUPLICATE" university keys she wore around her neck rattled as she put them away.

"Dr. Chen?" she called.

"In here, Chrissy."

She followed the voice to his office. Dr. Robert Chen was on the telephone. He waved but didn't flash his usual smile. With his graying hair, hopelessly out-of-date eyeglasses, and pale, skinny feet in a pair of huaraches, Dr. Chen reminded Christina of her father, who was also a fashion-clueless scientist of a certain age. She went to her desk and unloaded her backpack.

"Don't get comfortable," Dr. Chen said, emerging from his office with a look of distress. "There's been an accident at the *Syntrophus* test site."

"What kind of accident?"

"Fire," Dr. Chen said, "and possibly an underground explosion."

"Oh my God," she said, stunned. The *Syntrophus* test—which Mickey had been so interested in—was the centerpiece of her Ph.D. thesis project. With CaliPetro's help, Dr. Chen had won approval from the city to use a brownfield site for the work, at a bankrupt gas station in south central L.A. Setting up their mock tar sand in the underground storage tanks had been costly, and as of yet, they hadn't reaped any meaningful data. What if the experiment was ruined? Selfishly Christina wondered how many extra years this accident would put between her and graduation.

"We need to check the damage," Dr. Chen said. "I rode my bike today. Did you return the car?"

"I did, but it's almost out of isobutanol."

"The bugs made a fresh batch. We'll fill it up and meet the CaliPetro rep in Jefferson Park in an hour."

⋆ ⋆ ⋆

Christina stared out the window of the little X-car as Dr. Chen drove past a vacant lot and an unkempt auto repair shop that was barely distinguishable from the adjacent junkyard. The street had a bombed-out look to it already; she wondered what they would find at the test site.

The old gas station didn't look much different from its usual state of decay, except for an array of new-looking cars bearing logos for various government agencies parked in front. Christina and Dr. Chen joined the coterie poring over the site.

"I don't see any damage," she said.

"Let's check the access portal," Dr. Chen replied.

As they walked toward the hole which led to the underground gasoline storage tank, Christina noticed scorch marks on the concrete. Blackened tufts of burned weeds curled from cracks in the pavement. At the access portal, the cap which normally sealed it was missing.

"Hello, Robert," said a bespectacled man wearing a light blue polo shirt with the CaliPetro logo on the left chest.

Dr. Chen shook the man's hand. "Morning, Sid."

"It's not good, Robert. From the reports it sounds like we had a big methane fire here last night."

Dr. Chen nodded solemnly and got down on his knees to peer into the hole.

"Anyone hurt?" he asked.

"We don't think so. They found a homeless encampment over behind the propane tank, but nobody was in it. Looks like the fire just burned from the portal, nowhere else, so unless somebody was standing over it at the time, things should be okay."

"That's a relief," Dr. Chen said, standing up. "I can't see anything down there. The detection system is completely gone."

"We found part of it earlier, blown out and burned almost beyond recognition."

Dr. Chen nodded again. Christina saw the heavy disappointment in his face.

"I suppose the good news is this means our bacteria worked," she said.

Sid from CaliPetro looked at her. "Excuse me?"

"The methane that fueled the fire must have been produced by Dr. Chen's bacteria," Christina said. "We designed the *Syntrophus* bacteria to break down heavy crude oil, and then convert the products into flammable methane gas. This fire proves the system works. The bacteria made enough methane to cause an accident."

"True enough, Chrissy," Dr. Chen said. "But it won't do us any good now."

"Why?" she asked.

Sid answered. "This incident proves your energy harvesting strategy is too dangerous. CaliPetro can't have explosions and fires at a production site."

"But this was an artificial system—a contained storage tank. Surely in a real tar sand you could find ways to manage it safely," she said.

"Perhaps," the rep said, "but CaliPetro won't be financing the research to figure it out. Absent any encouraging findings, we've reached our funding limit for this technology. We're more interested in spending our R&D dollars these days on renewables. You've got a good idea here, but the Institute will be focusing on cellulosic ethanol from now on."

"But—" Christina said.

Sid ignored her. "I'm sorry, Robert. The tar sand energy harvesting project is dead—at least until crude hits $175 a barrel," he said with a chuckle suggesting this was a standard they could never expect to meet.

Christina gave her boss a look imploring him to argue, but Dr. Chen simply shook the oil man's hand and said, "I hope we can work together again sometime."

"I'll be in contact with you about the mess. CaliPetro agreed to pay for cleanup of this site when the experiment ended. We'll meet that obligation, but if the storage tank was damaged by the fire, remediation is gonna cost us a helluva lot more than we expected."

Before Sid wandered off to talk to a city official, he turned to them and said, "Maybe you can get the Canadians to help you out. They have the most to gain from your process."

Christina knew that Dr. Chen had already contacted a Canadian oil company, one that operated in the vast Alberta tar sands, but the company wasn't ready to commit funds until Chen's project was further along. That would never happen now.

Chen wandered about for a few minutes. Christina prayed for a miracle to resurrect the project.

"There's nothing we can do here, Chrissy," he said. "Ready to go back to the lab?"

She nodded despondently, and they returned to the X-car.

"Dr. Chen, what are we going to do?"

"Put the *Syntrophus* project on hold," he said, "or at least the field trial part. We can still study the organism. The genetic modifications we made to it may be useful in the future."

'In the future' won't help me finish my Ph.D. in the present, she thought.

As if reading her thoughts, Dr. Chen said, "Fortunately we have several projects to keep us busy. You can include the genetic engineering of *Syntrophus* in your Ph.D. thesis. But from now on, this will be your baby."

He patted the dashboard as he spoke.

"The X-car?"

"Not the car, the fuel that it runs on. Biodiesel produced by *E. coli* bacteria. The fuel of the future: renewable, carbon-neutral, and not food-based."

This was good news. She thought the biodiesel project was way cooler than the tar sand research. She'd wanted to work on it from the beginning, but Dr. Chen insisted it was too risky for her Ph.D. thesis.

"Making the bacteria photosynthetic, like little plants, is revolutionary," Chen said. "If we can get it to work—still a big if—it could change the world."

He paused, momentarily lost in a fantasy of dollar signs, Nobel prizes, or maybe both.

"I won't force you to take it on. You know what we're trying to do is extremely ambitious. It might never work."

"I want to, Dr. Chen. It's worth the gamble, even if I have to spend the next ten years in graduate school."

"Hopefully it won't come to that," Chen laughed. "Sometimes things move quickly. Look at our *Syntrophus* project."

"Fast work indeed," Christina said. "A little too fast."

Dr. Chen nodded. "I never expected they'd make enough methane to cause an explosion like that. I guess we're lucky the little buggers didn't blow up half the city."

The joke reminded her that in all the excitement, she hadn't yet spoken to Dr. Chen about the incident at La Brea.

"You heard about what happened at the tar pits on Saturday?" she asked.

"Of course. It was all over the news."

"I was there, you know."

"Really! That's right, you volunteer for their digs." He glanced at her as if searching for the answer to a question. "You haven't shaved your head so I guess you didn't get doused in tar."

"Fortunately not," she said. "The crazy thing is, nobody can explain what happened. Why was there such a huge bubble when normally the gas seeps up in smaller amounts?"

"I'm sure a geologist will come up with a model to account for it. If I remember the last time I visited La Brea, the gas bubbles varied quite a bit in size and frequency."

"They do," she agreed, "but this bubble was way beyond the normal range for size."

"In any random distribution—a bell curve—you occasionally get outliers."

"I know, but . . ." she said, her voice trailing off into uncertainty.

They turned into the campus of UCLA and Dr. Chen zipped the X-car into its reserved parking spot. He looked at his student.

"What's bothering you, Chrissy?"

"I witnessed the biggest bubble burst, but the gas from the bubble didn't change the odor in the air. Hydrogen sulfide gas is really stinky. If the bubble had released it, I would've noticed."

"Which means what?"

She hesitated, not wanting to school her P.I.

"It suggests that the gas rising from the tar pits in those anomalous bubbles was almost entirely methane."

"That's normal for La Brea."

"Well, yes, most of the escaping gas there is methane. I once saw a volunteer ignite a small leak in the grass and cook a hot dog over it. But normally the methane is contaminated with H_2S. This gas bubble wasn't."

Dr. Chen shrugged his shoulders as he exited the car. Even though he wasn't a tall man, he could easily lean on the X-car's roof and look over as she closed the passenger door.

"So they better not light any matches around Hancock Park for a while," he said.

She needed more reassurance. *Out with it.*

"Dr. Chen, I can't help wondering . . . I mean, we optimized our *Syntrophus* bacteria to degrade hydrocarbons . . . and the field test started a few weeks ago . . . and now the fire . . ."

"Are you suggesting there's a connection between my research and the incident at Rancho La Brea?" Dr. Chen said.

"Do you think it's possible?"

"Certainly not. And you of all people should know why."

She did know the reasons why. She helped design the safeguards in the genetically-altered bacteria. What worried her was she wasn't the only person to detect a hint of vinegar in the air on Saturday.

Chapter 7

The subway to the sea.

It was a splendid idea, an idea whose time had finally come. After almost three wasted decades, Brad Somerset was once again digging under Wilshire Boulevard.

Of course, Brad was a much younger man when he first worked for the Los Angeles County Metropolitan Transportation Authority on construction of the Purple Line subway in the 1980's. Then, he was twenty-two years old, vigorous and muscled, and the heavy manual labor of construction work merely gave him a big appetite. As he watched the men and even (*gasp!*) a woman laboring under his supervision, he knew such physical efforts today would give him a hernia. Fortunately a college degree and long experience in underground construction had freed him from the grunt work. He was a project manager now, more likely to push papers than a shovel.

Brad wasn't just an office man, though. He still spent a fair amount of time at the construction site, especially on days like today when the newly-excavated tunnel was being equipped with sophisticated wireless surveying instruments. These precision tools included seismographs, tiltmeters and inclinometers designed to detect the smallest changes in walls or ceilings in the tunnel and in the buildings or street above. The system was an important safety feature that they didn't have years ago. It could alert them to any destabilizing movements caused by minor earthquake activity or by the construction itself.

"I'm not getting a reading from that deformation monitor," Brad said, pointing. "Check the orientation of the prism; maybe the laser isn't hitting it right."

Working on the Westside subway extension was far more pleasant than work in a coal mine—something else Brad had done in his career—and for that he was grateful. The shallow tunnel was well-lit, and once the virgin section was properly equipped with a high-volume ventilation system, the air would be pretty fresh.

"Better," he said. "Calibrate it with the next one over."

The original Purple Line ran under Wilshire from downtown L.A. west to Western Avenue. That left the subway still thirteen or so miles inland, amputated from its manifest destiny of extending all the way to the Pacific Ocean. But unlike most unfinished transit projects, this one hadn't simply run out of money. Extension of the subway line further west was controversial, and the controversy reached all the way to Washington, D.C. Years ago, Brad was stunned when L.A. Congressman Henry Waxman pushed through a ban on funding new tunnels under a four hundred-block area of Wilshire between La Brea and Western Avenues, an area the feds designated a "gas risk zone."

A load of crap that was, he thought. Sure, this part of town had problems with natural underground gas, but he believed the ban was NIMBY politics played by rich folk who didn't want a subway line connecting their exclusive Westside neighborhoods with downtown. When a local Ross Dress for Less store blew up in a methane explosion in 1985, it provided the perfect political cover for the limousine liberals: stop the subway for *safety's* sake.

Well, another twenty-five years of growing congestion on L.A.'s roads had forced many people to rethink their position. Plus, the Public Works Department had successfully managed construction of sewer tunnels through an area heavily pocketed with methane gas. Experts now testified that it was possible to safely build and run a subway under the entire length of Wilshire Boulevard. With Waxman's support (*damn, how long had that guy been 'serving' in D.C.?*), the ban was repealed, initiating a series of events that ultimately led to Brad standing here today.

As he made programming adjustments to a small electrical unit on the tunnel wall, he noticed one of the workers stop in mid-stride and sit down on the floor.

"You okay?" Brad asked, walking over and putting a hand on the man's shoulder.

"I don't know," the worker said. "I feel kind of light-headed."

Then a second worker—the woman—also plopped to the ground. All of a sudden Brad noticed the air felt stuffy and close.

Abruptly lower air quality in a tunnel. Dizzy workers.

You didn't need thirty years of underground construction experience to know they had a problem.

He shouted to the foreman. "We've got a gas leak. Everybody out—now!"

Men abandoned what they were doing and scattered like rats for the nearest exit to the surface.

"Be careful of sparks! Don't turn anything on!" he shouted, terrified of igniting an explosion.

"What the fuck happened to the methane detectors?" the foreman yelled.

"I don't know. They should've sounded long before it got this bad."

A traffic jam ensued on the ladders. *Shit, we haven't got much time.* Brad screamed at the men to hurry—as if they needed encouragement. Rather than just standing at the end of the line waiting for his turn, he surveyed the area for stragglers.

The woman was now lying prone and unmoving where she fell.

Knowing he couldn't carry her unconscious body up a ladder alone, he grabbed the foreman's arm and the two of them raced to her side. They struggled, wasting seconds as they tried to find the best way to pick her up and share the load. For a moment Brad remembered when his kids were little, how much heavier they were asleep than awake. He helped raise the woman high enough to sling her torso over the foreman's shoulder.

They were halfway back to the ladder when the foreman collapsed. Conflicting impulses toward self-preservation and altruism made Brad pause. The opportunity for decision passed when he too was overcome by the foul air.

As he slipped into unconsciousness, he made a strange olfactory observation.

Not rotten eggs . . . sauerkraut?

CHAPTER 8

Fifteen dollars for a salad?

Christina gulped when she looked at the lunch menu on display and reminded herself that the biotechnology giant Bactofuels was picking up the tab. Surely the company rep knew this place was pricey when he chose it for his meeting with Dr. Chen. But did he know he'd be paying for a graduate student, too?

The menu for The Restaurant at the Getty Center extolled the virtues of local, sustainable food, but Christina knew the real reason you needed a reservation to eat here was the view. The Getty Center Museum was a stunning architectural masterpiece in the Santa Monica mountains of Los Angeles, perched nine hundred feet above the 405 freeway which snaked away southward below them. On a clear day like today, the view from The Restaurant was breathtaking, trumping even the exquisite collection of European art on display inside the Getty's Italian travertine walls.

This was not Christina's first visit to the Getty. The world-class attraction was only a three-mile bike ride from the UCLA campus. Thanks to the philanthropy of J. Paul Getty and his ten billion-dollar trust, the tram ride up the steep slope from the parking lot, and admission into the gardens and museum, were free. For an intellectual young woman on a grad student budget, that added up to an irresistible deal. She visited several times a year.

But she'd never eaten at The Restaurant. Standing in the sun outside the entrance, Christina checked the time: five minutes past their reservation. The restaurant was busy, and the hostess turned away a middle-aged couple who complained loudly in some foreign language as they marched toward the long line for the cafeteria. Christina fretted that The Restaurant would give away their table. She searched the crowd for Dr. Chen and Jeff Trinley, their contact from Bactofuels.

She spotted her boss and promptly forgot any concerns she had about being underdressed in her Lycra skort. Dr. Chen was wearing hiking shorts and a T-shirt with a biochemical pathway cartooned on the back. His companion was also in shorts but his Tommy Bahama camp shirt was significantly more stylish.

"Parking lot was full," Dr. Chen said. "We had to use the remote lot and ride the shuttle. It would've been faster to walk from the lab."

Christina knew Dr. Chen disliked driving, and the only reason he'd arrived by car was because Trinley had picked him up. She, on the other hand, had come on her bike an hour earlier to enjoy the museum for a while.

Dr. Chen smiled and put his hand on Christina's shoulder. "Jeff, I want you to meet Miss Christina González, Ph.D. candidate in my lab. Since the fiasco with the tar sands project, I'm putting her to work on *E. coli* isobutanol."

Trinley glanced at her with a vacant expression. She offered her hand and said, "It's nice to meet you."

He didn't bother to make eye contact when he gave her a limp handshake.

I guess he didn't know the graduate student was coming. She felt intensely awkward.

The hostess led them to their table. Christina politely took her seat on a chair with its back to the glorious windows so the others could enjoy the panoramic view. The seat was also in the sun, which felt good. She was dressed for summer biking, not for air conditioning, and the restaurant seemed excessively cold.

Trinley ordered a beer and looked out at the landscape, his gaze passing through Christina as if she were as invisible as the glass windows themselves.

"So Robert, what happened with the *Syntrophus* project?" Trinley asked.

41

Dr. Chen grimaced. "Not much to tell, Jeff. You know we had an experimental model set up in an underground gasoline storage tank. We put our bacterial cultures in and let it cook. Then it blew up." He made a *poof* gesture with his hands.

"CaliPetro couldn't have been too happy about that."

"No, Jeff, they weren't," Dr. Chen said with a sigh. "Neither was I, nor was Christina. Disappointing, for sure."

"Especially since the microbiology worked really well," Christina said, trying to join the conversation. "I'm sure it was just the engineering that failed."

Trinley gave her a cold look. "*Just* the engineering? You'll find that when you want to scale up a laboratory project to an industrial level, practical problems with design and production are far from trivial. In fact, they often make the basic science look easy."

He turned to Dr. Chen. "Bactofuels has a lot of experience with this kind of thing, Robert. Large-scale production of proteins and enzymes is what we do best, and we've got customers in industry, agriculture, and medicine. I can't say I'm surprised that CaliPetro wasn't up to the challenge. They may know how to drill for oil, but what do they know about microbiology?"

Dr. Chen shifted in his chair. "They know enough, Jeff, and as their consultant, I gave them good advice. I still don't understand why the reaction was so unpredictable."

"I'm not going to argue with you," Trinley said, waving his hand to symbolically sweep away Chen's affiliation with the other sponsor. "But I suppose this incident leaves a bit of a gap in your institute's finances."

"In the short term, yes."

"Then you'll be happy to know Bactofuels is prepared to fill the gap. We're very optimistic about the progress you've made on the photosynthetic *E. coli*. By devoting more resources to the project, we hope to speed it up. With additional funds, perhaps you can even hire a qualified assistant."

The comment, though not overtly directed at her, made Christina burn. *Who does this guy think he is? I may be the student today, but I'll be the professor tomorrow.*

Dr. Chen perceived the slight as well. "Christina will be on this project full-time from now on. She's an outstanding scientist and I know we can count on her to do things right."

"I'm sure," Trinley said, and turned to address her directly for the first time. "Miss González, do you know what Bactofuels does?"

Sensing a test, Christina marshaled her considerable academic talents and answered him. "You sell enzymes and bacterial cultures. Farmers use them to break down manure. Hobbyists use them to clean their fish tanks. Your genetically-engineered bacteria manufacture human proteins for use in pharmaceuticals. Organic farmers buy your biopesticides. And now you're working on biofuels."

"Very good, all true," Trinley said with a hint of honest praise. "But I want to emphasize the overall theme of our work. Bactofuels is a world leader in synthetic biology."

"The application of engineering principles to living systems," Christina interrupted, unafraid to assert her competence. "For example, taking a naturally occurring biochemical pathway, or series of enzymatic reactions, and altering it to produce something useful to humans."

"Or even designing and manufacturing a living cell from scratch," Trinley said. "We're not there yet, but this photosynthetic *E. coli* project is the closest we've come. The project is very important to us."

The waiter placed a beautifully arranged plate of baby salad greens, sliced heirloom tomatoes and fresh mozzarella cheese in front of Christina. She estimated the actual cost of the ingredients to be about two bucks.

"Fresh ground pepper?" the waiter asked.

"Please," Christina replied.

As the waiter made a showy display of operating an oversized pepper mill, Trinley spoke to Dr. Chen.

"I'll tell you the truth, Robert. We don't really expect the isobutanol to be commercially viable. No matter what modifications you make, using bacteria to produce biodiesel will be too expensive compared to oil unless a major war breaks out in the Middle East. What Bactofuels wants is an organism that we can patent and use as a basic model for producing other, more costly chemicals. *Escherichia coli* is the best-understood bacterial species on the planet. It's versatile, hardy, and generally harmless. By giving it the ability to use sunlight as an energy source, you're creating the perfect biological factory. With the proper genetic modification, Bactofuels can use *E. coli* to manufacture just about anything."

Christina listened with fascination. She thought producing ecologically-friendly fuel for vehicles like the X-car was the whole point of the project, but Trinley's goal was even bigger. He wasn't thinking about just one product, but about the process. Instead of selling biodiesel, he wanted to build a microbial factory with a genetic assembly line that could be tweaked to produce any number of different organic substances. She had to admit that was pretty smart. Gas sold for a few dollars a gallon, but some proteins were worth tens of thousands of dollars an ounce.

"With your financial support, I'm confident we can engineer these bacteria to meet your requirements," Chen said. He winked at Christina.

"Thank you, Robert," Trinley said, taking a bite of ahi tuna.

"And don't write off the isobutanol yet," Dr. Chen said. "The price of oil is volatile, and who knows what people might be willing to pay for solar gasoline?"

Christina couldn't answer that question, but she did know that there was big money in oil. The museum complex around her cost a *billion* dollars to build, and that was only a drop in the bucket of the Getty Oil fortune. If Dr. Chen's technology could siphon off even an infinitesimal fraction of the conventional fuel business, they'd be set for life.

CHAPTER 9

"Charcoal's ready," Mickey announced.

Until she moved to L.A. for graduate school, Christina had lived her entire life in the Midwest. As she stepped out the sliding door to the patio of their first floor apartment, she repeated her daily pledge to never take the weather for granted.

It was a perfect night: warm but not hot, dry but without any wildfires to cloud the area with smoke. The oleander bushes behind her building were covered in pink and white flowers. With the sliding door open, there was nothing to separate indoors from outdoors. No screen was needed; the paucity of mosquitoes in L.A. was a touch of divine grace.

Mickey leaned over a miniature Weber grill, stirring the red-hot coals with a stick. Christina handed him a platter of raw chicken breasts that she'd marinated in a spicy Mexican adobo sauce. It was a family recipe that both she and River enjoyed growing up.

The threesome kicked back in plastic chairs on the patio drinking ice-cold diet soda from colorful picnic cups, and Christina felt content. Despite the occasional irritation—or trip to a police station—she enjoyed living with her cousin. And Mickey was such a regular fixture at the apartment that she'd grown fond of him, too, though a boyfriend of her own would be better. Mickey had a good sense of humor, and he was handy with a grill. She could forgive a lot in a man who cooked.

"How's work, Chrissy?" River asked.

After the accident that ended her tar sand project, Christina had felt some genuine sympathy from her cousin. Before, River seemed to take for granted that her studies would automatically lead to graduation in about six years. Christina's obvious distress when her thesis project collapsed must have forced River to recognize the challenges and unpredictability her cousin faced in her quest to earn the title "Doctor."

"Things are looking up," she said. "Dr. Chen signed an agreement with another sponsor, Bactofuels, to make up the grant money we lost from CaliPetro. That means he can keep paying me, and—," she couldn't resist the jab, "—you can keep a roof over your head."

"What do they want for their money?" Mickey asked.

"Photosynthetic bacteria that they can use as factories to manufacture enzymes."

"Photo who?" River said.

"Photosynthetic. Like, photosynthesis? As in, plants and the bottom of the food chain and all that?"

River gave her a blank look.

"Geez, River, you're a college graduate! Don't they teach science at Claremont Pitzer?"

Mickey snickered. "Not in the Gender Studies field group, they don't."

"Maybe I should rent some episodes of *The Magic School Bus* for you," Christina said.

"Don't be a jerk, Chrissy. Not everyone is a science nerd," River said.

She bit her tongue, remembering that while she might not approve of River's educational choices, her cousin was every bit as smart as she was.

"Photosynthesis is the process by which plants convert the energy of sunlight into the chemical energy of food. It's the basis for almost all life on earth. Photosynthetic organisms make food, and then they become food for other life forms—plant-eaters—and on up the food chain to meat-eaters."

"Like us," Mickey said, flipping a boneless, skinless piece of poultry over the coals.

"The bacteria I'm working with, *E. coli*, are more like animals than plants. They need to eat to survive. But Dr. Chen put the genes for photosynthesis into them, and now they're green and can make food from sunlight, like plants do."

"Are those the bacteria in the X-car?"

"They're not in the car, but they make the fuel for the car. We also designed them to convert sunlight into isobutanol. That's an alcohol—related to ethanol—and it makes a great fuel for diesel engines."

"And it's eco-friendly, right?" River said.

"It is when it's made this way. When my photosynthetic bacteria produce isobutanol, they take CO_2 out of the atmosphere. When the fuel is burned, CO_2 is released but it just replaces what the bacteria took out. It doesn't add to global warming."

"Cool," River said.

Mickey stoked the charcoal and picked up an alternative newspaper River had laid on the table.

"But we still have a lot of work to do," Christina said. "The bacteria make isobutanol but we have to feed them. Sunlight alone doesn't work—not yet."

"That's good for you, though, because you need a research project."

"I guess so."

"I hope you figure it out, Chrissy," Mickey said, suddenly animated and waving the newspaper. "This gasoline bullshit can't go on forever. It's bad enough that the oil companies are getting rich while wrecking the environment with their drilling and spilling and carbon emissions. Now they're bleeding the little man by watering down his gas!"

He slapped the newspaper in front of them, pointing to an article titled, "Jefferson Park Station Sold Bad Gas."

Jefferson Park?

Intrigued and a little worried, Christina skimmed the text. According to the report, a number of cars that had filled up at an independent gas station in the Jefferson Park neighborhood broke down and suffered costly engine damage because the fuel had been diluted.

"The nerve of some people!" River said.

"Let me see that," Christina said, snatching the paper to read the whole article.

The owner of the station denied tampering with the gasoline, and said that testing of his underground fuel tanks would prove the gasoline was fine. He blamed any problems on the decrepit condition of his customers' cars.

"Strange," was all Christina said, though she was thinking a good deal more than that.

"I mean, did this guy think he could get away with it?" Mickey said. "Did he think because his customers were poor, no one would notice? Aaah, he probably will get away with it. I bet the cops won't even shut him down. Neil oughtta blow his tanks, too."

A razor-sharp glance flew from River to Mickey, and Christina watched his face turn beet red. He mumbled something and turned away to fuss with the grill. River smiled and folded up the paper, but it wasn't a real smile. Christina had seen enough family photos to recognize River's fake camera grin.

"That's such a shame," River said lightly. "By the way, did I tell you about the civil rights march I'm organizing next month?"

"What do you mean, 'blow his tanks, too'?" Christina said slowly.

Mickey kept his back turned. River took on a glazed, deer-in-the-headlights expression. Christina felt the blood drain from her face. She recalled the two-thousand-year-old words of Judas Iscariot. *The one I will kiss is the man.*

Was she breaking bread with her betrayers?

"It wasn't an accident?" she whispered.

They shook their heads and acted confused. "What wasn't?" River said, but River was a terrible liar.

"The accident with my tar sand project—it wasn't an accident?" Christina said, the volume of her voice rising with her growing fury. "Somebody—what did you say, Noah? Neil?—he blew up my experiment? You know who destroyed my experiment?"

"Chrissy, we—" Mickey began.

She didn't hear a word. "Are you out of your minds? Did you tell him where it was? Oh, God," Christina smacked her forehead, "I told you the test site was in Jefferson Park. I think I even pointed it out to you once. Is Neil one of your ecoterrorist friends? What did you do?"

She was shrieking now, her normally even temper boiling like the surf in a hurricane.

"I knew those people you hang out with didn't approve of my project. But I never would've thought . . . How could you?"

Tears flowed down her cheeks. To think that her loved ones were traitors was a hundred times more painful than the sabotage itself. River and Mickey—or their "friend"—had committed an act of violence against her and her sponsor. By using information she gave them, they'd made her an unwitting accomplice. What would Dr. Chen do if he knew? Could he ever trust her again? Might she lose her position at the university?

Would River and Mickey go to jail, only this time for real?

Torn between vengeance and fear, there was no way to sort out her feelings—or decide what to do—while the guilty parties were sitting at table with her.

"Get out," she said.

"What?" River said.

"I said get out, both of you. Get out of this house. If you're not gone in five minutes, I'm calling the police and telling them everything."

"But—"

"Just leave. I mean it. Mickey has a place somewhere, doesn't he?" She buried her face in her arms, her anger morphing into a plea. "Go away."

She didn't look up until the sound of shuffling feet quieted, and the front door had clicked shut. Then like a disconsolate child, she went to her room and curled up on the bed with her head sandwiched between two pillows.

One of their friends sabotaged my experiment. They betrayed me.

Before leaving, Mickey had taken the chicken off the fire and neatly arranged it on the platter. All night the perfectly cooked meat lay there spoiling, and feeding the flies.

CHAPTER 10

The next morning was Saturday, Christina's day at La Brea. Things had settled down at the tar pits—no more asphalt geysers—and Linda had called to tell her that the volunteers were working Pit 91 again. Christina planned to go, and when the alarm woke her she saw no reason to change her mind.

She poured a bowl of cereal and sliced some strawberries. The silent emptiness of the apartment was oppressive; she turned on some music. She'd spent a restless night agonizing over her moral dilemma. That Mickey was involved in an environmental activist group, she knew. She didn't think his group was affiliated with any larger organization. It was more a gang of buddies who instead of tossing down beers at a bowling alley preferred to disrupt government hearings about new coal-fired power plants. Christina had met some of the guys before, but she couldn't remember a "Neil." Maybe he was new, or maybe he was part of another group. Either way, he must be a lot more radical than Mickey and his pals.

At least, that's what she hoped. She didn't want to believe that Mickey himself was mixed up with explosives and industrial sabotage. That stuff sounded like a felony conviction, and Mickey wasn't a felon. A pinhead maybe, but not a felon.

What am I going to tell Dr. Chen?

Dr. Chen needed to know that the tar sand experiment didn't explode on its own. The energy harvesting technology might be safe to use after all. Maybe they could convince CaliPetro to sponsor a new field test.

But how could she explain what she knew without revealing how she knew it? If Christina ratted, the police would investigate. What if they figured out who was responsible and arrested her cousin? What if the trail led them to back to her, and she was implicated? After all, Neil learned the crucial information about the test site (indirectly) from her.

Despite a full night of contemplation, the answers to these questions eluded her.

To make matters worse, her motivations were confused. While cursing their actions, she fretted about River and Mickey, felt sorry that she'd forced them out, wondered if they'd made it safely to Mickey's place. Around midnight she nearly got out of bed to call and make sure, but decided that would send the wrong message. She loved them, but that didn't let them off the hook.

She cleaned the kitchen and wheeled her bike to the door for the combination bus/bicycle ride to Hancock Park. Some manual labor in the tar pit would be good for her; it might help her think.

A wide perimeter around the Lake Pit was closed to visitors, but the rest of Hancock Park was open. The day was sunny but Christina noticed fewer people strolling about than usual. That was understandable. No adequate explanation had been offered for the giant gas bubble eruption, so no one could predict whether it might happen again. Christina vowed not to go anywhere near Lake Pit.

Linda was already at work in Pit 91. Christina waved at her, and Linda smiled a greeting.

"I'll join you in a sec," Christina said, ignoring the usual sulfurous odor.

She changed clothes in the shed and donned a large pair of fireman's boots before descending into the pit.

"Watch your step," Linda said. "The tar's a little slippery today."

Christina noticed it right away. The tar, which normally was heavy and thick, felt thinner, more watery. That made the floor of the pit slick and oily rather than sticky and goopy.

"What's up with that?" Christina asked as she gingerly stepped across the coated planks.

51

"I don't know, maybe it's the heat?" Linda said. She gestured toward a tray of small bones next to the base of the ladder. "Take a look at those. The dig leader uncovered them yesterday. They may be skull fragments from a Merriam's Terratorn. See the beak part?"

Christina examined the fossils. Merriam's Terratorn was an extinct bird of massive size. Specimens from La Brea suggested it had a twelve-foot wingspan, making it even larger than modern-day condors. Fossils from this organism were rare; if she and Linda excavated more of the skeleton today, it would be exciting.

The bones were stained the usual rich, varied brown color imparted by the tar to all the fossils preserved in it. Christina picked up the beak fragment to observe it more closely. Then she dropped it with a start.

"Linda, did you say these were dug up yesterday?"

"Yes. Quite a find, eh?"

"When were they cleaned?"

"Cleaned?"

"Yeah. The asphalt coating's been removed from these bones. Normally everything we dig up has to be treated with solvent at the museum laboratory to make it look like this."

Linda set down her tools at the grid section where she was excavating and half-walked, half-skidded over to Christina.

"Huh, you're right. I swear they weren't that clean when I got here an hour ago."

Christina felt a vague sense of unease in her gut.

"Do you think it has something to do with the tar being more liquid today? Like, it just dripped off?" she said.

"Maybe. I can test that," Linda said, skating back to the open pool of tar.

A small bubble broke the surface of the tar. Christina turned to watch Linda's experiment and noticed that despite the relative fluidity of the tar today, the bubble left a hole in the surface of the tar. She thought the hole was even making a small sound, like a tiny teapot whistle.

What the . . .

When the faint smell of vinegar reached Christina's nose, her scattered thoughts suddenly fell into place.

"Linda, wait—"

But even as the words left her mouth, Linda was picking up her chisel and file. The small metal tools clinked together.

And Linda's outstretched arm burst into flames.

"NO!"

The fire spread so quickly that Christina never saw Linda's expression change from surprise to fear. The surface of the tar ignited, engulfing Linda. Then the oil slick which covered the wood floor Christina was standing on also caught fire. Flames licked her feet and the air in the pit thickened with black petroleum smoke.

"Linda!" Christina screamed, but it was already too late. If she hesitated another second, she wouldn't escape.

Ascending the ladder out of the pit was treacherous under the best conditions. Now, she was fleeing for her life, climbing blind through acrid smoke. She reached for the rung above her head and grasped it tightly while raising one clunky boot.

The tar-encrusted boot was on fire.

Summoning every ounce of self-discipline she possessed, she planted one burning foot after the other and rose above the inferno without slipping. The skin around her knees seared in pain where the flames danced over the top of the boots. She reached the lawn, collapsed on the grass and rolled away, kicking off the boots. Screaming and crying, she crawled back to the pit. The heat and smoke formed a virtual wall that rose parallel to the pit's edge. She could not penetrate it, and though she sat ready to extend a hand and pull her friend to safety, the ladder remained empty.

CHAPTER 11

"Thank God you're all right," River said, placing her hands on Christina's cheeks and kissing her forehead.

Christina lay on a bed in a small emergency room bay defined by gossamer "privacy" curtains. River claimed the only chair and slid it close to the bed to hold her hand. Mickey stood awkwardly with his hands in his pockets and leaned against the wall.

"My friend died in the fire," Christina said, her eyes wet with tears. "All I got was some minor burns and smoke inhalation. I tried to go to her, but I couldn't . . ."

She couldn't hold back the sobs as the horror of those few seconds played over and over in her mind.

"Shhh," River said, stroking Christina's hair. "There wasn't anything you could have done."

Christina nodded and wiped her nose on the hospital gown. "Thanks for coming," she said softly. She was grateful for this reversal of their usual roles, with River playing the part of comforting mother.

River smiled. "Of course. We're family."

Blood is thicker than water. When the ambulance brought her to the hospital, she called her cousin without hesitation. What happened yesterday didn't matter. She needed support, and she needed it now.

"The doctor told me to stay off my feet for a few days," she said.

"That's not a problem. Mickey and I can take care of you," River said, then added, "I mean, if you'll let us."

The elephant in the room had made its presence known.

"Please come home," Christina said.

River squeezed her hand.

*   *   *

At the apartment, Mickey busied himself in the kitchen while River helped Christina wash the smoke from her hair and get into bed. She was barely settled when a knock came at the door.

"I'll get it," Mickey said.

A minute later, he poked his head in Christina's bedroom and said, "Are you decent? LAPD wants to talk to you."

"Not in here," she said. "I can sit on the couch."

The police officer in her living room looked like he'd walked out of a Marine Corps recruitment poster. He was built as solid as a rock and as straight as a Ponderosa pine, with certainty and strength in his expression.

"Lieutenant Jerry Branson, ma'am," he said, shaking her hand. "Would you mind answering a few questions about the incident at La Brea this morning?"

"It was more than an 'incident.' A woman burned to death," Christina snapped, her manners as singed as the skin on her legs.

"I'm aware of that, ma'am. My condolences," Branson said. He paused to emphasize his sincerity, then continued. "I understand you were the only other person in the tar pit with the victim. Can you tell me what happened?"

"Linda was leaning over the tar. I was about ten feet away, right next to the ladder," Christina said. "That distance saved my life but I was too far away to help . . ."

She choked on her words. Branson waited impassively for her to continue.

"Just before the fire, I noticed a small gas jet open up in the tar. Linda was holding her tools; I think they sparked and ignited the gas."

"Did you see the gas jet burn?"

Strange . . . no, she hadn't.

"No, it happened too quickly. The first flame I saw was the fire on Linda's sleeve. Then with all those petroleum products in the pit, it spread like crazy. I made a run for it and barely got out."

55

"You're sure you didn't see a blue flame coming from the tar?"

"It all happened so fast . . ." Christina repeated.

Branson nodded with understanding.

"Were there any other witnesses?" he asked.

"No. The pit is hidden from general view, and the observation platform was vacant."

River jumped up, defensive. "Are you accusing my cousin of lying?"

Branson looked surprised at her outburst, then gave River a calm and weary smile that suggested she watched too much TV.

"No, ma'am, not at all. No one suspects this was anything but an accidental death. But you may have heard that this part of town has had a series of unfortunate accidents in the last two weeks. These accidents all have one thing in common. Gas."

What's this? Christina thought, and inquired further.

"I don't pay much attention to the news, officer. Can you tell me what else has happened?"

"Well, it started with the tar blowout at La Brea, which you must know about since you work there. Then there was a home explosion—two homes, actually. And a couple of days ago, three workers nearly asphyxiated during construction of the Westside subway extension. And now this."

Christina noticed he didn't mention the Jefferson Park accident, or, well, whatever it was. She fervently hoped it wasn't connected to the incidents Branson had just described, but her doubts were growing.

"You believe these were all methane leaks?" she asked.

"That's the most logical explanation," Branson said, half to himself. "This whole area sits on top of an oil field. We know it's releasing methane gas all the time."

"Right. Like the bubbles at La Brea," Christina said. She could see the qualifier "but" written on Branson's face, and spoke it for him. "But . . ."

"But only trace amounts of methane were detected in the subway tunnel. Whatever the gas was that overcame those workers, it diffused away quickly."

Christina straightened up with a sudden urgency.

"What did it smell like?" she asked.

"What did what smell like?" Branson said, not used to being questioned.

"The gas in the subway. Did the workers say it smelled like rotten eggs?"

Branson eyed her keenly. "As a matter of fact, it didn't. One of them said the smell reminded him of sauerkraut."

"Oh," she said, trying to conceal her agitation. "Well, then I guess it probably wasn't methane. At La Brea, the methane always smells like rotten eggs."

Don't tell him what you suspect.

She put on a pained expression even though the prescription narcotics were still doing their job. "I feel just terrible, officer. Is there anything else you need to know?"

Branson rose to his feet. "No, ma'am. Thanks for your time. If I have any more questions I'll call."

River steered him toward the door, giving Christina a queer look as she passed.

"Okay, good-bye," she said and practically caught Branson's heel as she closed the door behind him. Then she sat down on the lounge chair and fixed her eyes on Christina.

"What's going on?"

"Huh?" Christina said.

"Don't play me for a fool, Chrissy, I know you too well. Something about all that gas business freaked you out."

"Yeah, and what the hell is sauerkraut?" Mickey said.

"It's pickled cabbage," Christina said, "and a clue. A clue to the consequences of your damned foolish actions."

She wagged her finger at Mickey.

"Me? What's this got to do with me?"

"You wouldn't know, would you? You and your stupid friends with your green religion, meddling in things far beyond your understanding."

"No need to get nasty, Chrissy," River said.

"Oh, I'm only getting started with nasty. The two of you betrayed me and broke God only knows what laws."

"I thought we were past that," River said.

"Past it? We never even discussed it! You told some associate of yours about my tar sand project. He convinced you that

57

tapping the energy of otherwise inaccessible petroleum was bad for the planet. You decided to do something about it."

"It wasn't my idea," Mickey said.

"But you told him where the test site was."

"Well, kind of, the general vicinity."

"You told him enough. Were you with him that night? Did you bomb the storage tanks?"

"No! No, I wasn't there. He had his own deal. I told him it was a bad idea."

"It wasn't that bad of an idea," River said, defending their actions. "Get off your high horse, Chrissy. There are bigger issues here. I'm sorry your thesis project was set back, but that was pretty temporary, wouldn't you say? Sure, CaliPetro lost some money, what, like, five minutes' worth of company profit? Our 'associate' was acting for the greater good and nobody got hurt."

"The greater good?" Christina fumed. "If Dr. Chen's project had worked, it would've been a major step toward energy independence! You don't like sending billions of dollars to the Saudis, do you? In Saudi Arabia they oppress women! You couldn't even drive a car there, much less gad about publicly with your boyfriend."

"If global warming continues, we'll all be dead and human rights won't matter much," River retorted.

"That's it. I'm calling the cops."

"Whoa, there, ladies," Mickey said, raising his hands in surrender. "Chrissy, I'm sorry. I really am. I should have shown more respect for you. And River, you have to admit we suspected Neil was trouble. We never should've confided in him."

Christina glared at her cousin.

"Fine," River said at last. "I *apologize* that I put the health of our entire planet ahead of corporate interests. I'm *sorry* I had something to do with the destruction of a deserted gas station, and I won't do it again."

"Fine," Christina said in a huff. "Now let me tell you a story about unintended consequences. Something is going on with the subterranean microbiology of this area."

River rolled her eyes.

"Listen to me," Christina said. "It may be related to you and your little terrorist plot. That police officer described events that all involve underground gas leaks: in a subway tunnel, beneath a house, deep in the tar pits. Now, in this part of L.A., we expect occasional methane leaks. They're a natural result of bacteria breaking down the oil that lies below us. But methane isn't the only gas made by bacteria that eat oil. Around here, they also release hydrogen sulfide, which stinks like rotten eggs. Methane bubbling to the surface at La Brea is always contaminated with hydrogen sulfide. You can smell it."

"That's why you asked the cop about the smell," Mickey said.

"Right. The day that Lake Pit erupted on those people, I was struck by the *absence* of hydrogen sulfide in the air. And I noticed something else. The smell of acetic acid."

"What's your point, Chrissy?" River asked.

"Acetic acid is the key ingredient in vinegar. Store-bought sauerkraut smells like vinegar."

"So you think the gas leak in the subway and the big bubble at La Brea are related," Mickey said.

"Yes. And more importantly, I don't think the primary gas in either case was methane."

"What, then?" River demanded with more interest than Christina expected.

"I think it was hydrogen. The police think so, too."

"How do you know that?" River said.

"Because that officer specifically asked me whether I could see the flame that ignited Linda's sleeve. Methane burns blue; you can easily see it when you light a natural gas stove. But hydrogen flames are invisible in daylight. You could walk right into a hydrogen gas fire and not know it was there until it was too late. Branson wanted to know if the gas leak this morning was hydrogen or methane."

"Does it matter?" Mickey said.

Christina nodded. "It matters a lot. Oil is rich in energy, right? Well, some bacteria are able to eat oil as an energy source the same way that we eat sugar or fat. Now, depending on a number of factors—for example, the petroleum source and the kinds of

59

bacteria present—different waste products are left over after the bacteria eat the oil. Normally in the ecosystem of the Los Angeles basin, the main gaseous waste product is methane. A sudden switch toward hydrogen production suggests a change in the underground ecosystem."

"The oil changed?" River said.

"No, the oil field can't change over a couple of weeks. The change must be in the population of oil-eating bacteria."

She stared at River and Mickey, waiting for them to connect the dots.

"Is that bad?" Mickey asked.

She grew impatient.

"My experiment at the gas station in Jefferson Park—the one you blew up—had special oil-eating bacteria in it, bacteria we engineered to be really efficient at breaking down hydrocarbons and turning them into hydrogen gas and acetic acid."

River went pale. She gets it, Christina thought.

"But . . . but . . . I thought your project was supposed to harvest methane from the tar sand," River said.

Christina leaned forward with an accusatory glance. "I gave you the Cliff Notes version of the project. The biochemistry is actually more complex. More than one species of bacteria is involved. In my experiment, they lived together in an underground community. One species, *Syntrophus*, breaks down the oil. Then a second kind of bacteria takes the *Syntrophus* waste and turns it into methane, water, and carbon dioxide. Our goal was to harvest the methane at the end."

"So you're saying—" Mickey said and stopped, unable to discern her point.

"I'm saying you messed with things you don't understand. You blew a hole in an underground tank of genetically-altered bacteria, and now they're taking over."

"The 'syn' ones?" River asked.

Christina nodded. "If my *Syntrophus* bacteria spread widely in the oil field beneath our feet, then we would expect new hydrogen gas leaks in the neighborhood. And it looks like that's what is happening."

"Subterranean bacteria? An ecosystem in an oil field?" Mickey said, shaking his head like it hurt from thinking too much. "What are you talking about? Nothing lives underground."

Christina snorted. "There may be more life underground than above. The biomass of microorganisms in the deep biosphere probably exceeds the entire biomass of all plants and animals on the earth's surface."

She faced them squarely and delivered her knockout punch. "You've committed a cardinal sin of the green movement. You introduced an invasive, genetically-modified organism into a delicate ecosystem, and no one can predict the consequences."

River sat still, a pensive look on her face. She swallowed hard, and when she spoke her voice was soft and shaky.

"Mickey," River said, "we killed Linda."

CHAPTER 12

The six thousand-gallon tanker truck swung wide to make a left turn into the GasMan independent filling station in Jefferson Park. Ronny, the driver, deftly maneuvered the huge truck past a palm tree and a parked car and rolled to a stop at the access portal for the station's underground fuel storage tanks. GasMan was the first stop on his daily rounds delivering gasoline to retail outlets in this part of L.A. Today he was carrying unleaded, 87 octane, summer blend.

The phrase "summer blend" made him laugh, as if the gas were some kind of specialty brew from Starbucks. Most motorists didn't know that the gas they bought between June 1st and September 15th had a different formula from the normal stuff. In the heat of summer, the volatile components of gasoline boil off more easily and pollute the air. To reduce summertime smog, Los Angeles oil refineries change the gasoline they produce to a low-evaporation blend.

Moving with limber grace from long experience, Ronny swung down from the cab and released the gasoline hose from its secured position on the truck. He dragged the hose to the fill port and lifted the small, heavy lid. After confirming the spill bucket inside the port was empty, Ronny hooked up the hose and started to pump gas into the underground tank.

While he waited, Ronny kept an eye out for the station's owner, fervently hoping the guy wasn't there. The owner had gone ape-shit when he was accused of selling tainted gasoline. He blamed the distributor, but tests of the fuel in the underground storage tank got everyone off the hook: nothing wrong with the gas. Ronny expected there would be lawsuits anyway, so the owner was on edge. This was Ronny's first visit to replenish the station since the news broke, and he didn't want to be the person the guy vented on.

A flashing red light on the side of the building caught his eye. *The overfill alarm. That can't be right.*

Sticking to protocol, he immediately cut off the flow of gas into the tank. The overfill alarm was designed to prevent spills, and it was triggered when the underground tank was 90% full. Ronny knew the GasMan storage tank had a capacity of six thousand gallons. He checked his instruments: only about two thousand had gone in. Normally, he delivered over five thousand gallons of 87 octane to GasMan.

Must be the bad press, he thought. If customers were avoiding the station, that would explain why less gas had been sold.

Leaving with an extra three thousand gallons in his truck was a pain in his ass. Retains, as such incidents were called in the business, cost money. Rather than haul the gas back to the refinery, he'd try to top off some of his other customers in the area. But before he did that, he wanted to verify that the GasMan tank really was full. He didn't have a lot of faith in electronic monitoring systems, so he fetched a bit of old-fashioned technology from his truck: a gauge stick.

When unfolded, the gauge stick was twelve feet long. Ronny lowered it through the port and dipped it into the gas. The overfill alarm was right; the tank was nearly full. He refolded the stick and kept it handy because he'd be using it at the stations he visited next. Then he sealed the access port, packed up the gas hose, and wheeled his tanker truck back on the road.

CHAPTER 13

After a couple of days' healing rest, Christina was back at UCLA. When she arrived on campus, she ordered the largest size soda at the Court of Sciences plaza café. She needed the caffeine to counteract the sedative effect of the mild painkillers she was taking for the burns on her legs.

The building directory still read "UCLA-CaliPetro Bioenergy Institute." Christina wondered if Bactofuels would get its name up there soon.

"Good morning, Dr. Chen," she said, bouncing into the lab.

"Chrissy! Welcome back," Dr. Chen said. "It's too quiet around here without you. How are you doing? Are you sure you're ready to be on your feet again?"

His voice conveyed genuine concern. When Christina chose to work with Robert Chen, she won the P.I. lottery. He was a good scientist and a good man.

"I'm fine, Dr. Chen. Plus my cousin is driving me crazy."

He laughed. "I know what you mean. I can't stand being sick; I start to lose my mind after two days at home. Well, I have lots of work for you to do. Jeff Trinley was here yesterday about the photosynthetic *E. coli* project. Bactofuels wants HPLC measurements of bacteriochlorophyll production and quantification of gene expression from the *crt* operon."

"I can do that," Christina said.

"That's what I told Trinley," Dr. Chen said, "even though he didn't believe it."

"Thanks," she said, grateful for her mentor's support.

"If you don't mind, I need to excuse myself for a few minutes. I'm in the middle of writing a review. Don't want to lose my train of thought."

"Of course," Christina said.

Dr. Chen disappeared into his office. Christina drained her soda cup and tossed it in the trash before approaching her lab bench. Though she was tidy, her workspace was probably contaminated with toxic chemicals. She would never bring food or drink near it.

She opened a laboratory protocols manual to review how to do the HPLC experiment, but found it hard to concentrate. She worried about the escaped *Syntrophus* bacteria—if that's what had happened. River and Mickey agreed that she ought to tell Dr. Chen about the gas leaks around town. Christina conceded that she would not tell him CaliPetro's experiment had been sabotaged. An accidental explosion sufficiently explained how the bacteria might have entered the subterranean ecosystem.

She hated to lay a burden of guilt on him; Dr. Chen would feel responsible for the accident and its consequences. But she couldn't rat on her family.

If I ever get my hands on that Neil character . . .

Using a flint sparker, Christina lit a blue flame in the Bunsen burner on her bench. The fire acted like salt on her emotional wounds from Pit 91.

Oh, Linda, she thought and wiped her eyes with the sleeve of her lab coat.

Natural gas was easy to ignite, but hydrogen gas was ten times easier. Ordinary static from a person's hair or clothes could do it. At the time of the accident, Linda was carrying steel excavation tools in one hand. They clinked against each other and sparked over a hydrogen leak. Linda didn't have a chance.

Christina cordoned off her grief and started to work. She picked up a bacterial culture needle—a thin platinum wire mounted on a pencil-like handle—and lifted the wire into the hottest part of the burner flame until the metal glowed red. After allowing the wire to cool in the air, she plunged it into a flask of cloudy yellow liquid: an old culture of the photosynthetic *E. coli* bacteria. Then she dipped the tip of the wire into a tube of fresh sterile broth. To the naked eye the wire looked clean, but Christina knew it was covered with thousands of invisible bacteria that would slip off into the fresh food and begin to grow vigorously, doubling in number every half hour. Only a touch was all it took to spread bacteria from one liquid to another.

"Chrissy?" Dr. Chen said. "I finished the abstract. You said you wanted to talk to me about something?"

She told him what she'd heard from the police officer about the incidents, and how they could all be explained by hydrogen gas leaks. She emphasized that acetic acid vapors were often present, and that methane was not detected in the subway accident.

"Dr. Chen, all these things happened after the explosion in Jefferson Park," she said.

Her teacher's expression was grave. "I heard on the radio this morning that there was a fire in the basement of a grocery store in Koreatown. That could be another one."

"Do you think our *Syntrophus* bacteria are responsible?"

"That's quite a lot of circumstantial evidence, so I'm forced to consider the possibility," Dr. Chen said.

"Should we test for it?"

"How? *Syntrophus* is anaerobic; exposure to air kills it. To get a test sample, we'd have to drill at least ten meters underground."

"CaliPetro could do that."

"I'm pretty sure CaliPetro doesn't want to know."

"So what are we going to do?"

Dr. Chen considered for a minute.

"Nothing," he said. "At least, nothing for now. We'll wait and see what develops. If our altered *Syntrophus* bacteria are feasting their way through the Salt Lake Oil Field, there's nothing we can do to stop them. Once they've eaten the uppermost layers, the system should naturally come into some kind of balance."

"But what about the danger of hydrogen leaks?"

Again, Dr. Chen was momentarily silent.

"Let's hope for the best. And stay out of any basements."

Chapter 14

"Triple-A emergency road service, may I help you?"

The caller dispensed with any niceties and launched into an expletive-laden tirade. Gary, the call center associate who'd answered the phone, let the man carry on until he had to stop for breath.

"I'm very sorry about the wait, sir. If I can have your member number, I'll get an update on your situation."

He typed in the number and scanned the report. The caller had been waiting over three hours for an American Automobile Association contractor to come and start his car. Gary saw the address: the malfunctioning auto was in central Los Angeles, 90006 zip code.

"Sir, I understand your frustration but we're experiencing an unusual number of service requests in your area. According to my records, you reported you were not in any danger. Is that still correct?"

The caller carried on a bit about the dangers of unemployment, but admitted he was safe at home, his car parked on the street out front.

"A service vehicle will be dispatched to your location as soon as one becomes available. But to be frank, sir, you may want to make alternative arrangements to get to work today."

The caller hung up. Gary shook his head in amazement. In eight years on this job, he'd never seen a day like this. Calls about stalled cars were pouring in at an unprecedented rate, as if Southern California were in the middle of a North Dakota blizzard. The opposite was true; the region was in the grip of a heat wave, with inland temperatures reaching into the low hundreds. The strangest thing about it, however, was that the stranded cars were nearly all located within thirty miles of downtown L.A., the majority concentrated in central L.A., south L.A., and the area around USC. Gary had seen a computer-generated map marking each call with a red dot. The dots were piled up like a volcanic cone in one area, and flowed out like lava from the center.

AAA was bringing in tow trucks from as far away as Long Beach to handle the situation, but the backup of customers was growing. On a normal day, most calls came from drivers with dead batteries, flat tires, or empty gas tanks, all of which could be handled fairly quickly on the spot. Today, most of the cars needed to be towed to a repair shop for a diagnosis, which was really tying up the service crews.

The calls kept coming. Gary wondered what the heck was going on in central L.A.

CHAPTER 15

Shawna White took both hands off the steering wheel and picked up her cell phone to compose a text message. After thirty minutes on the northbound one-ten, she'd traveled about four miles. This being Los Angeles, she usually didn't bother to seek an explanation for traffic slowdowns. They happened, like lightning bolts from an angry god. You couldn't predict them, prevent them, or avoid them if it was your fate to get stuck.

But today, the reason for the jam was pretty clear. In those four miles, Shawna had seen five stalled cars, and only three of them were on the side of the road. The other two were blocking lanes of traffic. In the maxed-out highway system of L.A., a slowdown could be triggered by a single driver carelessly changing lanes and forcing just one other car to hit the brakes. So it was no surprise that those stalls were wreaking havoc on the road.

Must be the heat, Shawna thought. It was so freaking hot out on the pavement that her car's air conditioning was having a tough time keeping up. She worried that the nine-year-old Chrysler might overheat, and decided to get off the freeway for a potty break and a soda. She took the exit for West Jefferson Boulevard and pulled in to a filling station with a minimart.

Technically it wasn't afternoon rush hour yet, so after topping off her tank and buying a bottle of Sobe, Shawna opted to try her luck on surface roads. As she expected, the going was slow (red light . . . red light . . . red light) but she was heartened by radio reports that the traffic jam on the one-ten was getting worse instead of better. For once she'd made the right choice of route.

After another wasted forty-five minutes, she reached her home in Westlake, near Wilshire Boulevard. She had two hours before the start of her shift as a cashier at Food 4 Less.

Shawna knew stop-and-go driving like that was hard on a car. She couldn't remember the last time she'd had the oil changed. The car was a clunker, but it was paid for. Money was tight; she couldn't afford to have it break down. Better to spend a little now than a lot later. She decided to stop at a quick lube joint before work.

A lanky young man in greasy overalls took her keys. Shawna watched him drive her car into the open-air bay and seated herself in the waiting room. A tattered copy of *Us* magazine dated three months ago lay on a table. She stuck a quarter in a candy machine and turned the crank for a handful of generic M&Ms.

It came without warning. The explosion rattled but did not break the floor-to-ceiling windows in the waiting room. Colorful little candies scattered across the floor as she dropped them in surprise. A metallic boom and the sound of shattering glass came from the garage. Men shouted. An alarm went off. Shawna and the other customers in the lounge dashed for the exit and gathered on the sidewalk outside. Smoke billowed from the work bay.

She recognized her car. It was suspended in the air on a post lift, engulfed in flames like an overheated marshmallow on a stick. She stared at it in disbelief.

Then with the black humor of a person accustomed to bad breaks, she said, "So much for preventive maintenance."

CHAPTER 16

An electric cart with Chevron's blue and red logo on its side zipped through a maze of pipelines in a bewildering industrial jungle. Wearing a blue jumpsuit, white hardhat and steel-toed boots, Ken Khadder steered the cart under the shadow of tall stacks emitting white clouds of steam. Ken had been a reliability engineer at Chevron's El Segundo refinery for so long he could practically navigate the one and a half square-mile facility blindfolded.

Ken knew as much about Chevron's main Los Angeles oil refinery as anyone alive. At some point in his career he'd worked on every system at El Segundo. From the offshore Marine Terminal where oil tankers unloaded their crude into pipelines that ran under Santa Monica Bay, to the distillation towers where the refining process began, to the cat cracker that converted heavy petroleum into gasoline: Ken knew how El Segundo worked. He was even the refinery's unofficial historian, happy to tell visitors about Standard Oil choosing this site for their second California refinery in 1911 to produce kerosene for lamps.

In 1911, El Segundo was an unpopulated hinterland on the Pacific coast south of Los Angeles. The city grew up around it, a relentless urban sea that lapped at the refinery's borders. Los Angeles International Airport was less than a mile to the north, and this proximity made LAX an important customer. El Segundo supplied 40% of the jet fuel used at LAX.

Jet fuel was on Ken's agenda today. He rolled the electric cart to a stop beside what looked like a giant erector set. The complex metallic structure was the refinery's hydrocracking unit. It converted heavy petroleum into jet fuel, a sophisticated chemical process that used a patented catalyst to break or "crack" large hydrocarbon molecules into smaller ones. Ken spoke to a supervisor at the hydrocracking unit, reminding him about the pipeline maintenance scheduled for that afternoon. Then he continued to the storage tank area, where he met another engineer wearing a jumpsuit that was stretched tight over his expansive belly.

"Did you bring the pig, Al?" Ken asked.

"Wouldn't be doing my job if I didn't," Al replied. "I'm the pig keeper."

They both smiled at his joke.

"These smart pigs are my babies," Al continued. "The one in the truck is new. I used it for the first time yesterday. Worked like a charm."

"Which in-line inspection did you use it for?"

"We ran the pig through the gasoline delivery pipelines. Got data on the integrity of all the 87 and 89 octane pipes, from storage tanks to trucks."

"Then I expect the pig will do a good job again today. We'll run it through the jet fuel pipelines from here to LAX. Program the pig to record information on metal loss and corrosion, and temperature and pressure in the pipe. Of course if there are any early signs of fracture, I want to know. Get pictures, if you can."

"It's as good as done," Al said.

The two men walked to the bed of Al's truck, where he opened a large plastic case approximately the shape of a pipe. The smart pig was inside.

Al made an oinking sound, but of course the pig didn't squeal. A pig, or pipeline inspection gauge, is a tool inserted into a pipeline to perform a task, such as cleaning the pipe, separating batches of different liquids flowing through the same pipeline, or in this case, inspecting the pipeline as part of routine maintenance.

"Nice pig," Ken said.

"A beauty, isn't she?" Al said. "Looks like a cross between a jet engine and a sandworm from *Dune*."

"Yeah. A real beauty," Ken said with a laugh. "Let's get her in the trap."

The pig trap, or launcher, was isolated from the main pipe by a valve above and a valve beyond. Al made sure the trap was depressurized, then inserted a key to open the trap closure lid. Together they lifted the pig and shoved it through the opening. Then Al sealed the lid behind the pig. Next, he opened the kicker connection which isolated the trap from the main pipe. Pressurized jet fuel rushed from the main pipe into the trap behind the pig. This flow pushed the pig forward, but the pig couldn't enter the main pipe until Al opened the throat valve. When he did open it, they heard the pig surge down the pipe, propelled by flowing jet fuel.

"Done," Al said as he reset the system and depressurized the trap. "This little piggy went to market."

Ken waved approval and departed to continue his rounds on the electric cart. Hours later he got a call from Al.

"I retrieved the pig and downloaded the inspection data," Al said. "I'll send you the file but the bottom line is the LAX pipeline looks great and the pig performed flawlessly. Just like yesterday in the gasoline pipes."

"Glad to hear it, Al. We wouldn't want any problems getting jet fuel to the airport. Summer travel season is in full swing," Ken said.

"If LAX has a problem, it won't be our fault," Al assured him.

Before leaving work for the day, Ken checked a traffic report. The news was bad. He groaned and called his wife to let her know he'd be late.

CHAPTER 17

"This is bullshit," Mickey said, rising from his seat on the Metro Bus.

"Sit down, Mickey," Christina said, embarrassed. "Don't make a scene. There's nothing we can do about the traffic."

River rolled her eyes. "You're always so passive, Chrissy. We've been sitting here for twenty minutes and haven't moved an inch. I think it's time to do something." She gathered up the tote bags that were scattered on the bus floor around them. "At this rate, the milk will be spoiled before we get home."

"At least it's air conditioned in here. The milk definitely won't survive the walk to the apartment. I bet it's ninety-eight degrees outside," Christina said.

"I'm getting off," Mickey said impatiently, and extended a hand in invitation to River.

Christina looked out the window at the stack of cars on Wilshire. "You can't just get off in the middle of the street."

"Oh for God's sake, Chrissy, nothing is moving," River said. "Whatever is blocking the road isn't about to magically go away. This bus is a trap." She found the two heaviest grocery bags and draped them over Mickey's arm.

"You can sit here if you like, but we're leaving," she said, and gestured to Mickey to move to the front of the bus.

Christina was scrupulously rule-abiding, and disembarking in this way felt a bit mutinous. But River was probably right; the bus was going to be stuck for a while. Christina grabbed the last of the groceries and followed her cousin toward the driver. To her surprise, the driver opened the door and freed them without comment.

"Bet he wishes he could walk away, too," Mickey said as they traded the cool comfort of the bus for the heat of the pavement.

The trio began the trek to the apartment on foot. Christina estimated a thirty-minute walk from where they were. She arranged the bag straps more comfortably on her shoulders. Mickey removed his shirt.

As they walked down one block after another, Christina got a better view of the magnitude of the traffic problem today. She'd never seen anything like it. Wilshire Boulevard was completely jammed. Intersections were gridlocked. Parked cars, and cars trying to exit parking garages, were trapped in place. Because of the heat, most of the drivers were keeping their cars running for the A/C. The air was thick with hot exhaust fumes.

"What a nightmare," River said.

"Triumph of the internal combustion engine," Mickey said. "Serves all those car owners right. It's just too bad they're taking the public buses down with them."

Christina never demonized cars, she simply couldn't afford one. But despite the long walk in the heat, she was relieved not to be in a private vehicle today.

They turned down a side street to escape the pollution on Wilshire, and discovered that traffic was backed up in every direction. Shade was more plentiful on the other side of the street, so they turned to cross over.

"Is that car empty?" River said, shielding her eyes to peer into a silver Toyota Camry that was stopped in the middle of the street.

Mickey and Christina checked the passenger side and back seat.

"Totally," Mickey said. "Where's the driver?"

The car wasn't running, and the doors were unlocked.

"Maybe the air conditioning gave out and he couldn't take the heat," River said. "There's a puddle on the ground under the car. Maybe it's Freon."

"Freon's a gas, not a liquid," Mickey said. "Could be antifreeze, though."

Christina knelt down to look at the unknown liquid. As her nose dipped low to the ground, she was struck by an unmistakable smell.

Vinegar.

"Get away from the car," she said, standing up with deliberation to avoid any sudden movements that could generate a spark.

Mickey was on the other side, and either didn't hear or ignored her. He reached out for the car's roof. Christina yelped in dismay when his hand made contact with the metal of the car.

"Mickey, get away from the car," she said urgently.

He continued to ignore her. "If other people are ditching their cars, too, it'll take forever to clear this traffic jam," Mickey said and opened the passenger door.

"No, Mickey!" Christina shouted.

She dropped her groceries and ran at him. He wasn't expecting to be tackled, and the momentum of her crashing into him knocked them both down, away from the car. Canned beans and frozen orange juice rolled down the street.

"What was that for?" Mickey yelled as he shoved Christina off and stood up.

"Please, listen," she said. "Stay away from the car."

The pleading in her voice affected him, and he didn't move. "Why?"

She picked up the scattered food items and led River and Mickey to the opposite sidewalk.

"That car is leaking acetic acid."

River's eyes widened.

"Hydrogen," River said. "You told us acetic acid and hydrogen went together."

"Yes," Christina said. "There may be a hydrogen leak around the car. Mickey, the slightest thing could set it off."

They continued walking in silence, passing more cars stuck in the traffic. Some of these were empty, too, but the drivers were loafing nearby, talking on their cell phones as they waited for a chance to escape this extraordinary mess.

"Chrissy," River said at last, "what is going on?"

She sounded afraid.

"Nothing. I mean, I don't know. Really bad traffic," Christina said.

"Chrissy," River continued, "I thought those bacteria of yours—the ones that eat oil—you said they live underground."

"They do," Christina said. "*Syntrophus* species are anaerobic. That means they're killed by oxygen. They can't survive in the presence of air any more than we can survive without it."

"Then why was that car leaking vinegar?"

"Well, acetic acid is corrosive. It'll eat through metal pretty quickly."

Then River's point penetrated Christina's willful ignorance. She stopped walking and felt her stomach tie up in a knot.

"No, that's impossible," she said, arguing out loud with herself.

"Chrissy," River said, her voice trembling on the verge of crying, "what would happen if your bacteria got into a car's gas tank?"

"They would die because of the air."

"But what if they didn't die?"

Christina closed her eyes and recited.

"*Syntrophus* converts crude oil into hydrogen, acetic acid and carbon dioxide. The reaction is energetically unfavorable unless a second species of bacteria consumes the hydrogen and carbon dioxide. *Syntrophus* lives underground, where there isn't any air and temperatures exceed a hundred degrees."

"It's hot today," River said.

"But the air . . ." Christina said.

Mickey's mental wheels turned more slowly, but he was catching on.

"Wait a minute," he said. "Those bacteria eat gasoline? And turn it into vinegar?"

"No," Christina said, "I mean, yes, they can, but not in the presence of air, not in a car."

River fixed her eyes on her cousin.

"What if they survived?"

Christina looked away. Avoiding further eye contact, she picked up her bags and marched away.

"They can't do that," she said, as if it were the final word on the matter.

But the ominous statement she herself made a few days ago echoed in her mind.

No one can predict the consequences.

CHAPTER 18

"This is the captain speaking. We're number one for takeoff. Flight attendants, please be seated."

Mariah Donahue, head flight attendant for Qantas flight 101 from LAX to Sydney, Australia, made a final fuss over the passengers in the Boeing 747's first class cabin and sank into her seat. She was tired already, and they still had a fourteen-hour flight ahead of them.

The delay on the tarmac had put everyone on edge. Mariah had to keep the passengers strapped in their seats because regulations demanded no one get up while the plane was on an active runway. The passengers grew restless because no one could tell them exactly how long they'd be stuck. The delay had grown from fifteen minutes to fifty-five, and she'd had to deal with several incidents of people getting up to use the toilet or opening the overhead bins to fetch something. At least they were on their way now.

Mariah listened to the familiar sound of the jet's powerful engines revving and felt the g-force as the plane accelerated forward. Finally it will cool off in here, she thought. Los Angeles was blazing today, and the plane's air conditioning was no match for the scorching pavement. The crew had asked the passengers to close their window shades to block out the sun, but it still got pretty stuffy, especially in the crowded coach cabin. The flight attendants back there were preparing to serve glasses of water when the takeoff clearance finally came.

A minute after lifting off the plane was over the ocean. For the rest of the flight, the view from the window seats would be endless blue or black of night. Mariah unbuckled and started the in-flight entertainment with previews of the movies to be shown. She and her fellow crew members had a dozen small tasks to complete while the jet ascended toward its cruising altitude of thirty-five thousand feet.

Twenty minutes into the flight, she got a call from the flight deck. The first officer was speaking.

"Ms. Donahue, report to the cockpit at once."

It was an unusual request and the first officer's voice sounded tense. But Mariah was unruffled; she'd logged more than a million miles of flying during her career and had complete confidence in the aircraft and its crew. She glided to the front of the cabin and inserted her key into the reinforced cockpit door.

"We're going back," Captain Mackenzie said after the door closed behind her. "I'll make an announcement to the passengers momentarily."

Mariah had flown with Mackenzie dozens of times. He was about as experienced a pilot as you could find; he'd been flying for Qantas for twenty-eight years. She liked his style: stern when necessary, gracious when appropriate. He delivered this news with cool professionalism.

"What's wrong?" she asked.

"We're losing fuel. We loaded fifty thousand gallons of Jet A at LAX. Sensors say we've lost one-fifth of that volume. At the same time, I'm reading a massive increase in vapor pressure in the tanks."

"It doesn't make any sense!" the flight engineer exclaimed without Mackenzie's emotional restraint. "If fuel is leaking out, the pressure should bleed off into the atmosphere."

The Captain kept his eyes on his instruments while he spoke. "I agree, I've never seen anything like this. These readings break all the rules. Air traffic control is aware of our situation and they're clearing the airport for us. I've got experts at Qantas and Boeing scrambling to give me a scenario analysis. In the meantime, Mariah, I need you to prepare the cabin for emergency landing. I expect to touch down at LAX in twenty-eight minutes, but I want the passengers ready for a water landing just in case."

"Yes, sir," Mariah said. She left the cockpit with her heart in her throat.

She'd only just finished informing the other flight attendants when Captain Mackenzie's voice came over the intercom.

"Ladies and gentleman, we're experiencing a problem with our fuel tank. As you know it's a long way to Sydney, so for everyone's safety we're going to turn around and return to Los Angeles. It's particularly important at a time like this for you to remain calm and give your full attention to the flight attendants, who will now prepare the cabin for landing. Thank you."

His words were bland and his voice sounded calm. Many of the passengers seemed more concerned about another delay than about a mechanical problem. But when Mariah instructed everyone to put on a life vest, the tension level in the cabin skyrocketed. Several passengers started to weep; one even wailed out loud.

"In the event of an emergency evacuation, leave all personal—"

Mariah faltered for a moment and listened. The sound of the aircraft was wrong. It was too quiet. She felt the nose tilt forward slightly.

"—belongings underneath the seat—"

It happened again. Mariah realized the stepwise silencing of the background noise was the sound of engines dying. They'd just lost starboard engines one and two.

The 747 had only two engines left.

That's enough, she reassured herself. We can make it just fine on two, or even one.

She continued her speech. A murmur rose in the aft left side of the cabin; some of the passengers had noticed the silence. She hoped they didn't start a panic. If everyone just stayed in their seats . . .

The loss of sound wasn't dramatic like an explosion would be, but its significance was equally profound. Mariah realized the silence was now complete. Engines three and four had also failed.

The plane yawed a little, then corrected. Trying not to look like she was in a hurry, Mariah entered the cockpit.

"Roger, we've lost all four engines," Mackenzie was saying. "Possible vapor lock with sensor malfunction. Fuel tanks still reading half full."

"There's nothing wrong with the engines!" the flight engineer said. "We still have plenty of fuel! What the hell is going on? Boeing, can you explain these readings?"

"Sir," Mariah said gently.

"Eight minutes," Mackenzie said to her. "I'm going to bring her down on the water. We've got about eight minutes glide time. Strap yourself in."

Either bravery or denial allowed the flight attendant to inform the other members of the cabin crew, assist several passengers with their life jackets, and get herself seated before sickening terror filled her belly. Five minutes after leaving the cockpit, Mariah was in her chair, watching the choppy sea come closer and closer. She tried to swallow.

I'm a professional. These people need me.

Emergency drills, memorized in comfortable classrooms and simulated crashes, scrolled through her mind like text at the bottom of a CNN broadcast.

Unlike the placid Hudson River that cradled Captain Sully's plane, the sea below Mackenzie's Boeing churned with huge waves. At first contact with the water, the plane jerked violently. Metal groaned. Plastics snapped. Passengers screamed. Mariah clenched her seat. The aircraft was breaking up. She waited helplessly for salty water to stream into the fuselage.

But drowning was not her fate. Forty-eight minutes and twenty-two seconds after takeoff, the central fuel tank on Qantas flight 101 exploded, shredding bodies and scattering debris across a square mile of the Pacific Ocean.

CHAPTER 19

Mickey heaved his grocery bags into the kitchen and dug out a half gallon of milk. He opened it and drank straight from the carton.

"Gross," Christina said as she delivered her load to the counter.

"Hey, the milk's warm," he said. "Better to drink it than dump it."

River straggled in and made a beeline for the window air conditioner, turning it on as high as it would go.

"Save energy, save money," Christina chided her.

"I'll pay for it," River replied. She collapsed sweating on the couch, leaving Mickey and Christina to unpack the food.

Since their encounter with the stalled car Christina had been an automaton, unwilling to acknowledge the meaning of what she saw happening around her. The heat, the fumes, the angry drivers, the abandoned cars—the walk home was like a scene from a disaster movie. She was relieved to be inside the apartment where she could close the door and ignore the terrible doubts nagging her conscience. Mechanically, she emptied a five-pound bag of rice into a storage container and made room in the cabinet for jars of pasta sauce.

River turned on the T.V.

"—has gone down eighty miles offshore in heavy seas. The pilot of the 747 reported a series of puzzling sensor readings and was returning to LAX when the plane may have exploded in mid-air. The search for any survivors will be delayed because in a shocking coincidence, a second aircraft, reported to be a Hawaiian Airlines Boeing 767, has made an emergency water landing about thirty miles from shore. We've been told that inflatable rafts were successfully deployed from the Hawaiian Airlines flight, and rescue crews are being dispatched to the scene."

Christina dropped what she was doing.

"What are you watching?"

"It's the news, and it's on all the channels. Something about airplane crashes out of LAX."

"Crash-*es*? As in plural?" Mickey said.

Christina took a seat next to River on the couch, her eyes glued to the set as she listened to the newscaster.

"We're trying to bring you the most accurate information," he said, "but the situation is changing quickly. Right now, we believe two aircraft have gone down in the Pacific. Another two aircraft have been lost over land, and three have successfully made emergency landings at LAX, Burbank and Ontario Airports. The affected flights all departed LAX after 2 PM today. All flights from area airports have been suspended, and flights out of LAX that are currently in the air have been ordered to land at the nearest airport."

"It's like September 11th," River said.

"Do they think terrorists are responsible?" Mickey said.

"Shh," Christina said.

A round-faced female official from the Los Angeles Department of Transportation appeared on the screen. A reporter questioned her.

"Does your department believe there's a connection between the chaos on the freeways and in the air?"

"Well, ATSAC, our automated traffic surveillance and control system, tells us we have widespread disruption of the road network. The worst problems are in central L.A., where we've got blockage of all major freeways and most surface roads as well. The cause appears to be an unusual number of breakdowns. People's cars are just stopping, and we can't clear them fast enough to keep the roads open. We've also had reports of car fires in at least three locations. Now, we don't have an explanation, but it's hard to believe that the simultaneous problems at LAX and on our roads are just a coincidence."

"Can you speculate on the connection?" the reporter asked.

The dark-haired woman cleared her throat. "One possible connection is the fuel supply."

"Is the city prepared for a terrorist attack on the fuel supply?"

The official twisted in her chair. "I don't think we're looking at an attack here. Even if someone tampered with our city's pipelines or refineries and sabotaged the fuel, we don't think the consequences could be this widespread."

"But it's possible?" the reported pushed.

Christina grabbed the remote and changed the channel. Another station was broadcasting images of a car fire on the one-ten freeway. A photojournalist described the pandemonium.

"Our van is trapped in this frozen river of cars that you see around me," she said. "About forty-five minutes ago, a stalled Mercedes C230 maybe two hundred yards ahead of us started on fire." She gestured and the camera panned from her to the burned-out shell of a car. "We have yet to see any firefighters or police on the scene."

Mickey started talking at the T.V. "They can't get there. Nothing can move."

The story was the same on every channel: airplane disasters, stalled cars, fires, and complete gridlock. The situation was worst in central L.A.

Without asking for permission, Christina turned off the television. The three of them sat in silence. Finally River spoke.

"Jefferson Park is in the center of it all."

"Oh, come on. You don't think we're responsible for this," Mickey said. "Chrissy already told us her bacteria can't survive in air."

"I know what she told us," River said, looking expectantly at her cousin.

"Maybe someone put something in the oil supply," Christina said. "A poison of some kind that ruins the gas."

"Chrissy, how much poison would it take to contaminate that much gasoline? And jet fuel, too?" River said. "A huge amount, an impossible amount, spread all over the place. Nobody could pull that off."

"Maybe an oil company made a mistake," Christina said desperately. "Maybe they mixed up their fuel shipments, like, diesel instead of gasoline."

"Normally I'd be happy to blame Big Oil," River said, "but face the facts. Whatever is happening in Los Angeles is growing and spreading. Poison can't do that. Delivery mix-ups can't do that. But your bacteria can. They grow. They spread."

"They're killed by oxygen!" Christina said.

River rolled her eyes. The telephone rang. Christina hastened to answer it.

"Chrissy, it's Dr. Chen. Can you come to the lab right away?"

"I think so. My bicycle still works. What's up?"

She could hear his incredulity in the silence.

"You of all people should know," Dr. Chen said.

CHAPTER 20

Christina steered her bike through the paralyzed streets on her way to UCLA. She refused to think, and concentrated on the novelty of not having to dodge moving cars while bicycling. When she arrived, the softness of a Southern California evening lay on the campus. Dwindling sunlight and a gentle breeze came from the direction of the ocean. She locked her bike on the usual rack, but changed her mind about leaving it unattended. In today's traffic situation, her wheels were worth more than a car. She took the bike up to the lab with her.

Hardly anyone was on campus. Christina wondered how many students and professors had made it home, and how many were stranded. The door to the lab was locked. She dug her keys from her backpack.

"Dr. Chen?"

"I'm here, Chrissy," he called from the media prep kitchen in the back.

Christina noticed someone had printed out three journal articles and laid them on her desk. The titles said they were about lateral gene transfer in bacteria. She didn't know why they were there.

Dr. Chen emerged, wiping his hands on a paper towel. He tossed the towel in a trash can, crossed his arms, and leaned against the hard black surface of the lab countertop. His brow wrinkled as he seemed to struggle for the right words.

"If our *Syntrophus* bacteria are in the city's gasoline, I . . ." he began, then faltered and lowered his head.

Christina felt tears welling up in her eyes.

"Our bacteria didn't do this," she said. "They're anaerobes."

Dr. Chen laughed, a mournful, hollow laugh.

"Christina. At some point in the past, all life on earth was anaerobic. But it didn't stay that way."

She didn't want to believe.

"We must consider the evidence," Dr. Chen said. "First, the time correlation. The explosion at our test site preceded the hydrogen leaks. The hydrogen leaks preceded the corruption of the city's oil supply. Second, the presence of acetic acid. Did you smell any stalled cars today?"

"Yes," she said meekly.

"They're leaking acetic acid. *Syntrophus* converts hydrocarbons into hydrogen, acetic acid and carbon dioxide. Third, the weather."

"The weather?"

"Today's disasters coincide with an increase in the ambient temperature. *Syntrophus* is thermophilic; it grows best when it's hot."

Christina nodded. "But how—"

"We'll speculate about how later. Tonight we need to ascertain the facts. We need to know whether the Chen-González strain of genetically-modified *Syntrophus* bacteria is present and alive in commercial gasoline."

He reached for a rack of test tubes on the bench top. Each tube held a few milliliters of liquid, about two tablespoons.

"These are samples of gas I siphoned from randomly chosen cars between here and my house. If the car was stalled or smelled of vinegar, I made a note of it. As a control I also have a sample from my own car, which I haven't refueled in twelve days. It should be clean, a good negative control."

He handed her the rack of tubes.

"Tonight, you're going to do DNA studies to look for our bacteria in these samples. You will also attempt to culture bacteria from the gasoline in the presence and absence of oxygen. Meanwhile I'll do the biochemical studies to figure out what's happened to the molecules in the gasoline, to understand why it's gone bad."

Christina accepted the tubes of gasoline with trepidation. Then she went to work. Using scratch paper, she mapped out the experiments to be done, planning for appropriate controls. She checked the lab freezer to make sure they had the reagents she needed. She would use PCR, or polymerase chain reaction, as the most sensitive test for *Syntrophus*; PCR could detect as little as one single bacterium in the material tested. Added to that, she would use DNA hybridization in a microarray to detect the DNA sequence changes that she and Dr. Chen had introduced into their strain. For good measure, she also decided to run enzyme-linked immunosorbent assays, or ELISAs, which used antibodies to detect proteins in the bacterial cell wall. Finally, she would set up cultures, but it might take days to get the results on that.

Dr. Chen disappeared into another part of the building to use the mass spectrophotometer, leaving Christina alone with her thoughts. She meticulously followed her experimental protocols, but her mind churned with anxiety. It couldn't be true. Dr. Chen was such a nice man, and she was an honest, well-meaning student. Their scientific work was intended to help humankind. They didn't send hundreds of people plunging to their deaths today.

But what if they had?

She programmed the thermal cycler for the PCR and put the microarray in an incubator. While waiting for results from those experiments, she did the ELISA. The test was easy to read. A strong positive turned blue. Negatives didn't.

Adding a drop of this, then a drop of that to each reaction, Christina watched her timer count off the seconds. The liquids swirled together. A faint hue appeared in the solution. Christina's heart sank as a deep indigo color developed in several of the samples.

They would get more details from the DNA tests and the chemical analysis of the gasoline, but Christina could no longer deny the facts. Her bacteria were eating L.A.'s gas.

*   *   *

Just before dawn, Christina and her boss shared their data with each other. In laboratory science, results were often ambiguous or conflicting, but their efforts tonight had produced clean data and an inescapable conclusion. Dr. Chen looked defeated, his shoulders sagging and his face wooden.

"I have to contact the authorities. If the infection spreads . . ." He paused, and shuddered. "The oil-eating bacteria must not escape the L.A. basin. The city must be quarantined."

Christina wondered how they were going to do that. These germs would spread as easily and relentlessly as the flu, a plague of petroleum instead of people. Humans didn't carry the bacteria in their bodies but in their transportation machines, in their automobiles, railroad cars, pipelines and ocean-going tankers. In things that moved, things that traveled to places the bacteria hadn't reached yet. The nozzle on every filling station pump in Los Angeles could transmit the infection. You might fill up at Shell in Los Angeles today and contaminate an Arco station in San Francisco tomorrow. Every car that used the pump after you would also be infected in an unstoppable epidemic against which they had no vaccine, and no treatment.

"Who will you call?" she said.

"Everyone I can think of," he said, "starting with CaliPetro, then the university chancellor, I guess. She'll know how to get the information to the right people."

Christina considered what would happen next. Dr. Chen would be blamed for a disaster whose scale was yet to be determined, but already had taken hundreds of lives. So would she, for that matter, but she was a lowly graduate student, like an army private following orders. At best, Dr. Chen's career was over. At worst, he might go to prison.

She couldn't let that happen. The bacteria's escape from the test site wasn't his fault.

"Before you call CaliPetro I have to tell you something."

He looked at her with dull eyes. She swallowed hard.

"You mustn't let them blame you."

"But Chrissy, I'm responsible. The bacteria were engineered in my laboratory. I directed the test that blew up and released *Syntrophus* into the environment."

"Yes, but—" Christina hesitated, "—but the explosion at the test site wasn't an accident."

Curiosity brought a flicker of life to the professor's expression.

"What are you talking about?"

"The tank was sabotaged by an eco-terrorist, someone named Neil. Neil did this, not you."

"How in the world do you know that? And why didn't you tell me before?"

She told him about River and Mickey, how they were loosely connected to the guilty party, how she didn't want them to get in trouble but she could keep silent no longer.

"Your cousin did this?" Dr. Chen said, his face now fully animated by anger. "And you didn't tell me?"

"I'm sorry," was the only thing she could think to say.

A tall, narrow cardboard box marked with drawings of broken flasks stood against the wall nearby. Chen kicked it with all his might. Glass waste inside tinkled and shattered as the box crumpled. He kicked it again and the box tipped over, spilling sparkling shards on the laboratory floor.

"I can't believe this," he said.

Christina kept silent.

Chen paced back and forth a few times. Then he righted the bin of broken glass and rubbed his scalp.

"I understand," he said heavily. "It's not your fault. But ultimately, the whole affair is my responsibility." He folded his hands in front of his face. "And whether or not this young fool is found and punished, no one can undo what he's done."

Chapter 21

At 5:40 AM, Los Angeles Mayor Felipe Ramirez stared out the window as the light of early dawn illuminated sporadic columns of smoke rising from parts of his city. He rubbed his trademark goatee and stroked his carefully coiffed ebony hair, longing for the good old days when budget deficits, teachers' strikes, and police misconduct were his biggest problems. In other words, any day before this inexplicable, multifaceted transportation crisis crippled his constituency.

"You think those are car fires or structures?" he asked his chief of staff Nelson Molton, one of the advisers gathered around him inside L.A.'s City Hall tower.

"Hard to say, Mr. Mayor. We've got reports of both all over town."

Ramirez wondered how many were the result of gas leaks, and how many were arson. Setting things on fire seemed to be a natural human response to any breakdown in authority, and after a long night on the job, he knew Los Angeles was perilously close to anarchy. Virtually every road in the city was blocked by stalled vehicles, so even though many cars were still functioning, they had nowhere to go. Police and fire crews were paralyzed like everyone else. Ramirez hoped to God people didn't start looting. He remembered how well-behaved New Yorkers were on 9/11 but didn't expect as much from his fellow Angelenos. This crisis had stolen their mobility, and nothing was more likely to piss off a Southern Californian than taking away his freedom to hit the road.

"What's the latest from LACMTA?"

"That's the one bright spot in the picture," Molton said. "The Transportation Authority confirms that light rail and subway lines are still operational. They've had to clear abandoned cars from some surface intersections, but the trains are moving. The crowds weren't too bad during the night, but they're expecting problems with excessive passenger loads today."

"We need to secure those rail lines for use by emergency services," the mayor said.

"Absolutely. As you know, sir, we mobilized the local National Guard during the night. One of their first priorities is to get troops in all the Metro stations. That's happening as we speak."

Ramirez stifled a yawn and emptied his cup of coffee. "Let's give them another hour to get in position. Then we'll have to decide who gets to ride, and who doesn't."

"It could get ugly, sir."

"What do you mean, 'get' ugly? How many hundreds of people died in those plane crashes yesterday? More died in an ambulance, or at home, because they couldn't get to a hospital."

He pounded his fist on the desk. An Army veteran and only 42 years old, Ramirez was a vigorous leader who always preferred action over hesitation.

"What the hell is causing this? Who's responsible? And how can we fix it?"

"LACMTA gave me another clue," Molton said. "They checked their entire fleet of compressed natural gas buses, and the engines are working fine. Granted, they can't drive anywhere because the streets are impassable, but no mechanical problems at all."

Ramirez put his hands together. "Compressed natural gas," he repeated. "More evidence that whatever is happening is linked to gasoline. Someone put something in our gasoline."

"And jet fuel," one of the advisors pointed out.

"Product tampering on an unprecedented scale," Molton agreed.

"Fucking al-Qaeda, I'll bet," he said. "A dual-purpose attack. Massive economic disruption and an assault on a potent American symbol: the car, in Los Angeles. Homeland Security should've seen this coming."

"You can ask the President. He's supposed to call in about eighteen minutes."

"What, you think I forgot? Christ. After I talk to him, I want a conference call with every oil company executive in town. They have to figure out what's in the gas and how it got there. Then they better make a plan to purge the bad stuff and get fresh supplies from somewhere on the double."

The telephone on Ramirez's desk emitted a light pinging sound.

"The Prez checking in early?" Molton said.

Even though the meeting was over the phone, Ramirez automatically adjusted his tie before picking up. After half a minute of listening he said, "Hold on, I'm going to put you on speakerphone so my advisors can hear this." He made the proper adjustments and said to the group, "Different president."

A woman's voice, powerful yet somewhat strained, came from the phone.

"This is Dr. Elaine Hampton, Chancellor of UCLA. I know what's causing the city's petroleum problem, and it's worse than you think."

Chapter 22

Sunlight fell on Christina's laboratory notebook as she recorded her final observations. The liquid ink pen she used only for this task made a scratching noise that seemed loud in the quiet of the lab. She'd worked all night, but the heavy drowsiness that afflicted her in the predawn hours lifted as her body sensed that it was once again the proper time to be awake. Concentrating on her work, she didn't hear Dr. Chen approach.

"Go home, Chrissy," he said. "Prepare for a siege. If it's not already too late, stock up on provisions on your way. Get as much as you can carry."

She looked at him stupidly, her mind still focused on molecules and oblivious to real life.

"This crisis is only beginning," he said. "I don't know what will happen once everyone realizes they can't just refill their gas tanks and go on their merry way."

"The bacteria are here to stay, aren't they," Christina said, a statement more than a question.

Dr. Chen nodded. "Yesterday the media were speculating about terrorists putting something in the fuel supply. I wish they had! A simple contaminant could be diluted, washed away. *Syntrophus*, on the other hand, will have colonized the entire petroleum infrastructure: individual car tanks, gas stations, pipelines, tankers. Adding fresh petroleum will only stimulate their growth. The more you feed them, the more they'll multiply."

"Guess I'm lucky to have a bike," Christina said.

"Transporting yourself around the neighborhood isn't the problem. Think about the less obvious ways you depend on petroleum. The most immediate issue will be food. Without trucks making deliveries, stores are going to run out fast."

A primal sense of fear rose in her as the enormity of the situation dawned on Christina. She had to tell River and Mickey. They must turn the apartment into a bunker and protect themselves. Too bad none of them owned a gun.

"We'll start rationing our food right away," Christina said, thinking about how long they could survive on dried ramen noodles. "But water . . ."

"You didn't notice the water and electricity are still on," Dr. Chen said.

Sheepishly Christina acknowledged that they were. How easy it was to take them for granted.

"Those utilities don't depend directly on petroleum," Dr. Chen said, "but without gasoline it'll be difficult to make repairs to the system. You'd better fill every container in your house with drinking water just in case. But enough talking. Get yourself out of here."

"What about you?"

Her mentor's face clouded. "I'm staying in the lab."

"But there's hardly anything to eat."

He shrugged his shoulders. "I'm not leaving until I find a cure."

"I can help you."

"No," he said forcefully. "I can do the work alone, and I don't want to be responsible for you. As you pointed out, there's no food."

Dr. Chen escorted Christina and her bicycle down the elevator and to the main entrance of the building. The campus was quiet, with no obvious threats. He sent her on her way.

"If it turns out you'd be safer here, then by all means come back. But I think for now the best place to be is in your own home," he said.

With a combination of regret and relief, Christina pedaled away toward Westwood Boulevard, which led out of UCLA and connected the campus to the rest of the city. Every lane of the street was clogged with traffic. At first glance, it looked like a typical rush hour—except the cars were silent and empty, like the day after the Rapture in a city populated by saints.

She half-expected to see a Hollywood film crew.

Images from disaster movies came to mind, but she'd never seen one like this. In theaters and on late-night TV, Christina had vicariously experienced nuclear wars, unstoppable plagues, earthquakes, tsunami, alien invasions, and more. The weird thing about this catastrophe was the absence of death and destruction. On the eerily still streets of Los Angeles, the only dead things were cars, and the worst damage was hidden inside internal combustion engines.

*   *   *

Dr. Chen's call interrupted her trip home. She stood astride her bike, mouth agape.

"I can't. I'm only a student."

"You're a scientist," Chen said, more harshly than she expected. "You're talented, knowledgeable, and you communicate well. Whether you believe it or not, you're capable of doing this." He paused and softened his tone. "I'm sorry, I know it should be me. If the stakes were any less, I would handle it. But Chancellor Hampton insists that someone who understands the *Syntrophus* project must answer the mayor's questions, and I can't leave the lab. That means you have to go in my place."

She wanted to say, I'm too ashamed. Don't make me share responsibility for the petroplague. Let me go home and hide while you make everything okay.

Instead she said, "Downtown is too far to go on my bike."

"They're expecting you at the Wilshire and Western Metro stop," Dr. Chen said. "Someone will escort you to City Hall. When the interview is over, they'll get you back to the Metro."

How can I explain the impossible? How can I give them hope when we have nothing to offer?

"Okay," she said, though she meant nothing of the sort.

*   *   *

Mayor Ramirez was not the kind to sit still in a crisis. As the meetings at City Hall rolled on hour after hour, he paced the room. Movement energized him and he looked forward to knocking some heads when the nerds from UCLA arrived. The chancellor had promised to supply him with an appropriate target for his ire. Those eggheads at the university had landed the city in this mess. They'd have to do some smooth talking to walk out of his office with their asses intact.

"Mr. Mayor, the scientist from UCLA is here."

"Send him in," he said and temporarily took a seat at the head of the conference table with a dozen of his top officials. "Only one?"

"Yes, sir."

A poised young woman of Hispanic origin stepped into the room, her shiny hair secured in a ponytail that drew full attention to her eyes, which were rich and dark and intelligent.

"You're the scientist from UCLA?" Ramirez said with surprise as he rose to his feet.

"My name's Christina González, your honor. I'm a Ph.D. candidate in the laboratory of Dr. Robert Chen."

He looked past Christina to see if someone accompanied her, but she had come alone. It was most disconcerting. The head-knocking and ass-kicking he'd anticipated no longer seemed like a good idea.

"Where is this Dr. Chen?"

"Working on a solution to our problem," she said. "He won't rest until he's found one."

Ramirez wanted to rail against her and vent his frustration over the petroplague, but she made a terrible scapegoat. Attacking the polite, lovely student would make him look like a bully. He'd have to settle for information instead of revenge.

"Tell me about the petroplague germs," he said.

She spoke earnestly, thoughtfully, using language the laypeople could understand. She explained the original purpose of the work, and told them about the field test in Jefferson Park. He listened and asked questions, impressed by her composure and depth of knowledge. He considered himself an excellent judge of character, and she seemed to be reliable and honest.

He also couldn't help noticing that she appeared ignorant of her attractiveness. She wore no makeup, yet her face was captivating. In his experience of L.A., her combination of brains, humility, and good looks was unique.

"I'm sorry we don't have all the answers," Christina said, "but if there is anything else we can explain for you, please call me or Dr. Chen."

"Thank you, Ms. González," he said. They shook hands; hers was trembling. He addressed an aide. "Please make sure she's allowed to board the Metro."

She departed and the mayor resumed his pacing. Though the messenger from UCLA was surprisingly pleasing, her message was not. Los Angeles was in for a heap of trouble, and Ramirez couldn't rely on the scientists to fix things anytime soon.

CHAPTER 23

People magazine. That's how Christina knew the mayor preferred boxers to briefs, and this silly bit of trivia had helped her stay calm through the nerve-wracking interview. *People* had published a feature on Ramirez in their "most eligible bachelors" issue, an issue she guiltily enjoyed. Like many bachelorettes she'd daydreamed about meeting a man from the list, but today when it really happened it was more ordeal than fantasy. At least he had treated her with respect, probably more respect than she deserved considering her complicity in recent events.

But her testimony was over and now she had more pressing concerns. Riding her bike toward the apartment, her number one concern was food.

"We're still checking, Chrissy, but all the stores in the area are closed," River's voice whined from Christina's cell phone.

"How far are you from the apartment?" she asked.

"I've covered about a mile. Mickey's gone a little further in the other direction."

"Damn," Christina said. "We should've bought more stuff at the grocery yesterday."

"Yesterday we weren't relying on FEMA to provide our next meal," River said. "How long can we last on what we've got in the pantry?"

"With or without Mickey the Bottomless Pit?"

"I won't let you turn him out, Chrissy."

"I'm kidding. But we're all going on a diet real soon. I'd say we've got maybe three days of rations, plus whatever's buried in the freezer."

"That's not much. Will the roads be open by then?"

"No, River, I don't think they will. The truth is, they may never open. Even if all the dead cars are pushed aside, the oil-eating bacteria can't be exterminated. Anything gasoline-powered simply won't work here. Not ever again."

"That's impossible. Los Angeles can't exist without cars and trucks."

"You said it, not me."

The young women were silent for a moment.

"Chrissy, do you remember New Orleans after the hurricane? The roads were all blocked there, too. By water. People went kind of crazy."

"I know. That's why I want to stock up on supplies and barricade ourselves in the apartment, before everyone else realizes how bad it is."

"We have to get more food, Chrissy."

"Then find an open store! I'll keep looking, too, but I don't want to stay out here any longer than necessary. I'm afraid somebody will try to steal my bike."

Conversing on her cell phone took Christina's attention away from where it needed to be: on the road ahead. She swerved to narrowly avoid crashing into a car's side-view mirror but lost her balance. The bike tipped over. She rubbed her leg and stood up, bruised but otherwise unhurt. The street was quiet—too quiet. She felt exposed and vulnerable. Her pulse quickened; she recovered her phone and mounted the bike. Like a mouse fleeing a bird of prey that it fears but cannot see, she sped away.

"Chrissy, are you alright?"

"Fine, just dropped my phone."

"I have an idea," River said. "Meet me at the Seven Eleven by the apartment."

"You said nothing was open."

"Just meet me there, okay?"

*   *   *

Twenty minutes later, Christina coasted up to the convenience store and saw River and Mickey sitting on a curb in the parking lot. The store was locked and dark. As she got closer, she noticed River was holding a pile of bags. Mickey had something large and heavy on his lap. They rose to greet her, and Christina recognized the object in Mickey's hands. It was a cast-iron Dutch oven cooking pot from their kitchen.

A sense of foreboding crept over her.

"We should go home," Christina said, willfully ignoring the odd implement Mickey was holding.

"We have business here first," River said.

Christina looked again at the locked storefront, and at the Dutch oven.

"No, River. You can't."

"Yes we can, and we will. You know it's only a matter of time. Remember New Orleans."

Mickey chimed in. "If not us, somebody else will."

"No. No! It's a crime. We'll be fine with what we have. Just forget it," Christina said, turning her bike toward home.

River grabbed the handlebars. "You said yourself that it'll be a very long time until the roads reopen. Who do you think is going to take care of us? The government?"

"Fuck that," Mickey said. "I say we take care of ourselves."

And with that, he flung the iron pot against the door.

"Stop! What about the police?"

"Don't be a fool, Chrissy. There aren't any police, and they won't be coming anytime soon. Shut up and grab some bags," River said.

The door proved remarkably resilient as Mickey struck it again and again with his small battering ram. Christina shrank back against the side wall of the building, plastic grocery bags in her hands, shocked and confused by her own submission to this outrageous plan. She'd just testified at City Hall, for God's sake.

The sound of Mickey banging the glass seemed loud enough to summon a legion of police. On the third strike, he triggered an alarm. The high-pitched wail stoked her anxiety; she was certain they'd be arrested in minutes. But at last the door shattered, and the three novice burglars forced their way inside.

"Go for high calories and lots of preservatives," River shouted over the clamor of the alarm as she shoveled Hostess fruit pies into a bag.

Mickey was up to his elbows in the chips shelf. Sensible even in the midst of insanity, Christina targeted the nuts and dried fruit. Then she saw Mickey head for the beer section.

"That will not help us," she said.

He smiled and flipped her the bird.

Compared to the length of time it took to gain entry, it seemed to take no time at all to load themselves with all they could carry back to the apartment.

"Let's go," River said, and they exited the way they came in.

Christina draped bags over her shoulders and over the handlebars of her bike. The bags jostled and threw her off balance as she started to pedal. The bicycle wobbled and her foot caught on the ground. Rearranging the bags didn't help; the dangling weights made it impossible to ride. Already River and Mickey had sprinted halfway down the block; Christina was stranded near the broken door and screaming alarm. Surely, the police would be here any second. She'd be arrested. In a panic, she gave up trying to ride the bike. Instead she pushed it and the stolen food toward home as fast as she could on foot, her head swiveling as she scanned the area for pursuers who never came.

Chapter 24

The nervous tremor in River's voice belied the confidence of her words.

"That wasn't so hard, was it," she said, dumping a pile of Twinkies on the living room carpet.

Christina double-checked the deadbolt on the front door and closed the blinds.

"It was stupid and illegal," she said. "We're going to get caught."

"Lighten up, Chrissy," River said. "Even if the police can get to the scene, pretty soon half the neighborhood is going to follow in our footsteps. With a ransacked store and a hundred culprits, who's going to identify us?"

"Cameras, maybe," Christina said, but she guiltily acknowledged that the city's public safety officers had a lot bigger problems to contend with than a Seven Eleven heist.

"Welcome to the club, Chrissy," Mickey said.

"Club?"

"Lawbreakers, baby. River and I have a long and distinguished record of civil and not-so-civil disobedience, but I think this is your first. And it's a whopper." He gave River a high-five.

Christina felt her face flush. "I am not like you. Robbing a store was not my idea."

"If we'd waited until it was your idea, the place would've been cleaned out already," Mickey said. "Desperate times, desperate measures and all that. In a couple of days you'll be thanking me."

"I will not."

"Fine. Then you don't have to eat any of this stuff."

"I won't," Christina said stubbornly. She waved her arm over the scattered mess of junk food. "And for your information, you better hide all this because law enforcement is going to be on your tails."

"I told you, they're not going to find us," River said.

"I'm not talking about the Seven Eleven," Christina said with malicious delight. "They know about Neil and the sabotage at Jefferson Park."

It was satisfying to see the stunned expressions on their faces. She continued.

"Dr. Chen was going to take the fall for the gas tank explosion, so I told him the truth. Somebody is gonna want to interview you about your 'friend.'"

"You snitched on us?" River said.

"Heck yeah. But I didn't say you did it, I just said you knew the guy who did."

"You bitch."

River clenched her fists. Mickey quickly intervened, laying a hand on River's arm.

"Okay ladies, let's keep it cool," he said. "Chrissy, that was pretty low. But River, you have to admit the whole bomb thing was probably a mistake."

"No, I'm glad Neil did it," River said defiantly. "By stalling all those cars, just think how many tons of carbon those bacteria have kept out of the atmosphere. Christina says gasoline will never work again in L.A. If that doesn't force a change in the way we use energy, I don't know what will."

"You're so dumb," Christina retorted. "There's this thing called chemistry, River, and you just don't get it."

"Don't you dare—" River began, but Mickey stepped between them again.

"You two need to calm down," he said, giving River a bear hug that was part affection, part restraint. He faced Christina. "Do you want to explain something to us?"

"It's not worth the effort," she said.

River snorted and Mickey said, "Look, we've got nothing to gain and everything to lose by fighting with each other. As far as

I understand it, we're in for a tough time over the next few days. Maybe weeks. Can't we deal with it together? As a family?"

The magic word—family—drained Christina's fury. She sat down at the kitchen table.

"All right. Let me tell you what I learned in the lab last night."

River didn't speak, but she came to the table and took a seat. Mickey shuffled around in the kitchen making iced tea.

"First, you need to understand what Dr. Chen designed these *Syntrophus* bacteria to do," Christina said. "*Syntrophus* live deep underground in natural petroleum reservoirs, where there's no oxygen and no light. The bacteria break down oil for food. Now, crude oil is a complex mixture of different hydrocarbon molecules. The most valuable hydrocarbons in petroleum are simple straight-chain alkanes like hexane."

She grabbed a piece of paper and a pen and sketched the structure:

"But you also find branched alkanes, like isooctane."

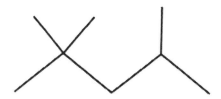

"And cyclic and aromatic compounds, which have carbon rings in them."

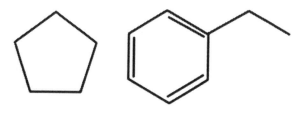

"Plus many, many other molecules. All of these hydrocarbons are potential food sources for oil-eating bacteria, but any one species of bacteria can't digest them all. In order to break down the different structures, the bacteria have to make the right enzymes."

"That's weird," Mickey said as he placed a tall, icy glass in front of each of them.

"People are the same," Christina said. "We break down sugars for food, but we can't eat all the different sugar molecules that exist. For example, we have the enzymes to digest starch—like you find in potatoes."

She outlined the shape of a molecule.

"But we can't digest cellulose, a very similar chemical that's found in cotton and wood."

Christina continued. "Dr. Chen's goal is to use bacteria to harvest energy from low-quality, hard-to-pump petroleum in tar sands. To maximize the energy produced, his bacteria need to eat a varied diet. The more kinds of hydrocarbons they can break down, the more energy they'll release. So he set out to create a superbug, a genetically engineered form of *Syntrophus* that could eat most of the different molecules found in petroleum."

"And he succeeded, I presume," River said.

"With my help, yes. Our *Syntrophus* bacteria are the most efficient oil-eating microbes on the planet."

"It never occurred to you that this might be a problem?" River said.

"No, because we had a built-in fail-safe. *Syntrophus* bacteria are killed by exposure to air. They can only eat oil in their natural habitat, deep underground."

"But not anymore. Something went wrong."

Christina fidgeted with her ponytail. "That's right, the bacteria aren't restricted to an oxygen-free environment anymore. Sometime after they escaped from our test facility in Jefferson Park, the bacteria changed."

"Mutated?"

"Not exactly. More like, they learned a new skill from some friends."

"We're talking about itty bitty microbes here, right?" Mickey said.

"We are, but even bacteria have ways of sharing information. The information is in the form of genetic material. Bacteria can actually give some of their DNA to each other in a process called horizontal gene transfer. It happens in the wild. Last night I found DNA in my *Syntrophus* that wasn't there before. The new DNA codes for aerobic survival."

"Life in the presence of air," River said.

"Yes," Christina said. "The whole sorry affair began when Dr. Chen and I brought our *Syntrophus* to a shallow underground location, at the gas station. Then your friend Neil freed the *Syntrophus* from their prison. Then *Syntrophus* met some of the local soil bacteria who shared everything they know about living with oxygen."

"So we're all to blame," River said.

"I suppose," Christina conceded.

"Shit. What a mess," Mickey said.

Chapter 25

Neil's chickens clucked softly when he extracted a freshly-laid brown egg from the nesting box in the stinky coop. Two Rhode Island Red hens left the feces-covered coop floor behind to scratch and peck the dust of the tiny back yard, performing a timeless two-step dance to uncover insects or worms. Neil wasn't sure whether urban chicken keeping was legal in this part of L.A., but the slum lord who owned the property didn't care as long as he paid his rent in cash every month. A Hmong family down the street kept a whole flock with a rooster so Neil never worried about his quiet little pair getting in trouble. And whatever the law said about it, recent events made it clear that backyard farming was the right thing to do.

The egg was still warm, chicken body temperature, as he rolled it through his fingers. He studied this small miracle, the hard-shelled egg. It was a perfect, nutrient-packed food source, naturally tested for hundreds of millions of years. But "progress" had made the simple, flawless thing needlessly complex. To eat an egg, other Angelenos got in their oversized cars and burned gasoline to drive to an air-conditioned grocery store brightened with fluorescent lights to buy a dozen stored in an electric refrigerator, packed in a petroleum-based Styrofoam carton, delivered by a diesel-burning truck from a mechanized farm a hundred miles away where the hens were fed recycled animal carcasses and antibiotics.

The petroplague had exposed the insanity of this way of living. Today in Los Angeles, sustainability wasn't a slogan. It was survival.

Because of me, Neil thought. This is my doing.

He looked at his hands in amazement, both proud of and appalled by the unexpected power he'd wielded when he arranged the bombing of the gas station on the strength of a tip from an amateur environmentalist named Mickey. His goals were not modest. For the planet, he wanted to prevent the release of untold quantities of carbon into the atmosphere. For himself, he wanted recognition and advancement within his organization, Earth Jihad. On the first count, the consequences of his action had exceeded his wildest dreams. On the second, he was unsatisfied.

Though it had no connection to Islam, Earth Jihad was loosely organized and decentralized in the fashion of al-Qaeda, partly for protection, partly because its members were generally anarchists. As a result, Earth Jihad had no clear chain of command to give orders—or honors—to the foot soldiers. Neil had heard nothing lately from the other members of his local cell, and he had little knowledge of anyone above him. Watching the petroplague unfold was gratifying, but he craved personal congratulations from his peers and superiors. He hoped it would come.

He plucked a few leaves of fresh oregano to garnish his egg and stomped into the dumpy little house in a pair of old Doc Martens, his scrawny white legs awkwardly connecting the heavy boots to a pair of cutoff shorts. He cracked the egg into a frying pan and tossed the shell into his compost collection jar.

The disaster presented a once-in-a-lifetime opportunity to transform a city synonymous with pollution and poor urban planning into a paragon of green living. The people would never have accepted the challenge voluntarily, but now it had been thrust upon them. Los Angeles could lead the rest of the world to a sustainable, oil-independent future.

He wondered, would the world follow?

His hand froze between his plate and his mouth, rich golden yolk dripping from a triangle of toast. The answer was clear. No, the world would not follow. Controlled by industrialists like his father, the world would unite to stop the plague, to make it a local problem for Southern California. They would never choose to suffer the birth pangs of a new economy liberated from cheap, dirty energy and useless manufactured goods. Someone would have to choose for them.

"I will do it," he said aloud like a mystic speaking to a vision.

The capitalists wanted globalization. He would give it to them.

CHAPTER 26

"We agree," Mayor Ramirez said. "The germ must not get out of L.A. Thank you for your support, Mr. President."

Ramirez ended his phone call with the President of the United States and rubbed his eyes. Their conversation had been distressingly frank. Until someone came up with an antidote to the petroplague, the man in the White House had one overwhelming priority: quarantine. Isolating the plague to Los Angeles was all that mattered in Washington, and the majority of federal assistance would be devoted to that task. Emergency services, food distribution, and clearing the roads were Ramirez's problems.

Deep down, he knew the President was right. But this was his city, and he was a fighter. He survived gang-infested streets as a child, and ambushes in Iraq during his time in the service. Los Angeles would not become Baghdad, not on his watch.

He rose from his desk and leaned against a floor-to-ceiling window in his office, forehead pressed against the glass. Los Angeles sprawled in all directions around him but an invisible noose would soon cut it off from the rest of the world.

He left his private office and joined a group of high-level officials in the conference room outside. It was time to prepare a battle plan, starting with a containment strategy.

Leaders display confidence to inspire confidence in others.

"Quarantine, people. How big do we draw the circle?"

"Better to over-shoot than under," said Molton, his chief of staff. "We should think in terms of concentric rings, drawing the outer ring quite large. Nothing leaves the center ring. Vehicles can move from outer rings to inner rings, but not the other way around. Where possible, movement within a ring should be allowed."

"How are we going to quarantine fifteen million people?" a second advisor said.

"We don't," Ramirez said. "Christina González said the germ doesn't infect people. It infects petroleum and anything the petroleum touches. The people of the greater Los Angeles area are free to leave the city, but they can't go in any type of vehicle that burns oil or gasoline. No cars, trucks, mopeds, lawn mowers, not any internal combustion engine of any kind. Let's make this perfectly clear: if those bacteria get out of L.A., the whole country is screwed, and it will be our fault."

"So people are supposed to walk across the San Gabriel Mountains?" someone asked.

"That's an option. Or they can stay put," Molton said.

"With the support the President just promised me," Ramirez said, "we can offer a few more choices than that. But staying put is the best option, and the one we should promote. We can't have thousands of people straggling across the desert in this heat. As long as we have utilities, Angelenos are safest in their own homes."

"What are the chances the lights will stay on?" an advisor asked.

Molton flipped through a stack of notes.

"The electricity and water shouldn't be directly affected by the germ. The Department of Water and Power gave me a breakdown of where they get their energy. Most of their generating capacity comes from coal-fired plants that aren't even located in California."

"Do the bacteria eat coal?"

"According to González, no. They'll eat gasoline, kerosene, jet fuel, and diesel, but not coal or natural gas. Which is good, because LADWP's second biggest power source is electricity generated from natural gas plants here in the Los Angeles basin. Even if those plants are contaminated, they should still function normally. The rest of our electricity comes from a variety of secure sources: nuclear from the Palo Verde plant in Arizona, and a variety of hydroelectric, solar, wind and geothermal projects."

"So virtually none of the city's electricity is dependent on petroleum," Ramirez said.

"Not the generating, anyway. Of course if there are infrastructure problems—downed lines or whatever—LADWP is going to have trouble getting things repaired in a timely fashion."

"And the water?"

"In theory, should be okay. The area's water lines are either standard gravity-fed or pressurized by electric or natural gas pumps."

"Thank God for small favors," Ramirez said. "If we can keep the water and electricity on, we can count on most people staying home, at least for now. Nobody panics when their TV, fridge and air conditioner are running."

"But those refrigerators will soon be empty," Molton said. "Without truck and rail transit into the city, we're going to run out of everything real fast."

"Let's talk big picture," Ramirez said. "The President agrees that the absolute number one priority is to contain the infection. Nothing that carries or touches petroleum is to leave L.A. If we can prevent the oil-eating bacteria from spreading beyond this area, it will buy us time to deal with our transportation problems while the scientists work on a solution. We've got one thing in our favor: any vehicle running on contaminated gasoline is going to die before it gets very far, so we have a natural quarantine effect."

"What about the Port?" someone asked. "Tankers shipping contaminated oil won't suffer engine failure."

"The Port of Los Angeles is closed, effective immediately," Ramirez said. "Any ships that haven't made physical contact with California should be diverted elsewhere. Any ships already in port will have to stay there to prevent spreading the germ. The President will order the U.S. Navy to enforce the ship quarantine. Of course the airports are shut down already."

"And the Port at Long Beach?"

"Same deal."

"Sir, you realize the impact these closures will have on the economy?"

"The President and I discussed it. The Port of Los Angeles is the busiest container port in the country. It handles twenty percent of America's imports and exports. Closure will be crippling, and the longshoremen will put up a fight, but what choice do we have?" he asked, throwing his hands up in frustration. "This isn't about money or a temporary economic disruption. It's not about poll ratings or political gain. Do you realize what will happen if this bug gets out? *Our entire civilization is based on oil.* We can't survive without it."

Gradually, the true magnitude of the crisis dawned on the city leaders. Their parochial concerns about Southern California were overshadowed by the global cost of containment failure.

"Ladies and gentlemen," Ramirez said gravely, "we have the authority of the President to use any means necessary. Whatever it takes, those bacteria must not escape."

CHAPTER 27

Neil scowled as he studied the quarantine plans outlined at a website hastily assembled by the mayor's office. The quarantine was distressingly complete and was being enforced by armed units of the U.S. Army and National Guard. He scrolled through a list of the major road blocks.

To the north:
> U.S. 101 between Carpinteria and Santa Barbara
> I-5 past Gorman at the 99 split
> State highway 14 north of Lancaster
> I-15 at Apple Valley

To the east:
> I-10 at Palm Desert

To the south:
> I-5 at Camp Pendleton Marine Corps Base
> I-15 south of Temecula

To the west, the Pacific Ocean served as the ultimate road block. In addition, military vessels were patrolling the coast to prevent the escape of any motorized watercraft. According to the mayor's statement, ships, aircraft, or vehicles attempting to run the blockade and pass from an inner containment ring to an outer one were subject to arrest or destruction.

Getting petroplague bacteria out of Los Angeles was going to be harder than he expected. He would need help. But from whom? The few Earth Jihadists he knew by name were no better placed than he was to implement the plan. One of them might get the cell leader involved, but then he would have to share the credit. He didn't want to. He started the petroplague— unintentionally, yes, but his action nevertheless—and now he wanted the plague to end the age of oil in human history. Stopping global warming would be his personal achievement, making him one of the greatest environmentalists of all time. A peer of Rachel Carson and John Muir; Al Gore would kiss his ring. He felt drunk with power and possibility.

The support he wanted was a few mouse clicks away. He had a contact in an online community of doomsayers, people separated by distance, class, politics, and religion but united in their imminent expectation of The End.

He needed the collapsitarians.

Chapter 28

Parallel lines of light shining on the television made it hard for Christina to see the images of chaos on the screen. She rose and adjusted the vinyl blinds drawn over the windows of the apartment. The lines disappeared. While she was at the window, she peeked out at the street.

"It's still quiet out there," she said with relief.

"Marx had it wrong," River said. "TV is the opiate of the masses."

"Plus the Internet and air conditioning," Mickey added.

With the room dark, Christina shuffled to the couch and curled up on the cushions. A day had passed since the three young people robbed the Seven Eleven store. As Mickey predicted, within hours of breaking in the store was completely cleaned out. Similar incidents occurred all over town.

"Any shootings?" Christina asked.

"No more than usual," River said, now on her fourth straight hour of watching the news. "It took a while for people to recognize the problem, so stores that were actually open sold their inventory. Looters like us," she taunted Christina with a grin, "mostly hit places that were locked up. No one there with a gun to run them off."

"Nobody's starving yet," Christina said. "The real test of civility will start in another day or two."

"Feels like I'm starving already," Mickey said, woefully rubbing his stomach. "Can't expect a man to be glued to the TV all day and not eat anything."

"You had lunch," Christina said.

"Yeah, but no chips or beer."

"We can't waste calories," Christina said. "You'll have to—"

"Check this out," River said, pointing at the screen.

Christina dropped her schoolmarm lecture and turned to the TV. Low-quality video showed a steady stream of people weaving their way through a gridlock of automobiles on a multi-lane freeway. In the background on one side lay wild, rugged desert; on the other, the endless blue of the Pacific.

"Is that Camp Pendleton?" she asked, knowing the Marine Corps base was about the only undeveloped piece of oceanfront left in Southern California.

"I think so," River said. "Those people are heading south on the five, trying to make it to San Diego."

The scene looked almost like a festive parade, a mishmash of unconventional locomotion. The fleeing Angelenos moved on bicycles, roller skates, scooters, and skateboards. A few horses carried riders. Many people walked, some pushed strollers or shopping carts, others pulled wagons. Some were decked out in full backpacking gear and strode easily with walking poles in their hands. All were moving toward the south, outside the quarantine zone.

"How are they getting these pictures?"

"Any way they can," River said. "Citizen journalists with cell phones, and stuff people are posting online. The stations' camera vans are broadcasting, too, but they're stuck in place. And their batteries are running out."

"What the hell . . . is that the other Mickey?" Mickey said.

The image focused on Disney's famous round-eared mouse logo, painted on the front of a white vehicle.

"That's a parking lot tram from Disneyland," Christina said. "Of course! The tram's electric, it doesn't have a petroleum engine."

The camera operator zoomed out to show the whole scene. The Disney tram was in the far right lane of a clogged freeway. A group of uniformed National Guardsmen preceded it and tackled the next car in the road. As Christina watched, they smashed a side window and entered the car. One man sat in the driver's seat and presumably released the parking brake and put the car in neutral. The others pooled their muscle power to roll the car out of the way. By this means, the crew had managed to clear one lane of the freeway behind them as far as the camera could see. Apparently the Disney tram was following along in the cleared path to provide support.

"A freeway lane won't be much use with the mayor's quarantine in effect," Mickey said. "No one is allowed to drive out."

"Alternative fuel vehicles can," Christina said. "Those Disney trams, for example. And most of the city buses are powered by natural gas. If they can clear space for them on the roads, the buses are exempt from the quarantine."

She thought about the trickle of able-bodied people venturing south under their own power, and the millions still trapped in L.A. For how long would they sit quietly in their homes, eating their cupboards bare? What about the sick, those in hospitals? What if a person needed an ambulance? Evacuating a few thousand people on foot and clearing one lane of highway was like treating a heart attack with an aspirin. It helped a little but did nothing to fix the real problem.

Mickey turned up the volume when the local anchorman appeared, his on-camera makeup wearing thin.

"This just in. Mayor Ramirez has ordered a curfew within all containment zones from 10 PM to 5 AM. No one is to be on the streets during those hours. It's not clear how this rule will be applied to people attempting to migrate out of the city. Also: LAX, Burbank, Long Beach and John Wayne airport in Orange County will be the first sites for shipments of emergency food supplies. The Federal Emergency Management Agency will coordinate the drops using Hercules C-130 cargo planes supplied by the U.S. Air Force. Because of the risk of contamination, the aircraft will not land but will use the vacant runways to drop several tons of food at a time. Details on what kind of food will be dropped, and how it will be distributed, are still sketchy. Stay tuned for updates."

"What do we do now?" River said.

"We're doing it," Mickey replied as he flipped channels.

"I can't just sit here," Christina said.

River searched her cousin's face. "Are you thinking about joining the refugees on the road out?"

"No, that's not it," Christina said. "I mean, I ought to be in the lab. This whole awful situation is partly my fault—and yours, too, of course—but unlike you I have the skills to do something about it."

River scowled but said nothing.

"Dr. Chen told me he wasn't going to leave the lab until he had a solution, a cure. I have to help him. I've been hiding here for too long."

"Suit yourself," Mickey said.

Christina abandoned the couch and searched the closet for her backpack. In her bedroom, she picked a few articles of clothing and tied a rolled-up yoga mat to her pack. The mat was thin but it would be better than sleeping directly on the lab's floor. When River and Mickey weren't looking she stole a bunch of energy bars from the kitchen and stuffed them in, too. Dr. Chen had been without food for over a day; she had to bring him something.

She pumped up her bicycle tires and donned a helmet. The pack wasn't large enough for what she needed to carry, and it hung in a swollen, distorted shape on her back.

"I don't know when I'll return," Christina said. Her heart brimmed with worry about being separated. They were a family; they ought to stay together. But she had to go.

"We'll be fine, but you be careful, Chrissy," River implored, her face pinched with concern. "It's the calm before the storm out there."

CHAPTER 29

The collapsitarians.

When by chance Neil met their *de facto* leader, he'd never heard the word before.

The lucky encounter occurred early in Neil's career as an extremist, after he'd begged and borrowed enough cash to join the throng of activists and policy tourists at the 2009 U.N. Climate Conference in Copenhagen.

Tens of thousands of them marched down Amagerbrogade toward Copenhagen's Bella Center, where representatives from over a hundred and ninety nations were negotiating a successor treaty to the Kyoto Protocol on global warming. Most of the protesters were young and white. They wore down jackets and wool beanie caps against the December chill and carried signs that read "There is No Planet B" or "Clean Coal is a Lie" or "Nature Doesn't Compromise." Nearly all the placards were written in English.

Neil shouted, "Corporations out!" in rhythm with the crowd. He shivered and stamped his feet; the Los Angeles winter clothing he'd brought felt paper-thin over his goose-fleshed skin but he had no money to buy a heavier coat. Fortunately the fire in his belly was more than enough reward for the discomfort.

This is what I've been searching for. These people, concerned citizens of the world, are my people. They are my brothers and sisters, my father and mother, more than those legal relatives I have back in California. I belong here.

A herd of costumed polar bears pushed forward through the parade, singing and dancing. Their leader carried a megaphone in one paw and in the other, a bottle of water labeled "Former Glacier." Polar bears and ice sculptures, the protesters' favorite symbols, were everywhere. Yesterday an artistic fusion of both elements, an ice-carved polar bear, caught Neil's eye; when he passed the spot again later the bear had melted and exposed a fossil-like bronze skeleton. So caught up was he in the carnival atmosphere, he nearly forgot that the goal of this Saturnalia was an international treaty to make significant reductions in CO_2 emissions.

"Governments lie, people die!" cried a group of protesters clad in white plastic suits as they collapsed to the ground in a "die in." He felt he might swoon in ecstasy.

The day progressed with speeches, teach-ins, and lots of chanting. A pretty Danish girl shared a Thermos of coffee with him and they used their cups to toast sham heads of state Barrack Obama, Angela Merkel, and Hu Jintao, who were seated at a table inside a giant glass box submerged to their necks in a mock rising ocean. Neil hoped the girl would have sex with him but they got separated when the police came to arrest some less-creative demonstrators who expressed their opinions by throwing bottles and breaking storefront windows.

Seeking refuge from the cold, he followed arrows to an indoor venue devoted to small-group lectures and discussions. He was sated by the sights and sounds and enthusiasm of the crowd, and only wanted a place to sit and rest for a while. A conference room with a number of empty chairs beckoned; he chose a seat toward the rear and leaned back with his eyes closed.

"Global warming is a hoax," said the speaker, a lean, energetic older man with a commanding voice and mischievous eyes.

Great, Neil thought. I picked the only wingnut seminar in all of Copenhagen.

"It is a folly embraced by the left and tolerated by the right to distract us from a larger and more certain disaster, a calamity so great that accepting its inevitability could lead to social collapse."

After a line like that, Neil couldn't help but listen.

"That's right, my friends. Whether we believe it or not, the end of the world as we know it is coming. Technology and globalization and overpopulation are wolves we've welcomed in the sheep's clothing of progress. The way we live now is unsustainable. Collapse is inevitable."

Neil opened his eyes and sat straight in his chair, stirred with sympathy for the speaker's dire claim. The man stepped away from the speaker's podium to get closer to his audience, and gestured emphatically with his hands and arms.

"Modern civilization rests on two pillars: growth and cheap energy. These twin supports are inextricably linked. The beginning of the Age of Oil in human history ushered in the era of growth. Oil made possible the Industrial Revolution and the population explosion. Standards of living in the West have now risen exponentially beyond what is needed to sustain life and happiness, yet still our economies demand growth. When we stop buying Happy Meals and plastic snow globes and electronic gadgets we don't understand and can't repair, when we realize that we own enough stuff, our governments scream, 'Recession!' and workers lose their jobs and debt rises and paper money is printed, all to feed an expansion. And 'more' becomes our highest aspiration, an unattainable goal that like a rainbow ever recedes before us, and we imprison ourselves in a perpetual state of consumer frenzy. Pollsters cite 'consumer confidence' as a measure of our society's well-being, while we shut out the natural world and willfully ignore the physical limits to growth."

Like a preacher, the man spoke with urgency and conviction; his voice climaxed and fell back. He exhorted his modest congregation, "My friends, economic growth acknowledges no limit, but the planet we live on is finite nevertheless."

Neil fought the urge to leap up and shout *amen!* and squinted at the podium to read the speaker's name: Preston Cobb from Hannibal, Missouri, USA.

"You came to Copenhagen because you care about the future," Preston Cobb continued, pointing, it seemed, right at Neil. "You know that the power of mankind to change the Earth exceeds our power to act with wisdom. But you've been deceived. Peak carbon—what you call global warming—might be real. I don't know. What I do know is long before melting polar ice drowns our coastal cities, the Age of Oil will be over. The peak will come before climate change, and it's the peak you need to worry about."

The projection screen at the front of the room lit up with a simple figure.

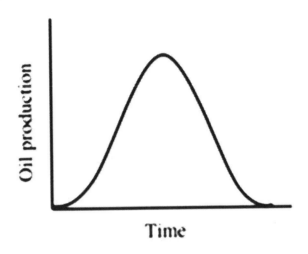

Time

"You're looking at the history of petroleum production," Cobb said. "When an oil field is discovered underground, extraction begins. In the old days, it was easy. You could find high-quality liquid oil close the surface. Punch a hole, and pressurized black gold would gush out. But over time it gets more difficult. Early wells get tapped out; you have to drill deeper. You have to drill more widely. The quality of the oil declines, it gets thicker, harder to pump to the surface. Eventually, production maxes out and then declines until it's too costly to work the field at all, and production stops. Oil companies search for new reservoirs. The next field will be harder, more expensive to exploit, maybe under an impermeable rock layer or five thousand feet of ocean water, maybe in a remote Arctic wilderness."

Cobb directed a red laser point at the graph. "The peak is reached, and production declines. Rising fuel prices and better technology may broaden the peak, but the shape is always the same. A petroleum geologist named Hubbert realized this decades ago. We call this graph a Hubbert peak in his honor."

Someone sneezed but the audience seemed spellbound.

"Do you get it?" Cobb challenged them. "Do you see? Whatever the delegates do or don't do at this climate conference doesn't matter. Oil production will decline. Hubbert peaks apply to individual wells, fields, countries—and the entire planet. Peak Oil will stop global warming. What we must prepare for is the wrenching impact of the peak."

A hand went up in the audience, and Cobb nodded.

"When?" the questioner said. "What if global warming destroys us before the oil peak?"

"The peak is closer than you think," Cobb replied coldly, and advanced to his next slide. "For some of us, it's already here."

U.S. crude oil production vs imports

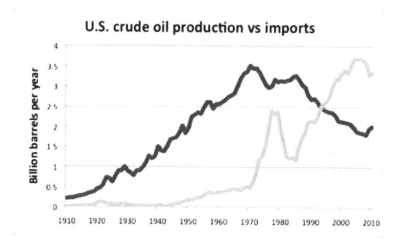

"Friends, my country reached its Hubbert peak back in 1970."

A murmur of astonishment drifted through the crowd.

"That's right. Peak oil for the United States of America was over forty years ago. All our drilling and spilling in Alaska and the Gulf of Mexico can't stop the decline. If imports hadn't taken up the slack, America's oil age would've ended with the gas crisis forty years ago. The International Energy Agency predicts we'll hit the planetary Hubbert peak as early as 2020. After that, even though there will be oil left in the ground, there will be no more growth. And I already told you what that means."

"Collapse," Neil whispered.

*   *   *

After the seminar-*cum*-revival, Neil lingered while the audience cleared out and Preston Cobb gathered his things. Neil still believed global warming was the bigger threat, but he wanted to hear more from this provocative thinker. He persuaded Cobb to join him at a café, just for a few minutes.

"Enjoying the party, young man?" Cobb said as a group of green-faced aliens strolled past an eight-foot earth-shaped piggy bank on the street in front of the café.

"It's not all fun and games, you know," Neil said, feeling self-conscious about the carnival excesses of the activists swarming Copenhagen. "I know you said global warming won't happen, but you're wrong. It is happening, right now."

Cobb stared disapprovingly at Neil's dreadlocks. "If you say so. I'd say peak oil is happening now, too. But here's the point. Whether Peak Oil or climate change comes first, the outcome is the same. Collapse. Are you ready?"

"No," Neil said. "We can stop it. That's why I'm here, to fight, to make change. Aren't you fighting, too?"

"I'm a doomer, Neil," Cobb said. "Even if it's not too late, I believe humans are too weak to make the changes that might save us. You obviously don't know, but I'm a celebrity of sorts. I have a following on the Internet—a blog, a book, a lecture tour. My claim to fame is preparedness. I'm not about politics. I'm about getting ready for the end."

"You've given up."

Cobb sipped his coffee. "You're just a kid. You don't know how bad it is. Go ahead, fix your greenhouse gas problem. I say it can't be done. But even if it could, then you've got to worry about Peak Oil. And more. The netizens who follow my blog worry about a whole list of problems that nobody can solve, any one of which alone could bring down the system. Peak oil, peak water, peak fish—"

"Peak fish?" Neil interrupted.

"The global catch of seafood by weight peaked in the late 1980's. It's been downhill ever since, and you don't think the number of people who want to eat fish has gone down, do you? Then you've got peak dirt—the degradation of our farmlands. And I know a bunch of ex-Wall Streeters who can't sleep because of peak dollars and peak debt. When you get right down to it, nothing we do is sustainable. We're at peak everything."

Neil's head was spinning and he didn't know what to say. Suddenly it seemed so much simpler just to focus on carbon emissions.

Cobb tossed a couple of ten kroner coins on the table and handed Neil his business card.

"I've got one piece of advice. Keep your health. It's the most important thing you can take with you through the collapse. Get vaccinated and stay fit."

That was the last time he saw Preston Cobb in person, but Cobb's ideas stuck with him long after the Copenhagen conference failed and he embarked on his eco-jihad. With his deeply rooted pessimism about the environment, Neil, too, was a collapsitarian. But until the petroplague, he didn't know it.

Chapter 30

The mayor's nighttime curfew is hours away, Christina reassured herself. *These people have as much right to be out and about as I do.*

But as she pedaled her way through the clogged streets of dead cars on her way to the lab, it became clear that many of those wandering around were up to no good. Only five blocks from home, she heard the sound of breaking glass and came upon a gang of four young men robbing an athletic shoe store. She turned a corner and sped away from the scene. Minutes later, she saw a solitary man strutting angrily down the sidewalk while shouting and brandishing a handgun.

Her heart beat faster and her legs pumped harder to cover the distance to UCLA as quickly as possible. *No women*, she thought, noticing the sinister absence of any females except herself outdoors. She felt distinctly unsafe, and wondered if she should turn back and go home.

But I've got to help Dr. Chen.

While riding down a street devoid of pedestrians, Christina wondered if she'd be safer on a major road. But the looters freaked her out; she decided to take her chances in quiet residential areas.

Reeking garbage cans waited in vain for the weekly pickup. Many were overflowing, and rotten globs of filthy paper and other debris drifted down the street. Christina struggled to navigate around the stalled cars and trash. Too late, she swerved to avoid a smashed whiskey bottle.

"Shit," she said when she heard a hissing sound.

She rolled forward a bit further and felt the pressure leaking from her rear tire. She dismounted and leaned her bicycle against a car. The inner tube was punctured. Thank God she had a patch kit, and knew how to use it. She reached to unzip the patch kit from beneath her saddle.

Then she smelled it. Vinegar.

A wet spot stained the pavement under the car.

She froze, then drew her hand back from the zipper. Her other hand rested on the bike seat; she used it to slowly pull the bike away from the car.

No sparks. No sparks.

Rather than let the front wheel flop and strike something, she risked a static discharge and grabbed the handlebars. Holding her breath, she walked the bike away from the potentially explosive vehicle, exhaling with relief when she was a few feet away.

A palm tree growing in a tidy yard nearby certainly wasn't leaking hydrogen gas. She tilted her bike against the trunk and concentrated on repairing the tube.

"Hey baby, you got a problem with your wheels?"

Christina jumped. In her rush to fix the flat, her awareness of her surroundings had slipped. Two men with baggy pants and baseball caps worn sideways were approaching from not far away.

"No problem," she lied, sweeping her tools into the sack and standing to face the men. The tube was patched, but not yet inflated. No other people were on the street. The men sauntered toward her. She strapped her pack on her back and prepared to ride off, flat or no.

"Nice bike," one said, glancing over his shoulder as if to confirm they were alone.

"Back off," she said in her most commanding voice. For an instant the gangstas paused. She hopped on her crippled bicycle and pedaled furiously. The young men dropped their pretense of friendliness and sprinted after her.

Normally she could easily outpace anyone on foot, but with no air in the back tire, the bike moved like she was riding through deep sand. Within two seconds she realized they would catch her before she reached the end of the block.

"Wait up, bitch."

Panic accelerated her thoughts. In a flash she wondered if they just wanted her bike. Should she drop it and run? But on foot she would be completely powerless.

The gap between her and her pursuers was down to three or four seconds and closing. A sob slipped from her lips. There was no escape.

Unless . . .

No time to analyze the risk.

Two cars ahead she saw the telltale dampness on the ground. She prayed the bacteria were still eating, still dumping their flammable waste. While moving, she lifted a foot from the pedal and reached for the kickstand. The metal stake popped into place. She steered the bike as close as she could to the side of the car. The men were almost upon her, shouting and lunging for her backpack. She allowed the bike to tilt slightly. The kickstand scraped along the ground. The bike wobbled but kept going. She turned sharply around the front of the car, encouraging the men to cut close around the fender.

The hydrogen flame she'd ignited was invisible but devastatingly hot. She never knew whether it caught one or both of the men. She rode away from the screams and didn't look back.

Chapter 31

Before he met Preston Cobb, Neil believed in change, in people power and in velvet revolutions that could change the status quo overnight. He did not believe collapse was inevitable. But Cobb's dark view of the future influenced him, and he kept in touch with Cobb. Occasionally he left posts at Cobb's survivalist websites, sharing tips about organic gardening and graywater recycling.

The petroplague made Neil and Cobb's people strange bedfellows. The survivalists were waiting—some of them impatiently—for the end. Now, for very different reasons, Neil wanted the end to come, too. He videophoned Cobb at his home in Missouri and found the collapsitarian leader in a bookcase-lined room, brightly lit through skylights. A bowl of green pears sat on his desk.

"This is the beginning of the end," Neil said. "Peak Oil is here."

"Technically this plague has nothing to do with the Hubbert peak, but I agree," Cobb said. "If L.A.'s quarantine fails, the age of oil is over. Which makes me a very busy man. You said you had something urgent to discuss?"

"I want to talk about the quarantine." Self-consciously Neil lowered his voice. "About breaking the quarantine."

Cobb whistled and looked Neil in the eye, his face expressionless.

"That sounds like a crime, Neil. One with very big consequences."

"Collapse," Neil nodded. "That's what you've been waiting for, isn't it?"

"I've been preparing myself and others," Cobb said noncommittally.

"You told me that after the peak, oil prices will skyrocket. The industrial economies will fail because they depend on cheap imported fossil fuels. There will be more wars over oil."

"More?" Cobb scoffed. "Those little showdowns in Kuwait and Iraq don't count. They're nothing compared to what will happen when the U.S. and China duke it out over the last productive oil fields on the planet."

"That's my point. Millions, maybe billions, of people will die in the oil wars. But what if we could prevent the wars?"

"War is an inevitable consequence of Peak Oil."

"But like you said, this isn't the peak, it's something different. If the petroplague goes global, of course there will be fighting. But big-time war—war fought abroad, between superpowers—that takes a lot of energy. Petroleum-based energy."

Cobb leaned back in his chair. "I'm listening."

"After a Hubbert peak, oil production declines but remains high for a while. That leaves a lot of resources to fight over. But the petroplague cuts off the peak. To zero. Right now, here in L.A., nobody's fighting over the last few gallons of gas, because there isn't any to fight over."

"A bloodless end to the oil age," Cobb said. "An interesting theory."

Neil put it on the line. "The end of oil is the end of global warming. That's what I want. You want the end of oil because you're tired of waiting for it."

"I don't want collapse. I merely expect it," Cobb said, but his eyes gleamed with an excitement that belied his words.

"Spreading the petroplague would be a mercy killing," Neil said. "We're gonna run out of oil soon no matter what. But with the petroplague, we make a clean break. You can't have a war over oil without oil. No armored Humvees, no drones, no battleships if there isn't any gas."

"Mercy killing is illegal," Cobb said, "but understandable at times."

"I'd do it myself," Neil said, "but I'm trapped in the city. I need someone on the fringe, someone who thinks like we do."

"Like you do," Cobb corrected.

"Well?"

"I don't condone extremism," Cobb said carefully as he scribbled on a piece of paper. "When I find it in one of my websites, I ask the offenders to leave."

Cobb held up the paper. It had a web address on it.

"What you're proposing is criminal, and I condemn it in the strongest possible terms," Cobb said.

But he winked. Neil saw the gesture and understood. Cobb thought he was being monitored for audio.

"You're right. I'll reconsider," Neil said, playing along. Then he hung up and went straight to the chat room Preston Cobb had suggested.

CHAPTER 32

Constantly monitoring her surroundings, Christina inserted her key into the research building at UCLA. Swiftly she drew her bike in behind her, like a sailor entering the pilothouse during a storm. She tugged at the door to hasten its latching. An uneasy quiet lay over the building. The lights and air conditioning were still on, and she saw no sign of vandalism. The elevator opened and she rode it to the Bioenergy Institute floor.

The door to Chen's laboratory was closed and locked but the lights were on inside. To avoid startling her mentor, Christina first knocked on the door and called out to him before unlocking and entering.

Piles of unwashed glassware and unemptied trash cans testified that much work had been done in the days since she left. She heard sounds in the next room.

"Dr. Chen? It's Chrissy," she called and walked toward the sound. "I'm back."

Robert Chen waved the mouth of a test tube through a Bunsen burner flame, capped it, and set the tube down in a rack. His haggard face lit up when he saw her.

"Chrissy! Hello! Welcome!" he said and gave her a hug. Then his expression clouded. "Is everything okay? Why did you come back?"

"Everything's fine," she said, ignoring the obvious complications of life in L.A. at the moment. "I just couldn't sit at home being useless anymore. I had to come help you."

"I'd be lying if I said I wasn't glad to see you. I've made progress, tremendous progress, but together we can accomplish twice as much," he said.

"I see you could use a dish washer. You're going to run out of flasks."

Dr. Chen laughed. "I have been going through quite a few bacterial cultures. Did a little research on the nutritional content of bacterial growth media, too. LB broth tastes a bit yeasty but it'll keep body and soul together in a pinch."

"You've been eating laboratory reagents?" she asked, shocked.

"Only a little, and all of it was sterile."

She immediately reached into her backpack and handed him a fistful of energy bars. He beamed, tore one open, and ate it on the spot.

"How's the work going?"

"I may be on to something, Chrissy. A possible cure."

"Already?"

"A lot of work needs to be done before I can say for certain."

"What is it?"

"An antibiotic that seems to affect *Syntrophus*."

"I thought we tested all the antibiotic classes and none of them worked."

"This is a new substance. I don't have a clue what it is, I just know that it's produced by one of the microbes in our collection."

"From an oil field?"

"Yes. Presumably these bacteria compete with each other in the wild, and one species evolved to make an antibiotic that kills the other."

"Like penicillin, which is made by a mold."

"Right. The good news is, it doesn't matter whether this chemical is toxic to humans because we won't be using it as a drug. To use it against the petroplague, we have to identify the substance, and someone will have to find a way to manufacture it in large quantities."

"But there's a chance it can be done."

"Definitely a chance," Dr. Chen said. He touched Christina's shoulder. "There's still hope."

"Tell me what I can do."

"Your job is to work on Plan B."

"Plan B?"

"A million things could go wrong with this antibiotic project. We need a backup plan. Remember your Ph.D. thesis project?"

"The photosynthetic *E. coli* for Bactofuels."

"If we can't beat the petroplague, we'll have to learn to live with it. Jeff Trinley has been calling me every day to remind me that our *E. coli*-produced isobutanol could be a very profitable substitute for diesel fuel."

The X-car, Christina remembered. Its internal combustion engine had never run on gasoline. They always fueled it with biodiesel from their experimental *E. coli* production system. She sketched the structure of the molecule their *E. coli* produced using energy from the sun.

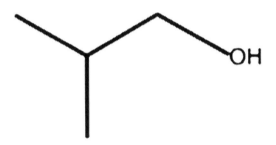

Isobutanol. Unlike petroleum diesel and gasoline, it wasn't a hydrocarbon. It was a branched-chain alcohol.

And *Syntrophus* wouldn't touch it.

"Trinley's right," she said. "The isobutanol will work even in an engine contaminated with *Syntrophus* bacteria. If it's the only transportation fuel available, people will pay almost anything for it."

"Which would solve Bactofuels' main problem. Before the petroplague, the cost of manufacturing isobutanol using *E. coli* was much too high to compete with oil."

"If price is no object, they can scale up the photosynthetic growth tanks."

"But only if you can get the thermodynamics right," Dr. Chen said. "We're still feeding the *E. coli* sugar to get them to produce fuel. You must wean them off the glucose and make them rely only on the sun."

This was a formidable scientific task, but she was undaunted. She plotted experiments, and while her ideas took shape, she pulled on some rubber gloves and washed the dishes.

CHAPTER 33

A rough, callused hand stained with soap-resistant dirt stroked a trimmed gray beard attached to a face leathered by sun. The hand dropped to a keyboard and typed.

"Got my beans, bullets, and Band-Aids. Thanks for all the advice. Goodbye and good luck to everyone."

After closing with the nickname he'd used for years, Tequila Jack logged off from the chat room. He was going to miss conversations with his survivalist friends and the Internet's easy access to information, but he was tired of waiting for the end of the world. It was time to do something about it.

Jack remembered exactly when his vigil began: May 26, 2008, the day gas hit four dollars a gallon at the corner Chevron station. It didn't matter that the price had fluctuated since then. Like Saul on the road to Damascus, Tequila Jack was a changed man once he learned about Peak Oil. He'd been preparing for the collapse ever since.

He sold his house and built a survivalist cabin in the wild, mountainous Angeles National Forest north of Los Angeles. When Barrack Hussein Obama was elected President, he withdrew all the money he had in banks and stocks, including his retirement account, and stashed it in a safe at home. When General Motors failed, he converted his cash into 24-karat Canadian Maple Leaf gold coins. When Obamacare passed the House and Senate, he quit smoking. When the Deepwater Horizon blew, he installed double-glazed argon/krypton gas-filled energy-efficient windows in the cabin, stockpiled iodized salt, started a bee colony, and got a dog. He purchased extra ammunition for his guns.

Until now, only the dog was paying dividends. The Labrador retriever's heavy black head rested on Tequila Jack's faded denim-covered knee, waiting for a scratch. Jack obliged, and Manley grunted with pleasure.

"We're going for a hike, boy," Jack said, rubbing the ears of his four-legged companion. He felt a kind of glee as he contemplated his mission. He'd been waiting for so long. And he'd sacrificed so much in anticipation.

Summer sunlight filtered through the trees of the canyon where Tequila Jack's self-sufficient, three-room cabin hid. The computer and refrigerator were the only electricity-dependent features in the house. They were powered by a generator because the cabin was off the main electrical grid. He was prepared to live without any appliances. The cabin was lit by natural light and he cooked in a solar box oven or on a high-efficiency wood-burning stove.

As the crisis in nearby Los Angeles unfolded, chatter among Tequila Jack's online acquaintances reached an all-time high. Giddily they exchanged their last messages and shared their final tips on home remedies, food preservation, and wilderness survival. Even though most of them owned portable generators or solar panels, they expected the elaborate electronic infrastructure of the World Wide Web to collapse and cut them off from one another. In the struggle for survival in a post-oil world, chaos would quickly overwhelm all complex systems.

Unfortunately, modern civilization was the most complex system of all. Its complexity and total dependence on oil made it a house of cards. Envirowacko's simple plan would easily bring it down.

Envirowacko had entered the online chat room a few days ago. The chatters were a suspicious, paranoid group; they moved to kick him out. But Preston Cobb vouched for the newcomer, and they let him stay. Envirowacko lived in Los Angeles. As he watched the petroplague strangle the city, he glimpsed an opportunity to change the course of history. Were the Peak Oilers interested?

Unanimously, they were. All of them would play a role in Envirowacko's plan, but geography dictated that one of them

139

would be the linchpin: Tequila Jack. Jack embraced the leadership role. They agreed on a date: fifteen days from now. Enough time for Jack to hike out of the quarantine zone and for the shipments to arrive. Enough time for the others to get their affairs in order.

Tequila Jack smiled and petted his dog. The years of waiting were almost over.

CHAPTER 34

One unbreakable rule governed the San Ysidro-Tijuana international border crossing a few miles south of San Diego: it's easier to enter Mexico than to leave it. Mexican border control offered southbound drivers on I-5 five lanes and little or no wait. Northbound drivers were regularly confronted with more than twenty lanes, long lines, and lengthy delays when they tried to enter the U.S.

But not today.

Diana Torres locked the doors of the Nike store at Las Americas Premium Outlet mall in San Ysidro, on the American side only a few hundred feet from Mexico. With the chaos at the border, business as usual was impossible. As the store's general manager, Diana agreed with mall management's decision to close and focus on security until the traffic cleared.

Like many of her customers, Diana was a Mexican national who lived in Tijuana. She always walked to work from the bus stop on the south side of the border. As she approached the crossing on foot to go home, she joined an enormous crowd of pedestrians waiting for permission to enter Mexico. On a typical day, there would be only a handful of camera-toting American tourists, well-to-do Mexican shoppers laden with bags from Banana Republic or Coach, and worn-looking day laborers going home to rest. Today, the people looked more like refugees.

Indeed, they were refugees of a sort. Mexico had responded to the petroplague crisis in nearby California with its own quarantine. The border was abruptly closed to all motorized traffic. Only pedestrians and bicyclists were being allowed to cross.

The disruption was massive and immediate. More than a million people crossed the international border every month, many of them in cars. When the road closed, traffic on the interstate locked into a jam almost as tight as the ones afflicting L.A. Stuck in traffic or unwilling to drive two hundred miles each way to the San Luis border crossing in Arizona, Mexicans stranded on the American side parked—or abandoned—their vehicles and walked home.

Diana stood on the hot pavement amid the sweaty throng and wondered when the mall might re-open. Her store hadn't received a shipment in a week, and neither her workers nor her customers could get to the store because of the traffic problems.

She did not consider the possibility that the disruption might be permanent.

CHAPTER 35

Tequila Jack's dog Manley skittered to his feet when Jack rose and headed for the kitchen area. The refrigerator in the little cabin was nearly empty. He grabbed the last can of beer. As he popped the top, he reflected that he could live without a lot of things in the post-oil future, but he was going to miss a cold brew on a hot summer day.

Back at his computer one last time, Jack read about the quarantine rules and the consequences for breaking them. He wasn't surprised that Democrat bastard Ramirez and his pal the President had imposed martial law in Los Angeles. State-sponsored violence and unconstitutional limits on citizens' freedoms were anticipated in most of the Peak Oil literature. The bit Jack found amusing was the delicate language in which the government described how they would murder you if you tried to drive your family to safety, out of the disaster zone, using your own car.

A slobbery blue rubber ball rolled past Jack's feet.

"You want to go to the lake, boy?"

Manley replied with a high-pitched bark and crouched with his head to the floor and his tail sticking up, wagging.

"In a minute," Jack said, taking a long swig. "We'll stop on the way down. But take it easy, we've got a ways to go."

He turned off the computer, finished the beer, and stepped into the back room of the cabin where it was ten degrees cooler. Jack had built this bedroom into the side of the mountain for natural cooling in summer. And in the winter, despite the cold at four thousand feet, the bedroom temperature remained survivable even without heat. On the bed lay a framed backpack, loaded for overnight trekking. He stuffed in a few more items, then hoisted it onto his back and headed for the door. Manley yelped and leaped for joy at his heels.

The man and his Labrador weaved their way down a narrow canyon, heading roughly eastward on an unmaintained fire road so pitted and strewn with forest debris that it was almost impassable by car. In the canyon there were enough trees of the Angeles National Forest to justify the name, but when they reached a more serviceable road, the trees were replaced by arid scrub. As they walked, Manley covered at least three times the distance Jack did, bounding forward and back, chasing birds and small lizards. The area was devoid of human activity—precisely the kind of place Tequila Jack was looking for when he made the decision to survive the collapse. It was hard to believe they were only sixty miles from downtown L.A. and the region's ten million people, but the mountains held back the hordes and their urban sprawl like a moat around a castle.

Pine Canyon Road turned into Ridge Route, and after an hour of pleasant walking, Quail Lake came into view. Manley took off at top speed. The "lake" was actually a reservoir on the west branch of the California Aqueduct which delivered water from Northern California to the desert areas of the southern state. At this time of year the water level was low, and ugly bathtub rings marred the shoreline. Manley plunged into the water.

While the dog frolicked in the lake, Jack strolled up the main highway. He saw none of the casual fishermen who typically showed up on weekends to try their luck on the reservoir, but he found what he was looking for. An abandoned car lay dead on the shoulder of the road. Using small tools extracted from his backpack, Jack pried open the gas tank cover and siphoned liquid from the tank. It stank of vinegar. He got enough to fill several one liter bottles.

"Let's go, boy," Jack called and whistled. Manley responded and soon was shaking his coat dry at Jack's side.

Tequila Jack gazed at the cloudy liquid he'd collected. He wondered where it originally came from, what messed-up country had profited when it was harvested from the underground treasure trove that the country neither earned nor deserved. Saudi Arabia? Nigeria? Venezuela? It didn't matter. Thanks to him, his friends, and Envirowacko, the age of oil was ending.

He buried the bottle in his pack and headed west toward Interstate 5.

"About twenty miles, boy," he said to the dog. "You up to it?"

The Wheeler Ridge oil field was the closest. After Wheeler Ridge, he planned to head west another twenty-five miles to the tiny Central Valley towns Maricopa, Taft and McKittrick—all legendary names in the history of California's oil industry. The oil towns persisted in the barren, sparsely-populated land atop the massive Midway-Sunset oil field, where Jack would have his pick of targets. The journey was long but he had a sleeping bag and enough to eat. The schedule allowed plenty of time to hit a number of oil wells and find a working post office. Before they knew it, he and Manley would be back at the cabin.

"How'd you like to sleep under the stars, boy?" he said.

CHAPTER 36

The beeping of the digital timer gradually worked its way into Christina's dream, then penetrated her sleeping thoughts, and finally woke her. Her body was stiff from sleeping on the thin yoga mat. She blinked and read the numbers on the timer.

"Crap," she said, fully awake the instant she realized the timer had been beeping for fifteen minutes already. Her experiments on the photosynthetic *E. coli* were tightly scheduled twenty-four hours a day, and she'd overslept.

She rose and stumbled to the light switch. The electricity was still on, something she no longer took for granted. If they lost power, the research would grind to a halt. She could barely remember whether it was day or night, and this windowless section of the lab that she'd claimed as her bedroom offered no clues.

Her hair resisted the comb that tried to tame her unruly tangles. A pair of recently-washed cotton bikini underwear and crew socks hung to dry next to a deep industrial sink along with an assortment of laboratory beakers, tubes and graduated cylinders. She felt totally gross after living and working in the same outfit for three days. Her body stank. At least she'd be able to change her underwear in a few hours.

She shuffled over to read the gas chromatograph of the latest output from her *E. coli*.

"YES!" she said, clapping her hands. She dashed off to find her boss.

In the main lab, the windows were dark, confirming that it was indeed nighttime. Dr. Chen was awake, laboring over a microscope. He looked scruffy and fatigued with an unattractive fringe of sparse whiskers on his chin. But he still managed to give her a smile.

"Good news," he said. "I have a pure culture of the microbes that make the antibiotic. Next job is to isolate the chemical."

"Then we're winning a double-header. My *E. coli* made some isobutanol today without being fed sugar." She handed him a printout of the chromatograph. "It's not much, but it proves that it can be done. With more work, I'm sure we can boost the yield."

A triumphant glow erased the weariness in Dr. Chen's face. "Great job, Chrissy. Trinley didn't think you could do it, but I knew you could. Bactofuels is going to be very pleased with this news."

A tinkling sound on the shelf above them prompted both scientists to turn their heads. A rack of test tubes was quivering slightly as if a ghost were passing through them. Christina noticed similar sounds coming from other areas of the lab, and she felt a soft vibration in the floor under her feet. Her eyes met Dr. Chen's.

"Earthquake," he said, jumping up.

In the time she'd lived in L.A., Christina had not yet felt an earthquake. The sensation was fascinating, gentler than she expected, yet more powerful and irresistible, like the momentum of a slow-moving river barge.

"Chrissy! Secure the lab!"

His command roused her. She saw him flying about, moving fragile objects away from edges where they might fall. But by the time she budged, the vibration and attendant rattling sounds had stopped.

"I think it's over," she said, touching her fingers to the lab bench to feel for movement.

Dr. Chen adjusted a couple more pieces of glassware and paused to gauge what was happening.

"I think so," he agreed. "Nothing major, thank God. That would be just what this city needs—a natural disaster on top of the man-made one we've already got."

CHAPTER 37

Los Angeles Mayor Felipe Ramirez noticed his chief of staff's disheveled appearance and wondered how bad he looked himself. He was avoiding mirrors like a vampire. The one good thing about the whole situation was the absence of camera crews at City Hall. Ramirez wasn't vain—he'd looked a lot worse in his Army days—but he was a politician in one of the most image-conscious cities on earth.

In fact, the whole crew assembled around the mayor's oak conference table looked like hung-over revelers awakened before noon on New Year's Day. Ramirez and most of his staff were sleeping in their offices. They ate whatever the National Guard brought in. They were exhausted and stretched thin. They desperately needed his leadership.

Especially with the news he just got from the U.S. Geological Survey.

"Mr. Molton, capsule reports please," Ramirez said. "Number one on our agenda: containment. What's the latest?"

"Our concentric ring strategy is working, sir," replied the mayor's chief of staff. "We've had no reports of successful blockade runners on land, sea or air. The Navy sank a vessel at sea when the captain failed to heed warnings to return to shore. There was no loss of life, all three people on board were picked up. However, a private single-engine aircraft was shot down after illegally taking off from Chino Airport in San Bernardino County."

Ramirez shook his head. "Damn fool. Did he think nobody would notice?"

"Might've been a kind of suicide by cop," Molton said.

"That idiot put a lot of people at risk," Ramirez said. "Any sign of the bacteria getting out?"

"None. Internal combustion engines just beyond our outer checkpoints seem to be working fine."

"Thank God. How are our emergency workers getting around the city?"

"Approximately forty miles of freeway have been manually cleared for one lane of traffic. These routes are being used by electric, fuel cell, and compressed natural gas vehicles either owned or confiscated by the city, county, state and federal governments. Some LACMTA buses, and the red and purple line subways, are operational. We've got shipments of bicycles and Segways arriving at containment border sites today."

"Segways?" Ramirez said skeptically. "Those goofy stand-up transports the mall cops use?"

"They work," Molton replied.

Imagining an LAPD SWAT team traveling on glorified toys unexpectedly filled Ramirez's eyes with tears. He laughed uncomfortably and wondered, what the hell are we doing? This is a losing battle.

He allowed himself a moment to regain his composure. Then he spoke to his people.

"Gentlemen, ladies, we're running out of time."

They looked at him expectantly.

"We've got to face the facts. Much of our effort is going to maintain the blockade, but the blockade doesn't do anything to fix our real problem. L.A. is paralyzed, suffocating, whatever you want to call it. We can keep the lights on and the water flowing, but without gasoline this place is going to die."

"Felipe, we all know the difficulty," Molton said softly.

"But there's more. I just talked to the local director of the U.S. Geological Survey. They're measuring increased subsurface pressures and tilt along the Santa Monica fault. The tremors of the last few days didn't relieve the stress, and the readings are still rising. They're predicting more quakes. Bigger ones."

"We're in no position to handle a major quake," Molton said. "Not now."

"Obviously. But God didn't call this morning and ask my permission. Whether we get hit with a big shaker or not, L.A. is on a one-way road to hell. We can't 'recover' from this petroplague the way we'd recover from an earthquake or fire. There's nothing to rebuild. We can clear the roads but that won't restore our transportation system. Cars and trucks, ships and airplanes are the life of this city, and they'll never run again."

Ramirez stared into the grim faces around him and offered hope.

"Only something radical, something totally outside the box, can help us. That something may be achievable."

"What is it?"

"A local biotechnology company is on the verge of producing a new transportation fuel, one that isn't affected by the plague. Better still, the stuff is renewable. It doesn't come out of the ground. It's made by bacteria turning sunlight into energy."

"They can do that?" Molton said.

"The company rep told me they made a breakthrough recently and it won't be long. I promised him our complete support. Whatever they need, if we can give it to them, we will."

"This could be our salvation," one of the counselors said.

"Not only could it save us," Ramirez said, "it could change the world."

CHAPTER 38

Heavily-laden trekkers walked northward along the five, some in gregarious groups, others quietly moving alone. Tequila Jack and his dog Manley blended in, just another pair of refugees escaping the stricken city of Los Angeles. Jack found it amusing to walk on an interstate highway and let Manley romp freely across lanes. The on-ramps were marked with ironic road signs, banning bicycles and pedestrians from the freeway and setting a minimum speed limit.

Relics of the oil age, he mused.

The weather was holding fine, sunny but not too hot. Along this canyon known as the Grapevine, I-5 linked Los Angeles with California's great Central Valley via the Tejon Pass at four thousand feet. The quarantine roadblock and inspection post, with armed guards and shoot-to-kill orders, was only a few miles ahead. Jack didn't expect any trouble at the containment border, but his mission was too important to take chances. His first task lay off-road anyway. He and Manley left the interstate and hiked west, climbing uphill over browned-out grasses in the occasional shade of a sprawling valley oak.

"We're on a mission of mercy, boy," Jack said to his faithful companion, scratching Manley's head as they rested under a tree. "You're a hero, just like those dogs on TV."

The shimmering California Aqueduct pointed toward Wheeler Ridge, part of the North Tejon Oil Field in California's oil-rich Kern County. They had only a few miles to go, and much of it was downhill.

"It's tough love," he continued. "Seems cruel, but it makes things better. We put some of this bad gas down a well and contaminate the whole field. We'll kill the field to save the people. No more oil addiction. No more bowing to rich Saudi kings. No more wars for oil."

A few hours later they reached the foot of the mountains and the arid, treeless flat of the San Joaquin Valley. Heat waves and smog distorted the view into the distance. Manley's tongue hung from his mouth, and he walked rather than trotted at his master's side. Jack gave him an encouraging pat when he spotted the first oil wells.

The pumpjacks—three of them at this site—rocked and rolled without rest. Jack scanned the horizon for a human presence, but the dirt road scratched in the valley's dust was empty. He could go about his business unmolested.

The pumpjacks' horse-like heads nodded up and down, driven by the teeter-totter action of the cross beam and rotating counterweight to which the heads were connected. The movement of the head raised and lowered a long rod which penetrated deep into the earth inside a cement-encased well. At the bottom of the well, oil seeped into the pump barrel and was gradually forced to the surface.

Two pipes stuck out from the side of the well where the rod entered. Manley lifted his back leg and peed on the pipes. Jack pulled a wrench from his backpack.

"Stand back, boy."

He adjusted the wrench to tackle the metal rings covering the top of the borehole where the rod entered the well. With some straining he managed to expose a small opening. Once he was satisfied that he had access to the interior of the well, he rummaged through his pack for a bottle of the cloudy liquid he'd siphoned from an abandoned car's tank on the day he left home.

"Here we go."

He poured about a half cup into the borehole, and the plague-infected fuel disappeared into the depths. Jack expected to repeat this process all the way to McKittrick. They'd replenish their food supplies in Taft. Then they'd complete their mission by looping back east across the valley floor to the city of Bakersfield and to the Kern River oil field where he knew pumpjacks covered the arid plain as thick as paparazzi around an A-list celebrity.

The rod on the contaminated pumpjack rose and fell, rose and fell as Manley and Jack strolled away.

CHAPTER 39

"Cheetos," Dr. Chen said, turning the bag over in his hands like a rare artifact. "Never thought I could be so grateful for junk food."

Jeff Trinley of Bactofuels then passed a bag of Doritos to Christina.

"It's the best I can do at the moment," Trinley said as he stepped out of the golf cart he drove to UCLA. "Goodies from my private hoard at the office. I'm almost out, though. Pretty soon I'll have to figure out how to get some of that government slop they're dropping from the skies."

To Christina's amazement, Trinley actually smiled at her. Her demonstrated success with his pet project must have won him over.

"You can't leave the cart out here," she said. "Someone will steal it."

Trinley tapped the roof of the car. "Solar panel," he said. "Without a recharge I might not make it back."

"Without a car you'll have an even harder time getting back," Dr. Chen said. "We'll prop the double doors open for you; looks like this thing will fit in the lobby."

"As you wish, Robert. This is your turf."

Trinley rolled the quiet electric vehicle into the research building and tucked it off to one side as best he could. Dr. Chen locked the doors behind them.

"On a sunny day like this—"

The professor's sentence was cut off, and Christina reached out to the wall for support. A tremor wobbled the floor beneath their feet in an uneasy rhythm. The degree of movement seemed about the same as with the earlier quake, but this quake lasted a little longer. No one spoke until it subsided.

"Did you feel the one yesterday?" Trinley asked.

"We did," Dr. Chen replied. "Must be an earthquake swarm."

"I hope it isn't a portent of things to come. We've got enough problems," Trinley said. "I'm taking the stairs, just in case."

They all agreed on this precaution and traipsed up to the Bioenergy Institute floor together. Christina's heart fluttered with excitement. Two earthquakes! She couldn't believe Trinley and Dr. Chen were so calm. In the Midwest where she grew up, earthquakes were thought to be terrifying events of mythic proportions.

Not always, I guess.

Still, she'd lived in L.A. for two years and never felt the ground shake. Why was it happening now, of all times?

"Where'd you get the golf cart, Jeff?" Dr. Chen asked as they entered the lab. "It's worth its weight in gold just now."

"From the Rancho Park municipal course, courtesy of the mayor's office," Trinley replied. "Bactofuels alerted the mayor that we may soon be in a position to offer him a solution to the fuel crisis, and he offered us his unconditional support."

"Excuse me?" Christina said. Her chips and lab keys clattered as she tossed them on her desk in amazement. "You told him what?"

Trinley fixed his eyes on her. "I told him, my dear, the same thing you told your boss."

"All I reported was encouraging findings with the isobutanol production. We're far from a 'solution,' as you put it. Even if we could do large-scale production of the fuel—which we can't—most ordinary cars can't use it without modifying their engines."

Trinley waved his hand. "So we dressed the news up a bit. The point is, Bactofuels is closer to a solution than anybody else, and any help we get brings us closer still. Hence the use of an electric vehicle to advance our cause."

Christina rolled her eyes, and Dr. Chen joined in her criticism.

"More than a little premature, Jeff," he said, "and you're wrong about being closer to an answer than anyone else. I have an extract of a chemical that kills the petroplague."

"You're still working on that?" Trinley asked in an accusing tone. "I thought we agreed—"

"I agreed to pursue the photosynthetic *E. coli* project to the best of my ability," Dr. Chen said, "and I have, with the able assistance of my graduate student. But one can't work on a single project twenty-four hours a day. There's down time, incubations and such. I was still able to search for an antibiotic against *Syntrophus*."

"And you found one?"

"I did."

Trinley's expression darkened. "Bactofuels is not happy about this, Robert. Remember, we're funding you for one hundred percent effort on our project, not on some pet idea of yours."

"I would hardly call a cure for this petroplague a 'pet idea,'" Christina said, incensed by Trinley's comment. "How can you possibly argue that Dr. Chen's time wasn't well-spent?"

"Because I'm paying the bills, and I didn't hire a student," Trinley said, lacing his last word with disgust.

Christina felt her face flush. Trinley turned to Dr. Chen and continued. "Besides, Robert, there's another issue here. The petroplague is a tragedy, yes, but it's also an opportunity. An opportunity to wean ourselves from oil once and for all. As long as oil is cheap, environmentally friendly alternatives can't compete in the marketplace. But if the price of oil goes up—which it has, of course, in the last few days—biofuels, and solar, and wind, and all the other renewable energy technologies out there will finally be adopted on a large scale. Think of the environmental benefits."

"And the financial benefits for you and your company," Dr. Chen said, his eyes hard. "I'd like to see carbon-neutral energy production as much as you, but I don't believe catastrophic destruction of the petroleum supply is a good way to reach that goal."

The two men glared at each other for a moment while Christina held her breath. Trinley backed off.

"Fine," he snapped. "When I make my next report to the mayor, I'll tell him about your antibiotic."

"That won't be necessary," Dr. Chen said. "When I have enough data, I'll contact the authorities myself."

Trinley nodded. "Is my sample of isobutanol ready to take for analysis?"

"I have it," Christina said.

"While you're at it, give me a sample of your new antibiotic producer. Bactofuels may be able to help you with the research, as a charitable contribution to the common welfare," Trinley said.

Chen ignored Trinley's sarcastic tone and took him at his word. "I'd appreciate that. Chrissy, would you mind preparing some vials for Mr. Trinley?"

"Sure, Dr. Chen."

Chen departed for his office, and Christina headed for a distant corner of the lab where the liquid nitrogen storage tanks were kept. To her irritation, Trinley followed her.

"You keep your stocks back here?" he said as they approached the tanks, which looked like squared-off beer kegs on wheels.

"The ones in active use are in the incubator over there," she gestured, "but you'll need a frozen stock for transport."

She donned a pair of oversized thermal gloves and unscrewed the top of one of the two tanks. Odorless white smoke spilled from the opening and drifted to the floor.

"What is that?" Trinley said.

"Nitrogen gas," she replied. "The specimens in the tanks are frozen in liquid nitrogen, at more than three hundred degrees below zero. When I open the lid, the nitrogen immediately starts to boil."

With her hands protected from the extreme cold, Christina lifted out a slender metal sleeve with eight small plastic tubes snapped to it. She popped two of them free and dropped them in a Styrofoam container of dry ice, then returned the sleeve to the subfreezing liquid and sealed the tank.

"You have any others stored around the lab?" Trinley asked.

"No, everything is in these tanks. But your isobutanol sample is in another room. I'll go get it."

"I'll wait."

Christina left the room, eager to get away from him. After he heard about the antibiotic research, his frosty, condescending attitude came back. Considering the progress she'd made on his photosynthetic *E. coli* project, she expected better. But at least he hadn't blatantly insulted her again.

She found the samples for Bactofuels and packaged them for the trip to the company lab. Then she returned to her desk.

Trinley wasn't there. Just as she started to get annoyed, he appeared.

He snatched the container from Christina's hand. "Tell Chen I'll be in touch."

"You're welcome," she said as Trinley turned his back to her and walked away. If he heard, he didn't react.

Prick, she thought, opening the bag of Doritos he'd brought. She'd had little to eat for days. The salty, crunchy snack was so satisfying that she temporarily forgave the Bactofuels rep his discourtesy.

CHAPTER 40

Tequila Jack stuck his thumb out pointing east on Highway 58. Manley lay patiently at his side, no longer wasting energy on playful detours. He fondly rubbed the dog's back. They'd covered the twenty-two miles from Maricopa to McKittrick in a single day. Drivers outside the plague zone were being generous to the refugees and it was easy to hitch a ride.

Too bad it takes a crisis to get people to work together, he thought. They'd have to do a lot more of it in the months and years to come if they were to survive the collapse.

He'd infected five pumpjacks over three separate oil fields on this side of the valley. Next stop was Bakersfield, where he would divvy up the petroplague-contaminated gasoline into vials and mail them to his survivalist allies. Early on the appointed day—eleven days from now—the recipients would fill their own gas tanks with clean fuel for the last time. Then at precisely 4 PM Greenwich Mean Time, they would begin contaminating as much of their local petroleum infrastructure as possible. The conspirators lived in eighteen states, Canada, Great Britain, and Italy. Jack wished he had contacts in Africa and Asia, too, but it didn't matter. The genie would be out of the bottle. No quarantine could prevent the petroplague from sweeping the globe.

A silver pickup slowed and pulled over. The driver, a Latino man in overalls and a baseball cap, gestured to the open bed of the truck and asked in accent-free English, "Where you headed?"

"Bakersfield."

"I'll stop to let you off."

"Thanks."

With only the slightest encouragement, Manley vaulted into the back of the truck. Jack followed and got the dog to sit with him near the cab. He gave the last of his water to Manley, who slurped it eagerly with his long pink tongue. The truck rattled down the highway.

*   *   *

Four people slouched ahead of Jack in line at the post office just before the 5 PM closing. While waiting, he made sure he'd written the same false return address on all the padded envelopes. He counted his money. Paying for postage would take most of his remaining cash but that was okay. After the collapse, the only thing paper currency would be good for was starting a fire.

"Anything liquid, fragile, perishable, or potentially hazardous?" the postal worker asked in a monotone while she glanced at the clock.

"No."

"Insurance?"

"No thanks."

One by one the fateful packages were metered and dropped carelessly into a postal bin.

"Will these go out today?" Jack asked.

"Yes," she replied.

Manley's entire body wagged when Tequila Jack returned to liberate the dog from the bike rack where he was tied.

"We did it, boy," Jack said. Manley licked his face in approval.

CHAPTER 41

After Trinley left UCLA, Christina called River and Mickey to see how they were holding up.

"You two knock over any convenience stores lately?"

"Too late, they're cleaned out," River said lightly.

"You doing all right?"

"Well, we haven't gone all Donner party yet," River said, "but if the TV quits we may have to kill each other just for something to do. What about you? Any progress?"

Christina told River all that had happened in the lab.

"That explains Ramirez's statement," River said. "His office put something out to the media hinting at a scientific breakthrough. I thought it was just hype to take our minds off the earthquakes."

"You've felt them, too?"

"Several. They're tiny so I shouldn't be worried, right? But I hear there have been a bunch more, too small for people to notice. It's making me nervous."

"Me, too," Christina agreed. "Now is not a good time."

River was silent a moment.

"Do you think there's any connection?" she said in a low voice.

"Connection to what?"

"To the petroplague, Chrissy. God, you can be so obstinate. Are you telling me it hasn't occurred to you that the timing of these quakes is more than a coincidence?"

"How could earthquakes possibly be related to bacteria eating our fuel?"

"You tell me, you're the scientist. All I know is my gut tells me it's fishy."

Christina was about to accuse her cousin of ignorance or superstition, but she hesitated when she realized she shared River's feeling.

"I guess it did cross my mind," she confessed, "although I don't see how the events could be connected. Unless . . ."

"Unless what?"

"Nothing," Christina said swiftly. "I'll ask my boss about it, okay?"

"Okay. Listen, there's something I need to tell you."

"Yes?"

"Mickey and I are thinking about bailing out, heading for San Diego."

"On foot?"

"Yeah, unless one of us sprouts wings. I'm giving you a heads up because maybe you want to come with us."

"I can't leave my work!"

Christina heard River fumble with the phone and say, "That's up to you. Does Dr. Chen really need you? You're just a student."

"Thanks a lot. Why doesn't anybody take me seriously? I'm doing good work, and I'm getting excellent results. I have something to contribute. I'm not going to run away."

"Can you bring the work with you, to another lab? Someplace where the cafeteria is still open?"

"Not really. The solar bioreactor here at UCLA is one-of-a-kind."

"Well, I'm just letting you know. Things have been pretty calm in the neighborhood, but Mickey and I think there will be some serious shit starting any day now. People can't sit in their homes day after day, eating up their last groceries, and not start to crack. We want to get out before that happens, while we still have a decent amount of food to take with us for the trip."

Christina silently considered what her cousin was saying. River continued.

"I don't want to leave you behind."

"Then don't go."

"We're going, it's just a question of when."

Though they'd been apart for days while Christina camped out at UCLA, Christina felt a sense of panic at the thought of being permanently separated from the people dearest to her.

"How much time do you need?" she asked.

"We've got the backpacks from our Sierra trip out and ready to load. We'd like to leave tomorrow."

"That's too soon," Christina said. "Can you wait one more day?"

"If you promise to join us, we'll wait."

Truthfully, Christina had no idea what difference it would make if she abandoned her post the day after tomorrow instead of tomorrow, but she wasn't ready to make a decision. Not yet, not with the antibiotic research and the *E. coli* biofuel project in full swing.

She noticed Dr. Chen leaning against the lab bench nearby, waiting to talk to her.

"I'll call you tomorrow." She turned to her mentor.

"Trinley just called me," Dr. Chen said. "He wants us to adjust the aeration cycle on the solar bioreactor."

"I can take care of it," Christina said, searching her desk for her keys to access the roof, where the bioreactor was.

Chen winced a little and said, "He specifically insisted that I do it, but I thought you'd want to help."

"What a jerk," slipped from her lips as she bent down to see if her keys were on the floor. The keys were nowhere to be found. "Sorry, I didn't mean that."

"You did, and you're probably right," Dr. Chen said with a sympathetic smile. "Let's go upstairs."

They climbed the stairs to the top floor and then one more flight up to the roof access. Dr. Chen unlocked the door. Brilliant sunlight temporarily blinded them as they stepped outside. The bioreactor was there, glistening in the sun.

"Check the temperature readings," Dr. Chen said.

Christina approached the bioreactor with a feeling of pride. The system had a futuristic beauty that bordered on art. Her genetically altered *E. coli* bacteria grew inside an array of what looked like oversized fluorescent light bulbs. The long glassy tubes were suspended one next to the other in a horizontal rack that gently rocked them back and forth. Because of the chlorophyll in the bacteria, the clear tubes were colored brilliant green. The movement caused constantly changing swirl patterns in the cloudy liquid in the tubes, which teemed with billions upon billions of microscopic life forms.

The air temperature on the roof was a hundred and two, several degrees warmer than the ideal for these bacteria. Water circulating through sealed chambers within the tubes cooled the cultures to the proper temp. In winter, heated water circulated through the pipes to warm the bacteria. Placing the bioreactor on the roof provided security and a shade-free supply of sunlight for the bacteria's photosynthesis. If their solar bioreactor didn't work here, it wasn't likely to work anywhere.

"Optimizing the oxygen and carbon dioxide flow," Christina said as she adjusted valves regulating pipes that fed into the solar bioreactor system. Dr. Chen inspected gauges displaying the effects of Christina's adjustments.

"A little more CO_2," he was saying when they heard the klaxon.

The grating, intermittent noise originated inside the building and escaped through windows and doors to reach their ears on the roof. The sound inside must have been deafening.

"That's the fire alarm," Christina said.

They sprinted for the door, Dr. Chen leaping down the steps ahead of her three at a time. Heavy fire doors isolated the stairwell and muffled the sound of the alarm. At each landing, she glanced down the hallways through small windows in the fire doors. She saw no smoke or flames.

When they reached the Bioenergy Institute floor, Dr. Chen reached for the door.

"You go outside," he said. "I'm going to check the lab."

"I'm staying with you," Christina said.

Chen didn't pause to argue, and flung open the fire door. The full blast of the klaxon exploded around them. She stuck her fingers in her ears. Every couple of months, the alarm went off in the building; in all the time she'd been at UCLA, there had never been an actual fire. But with the recent earthquakes and the problems of the petroplague, she feared the worst. If fire threatened their lab, they had to save whatever they could.

So much depended on their research, and the fire department wouldn't be pulling up in a shiny red engine within five minutes like it usually did. They were on their own.

They raced down the hall. Still no smoke in the air, but as Chen shoved his key into the lock and opened the door to the lab, Christina smelled a natural gas leak.

"Turn off the gas!" Dr. Chen shouted over the din as he sprinted left toward the storage area of the lab—into a billowing cloud of black smoke.

The master control valve for the lab's natural gas supply was to the right of the long room, about forty feet away. Christina stumbled around the corners of lab benches and flung aside a tangle of cords blocking the valve. She turned the handle and stopped the flow of natural gas.

"You got it!" she barely heard Dr. Chen shout from the other room. She ran to join him, picking up a small fire extinguisher along the way.

The smoke rising over her head triggered a flashback to the scene of Linda's death at the tar pit. She shook off her fear and kept going. Dr. Chen was wielding his own fire extinguisher, sweeping white mist over a section of bench top littered with burning debris that looked like paper. The flames extended down the bench almost in a straight line from a natural gas spigot at the wall, which Christina assumed was the source of the fire.

Though the situation seemed far less dire than the inferno at La Brea, panic induced by the memory brought her to a halt. She huddled behind a section of bench with a heavy stone countertop and cabinets beneath. It took her the span of three breaths to will herself to join the fight. Gritting her teeth, she stood up and looked over the bench top toward her mentor.

That's when she noticed the bottles of alcohol.

While Dr. Chen steadily put out the flames to his right, the fire was creeping to his left where the liquid nitrogen tanks stood, along with several bottles of two hundred proof, absolute ethanol.

Pure alcohol.

Easily ignited, extraordinarily hot when it burned.

165

"Dr. Chen! Get out of there!" she screamed over the blaring alarm.

He turned to her and must have seen her arm pointing wildly at the flames licking the ethanol bottles. But instead of fleeing, he lunged toward the danger, emptying the rest of his extinguisher on that part of the fire.

It was too little, too late. In a compressed second, she saw the extinguisher run out, and Dr. Chen's surprised face, and she dropped behind the protection of the bench simultaneously with the detonation of the first bottle. An amalgam of horrific sounds overwhelmed her. Dr. Chen's screams. The explosive shattering of glass. The unbearable loudness of the klaxon. Her own anguished moans.

More bursts rapidly followed as one bottle after another went off like Molotov cocktails. Burning alcohol splattered around her and she scrambled for cover. One fiery drop landed on her pants and instantly melted the fabric, but burned out just as quickly. The lab grew hot from the intense combustion of the alcohol, though unlike paper or tar, it produced little smoke of any kind.

She had to get to Dr. Chen and drag him away, but she had nothing to cover herself with. Frantically, she looked around for something, anything that might resist the fire. A lab coat?

Her search was interrupted by a massive explosion, like a bunker-busting bomb compared to the alcohol bottle's hand grenade. The noise ruptured her eardrum and she screamed in pain. Crumpled into a ball with her head between her knees and her hands pressed against her ears, she then endured a second gigantic blast. For an interminable period of time, she stayed on the floor, curled up and quivering, until the klaxon unexpectedly stopped.

Through the ferocious ringing in her ears, she could barely hear the lab's strange silence. There were no crackling sounds of fire. The smoke was thin and hovered near the ceiling.

"Dr. Chen?" she cried as she rose and staggered to the opposite side of the bench.

She choked at the sight of her mentor's mangled body. Jagged edges of shattered metal from the liquid nitrogen storage tanks protruded from bleeding holes in his torso and head. The exposed skin of his sandal-shod feet was the color of freezer burn on an old piece of beef. Singed spots of charred fabric dotted his clothes. One of his hands was blackened, the other was red with blood. In the span of perhaps a minute, Dr. Robert Chen had been cut by glass, scorched by burning alcohol, pierced by steel, and seared by freezing nitrogen.

Momentarily tearing her eyes from Chen, she scanned the area for threats. No flames were visible. The alcohol bottles were all broken. Because alcohol flames are hard to see in daylight, she moved forward cautiously, sweeping her hands before her, feeling for heat. A small puddle of liquid nitrogen from the tanks danced boiling in the corner.

"Dr. Chen?" she said softly, dropping to her knees at his side. She was afraid to touch him. He was not moving, not breathing. She looked in his damaged, unblinking eyes and knew he was dead.

Horror-struck, she fled to her desk and dialed 911. The only response was a busy signal. She dialed again and again, fear and despair consuming her, until she dropped the phone in surprise.

The fire alarm klaxon had started again.

"No!" she shouted. Another fire in the building? Maybe the earthquakes had damaged the natural gas lines, and gas was leaking somewhere else, too. The noise terrified her. The building wasn't safe. She had to get out, even though that meant leaving Dr. Chen.

She grabbed her keys and a few personal items from her desk and stuffed them in her backpack. The sleeping gear she'd brought would have to stay behind. As she wheeled her bike to the exit, she paused.

What if the building burned down? What would happen to their research?

In this one laboratory were two possible routes to salvation from the petroplague. She couldn't lose them.

Leaning the bike against the door, she tried to clear her mind of the panic brought on by the unsettling clamor of the alarm. Most of the isobutanol-producing bacteria were on the roof in the bioreactor, and she dare not go there. But in the lab she had a few lyophilized specimens—small samples of the *E. coli* that had been dehydrated in a way to keep them preserved indefinitely without refrigeration. She retrieved those while wondering what to do about Chen's newly-discovered microbe that made the antibiotic against the petroplague.

The frozen stocks had been destroyed in the fire when the nitrogen tanks exploded. That left only the live liquid cultures that were growing in an incubator. Christina sped to the machine that looked like a refrigerator but was warm inside.

Skidding to a halt at the incubator, she found the door open and the incubator empty. Plastic culture dishes and Pyrex test tubes were spilled on the floor.

The cultures were contaminated, useless.

"Dammit," she shouted.

The noise was driving her mad. She thought she smelled gas. Remembering that she'd given Trinley a sample earlier in the day, she decided to abandon ship. She shoved her bicycle out the door and dragged it down the stairs. When she burst into the fresh air of the university plaza, the campus was as still and empty as a graveyard.

Trinley better have taken care of that specimen, she thought as she pedaled furiously for home.

CHAPTER 42

The screeching of the building's alarm rang in Christina's ears long after she was past the range of actually hearing it. The pavement under her bicycle tires was sticky from the heat. Distant objects shimmered in the haze of the intense midday summer sun, as if being consumed by the pale flames of burning alcohol. She tried to block the grotesque image of Dr. Chen's corpse from her thoughts.

After being holed up in the lab for several days, she noticed a significant decline in civic order. The streets were still clogged with abandoned cars; most of the cars had now been vandalized, with smashed windows and spray-painted doors. So had many of the shops she passed, except for one supermarket that had a highly visible patrol of armed guards out front. A line of more than a hundred people stood near the entrance. She wondered what they were waiting for, what they had been promised. The city's food supply had to be running critically low by now.

She kept to major thoroughfares and rode her bike down the yellow center line whenever possible, avoiding piles of broken windshield glass as best she could. As she rode, she reconstructed a likely sequence of events in the tragedy at the lab. The natural gas leak started the fire and ignited the absorbent paper that lined the countertop. The fire reached the ethanol and the bottles exploded. The heat from the combusting ethanol warmed the ultra-cold storage tanks and boiled the liquid nitrogen into gas. Tremendous pressure built up and caused the tanks to explode. Finally the nitrogen itself extinguished the fires.

Dr. Chen was caught in the middle of it all. She squeezed the handlebars and choked back tears.

What the . . .

Her handlebars wobbled, the bicycle careened left, and she nearly crashed. She struggled to straighten her path, but she felt drunken, motion sick, as if the world were a rough sea pitching beneath her. She stopped to pull herself together, but the rolling motion continued.

Another earthquake!

Window panes on the upper floors of nearby buildings cracked and popped from their frames, fell to the sidewalk, and splintered. Flying shards of glass drove her to a vacant spot in the middle of the street. She knelt with her head down and fingers interlaced on top, the way the airlines suggest in preparation for a crash. This quake was bigger, much bigger, than the earlier ones. And it showed no sign of stopping.

Palm trees, adapted to hurricane-prone climates, swayed crazily, taking the movement in stride. An old hardwood tree nearby proved less flexible. A thick branch at least eight feet long dropped to the ground, the report of its fracture breaking the air like the sound of a lightning strike. She hugged her nose closer to her navel.

The sounds of destruction diminished as the earth waves gradually tapered off. Though her stomach still churned from fright and dizziness, she rose to her feet. Human cries rang anonymously from inside buildings, and car alarms went off in the distance. People previously huddled in their homes and offices spilled into the streets.

This was bad, very bad. Los Angeles was already crippled by the petroplague. The city couldn't handle this. Whatever calm still prevailed would dissipate in disaster-induced panic. She wondered if River and Mickey had delayed their escape too long on her behalf. They needed to start walking right away, with or without her. She steered her bike through the cooling spray of a ruptured fireplug and sprinted the rest of the way home.

From outside, the apartment appeared deserted, silent with the blinds drawn. The windows were unbroken, though the common lawn areas were covered with debris from trees.

Belatedly, she realized she hadn't called to tell River she was leaving the lab; her cousin would be startled at her arrival.

"I'm home," she announced loudly as she unlocked the apartment door. With an automatic motion of daily habit, she shifted the keychain from her right hand to her left and shoved it in a rear pocket. Inexplicably, she felt aware of the motion. Something about her keys . . .

"Chrissy!" a voice exclaimed from the darkness after the door closed. River turned the lights on and ran forward to embrace her cousin. Christina noticed fractured bits of ceiling tile on the carpet.

"Why are you here? Is something wrong?" River said, her face wrinkled with anxiety. She looked at Christina. "What happened?"

"There was an accident," Christina stuttered, "at the lab."

"Are you okay?" Mickey asked as he, too, appeared at her side.

She nodded. "But Dr. Chen is dead." The rush of adrenaline dried up and was replaced by a flood of tears. River and Mickey surrounded her in a comforting embrace while she cried, until she was ready to tell them what happened.

"So that's it, then. There's nothing to keep you here. We can leave for San Diego today," River said.

"I can't just leave," Christina protested. "Dr. Chen—"

"Is dead, honey."

"I know that," she said angrily. "But I can't leave his . . . his body lying there."

"You already did," Mickey pointed out.

River stroked Christina's hair. "What are you going to do, Chrissy? Carry him down the stairs and dig a hole in the courtyard with your bare hands? You respected him, maybe you loved him, but he's not your father. Even if he was, this is a crisis situation. That burned shell of a body lying in the lab isn't Robert Chen. The man is gone. You need to think about yourself."

Christina accepted a box of tissues from Mickey and blew her nose. She nodded.

"I thought that last quake was going to bring the house down," River continued with a gentle smile. "Mickey and I already decided we couldn't wait until tomorrow. We were planning to drag you from the lab and force you to come with us."

"Glad I saved you the trouble."

"We can cover a good eight miles before dark," Mickey said as he moved to prepare the third backpack. Christina laid a hand on the pack.

"I'll go," she said, "but not yet. You two should start without me."

"We won't do that," River said. "What are you waiting for?"

"I'm not waiting. There are things I have to do. Dr. Chen was this close to finding a cure for the petroplague, and before I leave I have to be sure the work is in good hands."

She pictured Jeff Trinley, and the image didn't inspire a lot of confidence. But certainly someone at Bactofuels would work on characterizing the antibiotic. Didn't Trinley have connections in the government, too? He would know what to do.

"I have to make a phone call," she said and retreated into her bedroom as Mickey flopped back onto the couch, his eyes on the TV. River watched her go.

Trinley didn't answer his cell phone, forcing her to leave a message. In a rushed muddle of words, she told him about the accident and demanded to know what he planned to do with his specimen. Frustrated, she sat on the edge of her bed and wondered what to do next. She absently started picking through her belongings, thinking about what she would carry with her when they evacuated.

Recent memories tumbled through her brain like clothes in a dryer. Robbing the convenience store; being chased by street thugs; her success with the *E. coli*; the accident at the lab; Dr. Chen's death; the earthquakes.

Minutes later, her phone rang. She jumped and looked at the number. It was the Bactofuels rep.

"Christina, thank God you're not hurt," Trinley said. "What happened?"

More clearly than in the voice mail, she detailed the events that followed Trinley's departure from the UCLA campus that morning.

"The earthquakes must have caused the fire," he said, his voice low and sorrowful. "This is terrible. Robert Chen was a great man."

"I shouldn't have left him," she confessed guiltily. "I panicked."

"No, by all means you had to get out of the building. It's unsafe and you must not return, especially not after that last quake. Robert wouldn't want you to risk your life for him even if he were still alive. I'll make sure the proper people are notified. He won't be abandoned."

"Thank you," she said with sincere gratitude. "With the lab . . . I mean, under the circumstances . . . I'm leaving town."

"I think that's wise. I'm hearing reports from the mayor's office that the situation around town is deteriorating. And they're expecting more quakes."

"More? How do they know?"

"They're getting data from underground sensors that suggest fault pressures are still rising."

Her jaw dropped. She remembered the question she'd meant to ask Dr. Chen but never got the chance.

"Are you afraid?" she said.

The words slipped from her subconscious seemingly under their own power, and she regretted saying them.

"Of what, a big quake? Sure, I guess, but the Bactofuels building is totally up to code. Don't worry about a thing. Just get yourself out of town."

"Before I go I need to know that someone is studying Dr. Chen's antibiotic. We need to know the structure, and how to do large-scale purification. If Dr. Chen was right, if it kills *Syntrophus* and stops the petroplague, he'll be a hero."

Trinley sighed. "The sample I brought to Bactofuels was damaged in transit. It's probably contaminated, ruined."

"What? How?" she asked, shocked. She'd prepared the specimen herself, taking every precaution so it would reach the other lab safely.

"I had an accident during the quake. But I'll take care of it. Tell me, where in the lab should I look for additional stocks?"

"There aren't any more! The fire was in our storage area. The liquid nitrogen tanks blew, and the incubator shook open and spilled the live cultures."

"That's terrible," Trinley said. "You're sure my sample was the only remaining bit of Chen's cure for the petroplague?"

"Pretty sure. I could go back and search the lab to be certain."

"Don't do that," he said urgently. "If there was one gas leak in that building, there will be more. You need to leave town. Now."

"Right," she said as her heart sank. Without Dr. Chen's antibiotic, Los Angeles would be quarantined forever. A successful conversion to Bactofuels' isobutanol might get people moving again, but they still couldn't risk spreading the petroplague.

"Where will you go?" Trinley asked.

"South," she replied. "To San Diego."

"Well, good luck. And don't turn back," he advised. "I'll take care of everything."

CHAPTER 43

"Magnitude 5.2," Molton said. "They're getting stronger, just as predicted."

Ramirez rubbed his hands together nervously. Lucky me, he thought. The first accurate earthquake forecast in history.

"What the hell is going on?" he said. "Why now?"

Molton shook his head sympathetically. "God only knows."

"Not only God," Ramirez said. His hands stopped dithering. "What do you mean?"

"I can't believe this seismic activity is a coincidence. I want to know why it's happening now, in the middle of the biggest crisis this city has ever faced." He frowned. "And the geologists have never been this accurate before. What's different this time? What are they seeing?"

His eyes narrowed, and he spoke with conviction.

"These earthquakes are not an accident. I want someone to tell me what's causing them."

*   *   *

The Pavilion for Japanese Art at the Los Angeles County Museum of Art was the assistant curator's favorite part of the museum. In contrast to the garish modernity of the Broad exhibit on the other side of the museum campus, the meditative East Wing was a place of serenity. Fiberglass panels instead of windows filtered the natural light and cast the works of art in a gentle illumination similar to the effect of a shoji screen in Japan.

The curator chose to sleep here, in the Japanese Pavilion. Her office was too cramped, cluttered with personal items and survival gear for the prolonged camp-out. When the petroplague shut down the city, she was one of a handful of employees who opted to live in the museum, keeping it safe, supervised, and maintained. It was an easy decision. The museum was her life. Staying here, surrounded by art day and night, was in some ways a dream come true. Though her body grew weary and hungry, her soul was nourished by the surroundings.

But as the days crept by with no sign that the crisis would end, she questioned her decision to stay. The electricity and water were still on, and there was still food in the cafeteria freezers, but the earthquakes frightened her. The staff's sense of isolation was growing, and they felt vulnerable. She had no weapon, and lawlessness was on the rise outside. What if armed robbers attacked the museum?

It was mid-afternoon and the beautiful light of the East Wing reflected off the gold leaf in a painting of a black horse with a flowing mane and taut muscles. Uncomfortably, the curator lay on her sleeping mat to read a book and possibly take a nap, when a smacking sound startled her to her feet. A shadow fell on the gold leaf. She looked to the "windows" and saw a dark stain on the outer surface. As she watched, more of whatever it was splattered the fiberglass panels. The sound of it striking reverberated through the room, and the light dimmed as the dirty splotches blocked out the sun.

Her running shoes gripped the floor as she sprinted for a real window where she could get a clear view of what was happening outside. She got a glimpse of Wilshire Boulevard to the south but the action was on the east-facing side of the Pavilion. The nearest window in that direction was downstairs. She took the steps two at a time and noticed an unpleasant odor before she reached the landing at a ground-level emergency exit.

An ugly black goop was spreading across the floor like spilled syrup. It was coming from the door. To her horror, the curator could see tar pooling on the ground outside, about two inches deep, slowly forcing its way into the museum.

*   *   *

"Chrissy, get out here. You've got to see this."

Mickey's voice reached Christina from the living room as she hung up on Jeff Trinley. *Yes, Trinley would take care of everything.* What did she, a graduate student with a dead mentor and a scorched lab, have to offer? Nothing. River was right, she needed to look out for herself.

Then she saw the dripping, black zombie on the television screen.

"Footage from somewhere near La Brea," Mickey said. "The tar pits are erupting big time."

The zombie was apparently a man covered in tar as thoroughly as a pretzel dipped in chocolate sauce. His clothing and features were indeterminate, obscured by the thick, sticky substance. While she watched, he fell to his knees. The image jiggled and pulled back, revealing a spreading stain of fresh asphalt on the sidewalk behind the man. Also in the picture, she recognized the corner window of a sandwich shop about two blocks from the tar pits.

The broadcast flickered and changed to a different video feed, this one from the air. She could discern the outlines of the Page Museum at La Brea, but it was awash in tar. Lake Pit had swallowed Hancock Park, and it was still expanding. Like an old-fashioned oil gusher, tar spewed into the air from at least three places in the image.

"They said there's tar in the halls of LACMA," Mickey said, referring to the tar pits' next-door neighbor, the Los Angeles County Museum of Art.

"Maybe they can spin it as a new modern art exhibit," River said as she appeared with a pack hanging on her back. While she adjusted the hip rests and tightened various straps, she glanced back and forth from Christina to the screen.

"What does it mean?" River said, looking at her cousin with an accusing stare.

"I don't know," Christina replied slowly, still hesitant to speak the truth.

"Of course you don't *know*. But what do you suspect?"

She had suspected for a long time, since all the troubles began, that there was a connection between her *Syntrophus* bacteria and the disturbances at La Brea. In science, a good theory had explanatory power, allowing one to make predictions about the future. The theory she'd hatched was proving to be quite good at explaining actual events—events like the earthquakes and this imbroglio at Hancock Park.

"The petroplague is causing it," she said finally, "and the earthquakes, too."

"How can that be?" Mickey said.

"The bacteria are native to underground petroleum deposits—oil fields, like the one that feeds La Brea. I think some of our genetically altered *Syntrophus* have gone home, colonizing the L.A. basin deep underground."

"Where they eat the oil," River said.

"And produce gas as waste. Lots of gas."

"So what?" Mickey asked.

"Gases are bigger than liquids," Christina said. "Did you ever put dry ice in a balloon?"

"No," Mickey snorted.

"When the dry ice gets warm it melts into a gas. The balloon swells and eventually pops. That's what's happening under L.A. The petroplague bacteria are converting liquid or semisolid petroleum into gas. The gas is expanding and causing a massive buildup of pressure."

"Enough pressure to force huge amounts of tar to the surface at La Brea?" River said.

Christina nodded. "And destabilize the Santa Monica fault."

CHAPTER 44

Ramirez scribbled his signature across another document. Even the petroplague couldn't kill red tape.

"You may be right about the earthquakes, Felipe," Molton said. "I've got a scientist on the phone. You can ask him if they're related to the petroplague."

"Who is it?"

"Jeff Trinley from Bactofuels."

Some answers, and perhaps good news.

"Does he have an update on that biodiesel he promised me? Put him on!"

Ramirez and his associates enthusiastically faced the speakerphone as if the Bactofuels rep were Jesus Christ himself.

"Trinley, I hope you've got the first good news of my day," he said. "We need that fuel."

"I know, Mr. Mayor, we're working on it and we're very close. But that's not why I called."

"Then why am I wasting my time with you?"

Trinley started talking faster.

"Sir, I need your help. Someone is threatening our biodiesel project."

"What? Who?"

"The same person who started the petroplague."

"What the hell are you talking about?"

"You're aware, of course, that the oil-eating bacteria which have us in their power originated in a laboratory at UCLA."

"I am."

"Are you aware that a student in that laboratory collaborated with a group of radical environmental activists to start this crisis?"

Ramirez shook his head as if to clear out his ears. "Excuse me?"

"The genetically altered *Syntrophus* bacteria first entered the environment when this student gave the terrorists the location of the research test site in Jefferson Park. With this information, the radicals bombed the test site and released the bacteria. The student denied any connection to the attack but recent events make it clear she is ruthlessly determined to keep the plague going."

Was Trinley talking about Christina González? The same Christina who gave testimony in this office?

"What events?"

"My colleague at UCLA, Dr. Robert Chen, who was also this girl's boss, is dead. Murdered in his lab by his own student."

Gasps of dismay rose from the gathered listeners.

"Chen was murdered?" Ramirez said.

"The girl rigged a lethal accident to stop his research. I'm afraid she might do something to sabotage the Bactofuels project as well."

Chen can't be dead, we need him. But he is dead? Killed by a girl?

"What girl, Mr. Trinley?"

"Christina González."

Ramirez felt the blood drain from his face. That sixth sense he'd long trusted, his ability to read people, had failed miserably. Christina was in league with the enviro-terrorists? She was a murderer?

"Why would she kill her mentor?"

"Chen was working on a cure for the petroplague. Some kind of antibiotic that would kill it. The girl couldn't let that happen. She whacked him and destroyed all the lab's samples of his antibiotic."

Ramirez didn't have time to digest this bizarre and disturbing tale right now, not with the plague raging and the earthquakes increasing. One word in Trinley's denunciation grabbed his attention. "Chen was working on a cure?"

"He was, but because of González it's gone forever. Your Honor, you've been extremely supportive of our research effort and it's paying off. I verified this morning that our photosynthetic *E. coli* are making isobutanol. We will provide you with a fuel that gets L.A. moving again. But I need your help."

"What do you want the city to do?"

"Arrest Christina González."

CHAPTER 45

Christina gripped the arms of the faded navy recliner as if another earthquake were trying to shake her from it.

"The photosynthetic *E. coli* project won't stop the seismic pressure buildup," she said. "Even if Bactofuels comes up with enough isobutanol to fuel the petroplague area, the earthquakes will continue."

"We have to get out of here," Mickey said.

"Yes, you do," Christina agreed.

"You?" River said. "Don't you mean we?"

"No," Christina said, her voice firm. "Dr. Chen's antibiotic is the only thing that can save Los Angeles."

"But you said his work was destroyed in the accident."

"I know. But there must be, there has to be, something in the lab that can be saved."

"You're going back to UCLA," River said.

"It's too dangerous," Mickey objected. "Last time you were attacked on the street and nearly blown up inside the building. Now the place is liable to collapse around you."

"Forget it, Chrissy. Let's pack up and leave. Now," River said.

Christina laughed, a mirthless laugh full of resolve. "Listen to you two, the dedicated social activists. Ready to stand up for what you believe, risk prison, fight for freedom and equality. But when there's real trouble, not an abstract, existential threat, you turn tail and run. Well, I won't, not as long as there is something I can do."

Though it was all true, she expected River to get angry. Instead, she seemed chagrined.

"This is different," River said.

"How, River? How is this different?"

"Because," River said. "Because it's you and not me."

Christina looked at her cousin, and finally got her meaning.

"You don't want me to get hurt," she said.

"Chrissy, ever since we were little, you were the responsible one," River said, the words flowing with emotion. "Your mom and dad, too. Not like me and my parents. We always had our causes, and they're important, but they change. I know that about myself. My causes are big and important and exciting, but they don't last. Your causes aren't as glamorous, but they don't change. You've always been steady, studious, dedicated to your family and your goals."

"Don't forget law-abiding," she said lightly, taken aback by River's sincerity.

"That, too," River said, now wiping tears from her eyes. "I know I don't always show it, but I respect you. And I hope you respect me. And I'm not telling you to run away because I'm a coward . . . well, in a way I guess I am. I'm afraid of losing you."

"Thank you," Christina whispered, and they embraced.

"There's no honor in futility," Mickey said.

"It's not futile. There's a chance," Christina said, releasing her cousin. "I remembered something about the bacteria and I think there may be a source of it still in the lab. I have to find out."

"Then I'll go with you," River said.

"No," Mickey interrupted. "I will. As a bodyguard, you know?" he said and smiled while he flexed his not-so-impressive biceps.

Christina put her shoes on. "There's no time to lose."

Chapter 46

By the time Christina and Mickey ventured out on their bikes, the shadows were long and the light was growing dim.

"It's so quiet," Mickey said. Hiding indoors for the last few days, he'd failed to notice this pleasant aspect of the end of traffic.

"Yeah," Christina said. The absence of car noise made her feel exposed. Each creak of her pedals announced their presence to unseen marauders.

Los Angeles was taking on the appearance of a third-world city, *sans* diesel fumes. Debris from the last earthquake and piles of unclaimed garbage littered the sidewalks. They rode down the middle of the streets and kept silent, moving at a fast clip. On one block, the power was out. They took a detour to stay in the glow of streetlights.

When the relative sanctuary of UCLA came into view, she felt a mixture of relief and anxiety. She had some concerns about the structural safety of her building, but mostly she dreaded seeing Dr. Chen again. Maybe someone had already taken care of his body. She could hope.

They entered the ground floor lobby and expelled sighs of relief that they'd made it unaccosted. The building alarm system was silent.

"Elevator?" Mickey asked.

"Why not live dangerously," she said, unwilling to haul her bike up the stairs.

The elevator doors opened on the Bioenergy Institute floor. Unexpected stripes of yellow decorated the hall.

"Police tape," Mickey said.

"Crime scene—Do not cross," Christina read the words emblazoned across the entrance to her lab.

"What's this about?"

"I don't know," she said, unsure what to do next.

Mickey reached for the doorknob.

"It says we can't go in," she protested.

Mickey rolled his eyes. The door wasn't locked. He pushed it open and gestured for Christina to lead the way. She hesitated, then wriggled through the tape, tearing some of the strips, and entered the dark lab.

The odor of natural gas was gone; in fact the air smelled fairly fresh. She'd expected a foul stench from . . .

"The accident happened over here," she said, flipping light switches as she went.

"Why did the cops come?" Mickey said.

"The alarms must have summoned them."

Christina had literally been living at the lab and knew every nook and cranny by heart, so it was obvious to her that people had been there. A stack of research journals had been rotated; a micropipettor had moved.

"The cops can't drive," Mickey said, "and the city's on the verge of riot. Why would they answer a fire alarm?"

"Maybe it was just campus police," she said, but as she gingerly made her way toward the accident, the impression grew on her that some kind of systematic investigation had been made.

"Oh!" she said.

Mickey was beside her in an instant.

"Where's Chen?" he asked.

"Gone."

The floor and walls were stained with blood, but Dr. Chen's body was no longer there. More yellow crime scene tape crisscrossed the room. A pile of broken glass had been swept into a corner.

Part of her was relieved that the poor man had been properly tended to, but the police involvement was worrisome.

Mickey stepped past her and scanned the room. Ostentatiously placed on the center of the bench was a business card. It belonged to LAPD Lieutenant Jerry Branson. Mickey held it up and waved it at Christina.

"You said it was an accident."

"It was. A gas leak, then a fire, then the liquid nitrogen tanks exploded."

"Seems the cops don't think so."

"Let's get what we came for, okay?" she said, her voice edgy.

They retreated from the site of the tragedy into the main part of the laboratory. Christina dragged a footstool to a bench next to an oversized refrigerator and reached for a three-ring binder on the top shelf.

"I have to find the right code numbers for the tubes," she said.

"What are you hoping to find?" Mickey asked as he patrolled the perimeter and peeked out into the hall.

"Oil."

Her finger scrolled down a handwritten list on the page until she found the reference she needed.

"What good is that?"

Mickey returned and hovered over her protectively. Like a big brother, she thought, and she was struck by the realization that this slacker boyfriend of River's was behaving differently. Exactly what was different she couldn't define, but she'd never seen him like this. More mature somehow. Almost responsible. She was glad to have him with her.

"At the very beginning of his research, Dr. Chen collected drill samples from oil wells all over the world. He wanted a library of many different bacteria that naturally live in oil fields. The *Syntrophus* bacteria that eventually became the petroplague came from one of these samples."

"Seems like we've got enough of that one," Mickey said.

"I'm not looking for *Syntrophus*. The antibiotic that Dr. Chen discovered comes from another species of oil field bacteria that lives in the same places. By going back to the source—the original oil field samples—someone can re-isolate Dr. Chen's antibiotic producer."

"Someone, not you?"

She put the notebook aside and started digging through racks of one milliliter plastic tubes.

"I'm skipping town, remember?"

Each time she found the number she was looking for on a label, she set the tube in a small cardboard box with paper dividers to hold the tubes upright.

"Mission accomplished," she said and gave Mickey a triumphant fist bump. "One of these has to work."

"What do we do now?"

"I'm going to give them to Jeff Trinley, my contact at Bactofuels. Their scientists can replicate Dr. Chen's work."

"And save the world," Mickey said.

In reply, Christina crossed her fingers. Then she called Trinley.

"Where are you?" Trinley asked.

"At the lab."

"I told you not to go back there! There could be more gas leaks!"

For a guy who treated her like she was lower than dirt, Trinley seemed surprisingly concerned about her safety.

"It's okay, the building is fine."

"But what are you doing? You were supposed to leave town."

He sounded agitated. She wished she could consult someone else, but at the moment Bactofuels was their best chance.

"I may have found some of Dr. Chen's antibiotic producers."

That shut him up.

"It's not a pure culture," she continued. "I have oil field samples from where the bacteria live in the wild. If I give them to you, can Bactofuels isolate the species?"

Trinley was still speechless.

"Mr. Trinley? Do you have people who can do this?"

"Yes, yes of course we do," he said at last. His tone had changed; he seemed much calmer now. "Give me the samples and we'll handle it. But you'll have to wait until tomorrow. The sun's gone down and the curfew is in effect. I'll meet you at UCLA at dawn."

"No," she said. "We don't have time to waste. I think my *Syntrophus* bacteria are causing the earthquakes. You have to get started on this right away."

"But Miss González—"

"I promised my cousin I would leave for San Diego as soon as possible. I want to give you these samples now. Tonight."

"Very well. Wait there."

"Not here," she insisted. Though no obvious dangers threatened them at the moment, she was afraid of the lab, and her anxiety was increasing. The accident that killed Dr. Chen kept replaying in her head, and the yellow police tape was disturbing. "I've got my bike. Can I meet you somewhere?"

"All right. Hold on a minute and I'll get a location. I have a place in mind but I want to make sure it's safe."

The line went silent and she waited. Mickey wandered over to a natural gas spigot and sniffed it. Christina paced back and forth. She thought she felt the floor tremble and she gripped the nearest lab bench. Finally Trinley returned and gave her an address. She ended the call.

"Bet he was psyched. You're going to make him a hero," Mickey said.

"I suppose," she said, wondering, "but he seemed kind of upset. Anyway, the arrangements are made."

"How far is it?"

"About six miles, I guess."

"Six miles?" Mickey exclaimed. "Chrissy, it's dark out. We can't ride that far, it's too dangerous. And the curfew—"

"I'm not spending the night in this lab," she said with her arms crossed.

"Can't you meet him somewhere closer?"

"That's already much farther for Trinley than it is for us. He said we shouldn't even start out for another twenty minutes so we don't have to wait for him."

Mickey frowned and tapped his foot. Then he broke into a grin.

"How 'bout we drive?" he said.

"Yeah sure, I'd love to," she said sarcastically.

"Doesn't the X-car still go?"

Ah, the bright green experimental Mini Cooper. She hadn't thought about it in a while. Leave it to Mickey; he loved that car.

"It doesn't belong to me."

"I don't think Dr. Chen is going to object. It's parked here on campus, isn't it?"

"Yes."

"And it's immune to the petroplague?"

"Right."

"Then what are we waiting for?"

"I'm just not comfortable with . . . and the streets are clogged . . ."

Mickey put his hands on her shoulders and rotated her to face him.

"Chrissy, it's not safe to ride the bikes around town. You want to finish this task and get out of L.A. Let's take the X-car. It's small enough we can drive it on the sidewalk if we have to."

"Okay," Christina exhaled, and she went to Dr. Chen's office to find the key.

CHAPTER 47

Even through the closed blinds, River saw the lights in the parking lot. There were several, and they were bright. Or maybe, with the absence of automobile lights lately, she'd simply forgotten how strong headlights could be. But she knew they couldn't be car lights, not with the petroplague raging.

Whatever was happening outside the apartment was more activity than she had seen in days, and she didn't like it. Activity, especially during curfew hours, was a bad sign. Of what, she didn't want to find out. She quietly extinguished all lights, including the glow from the computer monitor, and sat on the floor in the kitchen, listening intently.

The pounding on the front door was so sudden and so loud she nearly jumped out of her skin. Someone rapped on the windows as well, and a beam of light flickered around the room as a flashlight tried to penetrate the window dressings. The banging on the door continued. With that much force thrust upon it, River was sure the cheap aluminum frame would crumple.

"Open up! Police!"

Like hell I will, she thought. It was a nice trick. Some gang of toughs trying to find out which homes were still occupied. What would they do if they got inside? Robbery if the apartment was empty? Something more violent if they found a woman?

The pounding stopped and the lights danced. River heard voices of command and held her breath. She softly opened a drawer at head level and slid out a knife.

The door exploded inward amid shouts and flashing lights. She rose above the countertop to confront the invaders, knife in hand.

"Drop the knife! Police!"

Blinded by the bright beams shining in her eyes, River squinted and saw uniforms and utility belts. A row of handguns was drawn, pointing at her.

God, are they really cops?

"Drop the knife!"

She dropped it and raised her hands over her head, laughing. Cops, she could handle.

"What do you want?" she said lazily.

Four figures spilled into the living room; in the awkward light River thought maybe one of them was a woman. River stayed motionless in the kitchen while the officers located the light switches and turned them on.

The female cop approached and studied her face. River suppressed a sneer.

"This isn't her," the cop said. "Search the apartment."

"We ran out of pot last week," River said, taunting. She had no fear of the police. But what were they doing here, for Christ's sake? In the midst of the city's turmoil, they had the resources to send four cops to Christina's apartment?

"Where is Christina González?" the woman asked.

"I don't know. Why should I tell you?"

"We have a warrant for her arrest."

"Christina?" River gasped. *Fuck, was it the raid on the Seven-Eleven? Did they actually make an ID from a security camera or something?* "Christina's never done anything illegal in her whole life."

"Not according to this."

The female officer patted River down for weapons and then handed her some documents. As far as she could tell in a quick scan, she was holding papers that gave the police authority to forcibly enter the house if necessary for the purpose of arresting Christina.

On a charge of murder in the first degree.

CHAPTER 48

In anticipation of lengthy detours around impassable roads, Christina and Mickey departed immediately from UCLA even though Trinley had advised them to delay. It turned out the X-car was small enough to find a path down most streets or sidewalks. They had to stop twice to scrape aside stinking piles of trash—Mickey did it, God bless him—but they still arrived at the rendezvous early.

"Park over there," Mickey said, pointing toward a shadowy area under a broken streetlamp. "We may be waiting for a while and I don't want to be seen."

Christina rolled the car into place on the residential street half a block from the address where they expected to meet Trinley.

"We can watch from here. He'll probably be driving that electric golf cart he had before," she said, dousing the lights and sliding low into her seat.

They sat in silence, tensely watching for trouble.

"Shit! Cops," Mickey hissed and ducked his head below the level of the window.

Christina peeked over the dash and saw three LAPD officers rolling down the sidewalk on Segways. She put her hand over her mouth and wondered whether breaking curfew could get them arrested.

But the police didn't see them. They coasted to a stop some distance away.

"Isn't that the house?" Mickey whispered.

Christina straightened up a bit and squinted. Yes, the policemen had halted in front of their meeting place.

"I think so," she said.

The officers steered their personal transports toward the back of the property, then reappeared on foot. They seemed to confer and then dispersed, apparently taking up hidden positions in the immediate vicinity of the building.

"It looks like they're staking out the place," Mickey said. "You better call Trinley and tell him we'll meet him one block over or something. We can't get out here."

"What rotten luck," she said. As she reached for her phone, River's ring tone shattered the hushed silence in the car. Frantically she grabbed the handset to stop the sound.

"What is it?" Christina said.

"Chrissy, listen carefully. You're in a shitload of trouble."

"It's just a curfew violation and they haven't even seen us yet," she said, distracted and a bit confused.

"Who hasn't seen you?"

"The police."

"LAPD? Wherever you are, get the hell out!"

"I think we're okay. I'm going to call Trinley again—"

"Chrissy, listen. The cops are looking for you. They've been here, to the apartment. They have a warrant for your arrest."

"What?"

"For murder, Chrissy, for murder," River said, blubbering with sudden tears.

The phone drifted away from Christina's ear and she looked at Mickey as she tried to make sense of what she was hearing. Mickey stared at her, his eyes wide.

"They think I killed somebody?"

"Your boss. Dr. Chen," River said, snorting back phlegm. "They investigated your lab. Jerry Branson, that lieutenant who came here after Linda died at La Brea, he was involved. He said Chen's death wasn't an accident."

"Of course it was. I was there. I saw it happen."

"That's not good, Chrissy. Branson said the pressure release valves on the liquid nitrogen tanks had been tampered with. Sealed. When the tanks warmed up, the gas was trapped inside until they exploded."

"Why would they think I could do such a thing?" Christina said. She felt detached, as if watching a movie. The very idea was positively surreal.

"Branson didn't say."

"I know why," Mickey said. "It's because of me."

Christina met his gaze. It was steady.

"It all goes back to the sabotage at the gas station," he said. "To an outsider, it looks like you engineered this whole thing. You invented the petroplague in a lab. You conspired to release it by sharing the location of the test site with a radical environmentalist. Your boss is close to finding a cure, so you kill him—"

"Stop!" Christina said. "It's absurd, that's crazy talk."

"I know it's not true, but it kind of makes sense," River said.

I didn't—it was an accident—I have the cure in my hands!

"Where are you now, Chrissy?" River's voice brought her back to reality. Consciously Christina tried to master herself, to think like the scientist she was. She and Mickey were in a real pickle. She needed to be analytical, to think clearly without emotional taint.

"We're at a rendezvous to meet Trinley, but we have to call it off."

"There are cops?"

"Yes, apparently waiting for me to waltz in."

"Can you get away without being seen?"

Christina thought about the eye-catching little vehicle they were in.

"Not really."

"Doesn't matter. We can outrun them," Mickey said.

"That's true," Christina said. "On top of everything else I supposedly did, I stole the X-car, too. Those Segways are no match for the X."

"Then go," River advised.

"Where?"

"We should leave the city together, just as we'd planned. Since you have the car, come pick me up. We'll load the backpacks and get as far as we can before the fuel runs out."

"Agreed," Christina said and adjusted her posture to start the car.

"Wait," Mickey said. "Let me drive. We have to blast out of here, and you're way too cautious."

She smiled. Quietly, in the darkness, they crawled over each other and traded places. She was just pulling her left foot over to join the rest of her body in the passenger seat when the car began to tremble. By now she easily recognized the start of another earthquake.

The tremor quickly increased to a level of violence she hadn't felt before. A weird, low pitched rumble filled her ears and palm branches rained down on them. Two of the cops emerged from their hiding places.

"Go, Mickey!"

The X-car sprang to life. Without turning on the headlights, Mickey adroitly maneuvered the Mini into a clear path and hit the accelerator.

CHAPTER 49

Ramirez had a recurring nightmare about the fires in Iraq. The dream always began with the sensation of falling through choking blackness, and ended with the tumult of a helicopter crash. He would feel the heat and taste the sand in his mouth. The vision was steeped in a sense of powerlessness and its twin emotion, fear. When he had the dream in the years just after he came home from the Gulf in 2004, he would typically wake to a panic attack.

Dozing on the floor of his office, he had this dream again. He woke abruptly and needed a moment to remember why he wasn't in bed. The floor was trembling.

"Quake," he said.

From his window he saw a block of streetlights extinguish just before the trembling stopped. He would willingly trade a temporary, insubstantial panic attack for the concrete, troubling reality that confronted him. For a minute it seemed possible to fall asleep again, but a knock came on his door. It was Molton.

"Sir, we've got bad news."

Ramirez stretched and smoothed his dress shirt; he was sleeping in his clothes.

"That's such a surprise," he said and took a seat in his high-backed chair.

Molton slid a document across the desk.

"USGS reports rising pressures in the Wheeler Ridge and White Wolf faults."

"I don't need a sensor to tell me that. We just had another quake."

"The quake didn't come from Wheeler Ridge or White Wolf. Those faults aren't under L.A. They're on the other side of the Grapevine, over the Tejon Pass past Lebec," Molton said. "Forty miles from Bakersfield."

Ramirez stared at the report.

Molton kept his eyes fixed on the mayor and said, "Felipe, parts of them are outside the quarantine zone."

Ramirez spun to his feet.

"How? How did it get out?"

"We don't know for sure that it's out. There haven't been any engine failures in the Central Valley. The fault pressures may not be a consequence of petroplague contamination. One of our scientists said the geologic changes in L.A. could affect the faults in surrounding areas. But . . ."

"But the plague might be in the ground up there," Ramirez said.

"It might. And if it is, they tell me it's unlikely it got there on its own."

"A quarantine breach?"

"Possibly sabotage," Molton said.

Ramirez headed for the door. "Two of California's biggest oil fields—Midway-Sunset and Kern River—are near Bakersfield. Possibly a billion barrels of petroleum in them."

"That's a lot of plague food."

"We have to shut down the oil fields, stop the drilling," he said and lowered his voice. "But let's keep this quiet. The President is concerned we may have a China problem. If the Chinese think we've lost control of the petroplague, they may take matters into their own hands. There's a rumor they might use an electromagnetic pulse device to stop anyone or anything from leaving California and taking the plague with them."

"We have to do something," Molton said.

"Then get that scientist from Bactofuels on the phone. I want the cure the professor was working on when he died."

CHAPTER 50

"You're enjoying this too much," Christina said as Mickey whipped the X-car up one sidewalk and down another, twisting and weaving like a stunt driver.

"Anybody behind us?" he asked.

"I don't think so."

The tremor was over. She estimated it was no more severe than the previous one. Maybe the worst of the seismic activity was over. L.A. sat atop petroleum deposits, but they weren't famously large. Perhaps the underground *Syntrophus* activity had maxed out.

"I'll call Trinley. Hopefully he hasn't reached the rendezvous yet."

Trinley answered immediately. "I'm on my way," he said. "Are you there yet?"

"We have to change the location," she said. "The police are there."

"Miss González, you were right that we must start work on the antibiotic at once. I just learned from the mayor that your *Syntrophus* bacteria may have escaped the quarantine to the north. So we have little time. Please, meet me at the designated spot. This cure is far more important than a citation for violating curfew."

"It's not a curfew violation I'm worried about."

"What's wrong?"

"I think the police are looking for me."

"Paranoid delusions? Are you cracking?"

"No, I'm fine. I have valid reasons for wanting to avoid an encounter with the authorities," she said, growing assertive with aggravation. "Just tell me where you are and we'll come to you."

"I'm almost at the rendezvous, meet me there."

"I won't do that. Give me an alternative—"

She froze in mid-sentence. Trinley was right about one thing: she was cracking. If those policemen were indeed waiting for her, how did they know she was coming? She was distracted, traumatized, stressed out—but how in the world had she failed to see it before?

"You bastard," she said. "You killed Dr. Chen."

Mickey swerved the X-car hard to the left.

"You wanted to destroy his antibiotic work so Bactofuels could sell solar isobutanol at an exorbitant price. You borrowed my keys and tampered with the liquid nitrogen tanks at the lab. And now," her voice quivered with rage, "you've framed me for murder."

"I don't know what you're talking about. You sound very disturbed," Trinley said in an impassive tone. "Meet me—"

"At the ambush you arranged? Yeah, I'll just walk right up and introduce myself. Then you can destroy these specimens and act like Bactofuels' product is the city's only hope."

"Miss González, if you don't surrender those oil field samples, it will look very bad."

"It's going to look a lot worse when I take them out of the quarantine zone," she said.

"Hang up," Mickey shouted. She'd forgotten he was even there.

He reached over, snatched the phone, and disconnected the call.

"Take out the battery," he said, tossing the phone in her lap as he hit the brakes to navigate a particularly narrow gap.

Christina stared at him.

"Do it now!"

She fumbled with the handset as the car lurched forward.

"They can track your location through your cell phone," Mickey said. "Don't turn it on again."

Her anger dissolved into despair, and she cried while Mickey drove. Somehow, crying helped her to regain control. From under the seat she extracted a small Styrofoam box marked with bright orange biohazard symbols. Inside the box were the oil samples that she fervently hoped contained the secret of the petroplague antibiotic.

"What am I going to do with this?" she said.

Keeping both hands on the steering wheel, Mickey shrugged his shoulders.

"Forget about it."

"Is that an option?"

"Looking out for number one is always an option."

His choice of words rubbed her the wrong way. She'd been raised a good citizen among upright, God-fearing people. She believed in moral obligations, in self-sacrifice, in service to the community. The solution to the city's problem—the world's problem—lay useless in her lap, like the biblical lamp under a bushel basket. She wanted to help, but her hands were tied by Trinley's terrible treason.

"No, it isn't an option," she said, "not if Trinley is telling the truth about the petroplague being in Kern County. Do you know what that means? It means the quarantine failed. It means the rest of the country will eventually become like L.A. The petroplague will spread until there's no oil left."

"Chen wasn't superhuman. Another scientist will figure it out eventually."

"He was an expert on *Syntrophus*. No one else has a collection like this," she said, holding up the box. "Other scientists won't figure it out in time."

"In time?"

"This antibiotic might work as a fuel additive to keep the petroplague out of our petroleum infrastructure. But if the bacteria get established in big underground oil fields outside of L.A., there'll be no way to stop them."

CHAPTER 51

Neil stared at the page on his computer screen. A knot formed in his stomach as he read the *Los Angeles Times* article once more. He rubbed his eyes and tried to come up with a different interpretation, to deny what the words meant. He failed and became physically ill.

PETROPLAGUE MAY WORSEN CLIMATE CHANGE

According to scientists, the bacteria which cause the petroplague "eat" oil by breaking down the hydrocarbon molecules in it. As a result, they produce chemicals that are now recognized as hallmarks of contaminated fuel: acetic acid, which smells like vinegar; hydrogen, which is flammable; and carbon dioxide, which is an odorless and invisible gas. Under certain conditions, especially in underground oil fields, the acetic acid product is further broken down into methane, or natural gas. City officials speculate that the accumulation of these various gases in the Salt Lake Oil Field may be triggering the recent earthquakes, and the violent eruptions at La Brea.

In addition, climate scientists are now voicing concern about another effect of these petroplague-produced gases: they may accelerate global warming. Carbon dioxide is the most common greenhouse gas, but methane is twenty times more potent. Thus the consumption of petroleum by plague bacteria, especially underground, may be significantly worse for the environment than burning gasoline in internal combustion engines. This runs contrary to common sense, which wrongly suggests that the petroplague should reduce greenhouse gas emissions by ending oil consumption.

"I didn't know," Neil wept. "I didn't know."

His grandiose scheme to end global warming by spreading the petroplague was suddenly turned on its head. It wasn't salvation, it was suicide. What if the plague infected oil fields in other parts of the world? Could the bacteria survive in the Gulf of Mexico? What if Saudi Arabia caught the plague? How many billions or trillions of barrels' worth of carbon—or worse, methane—would spew into the atmosphere?

Instead of enviro-triumph, the success of Neil's plan now meant enviro-disaster bigger than Deepwater Horizon, Bhopal, and Chernobyl combined. He imagined he might be the architect of a calamity on par with the asteroid that killed the dinosaurs.

In a daze, he visited the chat room where he'd met Tequila Jack. The room was empty. Too late he realized his co-conspirators were anonymous free agents, flickers of cyberlife that he could neither identify nor contact in the real world. Desperately he called Preston Cobb.

"We have to stop the operation," Neil pleaded. "Can you find Tequila Jack?"

"I don't know what you're talking about," Cobb replied.

"Don't give me that shit," Neil said. "I made a big mistake. It'll be the end of the world. You have to contact your people and order them to call it off."

"I don't have people I can order around. The men and women who follow my blogs are independent, responsible individuals who want to prepare themselves and their loved ones for the collapse. Are you saying you've finally come around to believing that collapse is inevitable?"

"Listen, you bastard, I'm not talking about Peak Oil or Peak Dogshit or whatever else you've got. The petroplague is gonna cause global warming all at once. All of it, not over decades, but right now."

"You know I'm a climate change skeptic, Neil. I'm afraid I can't help you on that. If you think the end is near, why don't you visit my website and read about ways to prepare—"

Neil broke off the call. He raced to the bathroom and vomited, then kneeled sobbing over the toilet, resting his head against the hard, filthy porcelain.

What have I done, he wondered. Dad was right about me. I'm the biggest fuck-up that ever lived.

For an hour he wallowed helplessly in self-pity. The events that led him to this terrible predicament played over and over in his mind. Then he had an idea.

It all began with a scientist, some girl that guy Mickey knew. Neil couldn't stop the petroplague. But maybe she could.

Chapter 52

Mickey left the X-car's lights off as they crept up to the apartment. River told them the cops had left, but Christina kept her eyes open for any sign of surveillance.

"We have to move quickly," she said.

"River should be ready," Mickey said. "Get her and the packs. I'll stay with the car."

From a distance, the front door appeared to be closed, but when she reached it Christina saw the damage wrought by the LAPD. Absently, she wondered why River refused to let them in; she would have. The irony struck her. *I would've trusted them and opened the door, and they would've arrested me on a false charge.*

The lock mechanism was clearly broken. Christina knocked gently three times and then pushed. Trapped in the warped frame, the door didn't budge.

"River! It's me, Chrissy," she hissed into the crack.

She heard someone sidle up on the other side.

"I jammed the door," River whispered. "The packs are on the patio out back. Meet me."

Christina made a gesture of explanation to Mickey and dashed down to the corner of the building. River was already approaching, bent with the weight of both her and Mickey's gear.

"The red one is yours," River said.

Christina saw the hiking backpack on the concrete by the oleander hedge. She sprinted to it and found it shockingly heavy. She raised the pack onto a patio chair and wrestled her arms into the straps. The unfamiliar weight threw off her gait and she stumbled back to the X-car.

Mickey climbed out of the car and helped her stuff the pack into the tiny vehicle. River squeezed into the back seat, shoving her bag in ahead of her.

"Where to?" Mickey asked.

"South," River said, "as far as we can get until we run out of fuel."

"That won't be far," Mickey said. "We're pretty low already."

The night was still and quiet as Mickey piloted the Mini away from home. Christina slumped in the passenger seat next to him and gave River the devastating news.

"Trinley did it," she said weakly. "You know, the guy we were collaborating with at Bactofuels. He messed with the liquid nitrogen tanks and started the fire."

"And told the cops you did it," River said.

Christina nodded. "I can't believe they listened to him. I keep thinking that if I go to the authorities with the truth, we can straighten this all out."

"Are you mad?" River said. "It's anarchy out there. No lawyers, no supervision for the cops, probably no courts. You want to be locked up in a prison during a food riot? No, you can't talk your way out of this mess. You have to act."

In ordinary times, Christina had the highest faith in the integrity and accuracy of police investigations. But River was right; with the city's law enforcement in disarray from the petroplague, evidence to clear her name would be hard to come by.

"So I'm acting," she said. "I'm running away. What does that do for me? For the city?"

"It keeps you out of jail, and the city isn't your problem," River said.

"But it is," Christina objected, growing more distressed with the easy way out. "I helped engineer the petroplague bacteria. And I have the only stock of a possible cure."

She lifted the small box of samples and waved it at River.

"Forget about it, Chrissy. Get rid of those. We're going to walk out of the quarantine zone. You don't need to carry the extra weight."

"What's happened to you?" Christina said, angry that her cousin was pressuring her to abandon her ethics in favor of self-preservation. "A week ago you were the queen of civil disobedience, tuned in to suffering and injustice everywhere. Now you're all *me first.* Don't you realize, without this cure the city will suffocate? And the plague will spread unchecked. Trinley said some *Syntrophus* bacteria have already escaped the quarantine."

The X-car was moving in reverse as Mickey tried to find a path around a particularly tight blockage in the road.

"I have to convince Trinley to help me," she said. "The biofuel is wonderful stuff but it won't stop the quakes."

"He murdered your boss in order to destroy your cure," River said. "He's not going to turn into a model citizen just because you talk to him."

"He did that before we realized the petroplague was causing earthquakes. And I don't think he meant to hurt anyone. He knew Dr. Chen and I were on the roof when the fire started in the lab."

Ignoring Mickey's warnings ("I'll keep it short," she said), she reinserted the battery into her cell phone and called Trinley.

She fired her words like bullets the moment he answered. "This is your last chance to do the right thing, Jeff. We both know what happened at the lab, and why you did it. But your biofuel is only a partial solution to the problem."

"It's enough of a solution for me," he said in a calm, almost bemused tone.

"It won't stop the earthquakes," she snapped, wondering how long she dared stay on the line. "I'll leave samples of the antibiotic producers somewhere for you to pick up. If you isolate the antibiotic and give it to the mayor, you'll be a hero. Think about it. I'll call you back with the location."

And she hung up. Despite the cool night air sweeping over her from the open window, her armpits felt sweaty.

"You're just going to hand them over?" River said. "You can't trust him!"

"I need him," she said. Trinley was a traitor and a murderer, but only she knew that. He had the power to purify the antibiotic and get it dispersed with official support. She, on the other hand, was suspected of having started the plague on purpose. "I can't do it myself."

"Why not?" River demanded. "You've got the samples on your lap!"

"What, you think I can do a little microbiology while we're on the road?"

"Can't you use them just the way they are?"

"No."

"He's not going to help us, Chrissy."

"Us?"

"I'm not going to run and hide while you save the world. We're sticking together. As a family," River said. She squeezed Christina's shoulders from the back seat.

"Agreed. We stick together," Mickey said.

Christina felt a surge of hope.

"Thanks, guys. I have an idea how to get Trinley to cooperate. Mickey, take us back to UCLA."

CHAPTER 53

The yellow police tape no longer intimidated her. Christina ripped it from the door of her lab. River and Mickey followed her in.

"I'll leave the samples for Trinley here in the lab, where they'll be safe," she said as she opened the specimen box and removed a dozen tiny tubes from it. "I'm keeping six, just in case."

"You'd better," River said. "Mickey and I both think this Trinley guy won't change his stripes, no matter what trick you've got up your sleeve."

"We'll see," she replied. "Would you mind carrying these?"

She handed each of them a red plastic fuel jug and took a moment to rummage through a drawer of small tools. After finding a hammer, she led them out of the lab toward the stairs.

They climbed the stairs quickly, passing the top floor of the building and continuing to the roof. She unlocked the door and they stepped out into the night. The moon was bright and cast the strange scientific apparatus in a mystical green glow.

"This is what Trinley killed for," she said. "A solar bioreactor with photosynthetic *E. coli* inside. During daylight, the bugs crank out isobutanol, the fuel that will make him rich."

She unscrewed the caps on the jugs and attached the first one to a flexible metal mesh hose. "Fill 'er up," she said as she cranked open a valve and fuel flowed into the jug.

The first jug filled with isobutanol, then the other. Mickey raised one in a mock toast and said, "To the X-car!"

"One more thing before we go," she said.

Mesmerizing patterns of green liquid swirled through the bioreactor's long glass tubes as the tubes gently rocked back and forth. She flipped a switch to stop the rocking, and stood quietly beside the machine watching its hypnotic flow sputter to a halt. Giving the bioreactor an affectionate pat, she whispered, "I'm sorry."

"Stand back," she ordered River and Mickey.

The hammer in her hand rose, and with a squeal of exertion and regret she brought it down with all the force she could muster. The first reactor tube exploded, spilling warm, stinky green liquid on the gravelly roof. The second tube cracked and a thin spray of the same bacteria-laden fluid squirted out under pressure. Another blow from the hammer shattered more tubes and a puddle formed at her feet. Her clothing splattered with the remnants of her Ph.D. thesis project, Christina continued until all the vessels on the bioreactor were destroyed.

Mickey and River stared at her, wide-eyed with amazement.

"What are you doing?" River asked in a low voice.

"Buying an insurance policy," Christina said as she turned away from the demolished machine. "Once I collect a few tubes from the lab, I will control the last stock of Trinley's miracle bugs."

"Doesn't Bactofuels have some of the bacteria at their facility?" Mickey said.

"They don't, at least not any with the recent genetic modifications I made. This solar bioreactor is a one-of-a-kind prototype and we keep all the bacterial cultures on campus. Bactofuels routinely analyzes samples of the fuel we produce, but they don't have any of the cultures. Trinley will do anything to get these back."

"So that's your plan," River said. "You're holding his stuff hostage."

Together they left the roof and lugged the heavy fuel containers down the stairs.

"If Trinley won't play ball—or if I go to jail—his millionaire dreams will literally go down the toilet," Christina said while making a flushing gesture with her free hand.

Back at the lab, she scurried about from refrigerator to freezer to sink, emptying small tubes and flasks of Bactofuels' photosynthetic *E. coli* into a dirty beaker of bleach. She double-checked the storage areas to be certain she hadn't missed any. She spared five tubes from destruction, and carefully packed these hostages into the specimen transport box along with her antibiotic samples. Then she arranged the tubes she was leaving for Trinley on a piece of neon yellow scratch paper on her desk. Using a red Sharpie marker, she wrote "For Jeff Trinley" in large letters.

"I'll be ready to leave in ten," she announced to River and Mickey, who were speaking to each other in hushed whispers. Her companions embraced, long and hard. Christina was surprised to see a tear on River's cheek.

"I'm staying," Mickey said.

Chistina halted with her hand on a refrigerator door. "Staying? Why?"

"Neil called me. I have to see him."

Her jaw dropped. "Neil? You mean, *the* Neil? The tank-bombing eco-terrorist?"

Mickey nodded.

"I thought you didn't have any contact with him," Christina accused, stunned that the man responsible for all this had reappeared on the stage.

"I didn't. I told you the truth, Chrissy. I only met him a couple of times. He never even gave me his phone number."

"But he had your yours."

"Yeah," Mickey said, his expression grave. "I think he's done something awful."

"You mean more awful than starting the petroplague?"

"Yes. It sounds like somehow he transported plague-contaminated gasoline out of California."

"No," Christina said, looking up toward heaven. "Please, no. We need more time."

Mickey ran his hands over his face. "Neil said he needed your help to prevent a catastrophe. He sounded pretty freaked out but he definitely said 'prevent.' So maybe he hasn't done it yet."

"My help? Oh, that's rich."

"I'm not going to involve you. He told me to meet him at his house and he'd explain."

"Tell the police to get over there."

"I'd like to do that, and to beat the crap out of him. But he won't talk to cops. I have to find out what he's up to."

"And stop it if we can," River said.

"We agreed to stick together. We all go," Christina said.

"No," Mickey said vehemently. "You especially need to stay as far away from this guy as possible. My connection with him has already gotten you into trouble. I want you and River to take the X-car and get out of L.A."

River nodded in agreement. As much as she hated being separated, Christina knew they were right.

"You have to keep your cell phone off," Mickey said, "but River will turn hers on once an hour, on the hour, to give me a chance to contact you. If I learn anything from Neil I'll pass it along. And I'll catch up with you in San Diego."

He took the girls' hands and grasped them tightly. Christina hugged him and marveled at his transformation. The shiftless youth had become a man.

"You finish here," Mickey said. "River and I will fuel up the car, and I'll get my stuff out."

"Good luck, Mickey. Be careful."

Their departure left Christina feeling empty. Thank God River was traveling with her. She couldn't handle the pressure alone. That the petroplague had escaped the local quarantine, she knew. Ultimately she expected there would be no way to contain it, which meant the antibiotic was their only hope. But even with Trinley's cooperation, it would take time to isolate, manufacture, and distribute enough of it to prevent collapse. If Neil really had spread the plague further afield, the antibiotic would be too little, too late. She prayed that Mickey could convince the madman to abort his plan.

Packing tape stuck to her latex gloves as she sealed her specimen box. The box was marked with biohazard symbols, a distinctive pattern of bright orange interlocking rings. The box contained the potential cure for the petroplague as well as her leverage against Trinley: the last of the Bactofuels *E. coli*. After she and River were safely away, she planned to tell Trinley that he'd never lay hands on those *E. coli* again unless he turned over the antibiotic specimens to scientists who knew how to use them.

Carrying the only remaining samples of the bacteria that manufactured isobutanol was risky. What if the box got lost or damaged? What if she couldn't return the bacteria to Bactofuels when they were needed? She decided to leave a tube hidden at the lab and marked with a secret code. Trinley wouldn't know.

The tube was in her hand when she heard the door to the lab open and close.

River's back, she thought.

"I'm almost ready," Christina said, but she got no reply. "River?"

The only sound was a soft rustling followed by a click.

"River?"

Christina came around the lab bench toward the door. Jeff Trinley stood there with a gun in his hand.

"I told you not to come back," he said. His face was red and his hand trembled slightly.

"What are you doing here?" she said, wondering what the heck a guy like Trinley was doing with a handgun. He probably didn't even know how it worked.

"I don't need to ask you that question," Trinley said. "I've been on the roof. I saw what you did. I came to collect my property before anything happened to it but it seems I'm too late. Fortunately I'm traveling with protection. The streets of L.A. aren't safe at night."

He gestured with the gun. Christina raised her hands. The test tube dangled from her fingers.

"Is this what you want?" she said. "The billion-dollar bugs?"

Trinley's eyes widened. "Give it to me."

"On one condition. You promise—"

"You're in no position to make demands," Trinley said. He moved forward to snatch the tube from her hand.

Christina jumped back and warned, "One more step and I drop it. The tube shatters, and you're out of the biofuel business."

"What do you want?"

"I want you to do the right thing. The isobutanol isn't enough. Somebody has to develop the antibiotic, and they have to start working on it right away. I've got specimens for you, over there on my desk. Take them."

"Sure. I'll take them."

Trinley picked up the tubes. Looking her straight in the eye, one by one he popped off the lids.

"What are you doing? They'll get contaminated!"

Keeping the gun sort of pointed in Christina's direction, Trinley stepped to the sink and dropped the tubes in a bucket. As she watched in horror, he poured bleach over them.

"Now, my dear, if you want to save the world, you'll have to give me those *E. coli*."

He was rotten, rotten to the core. He was so tempted by wealth he couldn't see that his actions would be the ruin of them all. She hated him, hated his arrogance and greed, hated that the staggering responsibility for fighting the petroplague now fell on her shoulders alone. She pictured Dr. Chen's smiling face and remembered his horrible death.

"Fuck you," she said and let go of the tube.

The Pyrex cracked when it landed. She swiftly raised her foot and stomped on it. The precious golden liquid mixed with the dirt on the floor.

Trinley screamed and lunged at her. He struck her in the face with the gun; she put her arms up to protect herself but lost her balance and fell. He kicked her legs and her side. She felt dizzying pain and gasped for breath.

Then her attacker was knocked away. She wobbled to her feet, clutching her side. River was there. She wrapped her arms around Christina and pulled her toward the door. She saw Mickey pummeling Trinley and he shouted, "Run for it!"

"Can you walk?" River said.

"Yeah," Christina replied. "Wait!"

She couldn't leave without her specimens. Mickey and Trinley were grappling on the floor but she couldn't see Trinley's gun. She grabbed the box, took River's hand, and fled.

CHAPTER 54

Christina and River burst out of the science building and ran to the X-car under the light of halogen streetlamps. Dawn was still a few hours away. They jumped into the garish green car and Christina started the engine.

"Call the police," she said as she threw the Mini's engine into reverse.

"So Mickey can get sent up for Chen's murder? Or for starting the petroplague? I don't think so," River replied.

"But Trinley had a gun."

"Mickey can take care of himself," River said. Christina noticed that her cousin looked away when she said this. "He was walking me back to the lab when we noticed a golf cart parked near the door."

"Trinley."

"We were afraid there would be cops, too."

"Trinley didn't know I was there. It was just bad timing," Christina said.

"Well, Mickey told me to get you and run and not to bother about him. So I did," River said, her voice cracking. "Did he really have a gun?"

"He was carrying it for self-defense. He wouldn't actually use it."

River didn't argue with her.

Without maintenance, the university grounds were returning to nature. Unswept leaves and flowers blew aside as the young women made their escape. The only clear route for the Mini was off-road, but the ground was baked hard by the summer heat and felt almost like pavement. Christina spun the X-car's wheels on the once-manicured lawns of the campus. After years of careful habits behind the wheel, she had to force herself to drive recklessly.

"You were right about Trinley. He's a snake," she said. "He dumped the antibiotic specimens I gave him in bleach, right there in the lab while I was watching. Even if he changes his mind, he can't work on a cure now." With a tinge of remorse, she added, "Since I trashed the bioreactor, he can't do much on the isobutanol fuel either. He doesn't have any of the bacteria that make it."

"Do you?"

"Yes, I've got both kinds of samples. I'd give them to the authorities, but they think I caused the petroplague on purpose and murdered Dr. Chen to keep it going. They won't trust anything I give them."

"So it's up to us," River said. "You, me, and Mickey against the petroplague."

"Which means we have to change our plans," Christina said, turning right. "I have a good friend in a lab at UC Berkeley. She'll help us."

"Then forget San Diego," River said. "Take us north."

On the city streets, their path was often blocked by abandoned cars too close together to squeeze between. At one juncture, the gap looked tantalizingly close to being passable. Christina gingerly tested the space, nudging the X-car forward, and decided it was too tight.

"We'll never get anywhere like this," River said. "You need to be more aggressive."

"We'll never get anywhere if I wreck the car."

"I'm not saying you should wreck it, but you may have to scratch it up a bit."

"You think I should go for it?"

"Go for it."

They folded back the side-view mirrors and Christina pressed through the opening. Metal screeched on both sides and the Mini resisted, but she pushed the accelerator and they popped free.

"Which way are you going?" River asked.

"Four-oh-five is the most direct route," Christina said.

"That freeway was clogged solid even before the petroplague."

"Maybe they'll have a lane cleared."

"If they do, there will be people," River warned, "including police and soldiers. How do you think they'll react when we come tooling by in this thing?"

"We'll be fine. No one knows I'm driving this car."

"Chrissy, they may not be searching for you specifically, but I doubt they'll wave and smile when we pass. This car is about the only thing that still moves. If I were an official, I'd confiscate it."

"You think they can do that?"

"Pull your head out of the sand," River said. "They can do whatever they please. And you are a wanted suspect. Someone might recognize you."

"So what do you think we should do?"

"Take one of the canyon roads north, through Bel Air."

They weaved their way around obstacles into the ritzy, hilly residential area of Bel Air. The road climbed up, giving Christina a view of the Getty Center museum one dark mountain range over to her left. She remembered lunching there with Trinley and Dr. Chen—so recently, yet it seemed so long ago—and she felt the pang of loss. If only Dr. Chen were alive, this foolish mission would be unnecessary. People would have listened to him. He could've finished the research and presented his cure as a *fait accompli*, ready to deploy and save them all.

Like many places in Los Angeles, the canyon was desert-dry but this fact was masked by landscaping: gigantic celebrity homes with irrigated yards, and a golf course on Christina's right. The X-car followed the road as it traced the canyon bottom. Pale rays of dawn sunlight touched the western side. Fewer vehicles had stalled on this route, making it easier for them to proceed though Christina still had to make liberal use of sidewalks and front lawns. Under the streetlights ahead, she could see the road rising toward the mountain crest above the canyon. She wondered what the view would reveal.

"Look out, there's a fence in there!"

She was aiming for a path that skirted a tall hedgerow, expecting to push the shrubbery aside. She saw what River had noticed: the hedge concealed a wrought-iron fence against which the little biodiesel car had no chance.

"Try the other side," River said, but at this particular spot three cars were parked abreast across the road, including one which apparently had stalled while trying to do precisely what Christina and River were attempting.

"Impossible," Christina said. "The canyon's blocked."

"Back up," River said. "We passed a turn-off about half a mile ago."

The side road led steeply up another canyon. It was much narrower than the main road, and Christina was relieved to find it clear of abandoned vehicles. Minutes later, as they rounded a bend, she discovered the reason.

"Dead end," she said, perspiring as she looked at the odometer. They'd made little real progress, and this obstacle course driving through the mountains was going to limit the X-car's range. "I don't want to turn back. Our fuel is limited."

"We're not going back," River said decisively. "Let me drive. Please."

Christina didn't ask why because she didn't want to know. They traded places and River took them back toward the main road. River leaned forward to peer past Christina for a better view.

"The trees are all along the street. There aren't any on the canyon walls behind the houses," River said.

"The hills are too steep," Christina said. "Even allowing for some damage to the car, a Mini can't handle that kind of terrain."

River made no reply. They approached a shaded lot, but before coming to the main street, she slowed the car and turned right. "Tighten your seat belt," she said.

"River!"

Somehow the Mini cleared the curb and went off-road behind the homes backed against the steep canyon wall. Fences marked the rear property line and the outer reach of the homeowners' sprinklers. River steered the Mini on the bare, sloping dirt behind the lush backyards.

The canyon wall felt practically vertical in places, and the car tilted dangerously as they drove at a crazy angle. A more top-heavy vehicle would surely have tipped over, but somehow the spirited eco-car kept all four wheels in contact with the ground. Christina gripped her seat and door, too afraid to complain. Both young women instinctively leaned to the right at the worst parts as if their slender body weights could resist the car's temptation to roll.

From up here, Christina could see the main street and the blockage that had stymied them before. They passed it, carving their own way behind the houses. The car bounced up and down, making horrible scraping sounds each time its underbelly dragged on the earth. Slowly, they continued forward. Christina wondered how far they could make it like this.

"There," River said, pointing. The next house had no back fence; the rear of the yard was enclosed only by rosebushes. "We get back on the road there."

Christina swallowed and nodded.

River idled the engine a moment while she decided on the best line of approach, and then plowed the car into the roses. The beautiful plants gave way and the young women found themselves in the lovely oasis of some rich man's back yard, next to a cerulean blue swimming pool enhanced with underwater lights and a rocky waterfall at one end. An outdoor kitchen surrounded by thoughtfully-arranged lounge furniture invited them to give up their quest and just hang out.

"Sweet," River said. She nudged the car around the pool toward a shed at the edge of the property. "I bet there's a gate over there. It should open to the street."

River was right. Christina could see a short concrete driveway connecting the shed to a stylish wooden carriage door gate wide enough to accommodate the X-car.

"You have to move the furniture," River said. Blocking their way from the pool to the gate was a pair of cast-iron chaise lounges with fluffy orange cushions. They couldn't drive over or around them.

"Right," Christina said, nervously scanning the yard as she unbuckled and let herself out. The lounges were heavy, but they had wheels. She dragged the first one out of their way without difficulty.

A light came on in the house.

As she bent down to tug the second, she heard the sound of a door closing. She grunted and hastily flung the chair as far aside as she could and sprinted back to the car. River drove through the gap she'd created and lined up for an assault on the gate.

Out of the corner of her eye, Christina saw movement in the yard. A man appeared with something in his hand. He raised it and pointed it at them.

"River . . ."

Her cousin wisely decided that any further adjustments to their position were unnecessary. She floored it.

CHAPTER 55

When Mickey entered the lab, he expected trouble. He saw Trinley kicking Christina, instantly tucked into his best linebacker pose, and tackled him. Trinley went down and Mickey kneeled on his chest, punching him in the face as hard as he could. But the scientist was no slouch and got his arms around Mickey. They flopped against the hard laboratory cabinets and struggled while River and Christina disappeared.

Blood dripped from Trinley's nose. Mickey took a blow to the gut and doubled over. Trinley aimed a foot at Mickey's knee but Mickey barreled into him and knocked him down again.

The gun tumbled out of the scrum and skidded across the smooth laboratory tile.

Both men saw it go. Mickey dove for the weapon a fraction of a second before Trinley and got his hands on the grip first.

"You bastard," Mickey said as he tottered to his feet and backed away, breathing hard.

Trinley used his hands to push himself off the floor. He touched his face and glanced curiously at the blood on his fingers.

For a moment they both stood there, panting. Mickey hadn't been in a fight since junior high. In that quarrel, nothing was truly at stake; certainly neither combatant had a gun. But he remembered how terribly sore he was the day after. Considering how much his neck and ribs hurt already, tomorrow was going to be rough.

Trinley stared at the gun. A wicked smile curled his lips.

"Thanks for the alibi."

Mickey kept the weapon pointed at him. "Give me the keys."

Trinley dug a hand into his pocket and pulled out the key to the golf cart.

"Take it. I can add stolen vehicle to the list of charges."

"I didn't commit any crimes in this lab. But you did. You killed Christina's boss."

"The police don't think so. And my friend the mayor would never listen to such an accusation. But you've made it easy for me to prove that you were in this lab when the city's best hope for a cure was maliciously destroyed."

"You trashed Christina's stuff?"

"No, you did. Just like you conspired with Miss González to start the petroplague in the first place, and helped her arrange the death of Dr. Robert Chen."

"I don't have time for this shit. Toss the key," Mickey said.

Trinley did. "I'll have your face on the F.B.I.'s Most Wanted list by the end of the day."

"Go for it. Enjoy the earthquakes you didn't try to stop," Mickey said and walked away.

As soon as he was out in the hall, Mickey dropped the cool façade and took off at a run. He sprang down the stairs to the ground level, grabbed his backpack, smashed the key into the golf cart's ignition, and slammed the accelerator to the floor.

His getaway was comically low-speed, but the cart moved faster than either he or Trinley could run over a distance. That's all that mattered.

He glanced back to make sure the X-car was gone. Knowing that the girls were safe made it easier to face his next task. Neil was waiting.

CHAPTER 56

The X-car lurched forward. Christina didn't have time to brace herself before they hit the gate.

The gate blasted open and the lurid green vehicle shot onto the driveway. She squealed and covered her face. River held steady and aimed for the street, tires screeching as the car swerved hard right at almost forty miles an hour. They were well past the traffic jam that had forced them to take such an unconventional route. From here, the street was mostly clear. River pressed forward at speed.

Christina glanced back and saw no evidence that the homeowner was in pursuit. She rubbed her neck. Whiplash.

"You hit that gate so hard, we should be crumpled tinfoil in the driveway."

"A risk worth taking, considering the welcoming party at the house," River said. "Those gates are mostly decorative. The locking mechanism can't handle any real stress. My parents have one and my dad backed into it once. The thing opened right up."

Though it was running fine, the little car had visibly suffered from the adventure. "Mickey will be pissed," Christina said. "When he finds out you disfigured his pet—"

"I'm sure he has his own problems to deal with," River said sharply. A flash of worry crossed her face.

As the canyon came to an end, the road twisted upward. Soon they were driving on the spine of a mountain ridge in the hot morning sun. The view was excellent. Christina saw dry mountainside reflected in the surface of a reservoir to her right. She could also see the interstate running parallel to their present route.

"It looks like they have a lane clear on the four-oh-five," she said.

"We stay off the freeways until we must get on the five," River said resolutely. "That's still another ten miles."

They continued north and left behind the mountains and canyons of the scenic, exclusive neighborhoods. The wide, flat, heavily urban San Fernando Valley lay ahead. It was a region of perpetual congestion even in normal times, and getting from point A to point B had never been more challenging. Christina and River grew discouraged as they moved like rats in a maze, trying by chance to find a way through. Bottlenecks were everywhere, and their net northward progress averaged only a few miles per hour.

"We'd be faster on foot," River complained.

"Without the packs, we would be," Christina agreed. "But I'm not leaving mine."

Through the tedium and frustration, they gradually crossed the valley floor. The San Gabriel Mountains loomed taller as they got closer. The mountains hemmed in the city and abruptly separated urban area from wilderness. They also contributed to L.A.'s infamous smog by trapping air in the valley. The air had a dirt-colored tinge, but compared to what Christina had seen on other summer days, the smog today was thin. After another week without cars, the valley air might actually be clear.

When they finally made it across, she could appreciate how sharply the San Gabriels ascended from the flat valley floor. This natural barrier allowed for only one major road out of the L.A. basin to the north. Interstate 5 five snaked through a pass in the mountains that occasionally closed in winter due to snow. It was a shockingly tenuous escape route for a city the size of Los Angeles.

For Christina and River, the five was the fastest way out of town.

CHAPTER 57

The sun was rising as Mickey steered his "borrowed" golf cart down the sidewalks of L.A. He understood why Trinley had brought a gun on his trip to the university: having motorized transportation made you a target. Mickey had never touched a real gun in his life, so he handled the weapon delicately, like a piece of fine china, lest it go off by accident. It was comforting to know that in a pinch he had a way to defend himself. And the closer he got to Neil's place, the more comforting it became. Neil lived in a rough part of town.

He found the address and reluctantly parked the golf cart on the tiny front lawn. Even though he took the ignition key, he worried the cart would quickly disappear. Maybe Neil could help him lock it to something. He climbed two crumbling concrete steps to the door and rang the bell.

No response.

He rang again, listening to be certain the bell was working. After waiting several minutes, he pounded on the door and pulled out his phone to call the number Neil had used. The system directed him to an automated voicemail box.

The front of the house had a couple of windows. He rapped on them and tried to peek in, but they were covered by blinds. For a third time, he checked the address. This was the place.

His uneasiness grew. Neil had sounded desperate for this meeting. Why wouldn't he be here?

Maybe he's in the shower, or on the can, Mickey thought. It's not like we had an appointment.

He sat on the front step and pushed aside a spider web-covered doormat. Tucked under the edge of the mat was a folded piece of paper addressed to "M."

Well, it's not for Neil, he figured, and unfolded the paper. Written in large, left-handed block letters it read, "Come in."

"Okay," he said aloud and tried the door. The knob turned easily. Mickey entered.

"Hello?"

The room was sparsely furnished and smelled of stale curry. He closed the door behind him and called again, louder. "Neil?"

When no one responded, he raised Trinley's gun and cradled it uncomfortably at his chest. He moved deeper into the house, repeatedly announcing his presence. In a room off to one side he saw a blanket crumpled on the dingy carpet at the foot of an empty bed; he continued forward to the kitchen. Dirty dishes filled the sink but no one was there. Movement in the back yard caught his eye.

Ah, so he's out back. Mickey stepped into the yard.

A young man's body swayed from the branch of an oak tree, his feet almost touching a backyard chicken coop where two hens strutted, oblivious. An electrical cord was wrapped around his neck. Mickey waved off a flock of crows whose flapping around the body had attracted his attention. The distinctive dreadlocks were as good as a giant nametag. It was Neil.

"Oh, shit."

Panicked, Mickey ran back into the house. Neil had killed himself. *Why? What did he do? And why did he bring me here?*

Everything about the situation was wrong. He sorely regretted coming to the house. The girls had only been gone a few hours; if he left now, maybe he could catch up with them.

Then he saw an envelope on the kitchen table with his name on it. Turning his back on the dreadful scene in the yard, he opened it.

The suicide note detailed everything Neil knew about the plan he'd put in motion to spread the petroplague to the ends of the earth. Preston Cobb. The chat room address. Tequila Jack. The screen names of others involved in the plot, and some of their locations. The precise date and time of the plan's execution. In the message Neil confessed his despair and remorse over the perverse impact of his actions on the one issue that mattered most to him. He begged Mickey to warn his scientist friend so she could do something to save the planet.

Mickey double-checked the math. Five days. They only had five days. L.A.'s troubles and the local earthquakes were minor inconveniences compared to what was going to happen after 4 PM GMT in a couple of days. Christina needed to know. So did the authorities. Someone had to persuade them to trust her, to take her advice and use her samples to find a cure. If not, the plague would overwhelm them all. He stuffed the letter in his pocket and headed for the exit. River should turn her phone on in about twenty minutes. He ought to leave a message—

The golf cart sitting in the yard wasn't his.

"Hold it right there," a voice said.

Chapter 58

"End of the line," River said. "Let's eat."

Christina was stiff from hours in the passenger seat at River's side as the X-car wound through clogged streets on their way to the feet of the San Gabriel Mountains. Surface roads went no further, and in order to get out of the L.A. basin they had to get on the interstate—where they might be recognized and arrested as fugitives, or have their car confiscated. Given the uncertainties and the lateness of the hour, it seemed prudent to stop and eat.

She twisted into the back seat and managed to free a box of raisins and some potato chips from her pack. She offered them to River, who turned off the engine and stretched her shoulders.

"I'll never complain about ordinary traffic again," River said.

"Considering you don't own a car, that shouldn't be too hard."

"Hey, I've suffered through my share of jams," River replied. She took a drink from their water bottle and smiled. "Remember that mess in Mexico City?"

"How could I forget?" Christina said. "I thought Tío Marco was going to explode."

The pleasant memory of the summer after she graduated from high school lifted her spirits. As a gift, their mothers had arranged for Christina and River to travel to Mexico together to meet relatives and take some literature classes in Spanish.

"I swear there were more cars on that street than in my entire home town," Christina said. "Of course now that I've lived in L.A. I probably wouldn't be as impressed."

"They say the traffic has gotten even worse since we were there," River said, "but it's hard to imagine how that could be."

Their uncle had picked them up at the airport in Mexico City. They stayed with him and his family for a week and then traveled to Cuernavaca for the "study" portion of their trip. During their time in Mexico City, they were trapped in a traffic jam of cosmic proportions.

"The *calabaza* did it," Christina said. "Remember how we got a late start because I insisted I wanted a burrito made with squash flowers? Tío Marco was so good to us, he wanted to find the best place, which of course had the longest line."

"And the accident happened just before we finished eating," River said. "If we'd settled for tacos, we would've been outta there and saved ourselves about four hours."

Thinking about real food—fresh and colorful and hot—was torture.

"Right now I'd settle for just about anything the vendors were selling that day," Christina said, crunching on a chip. "Even if I couldn't wash it first."

"You were a real stickler about that."

"Budding microbiologist, I guess," Christina said. "Didn't do me much good. Diarrhea hit on day six."

"It helped you some," River said. "Mine started on day four."

They both laughed. Christina was about to tell another story when she saw River's smile fade. She followed River's line of sight and saw a man stagger out the front door of a bungalow three doors down the street. He clutched his side as if in pain and stumbled as he made his way toward the black-and-gold iron fence that enclosed the postage-stamp yard. Shouts came from inside the house, and a second man appeared in the doorway. He was brandishing a knife and stepped out to pursue his opponent, but a woman, screaming and crying, wrapped herself around the waist of the knife-wielder and dragged him to his knees. He struck her in the face with his elbow and she crumpled to the floor.

"Get us out of here," Christina said.

River had already dropped the box of raisins in her lap and turned the key. The players in the unfolding drama at the house paused and stared at the car like they were seeing a ghost. Christina didn't know or care to know what happened next. Whatever was going on, they did not want to be a part of it.

Minutes later, they found an on-ramp to the five.

"Fist bump for luck," River said. Christina's hand met hers and their car crept to the top of the ramp. Metal scraped on concrete as River pinched the Mini through a too-narrow gap between a burned-out wreck and the wall.

"It's open," Christina said with relief when she saw the freeway deck. At this critical point in the Los Angeles highway system, the right lane had been cleared wide enough for a large vehicle to pass. The Mini was home free. River joyously accelerated to a dizzying thirty miles per hour.

"The two-ten interchange is just ahead," Christina said.

River patted the dashboard. "Get us as far away from here as you can, little car. I don't like walking."

"Neither do they," Christina said, pointing.

A thin stream of pedestrians was trickling northward through the frozen automobiles. Some of them spotted the X-car and jogged toward it, thumbs out.

"We can't pick anybody up. There's too much at stake to risk entangling ourselves," River said.

Suppressing her natural desire to be helpful, Christina agreed and was about to say so when she noticed an orange and yellow striped barrier across the lane ahead. The barrier was erected just past the exit for I-210.

"Roadblock," she said. "Not from a stall. Intentional."

River decelerated, and Christina's apprehension grew when she saw uniformed National Guardsmen stand to meet them. The soldiers fingered their weapons, ready to raise them if the surprising little car didn't come to a stop.

"What are we going to say?" Christina asked, flustered.

"Depends on what they ask," River replied, slowing further to give them another few seconds to think before reaching the roadblock. "This might be the first containment ring."

"That's ridiculous! We're still in the city!"

"But once we pass the two-ten, this road leads only one way: out of town. It would make sense to stop traffic here."

"It's too soon! We have to get further north!" Christina said, panicking. If they were forced to abandon the car this far south, it would take them days just to walk out of the plague zone to a place where they could hitch a ride to the laboratory at Berkeley.

"Something tells me they don't care about our travel plans," River said. She put the car in neutral and rolled to the spot indicated by one of the guards. Two armed men approached each door of the car. River turned off the engine and said, "Let me do the talking."

"Please step out of the car," said one of the guards.

Christina and River exchanged a glance and then complied. To keep from fidgeting, Christina stuffed her hands in her pockets. The guards on her side of the car twitched and gestured for her to keep her hands visible.

"I'm sorry ladies, you can't go any further."

"Why not?" River said insolently. Christina cringed.

"Only electric-powered vehicles are allowed to leave the first containment ring. You'll have to turn back."

"Can't you read?" River responded. "This car doesn't run on gasoline. That's why it still works."

What is she thinking? Christina wondered, appalled by River's attitude. These are military people. They're not going to be cowed by a display of petulance.

Without making any sudden moves, Christina joined River on the driver's side of the car.

"Sir, this vehicle runs on an experimental biofuel that's not affected by the petroplague. It won't spread the germs. We will run out of fuel at some point but we just want to get as far as we can first."

"I'm sorry ma'am. Only electric-powered vehicles may pass."

"Okay, it doesn't have an electric motor, but it's like an electric car because it doesn't have any gasoline inside."

"That may be," the soldier said politely but firmly, "but my orders are clear. If you want to continue northward, you'll have to go on foot."

"That's ridiculous," River said, stamping the ground. "This is a free country!"

"We understand," Christina said, "but is there someone you can talk to? It's urgent that we get over the mountains as soon as possible. My . . . mother is very sick. A friend at the university let me take this car so I could be with her. I know nothing is allowed to drive out of the quarantine zone, but I thought we could at least pass the first ring. Since this car is like an electric."

"No exceptions," the guardsman said. "You'll have to turn back now. No loitering."

"But—" River said.

"No exceptions, no loitering," he repeated, the compassion gone from his voice. "You have two minutes before we confiscate your vehicle. If you attempt to break the quarantine, we are under orders to stop you by any means necessary."

Christina noticed the other guards had moved away from the car and assumed a ready-to-fire posture.

"But—"

"One minute, fifty-five seconds."

"Let's go, River," Christina said, bounding back to the passenger seat.

River muttered a curse but got back in the car. They backed away and made a U-turn.

"That was a disaster," Christina said. "We've got to get further north."

"It was stupid of you to suggest he contact a superior," River said. "What if he found out you're wanted by the police?"

"Not half as stupid as you throwing a tantrum like some privileged brat," Christina retorted. "He might've listened to us if you hadn't pissed him off."

"I didn't piss him off! You just rolled over and let him walk all over you."

"He was going to take our car."

"You should've been more forceful from the start," River said.

"Is that what—"

Christina stopped and took a deep breath.

"We shouldn't fight," she said. "No matter what we did, he wasn't going to let us through."

River nodded. "So what now?"

Christina pulled a map out of the tiny glove compartment.

"Get on the two-ten," she said. "There's one other way north."

"What other way?"

"That way," Christina said, pointing at the towering San Gabriel Mountains which separated Los Angeles from the Central Valley like a gargantuan wall. "We're going over the top."

CHAPTER 59

The earthquake specialist at the U.S. Geological Survey Field Office in Pasadena, California, was running on fumes: two hours' sleep plus a brief nap that left his cheek stained with ink from the papers on his desk. He'd slept more the night he and the kids camped out on the street to get a good spot for watching the Rose Parade.

He stood up and did twenty jumping jacks. The field office was short-handed, and he couldn't afford to be drowsy, not with all the seismic activity going on. When the petroplague paralyzed the city, several of his colleagues struggled home and didn't come back. He was glad he lived nearby and had kept to his post. In the last week there'd been more action than most earthquake scientists witness in a lifetime.

The USGS office was working closely with scientists at Caltech, the Jet Propulsion Laboratory, and elsewhere to process and interpret the large quantity of data flowing in from hundreds of seismic sensor stations all over Southern California. He analyzed a continuous stream of numbers and graphs from strain meters, deformation monitors, creepmeters, and motion sensors. The biggest activity had been concentrated in central Los Angeles. Until now.

"Whoa," the geologist said. "Priti, take a look at this."

A slender Indian woman in a brightly colored cotton skirt floated to his desk. She studied the data on his screen and double-checked the station locations.

"I'll call the mayor," she said.

*   *   *

It occurred to Ramirez that if they had a pressure monitor up his ass the thing would be redlining about now.

"The San Andreas?" he said. The woman was talking about the mother of all earthquake faults in California. Eight hundred miles long, the San Andreas fault defined the crash zone between the great Pacific and North American tectonic plates. "You're predicting a major quake on the San Andreas?"

"We are, sir, magnitude 8.0 or greater with a high probability in the range of days to weeks," the geologist confirmed.

The San Andreas fault. Source of California's largest earthquake in modern times: the Fort Tejon quake of 1857, estimated intensity of 7.9 on the Richter scale. It left over two hundred miles of surface scar that could still be seen today, marking where the ground ruptured when the plates jumped in opposite directions.

"You're telling me the Big One is coming," the mayor said.

"Earthquake prediction isn't an exact science."

"But you believe it's imminent."

"The data suggest a substantially increased risk in the short term."

"Goddammit."

"A San Andreas quake may cause less damage to Los Angeles itself than a big one on the Santa Monica," the woman said, trying to sound hopeful. "The San Andreas fault lies mostly to the east and north of downtown."

"Under Palm Springs, San Bernardino, and Palmdale, where millions of people live," he snapped. "Keep me informed."

He looked at Molton. "Any chance we can blame plague here in the city?"

Molton shook his head. One of the advisors said, "Highly unlikely, Mr. Mayor. I've got reports of vapor lock in pumpjacks around McKittrick. The changes USGS describes almost certainly mean the petroplague is in Kern County."

Kern County. Outside the quarantine zone.

There goes my run for governor, he thought, trying to make light of this dreadful news. It didn't work.

"We're losing," he said. "We need a cure and we need it quick. Get that Trinley guy in here right now."

CHAPTER 60

Cops were the last thing Mickey needed, but two L.A. police officers rose from the golf cart to intercept him. Suddenly one of them leaped behind the cart and drew his revolver.

"Drop the gun! Drop the gun!" he yelled.

His partner did the same thing and both of them pointed their weapons at Mickey. Mickey was so surprised that for a moment he didn't understand what they were talking about. Then he felt Trinley's gun in his hands and dropped it like a hot potato.

"Put your hands on your head!"

Mickey complied and the officers came around and cuffed him.

"I need to make a phone call," Mickey said. He sure hadn't expected Trinley to get results this fast.

"Too bad, hotshot. We've all got problems."

"But this is important—"

He was about to say, *it's about the petroplague*, but held his tongue. If he revealed too much, Christina and River might wind up in the same fix he found himself in. They ought to allow him a phone call at the station. He'd call River then.

For the second time that month, Mickey had his Miranda rights read to him. The words were the same, but everything else about the situation was distressingly different. Chaining River to a government building in the carnival atmosphere of a civil rights protest was a hell of a lot more fun than getting sent up for murder, or whatever Trinley had persuaded them to charge him with.

One of the cops, a steely-eyed thirty-something with several days of unshaven stubble on his chin, nudged Mickey into the golf cart.

"Sit down and don't stand up," he said, locking Mickey to the awning. "This isn't a Disney ride."

LAPD was taking him downtown in a *golf cart*. It was plain ridiculous. How could anybody take them seriously? He was mildly curious to see what silly improvisation they'd have to pull next.

Just as Mickey had done with the X-car, the cop steered the electric cart around and through the blocked streets. They were heading east toward downtown. An extraordinary number of people milled about on the streets. Many were carrying bags or dragging wheeled suitcases, a wary look in their eyes. Mickey discerned that few were traveling alone. The wanderers were assorted into groups, most likely for protection, like ancient tribesmen in a primitive world. When they saw the LAPD uniforms, people called out. Some complained, some cursed, others pleaded for help. The two cops pretended not to hear them, but Mickey saw the driver's knuckles whiten and his partner's right hand slip down to his holster.

The edgy, post-apocalyptic scene brought home to him how the thin veneer of civilization was breaking down. Even without a big quake, time was running out for Los Angeles.

"This is where you get off."

They had arrived at a Metro station, the Wilshire/Western stop on the purple line. The plaza above ground was patrolled by National Guardsmen with rifles slung over their shoulders. One of the cops separated Mickey from the golf cart and twisted his arms painfully tight behind his back to guide him into the shiny, polished steel cube that covered the elevator to the subway. They rode it down to the station level where the cop spoke briefly to a guard and they were waved through to the escalator, which wasn't moving. Mickey climbed down the stairs, trying not to stumble with his head pushed forward and his arms tied behind. The air rising from the subway smelled of sweat.

The subway platform was a scene of bedlam. Nearly all the people wore uniforms of some kind: LAPD, military, transit cops, EMS. Two ambulance stretchers bearing motionless bodies, one with an IV bag suspended above it, stood unattended a few feet from the track. The cop prodded Mickey down the platform toward what would be the end of the subway train when it arrived. There, one of the support pillars was wrapped with a simple small-link chain. Handcuffed to this makeshift security device were three other prisoners awaiting transport. Mickey made the group a foursome, one for each face of the pillar, like fish on a stringer. The officer who arrested him disappeared back toward the entrance.

"That ain't how they supposed to do it," one of the other men said. "They ain't supposed to let us be."

A clock on the wall said it was almost twenty past. In forty minutes, River would briefly turn on her phone, hoping to hear from him. It appeared Mickey wouldn't be making that call. He tried to sit down and was able to rest his buttocks on the tile floor but this lifted his arms toward his head, which was painful. For the next half hour, he alternated between uncomfortable sitting and standing. When the guy locked next to him urinated against the pillar and a trickle flowed in his direction, Mickey stayed on his feet.

"Here come the train," the chatty one said almost an hour after Mickey was left at the station.

A rush of wind and flash of headlights heralded the train's arrival. The pillar blocked most of his view of the ensuing activity on the platform. Apparently the prisoner transfer was a low-priority task; by the time a cop came to release the four men, everyone else was already on board. The escort uncuffed one of Mickey's hands and then locked it into the cuff of the guy behind him. In this way all four prisoners were secured into a small chain gang and loaded into the subway car.

The train stopped at each station, and by the time they reached the purple line terminus at Union Station, the accused had increased in number to ten. Mickey was fourth in line as they were led upstairs.

"It's less than a mile walk," said the police officer who met the train. "You'll get something to eat and drink when you arrive if don't give me any shit on the way."

The area around L.A.'s county jail hub was not pleasant for walking, but at least they didn't have to dodge moving traffic on the multilane streets as they passed one shuttered bail bonds operation after another. The hulking, windowless twin towers of the county correctional facility sucked the hope from Mickey's soul.

I don't want to go in there.

They passed through a barred gate at the perimeter of the expansive complex and were led into the inmate reception center.

At least this building has windows.

He knew from experience that police stations, like hospital ERs, were disorderly as a rule. But the scene that confronted him proved the criminal justice system in L.A. was stressed beyond its limits—and breaking. Inmates were locked to everything that didn't move. Uniformed officers were nowhere to be seen. The room reeked of urine. Posters on the walls delineated prisoners' rights and standard intake procedures, such as DNA testing and a medical exam for each man. But clearly none of the standard procedures was being followed. Men hollered for food and water.

The cop who brought them from the subway locked one of the inmates in Mickey's chain to the post of a molded plastic chair, and got the hell out. Mickey wondered how the prisoners would be identified, how they would be booked and charged.

As he surveyed the abandoned human flotsam around him, he had the chilling sensation that they'd been left here to die.

CHAPTER 61

Unlike I-5 with its glorious open lane, the two-ten offered only patches of clearing, and River was forced once again to bushwhack a path for the X-car.

"Wasn't it you back there who reminded me of this car's limited off-road capability?" River said. "Crossing the San Gabriel Mountains sounds about as off-road as you can get."

"We'll use roads," Christina replied as she scanned the map. "I see a couple that go all the way to the other side."

"Those aren't roads, they're mountain bike trails."

"No, some are roads. This one, Little Tujunga Canyon, is the one we want. If we take it all the way, it'll let us bypass the blockade on the five."

"You don't think they'll be monitoring these roads?"

"I doubt it, they're too remote. And technically they're inside the quarantine zone. If a car carrying the petroplague tried to get out this way, it would either break down in the mountains or be trapped at the next ring."

"That map doesn't look very detailed. Are you sure we'll be able to find our way?"

Christina crumpled the map into her lap with irritation. "No, I'm not sure. But do you have any better ideas?"

"Let me see the map," River said, stopping the Mini in a surreal background of motionless cars all facing the opposite direction. "It's going to take us forever to get through this section of the freeway, just to reach the exit for Tujunga Canyon. It adds miles to our route, miles we'll have to backtrack through the mountains once we get there. We'll burn so much fuel and time, we'd do just as well ditching the car with G.I. Joe at that roadblock and walking the rest of the way on the freeway."

"What do you suggest?"

"I say we take this one," River said, touching a finger to a spot on the map.

Christina squinted at the small print. "May Canyon Truck Trail?"

"Yep. It ends up in the same place as the road you picked, but will save us at least twenty miles."

"But it's a truck trail. What the hell is a truck trail?"

"I don't know, but it looks like a road to me."

Christina considered their options. River was right about Little Tujunga Canyon Road. According to the map, it was a huge detour. This truck trail was much more direct. If it wasn't too extreme for the X-car, it might shorten their eventual hike time by a day.

"All right, let's check it out," she said. "If it looks like the Mini can't handle it, we'll continue on to Tujunga."

They left the freeway and wound their way toward the mountains, which rose over three thousand feet above them, seemingly straight up. When they found it, the May Canyon Truck Trail started innocently enough as an ordinary paved road skirting the edge of a county park. As it ascended, it narrowed but still looked passable for the X-car.

They paused in front of a sign declaring "Angeles National Forest." River looked at Christina expectantly.

"Let's go for it," Christina said.

River reached to shift into drive but the car began to shake. She left it in park and took her hands off the steering wheel as if it were hot.

"Earthquake."

The previous quakes Christina had experienced displayed a certain musical pacing, starting softly and crescendoing to their peak before resolving. This earthquake lacked any such subtlety. Its tremors leapt from slight to severe in a single bound. Had Christina been standing, the motion would've knocked her down. An ancient valley oak leaned over the car, threatening to topple, but the shaking was so strong River was powerless to operate the car and move them to safety.

River ducked and put her arms over her head. Rocks tumbled down the mountainside, cracking and rumbling like lightning and thunder. Christina clung to her door and recited a Hail Mary prayer out loud. She was into the third recitation when the violent quake ended.

For a moment, the young women sat motionless, as if their actions might upset some delicate balance and trigger another quake. Strangely, Christina noticed that the noises continued: cracking, crashing, and now a low-pitched roar. The mysterious roar was growing louder.

"What is that?" River said tentatively.

"I—"

"Water," River said.

A shallow but broad stream of water suddenly filled the park and streamed over the road where they sat. The level was rising swiftly. Christina wondered if a water main had broken. Must be a really big pipe, she thought.

"Watch out!"

The water reached the car. It was flowing fast and getting deeper. The Mini didn't have much clearance from the ground, and at the rate things were going, in a minute or two the floor of the car would be underwater. River tapped the accelerator.

The wheels splashed water onto the windows and Christina heard the distinctive sound of water spraying the undercarriage. *Hang in there, little car!*

Because the truck trail rose sharply into the mountains, within a few yards they were on dry land again. They stopped and stared in amazement at the county park below them.

The park had become a pool.

"That can't be good," River said.

Even as they watched, Christina saw landmarks disappearing: picnic table benches, then the table tops. Trash cans, small trees, then taller and taller objects were swamped by the torrent which poured in from the east side of the park. Muddy, roiling water spilled in all directions. River inched the car forward to keep it above the ever-rising water line.

"That's no water main," Christina said, pressing the map against her knees to smooth the creases. She pointed at a blue splotch in their area. "It's this."

"Pacoima Reservoir," River read. "The dam failed."

CHAPTER 62

Like dogs left chained in a yard when the owner's away, the men at the county jail's intake facility were starting to bark.

Without food or drink, without access to toilets, and with only minimal supervision, the crowd of would-be inmates grew increasingly restive. A fight broke out not far from Mickey. Two men who were handcuffed to each other—and to more men, in a chain—grappled and kicked. The entire group was dragged to the ground, where they wriggled like gigantic worms in a bloody embrace.

This fracas finally drew out the first prison guards Mickey had seen in quite a while. Two of them emerged from behind a locked door, clubs in hand. They struck the combatants repeatedly, until the men curled up faces down in defense.

Then a guard pulled out a handcuff key to separate the belligerents.

The effect was as sudden as a spark in a room filled with hydrogen gas. The guards were set upon by a nearby group of chained men, and working as a team, the prisoners overcame their handicap and overpowered the guards. Mickey closed his eyes when the prisoners turned the clubs on the guards. Three more guards appeared, but the situation had already spiraled out of control. Too many prisoners were being held in a tight space, and too few jail personnel remained on duty to manage the task.

Handcuff keys seized from the guards started making the rounds of the room, and men fled the building. Mickey made every effort to keep his body passive to avoid antagonizing his neighbors. The room throbbed with the noise of shouting and banging. Small clusters of violence erupted here and there as the men fought over keys, but gradually a kind of order descended. One fellow took it upon himself to be master of a key, and instead of passing it on once he was freed, he systematically moved from one man to the next, expertly loosing their bonds. When he unlocked Mickey, he grinned and winked.

Mickey joined the wave of men flowing into the courtyard outside. Like spawning salmon trapped below a dam, they crashed against the prison gate, and he feared he might be crushed in the mindless stampede. Several minutes passed and the pressure increased behind him. Then a roar went up from the crowd as the gate slid to one side and the rioters spilled out. He never knew whether they'd forced the mechanism by sheer numbers, or whether they'd been released. But contrary to all expectation, he now found himself free.

Clearly, the forces of law and order were overwhelmed. On the bright side, maybe that meant no one would pursue River and Christina. On the not-so-bright side, the city was fast becoming a very dangerous place. He took stock of his situation. He had no food and no water. He was a suspected felon on the run. And most important, the clock was ticking on Neil's plot to globalize the petroplague.

What he wanted to do was walk to his old apartment and crash. What he had to do was tell someone about Neil. Someone with clout. Someone who could do something.

City Hall was less than two miles away.

They'll probably arrest me again, but if I give them Neil's note . . .

He walked to a bridge over railroad tracks and was part way across when the ground began to shake.

The bridge writhed beneath him and threw him off his feet. Lying face down on the pavement he could actually see waves rolling across the asphalt surface, leaving it fractured and torn. Images of the highway collapse during the Northridge quake flashed through his mind, and he braced himself for a fall if the road gave way. Abandoned vehicles around him jiggled and shifted from their original positions. He crawled to the clearest section he could find to avoid getting hit.

Compared to its predecessors, this quake was noisy. Mickey heard the screech of metal fatiguing and the cracking of concrete. A rumbling sound to the right drew his attention, and he looked up in time to see an old industrial building crumble into a pile of construction waste under a dense cloud of dust. He plastered his body firmly to the unstable ground and prayed for it to stop moving.

Chapter 63

Ramirez plucked his water tumbler off the floor and returned it to the conference table. The glass had danced over the edge during the quake but landed unbroken on the carpet. Based on the sounds he heard during the trembler, plenty of other damage had occurred.

"Reports!" he shouted at staff members as they hunched over laptops and fiddled with iPhones. "Magnitude! Origin! Was that the San Andreas?"

"No, sir, the quake was in the valley. Geological surveys report it came from the Sierra Madre fault. Epicenter in north L.A., southern edge of the San Gabriel Mountains. San Fernando area."

"Goddammit, it was strong."

There would be damage. There had to be damage after a quake like that. His mind was spinning. How bad? How would emergency services cope without transportation? He noticed that fortunately they still had power at City Hall.

"I've got reports of flooding in Sylmar," an aide said. "Water at least a foot deep in places. Level is rising."

"Water at the two-ten freeway," another added. "Flooding in San Fernando."

"What happened?" Ramirez said.

For a minute the only answer was the clattering of keys and murmuring into cell phones. Then someone spoke.

"The Pacoima Dam has failed, sir. Repeat: the Pacoima Dam has failed."

"The dam was at nineteen hundred fifty feet elevation," another aide said. "The reservoir is draining into the valley."

"What's the capacity?"

"About six thousand acre-feet."

Enough water to bury six thousand acres of land under water one foot deep. Not good, but not too bad in the grand scheme of things. The San Gabriel Reservoir, also in the Angeles National Forest about forty miles east of Pacoima, held eight times as much water.

"This time of year, it wasn't full, was it?" he said.

"No sir. Estimate reservoir was at . . . less than 50% of capacity."

"Three thousand acre-feet. We can deal with that."

Or more to the point, the residents of Sylmar would have to deal with that. There was precious little the county's public services could do for them right now. A couple of feet of water over an entire community was a helluva mess, but it shouldn't kill anybody, at least not right away.

Damage reports came in: damage to older buildings, cracked roads and sidewalks, palm trees down. The power was out in more than ten thousand homes. A few structures had collapsed. In ordinary times, heavy equipment would rush to the scene and rescue people trapped in those buildings. But L.A. was becoming Port-au-Prince. Earthquake victims were on their own.

CHAPTER 64

Christina looked back down the canyon. Water covered the park and the lower road that the X-car had travelled only minutes ago.

"We're cut off," she said. "The way back is flooded."

"Can't go over it, can't go under it, gotta go through it," River said, chanting the chorus from a popular children's song. "Though technically I guess we're going over, not through, the mountains."

"Unless the truck trail is a tunnel," Christina said, "which I doubt."

"I think we'll be lucky if we can tell the trail from the rest of the terrain," River said as she put the car in gear.

The road rose and twisted, and they lost their view of the city almost immediately. The pavement ended, and the Mini bounced along on dirt. Fortunately, summer was the dry season; if the road was wet, their little car would quickly be mired in mud. As long as River kept their speed at a crawl, it looked like the truck trail would lead them across the San Gabriel range.

Christina was amazed by the wildness of the place, so close to one of the world's biggest urban centers. Low-elevation forest shaded the steep, winding canyon chosen for the trail. Other than a few signs warning of twisty road and possible rock fall, there was no evidence of human activity. Further into the wilderness they drove. She saw an occasional hawk flying high overhead. Blackened branches appeared in some of the trees, and they came to an area completely burned by a recent wildfire.

"You're not getting car sick, are you?" River asked when Christina opened her window.

"No, I just wondered if it was cooling off," she said, sticking her hand outside.

"It will," River said. "After dark, the temperature probably drops twenty degrees. Even more once we make it to the higher elevations."

The sun was sinking low in the sky, and sections of the road were already in the dark shadow of the mountain. River turned the lights on.

"Want me to drive for a while?" Christina asked.

"I've got it for now," River said. "Are we going to stop for the night?"

"No," she replied, checking the odometer. "At this rate, we can't afford to lose time."

"Then you should take a nap," River said. "I'll give you the wheel in an hour or so."

Christina tilted the seat back as far as it would go—which wasn't at all far enough—and tried to sleep. The sharp twists in the road were making her a little sick. After days of bad food and high anxiety, her stomach was vulnerable to this fresh insult. She loosened her lap belt and curled up on her side. Miraculously, she managed to slip into a light slumber.

Crunch.

The sickening sound of impact wrenched Christina awake. Total darkness had settled outside. In the faint illumination from the dashboard, she struggled with her seat belt and tried to sit up. The car wasn't moving.

"What happened?"

River's face was ashen in the pale light. "Rocks."

One of the Mini's headlights was out. The other shone on a pile of rocky debris which covered the narrow trail from one canyon wall to the other.

River's voice cracked. "There was a bend—almost a U-turn—I was going slow, but it's so dark . . ." The words caught in her throat.

Christina opened her door and stepped out of the car. The night was black to an extreme, unfamiliar to city dwellers, and the air felt cold. Other than the sound of the idling engine, silence blanketed the canyon. She hugged herself for warmth and moved into the beam of the surviving headlight.

A jagged stone about twelve inches tall was wedged under the fender. It lifted the front of the car into the air; the front wheels no longer made contact with the ground. Many more rocks had tumbled off the main pile and lay scattered over the road.

Christina pushed the X-car, trying to nudge it off the rock and to the earth. Nothing happened.

"Looks like you ran over a rock," she said. "Can you back up?"

River gently engaged the accelerator, and the front wheels spun vainly in reverse.

"Help me," she said.

Her cousin joined her. She noticed how quickly River had regained her composure. Despite River's reputation as a gadabout, she could be tough and disciplined when necessary.

"We have to push it off the rock," Christina said. "On the count of three."

Both young women threw their full effort into shoving the vehicle clear, but it didn't budge. They tried to rock it back and forth, but the boulder was embedded in the chassis. The only way to free the car was to lift it straight up.

"I'll find a jack," River said and scampered to the hatchback.

While River unloaded the backpacks in search of tire-changing equipment, Christina clambered up the rock pile. Shivering, she looked around from the top.

The truck trail snaked away on the other side, but even if they could get the car moving again, they couldn't pass the rock slide. It probably happened during one of the earthquakes, she thought. *Rocks blocking us forward, water blocking us back. This journey was not going well.*

Her gaze wandered up the barren mountain slopes. While she slept in the car, they'd ascended above the forest. No trees, only hardy scrub, grew in this arid landscape. Tonight the moon was only a sliver of light, and the stars shone more brightly than she'd ever seen. Even the Milky Way was visible, and she marveled at how modern humans had lost touch with the heavens. She couldn't identify a single constellation, yet the ancients could track the movements of all the stars. Throughout human history, except for a blink in the previous century, night had been a time of darkness.

The noble silence and majesty around her made Christina philosophical. If the petroplague went global, humanity would be thrown backward in time to the pre-industrial era, when night meant darkness. But they would go crippled by modernity, lacking beasts of burden, and without any understanding of how the natural world works. They would not recognize the stars, or the heavenly signs that it was time to sow or time to reap.

Most of them would die.

"Found it," River shouted.

Christina slid down the rocks. River was under the car on her back with a flashlight, trying to find the best place to position the jack.

"I've never done this by myself," River said, "but I think it's not hard."

"Don't bother," Christina said. "We're ditching the car."

River sat up, inadvertently stabbing Christina's eyes with the flashlight.

"What do you mean?"

"There's no way around the rockslide, so there's no point wasting our time on the car," Christina said.

"We could turn back to the city and try another way."

She shook her head. "Even if the flood from the dam is over, we've burned too much fuel. Every mile we drive back is another mile we'll have to repeat on foot."

She dragged her backpack onto the road and unzipped the compartments, checking the inventory and familiarizing herself with where things were stashed.

"Chrissy, on foot we're, like, a week from getting out of this," River said.

"Don't you think I know that?" Christina said, standing up and glaring at her cousin. "I don't want to walk that far, but that's how it turned out, okay?"

She fetched the specimen box from the front seat and carefully secured it in her backpack. When she faced River again, her cheeks were wet with tears.

"If you want to go back to L.A., I'll help you with the car. But I have to keep going. I have to get these specimens to a lab."

River packed up the jack. "Of course you do. And we stick together."

Together, they helped each other hoist their heavy packs onto their backs.

Christina took a deep breath. "It's not over yet. Once we reach the freeway, maybe we can hitch a ride inside the containment ring."

River tightened a padded strap against her hip and said, "Nice night for a walk."

Chapter 65

Ramirez wondered how much caffeine you could take and still get a buzz; his chain-drinking must be pushing the limit by now. His eyes felt red and his heartbeat was rapid and shallow, but he took another sip of coffee. Sleep was not an option.

"Trinley's here, your honor," said one of the staffers. "Security radioed that he's on his way up now."

He stood and adjusted the cuffs of his sleeves. Early in the crisis, this scientist, Jeff Trinley, had made a bold promise. Ramirez had supported him, had given him extraordinary privileges to enable his work. It was time for the payoff.

The door opened and in walked a slick-looking man wearing khakis and a polo shirt. His face was bruised an ugly purple. Ramirez hadn't met Trinley in person before, but he recognized the voice when Trinley said, "Mr. Mayor?"

"Yes, Mr. Trinley. Thank you for understanding the urgency of my request for this visit."

"Sure," Trinley said, his eyes darting about nervously.

Ramirez noted an air of desperation about the scientist.

"Please, have a seat."

A dozen of the mayor's advisors took their places. Trinley sat with the look of a fox surrounded by hounds.

"I apologize, but we have no time for pleasantries. The situation has changed, Mr. Trinley, and not for the better. I need solutions, and I need them now. You promised me a breakthrough, a new biofuel that is resistant to the plague bacteria."

"We're working on it night and day, Your Honor," Trinley said, evading the mayor's gaze.

"But your production system isn't ready?"

"No, there's a—it's a challenge—more complicated," Trinley said. "We need more time."

"I told you, we're out of time. The petroplague has escaped the quarantine. It has infected the San Andreas. Without a cure, we may soon experience the biggest earthquake in California history."

"It's her fault!" Trinley said, slamming his fist. "That student, Christina González. She and her boyfriend smashed our bioreactor. They destroyed the bacteria that make the biofuel. The cultures we have at Bactofuels are all old versions, not the latest genetically-engineered product. I saw her boyfriend ruin the last specimen."

Ramirez had long believed he possessed a gift for reading people, for anticipating what they would do, for guessing what mattered to them most. Sometimes he was wrong—in the case of Christina González, spectacularly wrong—but Trinley, with his frantic, defensive attitude and wild claims, triggered alarm bells. The story wasn't convincing. The man was a liar.

If it was all a scam from the beginning, if there never was any biofuel, he would feed this guy to the lions.

"You witnessed this? Where?"

"In the lab at UCLA."

"Dr. Robert Chen's lab?"

"Yes."

"What were you doing in Chen's lab?"

"The girl hadn't been arrested yet and I suspected she might do something to my property. So I went to get my cultures. But I was too late. González and the boy were already there. He destroyed my company's work and then he dumped Chen's cure. I tried to stop him. That's when I got this," he said, pointing at the injuries to his face. "He stole my golf cart, too."

"Wait a minute. You told me Christina González destroyed Chen's cure when he died."

"Um, yeah, she did, but I guess there was some left—"

The conference room door burst open, and a scruffy young man flew in followed immediately by the grasping arm of a security guard in full pursuit.

"Mr. Mayor, listen to me! The plague is out!" he shouted just before he was tackled. The security officer tried to drag him away.

"There's a conspiracy—"

Thwack. The guard hit him.

"A terrorist is planning to spread the plague all over the country."

The guard yanked him to his feet, planted his face into the conference table and twisted his arms behind his back. "But there's a cure," Mickey mumbled from mashed lips.

Trinley leaped out of his chair, his face contorted.

"He's the one! The student's boyfriend! He killed my *E. coli* and he murdered the professor!"

He ran at the immobilized youth and landed a punch in Mickey's exposed side. Mickey caught him with a kick before the onlookers pulled Trinley away.

"Quiet! Let's have some order in here," Ramirez said.

Reluctantly Trinley returned to his seat. "If anyone's trying to spread the plague, it's him."

The guard spun Mickey around and pointed him toward the exit. He struggled, unwilling to leave.

"It's true that I know the guy who blew up the gas station," Mickey said, shaking his head at the guard. "I didn't have anything to do with it, but he told me about a bigger plan, something he's doing right now. You've got to hear me out."

Ramirez glanced from Trinley to Mickey and then caught the eye of his advisor Molton, who nodded agreement.

"Let him stay," he said to the security officer, who kept his grip on Mickey's arms but turned the prisoner to face the mayor. "What do you know, young man?"

"He left me a note—it's in my pocket—it talks about his plan. We have less than five days to stop it."

"Give it to me."

The guard released Mickey, who handed the document to the mayor. Ramirez's stomach flipped when he read it.

"You're supposed to be in jail!" Trinley said. "LAPD arrested you. Did you kill a cop?"

Mickey threw Trinley a dirty look but spoke to the mayor. "There's hope. Dr. Robert Chen at UCLA discovered an antibiotic that kills the petroplague. Christina González—who is not my girlfriend—tried to give Trinley a sample of it to work on. He destroyed it. But Christina kept one more sample that he didn't know about."

"Yeah? She's probably using it as a cover to spread the petroplague. She started it and she won't stop until it's—"

"Mr. Trinley!" Ramirez interrupted. "What do you know about Chen's cure?"

"There isn't any cure," Trinley said. "This hooligan is making it up to save his ass."

"Bullshit," Mickey said. "You had it in your hands and you dumped it down the drain because you want to sell your fuel. Mr. Mayor, ever since the crisis began, this man has been trying to advance his own interests with complete disregard for the public good. Robert Chen died as a result."

"Christina González killed Robert Chen!" Trinley said. "And what do you know about microbiology? Nothing!"

"It's true I don't know anything about science," Mickey said, "but Christina does. And she has the last sample of Dr. Chen's cure."

"Where is she?" Ramirez said.

Trinley looked at the mayor in dismay. "You're not listening to him, are you? This punk is one of the ecoterrorists who started this whole thing!"

"Mr. Trinley, can you give me the biofuel now or not?"

"No. Him and his friends destroyed my facility at the UCLA lab."

"Then we have nothing more to discuss. Get out of here."

"You're making a mistake. My fuel is the only thing—"

"Please remove him," Ramirez said, turning his back on Trinley, who was promptly escorted from the room. The mayor faced the earnest young man who now stood freely in his presence. His sixth sense urged him to believe the youth. He wanted to believe that a cure for the petroplague existed. He wanted to believe Christina González was the person he saw when he met her, not the person Jeff Trinley said she was.

"What's your name?"

"Mickey Winston."

"Well, Mickey, I don't know whether you're telling the truth or not, but we're stuck between a rock and a hard place. Tell me where your friend is and we'll find out whether Chen was on to a cure or not."

CHAPTER 66

Christina and River trudged through the darkness, weighed down by the heavy packs. When the road went uphill, sweat formed on Christina's back. When she arrived at a level section and walked easily, her shirt felt cold and clammy.

"We brought too much," River said, leaning against a boulder and removing her pack. "Never make it with this load."

"Ditch the tent," Christina suggested. "It's not going to rain, and we don't have time for real camping anyway."

"Agreed," River said. She detached the nylon bag containing the tent and poles and laid it on the side of the road. "Much better already."

To lighten her load, Christina discarded an extra pair of shoes and a spray can of insect repellent. For good measure, she doused herself and River with the spray before tossing the can aside. She felt an absurd twinge of guilt for littering in a national forest.

"Let's get moving," she said, yawning.

With her eyes fully adjusted to the darkness, the moon provided enough light to guide her steps on the pebble-strewn road. They descended to a lower altitude and re-entered a section of trees. The moonlight cast sinister shadows, and it was harder to see. The young women followed the road blindly, with forest on both sides.

"It's creepy out here," River said. Her voice sounded surprisingly loud in the quiet night.

"You're such a city girl," Christina teased, but she shared her cousin's feeling of unease. She wasn't afraid of true solitude, but the teeming metropolis wasn't far away. What if they were not alone in the forest?

"Did you hear that?" River hissed, putting a hand out to halt her cousin.

Her footsteps silenced, Christina listened with intensity sharpened by the weakness of her vision. "Hear what?"

"Something in the trees."

By temperament, Christina was calm and rational. She'd sit in the thirteenth row of an aircraft, or fearlessly open an umbrella indoors. But in this place, at this time, it wasn't unreasonable to be afraid. Her muscles tightened.

"They sometimes find mountain lions up here," River whispered.

"It's not a mountain lion," Christina said, but she raised her voice to make noise lest they startle some living thing with their hushed approach. "Just keep walking."

Side by side, they took a few more steps when the noise of a large animal crashing through the forest shattered the silence. Christina's heart leaped into her throat. The sound was ahead of them. Instinctively, she stopped and grabbed River's arm.

What do they say you're supposed to do if a mountain lion attacks? Run? Play dead?

But it wasn't a mountain lion that emerged from the trees. It was a man.

"Qué pasa, señoritas?"

He was dark-haired and sinewy as if he'd done hard work and lived a hard life. Even in moonlight she could see his face was dirty, with a poorly-tended mustache. An unlit cigarette stuck out the side of his mouth. He wore jeans and a long-sleeve cotton shirt.

But her attention was drawn to the rifle hung by a strap around his neck. His hands rested easily on the weapon, which was approximately aimed at them. It didn't look like he'd been out deer hunting.

Christina and River froze. *I guess playing dead isn't an option.* Running didn't seem terribly wise either. In a women's self-defense class they'd taught her to never surrender to an assailant even if he was armed, because you had a better chance of dodging a bullet on the run than surviving after you got in his car. *Easier said than done.* Out here in the wilderness, nobody was going to dial 9-1-1 when they heard shots.

"Buenas noches," River said noncommittally. "Lovely evening, isn't it?"

River's moxie snapped the band of fear that momentarily paralyzed Christina. She'd assumed this man was a threat, but maybe the gun was for self-defense. *If I owned one, I would've brought it with me.*

Then a second Hispanic man, stockier than the first and with teardrops tattooed at the corner of one eye, stepped into the moonlight. He, too, was armed. When a third man appeared and closed the circle around them, Christina gave up hope that the men were simply refugees from the petroplague.

"What are you doing here?" the tattooed one said with a thick Mexican accent, stepping toward them with his gun barrel pointing at River's stomach. "Están solas? Are you alone?"

He had his eyes on River when he spoke. She stared fiercely at him, but did not answer.

"Our car broke down," Christina said, figuring that much was obvious. "We're trying to get out of L.A." Dialogue, she thought. We have to talk our way out of this. Briefly, she wondered if all the crap she was carrying would be enough to stop a bullet in the back if she turned and ran, but she was pretty sure it wouldn't.

"You made it, eh? This is not L.A.," Teardrop Tattoo said. He prowled like a cat, circling River and poking at her pack with his gun. His henchmen stayed put with their weapons raised. "It's a long walk out of the mountains. Are you ready for a long walk?"

"We can handle it," River said.

In Spanish, Teardrop told one of the men to search the road for the car, and to figure out if the girls were traveling with anyone else. The man sprinted off. Christina listened and felt her fingers tingle as the fight-or-flight response clamped down blood flow to her extremities. *This is not good.*

"Can we go now?" she said politely. *Can't hurt to ask.*

"Tenemos hambre," growled the man standing guard.

"Sé," snapped Teardrop. "Yo también."

So that's what they want, Christina thought. Our food.

She hoped food was the only thing the men were hungry for.

"Here, you can have what I've got," Christina offered, releasing the front clasps that strapped her pack to her body.

Teardrop spun away from River and drove the barrel of his gun into Christina's belly. She gasped.

"Don't move unless I tell you to," he said.

Christina nodded and raised her hands to her shoulders, swallowing panic.

"Muchacho," River said, "you want us to hang with you for a while? We could use a rest."

God, she sounds so cool and collected, Christina thought. She'd give anything for a minute to confer privately with her cousin. Did she have a plan? Or was she just putting on a brave face?

"Sí," Teardrop said. He kept the gun trained on Christina but backed up to River. He put his hand on her chin. River flinched but managed a half-smile. "You girls stay."

Like we have a choice.

A flashlight beam broke the darkness down the road as the third man returned from his hunt. He reported quietly to the leader.

"Is not safe, two chicas out here alone," Teardrop said. He waved his weapon toward the forest. "Vámonos!"

The sinewy man jumped at Teardrop's command and led the way into the scrub. River and Christina followed, with Teardrop close behind. Christina wondered if wandering into the woods with your captor was the suicidal equivalent of getting into a car with him. But considering the truck trail wasn't exactly a hub of activity, she decided they weren't much worse off for leaving it.

The dry, prickly scrub growing thickly on the side of the road scratched her legs as they plowed through. Soon, the brush thinned and a canopy of trees spread over them, blocking the moonlight. She struggled to maintain a sense of direction in case she had to find her way back out, but the leader followed a winding path that was invisible to her. She despaired of a swift and easy escape, and thought about the precious package she carried. She didn't allow herself to consider these men might harm her or

River, but she did worry about the delay. If the antibiotic wasn't ready in time . . . and they still had so far to go . . .

"Ah!" River cried as she stumbled and fell.

Christina rushed to her. A thick, gnarled root protruded from the dirt. River must have tripped on it in the darkness.

"Are you okay?"

River moaned and grasped her lower leg. Teardrop shoved Christina aside and yanked River to her feet.

"Ow! Ow!" River said, protesting. "My ankle!"

She stood on one foot like a flamingo.

"Move," Teardrop said, giving her a push with his rifle. River lost her balance and fell again.

"Fuck," he said.

"Let me help," Christina said, inching closer to her injured cousin.

"No," Teardrop said. He called to the man at the rear, and ordered him to support River the rest of the way.

The rest of the way where? Christina wondered. She hoped it wasn't far. Every step took them deeper into danger—*no, don't think about that*—every step took them further away from their goal. She hoped River's twisted ankle would feel better soon. Real soon, because they had to rely on their own two feet to get out of here.

They stumbled forward a few steps with River hopping on her good leg but she soon collapsed again.

"It's too heavy," she said, meaning her pack.

Teardrop cursed again and told the skinny man to carry it. Christina tried to get close, to speak to River, but clearly Teardrop wasn't going to allow that.

"Get back," he said.

The skinny man was scrawny but strong. He lifted the pack as if it were no heavier than a loaf of bread, and returned to his position at the front of the line. They resumed walking, and River managed by leaning on the ruffian at her side.

The trees around them thinned out, yet the canopy overhead seemed to stay just as dense. The ground sprouted with plants, green and leafy, much different from the arid scrub near the truck trail. Christina squinted at the vegetation which grew thick and uniform, almost like a crop.

Though she'd never been a toker, she knew enough to recognize *Cannabis sativa* when she saw it.

It's a pot farm, she realized. These guys are drug dealers.

Well, that explained the guns and the vigilance. Illegal marijuana cultivation was big business in California. Christina had read about farms like this one popping up in wilderness areas all over the state, about rental homes converted into cannabis greenhouses with custom lighting and water systems, that only came to the attention of the authorities because of their unusually high electric bills.

It appeared the men had rigged some kind of jungle netting over the area to conceal the crop from aircraft. The netting might also hide the campfire she now saw burning ahead. Having open flames in the national forest during this dry season was incredibly dangerous. Either these guys were stupid, or the petroplague was making them desperate. Christina feared it was the latter, and she wondered what other risky things they might do.

"That's some good *mota*," River said as they entered the circle of light around the fire. "You sharing?"

Teardrop smiled but said nothing.

The campfire was not unattended. A fourth man, who looked like he might be brother to the scrawny fellow, was poking at the coals with a stick. He stood up and looked at the young women with surprise.

"Quién es?" he said, wondering whom his comrades had brought back with them.

Teardrop ignored him. River's escort released her and she sank to the ground, massaging her injured limb. Skinny waved his brother over and the two of them tore into River's backpack. They laughed and chatted in Spanish as snack packages and energy drinks spilled from its pockets. Their discovery of a pair of underwear among River's garments prompted a lewd pantomime.

Christina moved to sit down next to River, but Teardrop intervened and directed her to sit on the ground opposite her cousin. She obeyed. Their conversation would have to wait.

The men had all shouldered their guns; Christina relaxed a bit now that there wasn't a rifle thrust against her torso. She wriggled out of her backpack, keeping an eye on her captor to make sure he didn't mind, and laid the pack on the ground beside her. Chilly night air circulated over her sweaty back; the warmth of the fire in front of her felt good.

Teardrop double-checked that River's pack was completely empty. He allowed each of the men to select one item to eat, then stuffed the rest back inside. With a package of Oreos in hand, he pulled a canvas camping chair up to the fire and sat down. Warily he eyed River and Christina, as if trying to decide what to do next.

"What happened to the cars?" he said.

"We hit a rock," Christina said, "and the truck trail was blocked by landslide."

"Not your car," Teardrop said. "The cars in L.A."

How long have they been up here? she wondered. Do they even know about the petroplague?

"For one week nobody come to the mountains," he continued. "We hear the cars in L.A. not working."

"It's true," River said. "Nothing can move in the whole city."

"Why?"

"There's a germ," Christina said. "It eats the gasoline. The cars are fine, but there isn't any gas anymore."

"That's why we left," River added. "That's why we're walking over the mountains."

"But you say you have a car," Teardrop said, frowning. "Why your car still working?"

That would take some explaining, Christina thought as they fell silent. River gave her a look as if to say, your question, not mine.

"Well, it's a special kind of car. It worked for a while, but it doesn't work anymore."

Teardrop munched his cookies and tossed the wrapper into the fire. If he wasn't satisfied by Christina's answer, he didn't express it. One of his henchmen picked up River's backpack and carried it off into the shadows like a jaguar moving its kill. A light flickered on inside what Christina now saw was a large canvas tent. The man's silhouette flitted across the fabric wall. He lifted a whiskey-shaped bottle to his mouth.

"L.A.'s got big problems," River said. "There've been earthquakes. Floods. The police can't move. Nobody gives a shit about this anymore." She waved her arm to indicate the cannabis field.

"That's right," Christina said. "People just want to escape. Like us. Let us go. We won't tell anybody about you, and even if we did, nobody would care."

Teardrop didn't answer. He leaned over and dragged Christina's backpack to his chair.

Christina stiffened. *My specimens!*

ZZZIIIP . . . Teardrop peeled back the zipper of the main compartment and reached in. He pulled out Christina's provisions, sorting the food and drink into one pile, and her clothes into another.

ZZZIIIP . . . He opened the next section and found Christina's money, credit cards, and driver's license neatly packed in a waterproof sandwich bag. He grinned and nodded his thanks to her as he stuffed the bag in his pocket.

ZZZIIIP . . . In the uppermost chamber of the backpack, Teardrop came upon a mystery: a small Styrofoam box with strange orange markings on it. He turned it over in his hands. Panicked, Christina looked at River for help.

"Qué es esto?" Teardrop said as he tossed it toward his comrades.

"No!" Christina cried.

The fate of California rested in that small box. When it passed over the fire, she leaped to her feet. Her fingers knocked the biohazard container away from the flames, and it skidded into the darkness.

Instantly a fist smashed into her temple and she crumpled to the ground. Teardrop stood over her with his rifle drawn and the barrel against her crotch.

"I'm sorry. I'm sorry," Christina whimpered.

265

One of the scrawny brothers said something. Teardrop nodded and the man scampered off while his brother kept his weapon trained on River. Christina stayed curled up in the dirt with her hands on her head. *Stupid! Stupid! Stupid!*

The brother returned with a ball of twine and handed it to Teardrop.

"Sit up," he said.

Christina sat, one hand cupped over the swelling pain in the side of her head.

"Hands."

This was it. This really was the point of no return. He was tying her up. She couldn't let him! But with four men and four guns, an injured companion, and miles of wilderness in every direction, she had no choice. She lowered her hands together.

"Behind."

Reluctantly she parted and rejoined her hands behind her back. As she felt the thin cord wrap around her wrists, she watched them bind River's hands in the same way.

When the job was done, Teardrop left her and she sat uncomfortably with her legs crossed. River's face was pale and rigid.

He returned with the Styrofoam box. Christina was certain he didn't recognize the biohazard symbols. He sat in his chair again, the box on his lap. Christina stared helplessly at the box until she realized he was watching her.

"What is in the box?" he said.

"It's nothing of value to you, I swear," Christina said. "Please, let us go. You're welcome to keep all our stuff. Just let me take the box."

Teardrop smiled and drew a pocketknife from his jeans. The metal snapped as he opened a blade. Still watching Christina's reaction, he slid the knife into the seam of the box and severed the tape that held it shut.

"What is in the box?" he said again, and peeled off the lid.

Confusion spread across his face, and he took his eyes off Christina to focus on the contents.

What did you expect? Diamonds?

He lifted out a tiny, hard plastic tube to show his companions. They commented in Spanish. His fingers brushed over the tube as he tried to comprehend the obscure technical writing inscribed in Sharpie on the tube's side. Christina saw him position his thumb to pop open the top.

"Don't open it! Peligro! It's dangerous!" she said. This was a lie, but if he opened it he might contaminate the specimen.

He paused. The other men looked at him curiously.

"Dangerous," he said in a mocking tone, but he set the tube back in the box. Maybe the mysterious orange symbols had freaked him out a little, even if he didn't know what they meant.

"You tell me what is in the box, and maybe I let you keep it."

"I—I'm a scientist. Soy una científica," she added, wanting the other thugs to understand, too. "These are part of an experiment that only I can use. They're poisonous. Tóxico."

Teardrop seemed unconvinced but chose not to pursue the subject. He closed the box, stretched, and carried it with him toward the tent while instructing his men. Apparently it was their habit to take turns keeping watch at night. He told them to keep an eye on the girls.

The men argued briefly about whose turn it was to stay awake. The two who won gathered up the things from Christina's backpack and took them to the tent, where all was now dark. The scrawny guard quietly paced a circle around the area and yawned. Christina whispered to River.

"Silencio!" the guard barked.

Sighing, Christina lay down on her side. With her hands tied, repose on the hard dirt gave little comfort. She was thirsty and her stomach rumbled. She could no longer see her watch. *What time is it? How much time do we have?* The pressure of her anxiety rose in parallel with her mental picture of the gas pressures in the area faults, and she imagined she felt tiny tremors, harbingers of the Big One to come.

Chapter 67

Ramirez stood in his office and stared at his copy of Neil's suicide note and confession. He'd given the original to law enforcement, and by now the President himself might have read it. The F.B.I. and Homeland Security were over it like ants at a picnic, but they didn't have much time, and the plot to spread the plague had dozens of participants. If even one of them succeeded, they were screwed. In a few days, containment would no longer be an option. They needed a cure.

"Mickey, is Chen's cure at UCLA?"

"No, Trinley destroyed it. Christina and my girlfriend—her cousin—have what's left. But she said it's not ready, that somebody needs to work on it. She only took it with her because Trinley was being a dick."

"He said your friends were trying to spread the petroplague. Is that true?"

"No, of course not. They're just trying to get to San Diego. You know he has the police chasing Christina even though she didn't do anything wrong."

Ramirez gave Mickey a long, cold stare, waiting for him to squirm, but he didn't.

"Anyway, Neil's got the spreading part covered," Mickey said.

"We must find your friends. Are they traveling on foot?"

"No, they have a car. The X-car from UCLA."

"The what?"

Mickey explained. "It's an experimental vehicle from Chen's lab that runs on biodiesel—Trinley's fuel. The one that's not affected by the petroplague."

"They should be stopped at the first containment ring. Can you call them?"

"I can try," Mickey said, "but they're keeping their phones off so the police can't track the signals. River is supposed to turn hers on for a minute on the hour. We should be able to reach her then."

"That's almost half an hour from now," Ramirez said, checking his watch. "You try calling her, and keep at it until you get through. I'll see if my people can get any information from the border guards."

*   *   *

"A green car matching the description of the experimental vehicle was turned back on the five at Sylmar," Molton reported. "Two young women were inside. They did not get out and walk, but drove back toward the city. The guards believe the vehicle exited east on the two-ten."

"So they're going north," Ramirez said. "Where do you suppose they went next?"

Molton shrugged. "I think it's time to call and ask them."

Ramirez nodded. "Do we have someone ready to track the phone's signal in case she turns it on but doesn't want to talk?"

"We do."

They found Mickey dutifully pushing redial over and over without success. As the second hand on the wall clock ticked through its rotation, Ramirez started to sweat.

"Would we know if our people had a GPS lock?"

"Yes."

Another minute passed, and a third. Mickey shook his head. River's phone wasn't receiving calls, and the technicians monitoring it declared that the phone had never been turned on.

"What now?" Ramirez said. "Mickey, any idea where they would've gone on the two-ten?"

"I don't know, I thought they were making for San Diego."

"Somebody pull up Google Maps for me."

Mickey spoke up while the screen flickered. "The car's pretty distinctive. I mean, not only is it the only thing moving out there, it's neon green and has an advertising wrap all over it. If anyone saw it, they'd remember."

"Jackson, get in touch with every person with a pair of eyes in the San Fernando area. Find out if they've seen this car."

"Yes, sir. That's the area of the Pacoima flood, sir."

"I know. Let's hope they weren't caught in it."

Ramirez paced back and forth, stroking his chin, ready to get out there himself on a bike or Segway to look for that car if he had to. Chen's antibiotic was the only hope for Los Angeles. And if the eco-terrorist's plan succeeded, the need would go far beyond this city.

"This X-car is very special, right?" he asked Mickey.

"Yeah."

"And it's owned by the university."

"I think so."

"If I were the owner of such a car, I'd be worried about someone stealing it."

"We always were," Mickey said. "I mean, when Christina got to use it on some weekends, we were kinda paranoid about where to park it and stuff."

"If I owned such a car, such a valuable and attractive car, I'd have an anti-theft GPS tracking device installed."

Mickey perked up. "You're right. I would, too."

"Molton, get the Chancellor of UCLA on the phone. We have to track that car."

CHAPTER 68

When Christina's eyes flicked open, dark, foresty shadows filled her vision. Judging by the absence of any sign of dawn, her nap had been brief. The fire had burned low into a pile of glowing embers which radiated heat but little light. A faint smell of pot smoke lingered in the air. A breeze blew through the illicit drug farm, and the leaves of the cannabis plants made a gentle swishing sound. Periodic gusts stoked the campfire's embers to whiter intensity, which then faded. She watched nervously as one gust stirred bits of red-hot dust into the tinder-dry forest. Without moving, she listened for the guard.

Silence reigned. Cautiously, Christina sat up, a task made difficult by the binding of her hands. The twine had not been tied cruelly tight, but it was thin and coarse and was gradually wearing raw the skin underneath. Her shoulders ached from being held at such an awkward angle.

The guard was seated, leaning against a tree about ten yards away. The butt of a joint dangled from his outstretched hand, knuckles resting on the ground. She watched the regular rise and fall of his chest. He was asleep.

They're all asleep. This is my chance.

Chance for what? With her hands tied but legs free, Christina could slip away now and hope to find the road. But that would leave the two things that mattered most in the hands of the drug gang: the specimen box, and River. Unacceptable.

She glanced at the guard, trying to remember if he was the same one on duty when she drifted off. If he was, then the hour might be approaching for a shift change, and whatever she was going to do, she had to do it soon. The sleeping man was one of the scrawny brothers; she couldn't remember which. He snorted and shifted position. She dropped to the ground and faked sleep, but he did not wake.

If she could get her hands free, she'd have more options. With the full use of her arms, she could support River, sprained ankle and all, and the two of them could flee together. It would have to be without the *E. coli* or Chen's antibiotic producers . . . well, that was one possibility.

She scanned the vicinity for a sharp-edged rock or bit of metal to cut the twine that bound her wrists. Nothing was in view, but it was dark. Again she struggled to her feet and crept into the shadows, moving away from the tent where the gang was sleeping. Still she found nothing suitable; any tools the men possessed must be somewhere else, and the area had been cleared of rocks. She returned to the fire. The men had formed a ring around their fireplace using stones about the size of her fist. Most were worn smooth. Christina found one that had a broken edge. Though it certainly wasn't sharp, it was the only thing available.

Plucking the stone away from the fire, she laid it on the ground behind her back and tried to orient the broken edge facing up, adjusting it and then twisting around to check it. The rock didn't cooperate. No matter what she did, the rock tipped over so that the broken edge was down in the dirt. In that position, she couldn't use it as a blade.

She took a few deep breaths to restore her calm and quiet the noise of her panting. Then she picked up the rock with her right hand and tried to use the edge to saw through the twine.

After a minute of pressing as hard as she could, her right wrist cramped up and her left wrist was painfully scratched. The twine was unaffected.

This isn't going to work. What else?

Lacking a tool to cut the twine, and powerless to loosen the knot, what could she do?

Her gaze was drawn to the orange-red glow of the coals. *Fire.*

She could burn the cord.

Dry twigs littered the area. As she selected one to use as a match, she fervently hoped the twine was made of a natural fiber that would ignite easily. If it was synthetic, the heat would melt it to her skin.

Lighting the match wasn't a problem, but how was she going to apply the flame to the twine? She needed another pair of hands.

Christina barely breathed into her cousin's ear while she touched her hip.

"River."

River's eyes popped open, and thank God, she didn't make a sound. *If the guard is sleeping as lightly as she was . . .*

Not daring to speak, Christina silently performed a charade to illustrate her plan. River nodded, her face pinched with concern. They both knew what had to happen for this to work.

River took the stick in her hands and backed it into the dying fire. The tip of the desiccated wood ignited at once. Then she sat holding the match in her bound hands behind her, bracing it against the ground to immobilize the flame.

Christina closed her eyes and willed herself into a state of calm. If she cried out, all was lost. Craning her neck as far as she could, she could see the burning tip of the stick. She backed toward her cousin, pushing up her sleeves and extending her arms away from her body. She did not want to set her clothes on fire.

After one more deep exhalation, she reached for the flame. Heat triggered every nerve in her hand, and a primitive withdrawal reflex engaged before her conscious brain even noticed anything was amiss. Her arms jerked away clumsily, knocking the stick out of River's grasp.

An unvoiced puff of air escaped her lips. Her eyes darted to the guard; he didn't react. She knew she had to do better. Once the twine ignited, there would be pain. By force of will and concentration, she had to hold her arms still and make no sound. She repeated her breathing exercise.

River retrieved the stick and once it was burning brightly, she resumed her position with her back to her cousin and the match anchored to the ground.

At least she doesn't have to watch.

273

Again Christina reached for the flame. This time, she came at it from above, lowering her hands slowly, feeling where the heat was most intense, and adjusting her position. When the match flame felt centered on the twine between her wrists, she mustered her courage and self-control. She gritted her teeth, tensed her arms—and plunged her wrists into the fire.

Pain exploded in her hands but she resisted the reflex to pull away. Her eyes squeezed shut and tears leaked out, and she unwittingly held her breath as the fire seared her wrists. For several seconds she endured, then with a too-loud gasp pulled away and looked behind her.

Her hands were on fire.

Every natural impulse told her to smother the flames, to roll in the dirt. Somehow her conscious effort triumphed over instinct, and instead of putting out the fire she waved her arms to fan it. All the while, she tugged and twisted to break the twine.

River had turned and was watching, horrified and helpless. The seconds passed, and with every neuron in her brain screaming *stop!* Christina finally threw herself to the ground to frantically snuff out the burning twine. She rubbed and writhed on her back, wanting the torment to stop. Suddenly, her hands were free.

She scratched off the blackened remnants of the twine and looked at her hands. The fire was out, but the scalding pain continued unabated. Her fingertips were red and stinging—first-degree burns. The palms and wrists were worse, ragged and scorched with the lines of the twine, and encrusted with dust and ash.

Christina stared open-mouthed with shock at the sight of her own injuries, but River kept her wits and bumped Christina's hip to bring her back to reality. She looked up slowly and found her cousin's face against hers, an expression of alarm and warning written there. River jerked her head to point at something.

As awareness returned to her, Christina expected to see the guard bearing down on them with his gun drawn. But that was not what River was warning her about.

Fire!

CHAPTER 69

"You were right," Molton said triumphantly as he burst into the mayor's office. "The X-car has an anti-theft device."

"You have the car's location?" Ramirez said, jumping to his feet.

"Not yet. UCLA didn't install a live GPS tracking system so we can't call up the current location automatically. But they did put in a LoJack unit."

"Which means what?"

"We asked the state police to activate the car's device. Wherever that car is, it should now be emitting a signal."

"A signal. How does that help?"

"LAPD cars and helicopters are equipped with tracking computers to detect the signal. We just have to send somebody out to find it."

Even as Molton spoke, his face fell, and Ramirez dropped into his chair again.

"My friend, LAPD is having a small problem with its cars and helicopters."

"But by chance they might have a car in the right place. I've ordered them to check the tracking computers in every squad car in that part of town, even if the squad car is stalled."

Ramirez nodded and spun circles in his rotating chair. So close, he thought. The girl has a cell phone, but she won't turn it on. The car has LoJack, but LAPD can't track it down. He felt he might explode from sheer frustration.

"We don't have time for this. Once we find the car, and the cure, the scientists still have to do their thing. Who knows how long that'll take? The San Andreas could pop at any time."

Ramirez drummed his fingertips together. *Grace under fire.* That's what they tried to teach him in the Army. But he was a slow learner, and the last time the pressure got this high—over the desert sand—his performance was anything but graceful. Had the intervening years been long enough to learn the lesson?

He walked to the window and gazed at the deceptively placid night scene. City lights stretched in cornstalk rows in every direction. In observance of the curfew, the sidewalks were empty, and of course nothing moved on the streets.

My city, he thought. My city of angels. Despite all your warts, I love you.

"I'm going to find that car," Ramirez said, spinning away from the view.

"Excuse me?" Molton said.

"All aircraft were grounded because of the petroplague. Because they might be contaminated and crash or carry the bugs farther afield," he said with a gleam in his eye. "But that doesn't mean those birds can't fly."

"Are you suggesting—"

"LAPD's heliport is only a few blocks from here. I'm willing to bet at least one of their whirlybirds has a fuel tank that was filled before the outbreak. We'll use it to track the car's signal and fly that cure right to the university."

"Felipe, you can't be sure any fuel is safe. And even so, the military is under orders to shoot down any aircraft trying to leave the city."

"I'm not leaving the city."

"They won't believe you."

He stacked some loose papers on his desk and reached into a drawer for his sunglasses. "I'll take that chance."

"You're going to fly a helicopter?"

"The LAPD pilots have all been reassigned to food transports. Who else are we going to get right now?"

"It's been a long time since you flew," Molton said doubtfully.

"Once a pilot, always a pilot. Besides, I hear the new ones pretty much fly themselves."

CHAPTER 70

The San Gabriel Mountains were tinder-dry, and in the midst of their pyromaniacal exertions Christina and River had ignited some forest debris. A breeze blew light and steady through the grove, and already the hungry flames were marching downwind, devouring leaves and sticks and acorns. A spark drifted to a pile of pruned cannabis waste. The pile lit swiftly and poured marijuana-scented smoke into the air.

As the fire grew, so did the cracking and snapping of its flames. Christina grabbed River's arm and dragged her toward the trees upwind of the blaze. Unwillingly she cried out in pain when she tried to support River's injured side. To protect her hands, she thrust her arm under River's and lifted with her whole body instead of just her hands.

The commotion awakened the guard. He leaped to his feet and shouted. Christina expected to hear pursuit, even shots in their direction, but the man ran the opposite way. She glanced back and saw the fire crawling up a manzanita shrub adjacent to the tent, each newly ignited leaf flaring like a flashbulb as it burned and went out. He's going to save his buddies, she thought. Perversely, she was relieved to know they wouldn't be killed in their sleep.

"Let go!" River said.

They were secluded under the cover of darkness in the trees, and Christina noticed at last that River wasn't hopping on one leg.

"I'm fine," River said, gently extricating herself from her cousin's supportive arm.

"Your ankle?"

"I faked it," River said, grinning a little. "Thought it might be useful for them to think I was crippled."

"Damn it, River! If I had known you could walk on your own I wouldn't have fried my hands so I could help you."

The grin vanished. "Oh, Chrissy, I'm sorry. I assumed you had some plan to try to get the box back."

Ah, the box!

The flames were spreading with alarming speed. Shouts rang from the tent as sparks rained down on its canvas roof and the fabric began to smolder.

"You weren't going to leave without the cure, were you?"

"I was, to save you," she said. "How could I run away, if you couldn't follow?"

River's eyes glistened. "We can run together, but we can't leave it here to be destroyed."

Teardrop and his two henchmen emerged from the tent, hollering obscenities. They carried their guns and what looked like bottles. Christina didn't see the distinctive white and orange box in their hands. The roof of the tent ignited.

"Turn around," Christina ordered. She went to work on the knot securing River's wrists. The touch of the rough twine on her singed fingers burned, but she ignored it and struggled to untie the string. It was odd how the worst burns on her wrists, the areas that made her feel faint to look at, hurt the least.

In the distance, the drug gang fanned out away from the tent.

"Got it," she declared, and River wriggled her hands out of the bonds. The twine fell to the ground.

"They're out of the tent," Christina said. "If Teardrop left the tubes in the Styrofoam, they should be okay for a few minutes yet."

As if to hasten her decision, flames now licked the tent's walls.

"I'll go get the box. You stay here."

She didn't wait for an answer but scurried off toward the tent, taking care to stay several yards back from the clearing.

Smoke stung her eyes as she approached the fire, which was spilling over the ground like floodwater from a broken dam. Automatically she raised a hand to rub her eyes but cringed when she remembered her tattered palms.

She tracked Skinny Bad Guy #1, the guard who fell asleep on the job, moving into the cannabis field with his brother #2. Bad Guy #3, who'd rushed out of the tent in his underwear, had raced off in what she thought was the direction of the truck trail.

Unfortunately, she had no idea where Teardrop was.

The thickening smoke made her cough, and she dropped to her knees to escape some of it. She wasn't worried about being heard; the noise of the fire was loud enough to muffle the sound of her movement. The light cast by the flames was a bigger problem. Crawling was her best bet, but she couldn't use her hands and had to waddle as low to the ground as her legs could manage.

The tent stood only seconds away from her. It was thoroughly on fire now. Christina identified the side with the entrance flap. The entrance was tall, a walk in-walk out design, and she prayed it wasn't zipped. She was marshaling her courage to dash into the burning structure when she saw Teardrop coming her way.

He jogged toward the tent with one hand on his rifle and the other carrying a satchel or money bag of some kind. He didn't appear to see her yet.

Shit. As soon as she made her move into the clearing, he would see her. The thick Styrofoam was a good insulator but it wouldn't protect the samples forever. If she didn't get that box out of the tent soon, Dr. Chen's cure for the petroplague and the fuel-making *E. coli* would be lost.

As Teardrop approached, a flaming limb dropped from a tree and narrowly missed him. He hesitated, perhaps wondering if whatever he sought from the tent was worth the risk. Then a loud noise—like a woman screaming—drew his attention. He took off at a run in the direction of the sound, which happened to be away from the fire—and the tent.

Last chance, Christina thought. She grabbed a stick and dashed for the entrance flap.

Out in the open the smoke was somewhat thinner, and in the brilliant light of the burning canvas, she could see well. Using the stick, she pried open the flap as wide as it would go. Then, holding her breath and steeling herself to the heat, she ducked inside.

Fire. Inside the tent was an inferno. The exposed skin on her face howled in protest at the heat. Flames rolled up the walls

279

like waterfalls in reverse. Her eyes burned, she wanted to close them. But she had to find the box.

Two sets of bunk bed cots defined the small space. Wool Army blankets lay rumpled on the beds. Christina snatched one and wrapped it around her head and face for protection, searching desperately for the white and orange box. She found it in an untidy pile of snack packages and beer cans, not yet aflame. Seconds later, using her covered head as a battering ram, she burst out of the tent into the relative coolness of the burning forest.

With the precious package in her arms, she was running toward where she'd left River when she remembered the scream. A woman's scream. It now dawned on her that the scream had come from this direction.

"River!"

Where was she? Where was Teardrop?

Frantically plunging through the semi-darkness, Christina literally collided with the answer. The box was knocked from her hands and she squealed in pain, then delight, when she recognized her cousin.

"River—" she began.

"Shut up and run," River said, grabbing the box and sprinting into the trees.

Christina ran. She didn't know where they were going or what was happening behind them, but she followed River without question. The crack of gunshots rang out over the din of the fire, and she heard a man yell, "Puta!"

River led her at top speed with no sign of a limp. A tree trunk splintered as they passed: a bullet had torn into the wood. He's close, Christina thought. Additional shots followed. River led them closer to the forest fire, aiming straight for a wall of flames. *What the hell is she doing?*

The temperature increased and Christina wanted to stop, to turn, but River kept going. They both coughed from the smoke; Christina covered her nose and mouth with the blanket. Just a few yards from the flames, River paused, looking for something. She found it, and plunged through a gap where it was safe—barely—to pass through. More gunshots chased them, but now hidden from Teardrop by the blaze, River changed direction.

Unexpectedly, the box tumbled from River's grasp. Christina, only two steps behind, picked it up, and they ran side by side into the wilderness. Whenever an obstacle appeared, like a brush thicket, a boulder, or a small hill, they detoured to put it between them and the route back to the pot farm. Gradually, the fire receded behind them and the air cleared. Christina no longer heard shots or sounds of pursuit. But the young women ran and ran, slackening their pace as they grew tired and the fear which propelled them diminished.

Her muscles were starved for oxygen. Christina had to slow to a walk.

"I think we're in the clear," she said, panting. "God, my hands hurt."

She went to give the box to her cousin to carry, when in the dim light she noticed that River was clutching her left arm to her chest.

"Are you okay?"

River sank to the ground, shaking her head no. Frightened, Christina came around and saw blood dripping from the fingers of River's right hand, which was pressed against the left arm, covering something.

"What is it?" Christina said. "Show me."

Gently, Christina peeled back the protective hand with her own gory mess of a mitt. Muscle and bone poked from River's torn sleeve, soaked in a pulsing stream of arterial blood. She'd been shot.

CHAPTER 71

"I'll alert the military and try to convince them to leave you alone," Molton said to the mayor. "Just stay on this side of the mountains, inside the first containment ring."

"That's my plan."

Mickey spoke up. "Your Honor, let me go with you."

"This isn't a joy ride," Ramirez said. "The fuel situation is dodgy."

"I know. But you need me. River and Christina are running from the cops. If you hunt them down with a police helicopter, they're going to hide. I can reassure them it's okay."

Ramirez didn't like bringing a civilian, but the kid had a point.

"The commander is here," Molton said.

"All right, Mickey, you're with me," Ramirez said, and they left City Hall together.

A police commander accompanied them to the heliport. Mickey trotted behind the two senior officials as they jogged the one mile from City Hall to LAPD's downtown Hooper Heliport, the world's largest rooftop helipad.

"Breaking my own curfew. How about that?" Ramirez said as the moon shone down on the deserted street.

"I'll issue a citation when you come back," said the commander.

Two workers—the only two left—met them at the police department's Air Support Division facility.

"We need a chopper that hasn't flown since before the outbreak began," Ramirez said.

"One of our Aerospatiale ASTARs fits the bill."

"Take me to her."

A sliver of dawn light was perceptible in the eastern sky as Ramirez strode across the concrete roof toward his craft. She was beautiful, looked to be brand-new with a killer black-and-white paint job. "LAPD" and "To protect and to serve" were emblazoned on her side. He choked up as he touched her nose.

"Can you handle it, sir?" the commander asked.

"I flew Apaches with the 82nd Airborne. I can handle this sweet little girl."

"Let me orient you," the air support technician said.

Ramirez climbed into the pilot's seat and powered up the controls. Digital panels and LCD screens covered the interior like wallpaper, except for the expansive clear windows that provided excellent visibility.

"This isn't a helicopter, it's a video game," he said when he looked around the cockpit. Upon closer inspection, he realized that the basics hadn't changed. He could fly it.

The technician pointed out the key readouts and control interfaces.

"Fuel tank reads full," Ramirez noted.

"That's a good sign," the tech said. "We noticed that several of the choppers lost fuel just sitting here. We figured that was proof of contamination."

"Agreed. I'll assume this thing can fly and only worry about not getting shot down."

Grace under fire. He fought back the sense of urgency, the desire to set the blades spinning at once. With forced calm, he familiarized himself with the aircraft. Minutes ticked by. Mickey, standing on the concrete, cleared his throat. Ramirez looked up.

"You ever been in a helicopter before?"

"No."

"Then get in, but don't touch anything."

He waved his thumb at the copilot's door, and Mickey dashed to the other side of the aircraft. Mickey struggled with the door's latch; Ramirez let him in.

"On second thought, I want you to run the tracking computer," Ramirez said. "Find your friends' car. I need to focus on flying."

"Have you flown a lot?" Mickey asked, his anxiety trumping politeness.

"Used to, but I'll tell you, the last time I flew one of these babies, I ate Arabian desert sand for lunch."

"You crashed?"

"Like Dumbo with his ears pinned back."

The tech introduced Mickey to the LoJack system while Ramirez finished his preparations.

"Do you know where you're going?" the commander asked Ramirez.

"San Fernando and the two-ten. Last known location of the missing vehicle. Ready, Mickey?"

"I'm ready," Mickey replied, fastening his seat belt.

The technician freed the helicopter from its restraints and stepped clear, giving Ramirez a thumbs-up. The rotor began to turn, swaying the cockpit and filling the occupants' ears with noise.

"Put this on," Ramirez said, handing Mickey a helmet with ear protection and a communicator. "Here we go."

The helicopter lifted off and hovered a few feet above the rooftop. Ramirez nudged it forward—or so he thought—but the aircraft bucked. His passenger looked at him in alarm.

"Ever switch from a clutch to an automatic?" Ramirez said.

"Yeah."

"Just getting used to how she reacts," he explained. Molton was right, it had been a long time, but familiar patterns and sensations were coming alive in his brain after years of disuse. The rush of memory made Ramirez feel almost super-human, as if he were downloading data like a computer. He steered the chopper away from the heliport.

"Looks like we've got fuel," he said. "In case Molton can't convince the enforcers to leave us alone, the plan is to fly close to the ground to avoid detection. As a bonus, that might help us if the engines fail."

They were only ten miles from their destination. With the unfamiliar controls, Ramirez didn't dare spare any of his attention scanning the ground but when they reached Sylmar, he noticed early morning sun glinting off floodwaters from the Pacoima Reservoir.

"I've got a signal," Mickey announced, bouncing excitedly in his seat. "That way, toward the mountains."

"Roger."

The signal transmitting from the X-car drew them north of the two-ten to the edge of the city. Ramirez held the chopper motionless about ten feet over a lake that yesterday was a park. The wind from the spinning blades stirred the water and filled the air with spray.

"Looks like they were trapped by the flood and headed up into the mountains," he said, pointing to a road that cut into a narrow canyon in the wall of the San Gabriel range.

"LoJack agrees," Mickey said.

Ramirez hesitated. It was one thing to test his rusty reflexes piloting over the wide, flat San Fernando Valley. It was something else entirely to take this unfamiliar aircraft into the dangerous and unpredictable air currents of the mountains. And this was the border of the first containment ring. Once they crossed it, they'd be forced to stay low to avoid getting blasted out of the sky.

He'd have to fly the canyon.

"No choice," Ramirez said. Slowly, he took them in.

Chapter 72

Oh god oh god oh god spun uselessly through Christina's mind. She stepped back, her stomach heaving at the sight of the mangled arm. River re-covered the wound with her hand and wobbled woozily. Christina clutched her shoulders and lowered her to the ground. A trace of dawn light illuminated River's face. It was ghostly pale.

Christina ignored the pain from own burns and struggled to think. Get a grip, she told herself. First aid. What do they tell you about first aid?

Though she didn't have any medical experience, Christina possessed enough common sense to know the immediate threat was blood loss. It sure as hell looked like River was losing a lot of blood. She couldn't use direct pressure on a wound like that. A tourniquet was the only way to stop the bleeding.

Neither of them wore a belt; that would've been too easy, Christina thought bitterly. A strap from one of their backpacks would've worked nicely, but of course that wasn't an option either. She was still carrying the wool blanket she'd taken from the burning tent. If she could tear off a strip of the fabric . . .

Fat chance. The blanket was as strong as steel. She wasted a minute searching the area for a cutting tool, either natural or something cast off by humans. It was hopeless.

What else can I use?

Christina's heart skipped a beat when she had an idea. *It's not perfect but it might work.* She stripped off her fleece top and removed her bra. Quickly, she put her shirt back on to keep warm, and wrapped the band of her bra around River's arm just below the shoulder. Around and around she tugged it so tightly she was afraid it would break. River gasped but nodded to encourage Christina to continue. Then Christina locked the undergarment in place with the hook-and-eye closures on the band.

"Better than nothing," she said.

River lay on the ground, whimpering. Christina stood next to her, trying to come up with plan. The situation was bleak and she grunted in frustration.

"All my life, I carry a freaking cell phone," she said. "Now when I really need one, I haven't got one."

"I do," River said.

"What? Wasn't it in your backpack?"

"No. I took out the battery and didn't want to have to dig for it. Kept the battery and the handset in my pocket."

"I thought they searched your pockets."

River smiled wanly. "I have a lot of pockets."

Christina ran her hands down River's leg. In typical style, River was wearing a pair of designer hiking pants by Mountain Hardwear. The pants had a variety of cleverly placed pockets, including some below the knee. There, Christina felt the shape of a slender handset and small battery.

"I guess they were only interested in your ass," Christina quipped as she reassembled the cell phone. She paused before turning it on.

They needed help, that much was certain. They were hopelessly lost, had no supplies or maps, and were crippled with potentially life-threatening injuries. They'd never get out of the wilderness on their own. The petroplague seemed like a vague annoyance, someone else's problem, compared to the immediacy of what they were facing here and now.

But with one call, all that would change. Christina faced a murder charge, and by failing in her quest to develop Chen's antibiotic, she also failed to clear her name. As far as the authorities were concerned, she started the petroplague; she killed Robert Chen; she destroyed Bactofuels' research; and she was fleeing with the city's last hopes for scientific salvation.

River must have noticed her hesitation.

"You should go on without me," River said. "I'll keep the phone. Someone will come."

"No," Christina said. "It's over for both of us. I'm hurt, and we're lost." She looked at the Styrofoam box, its whiteness easily visible against the dark ground. "We'll surrender the specimens. Maybe someone will believe me and do the work in time."

She touched the phone and the screen came to life. Christina squinted at its brightness; though dawn was breaking, the forest was still quite dark.

No signal.

Why this surprised her, she couldn't say. Maybe the feeling wasn't really surprise. Maybe it was shock, anger, desperation.

"No signal, right?" River said when Christina sat there like a stone. "Figures."

Christina swallowed hard. "Probably doesn't make any difference," she said unconvincingly. "With the petroplague, how would they get someone here to rescue us anyway?"

She draped the blanket over River and tucked in the edges under her body. Then she sat down to think. The sun peeked over the horizon.

"I pulled a Darzee back there," River said.

"What?"

"Remember, from Rikki-Tikki-Tavi? The tailorbird's wife pretends she's got a broken wing to lure the cobra away from the nest."

Christina remembered the scream, back at the pot farm.

"Teardrop was heading for the tent," Christina said. "You saw him, and drew him away so I could get the box."

"Uh-huh."

"Thanks," Christina said, looking at the box purchased at so great a price. It was worthless to them now.

She was betting that Teardrop and his pals wouldn't bother hunting them down. The drug thugs had already stolen the women's valuables, and the wildfire on their farm ought to keep them busy. On top of that, the Angeles National Forest was vast. The cousins would be hard to find.

Hard for rescuers, too, Christina thought. We can't stay here.

"I'm thirsty," River said, but they had nothing to drink. She coughed, and then Christina noticed an irritating smell tickling her nose.

Smoke.

She stood up and peered into the forest. Heavy smoke was rising from the trees in the direction from which they'd come, accompanied by a dull orange glow that mirrored the sunrise in the east.

"The fire's coming this way," she said.

The breeze was carrying smoke toward them; the flames would follow the same path as the wind. Christina knew that wildfires in Southern California could move with astonishing speed. To be safe, they needed to get out of its way.

But where?

We should travel perpendicular to the wind and look for a clearing. Or better yet, higher ground. We might get a cell phone signal there.

"River, we have to move."

"I'm cold."

"Walking will help. I'll wrap the blanket around you."

She helped lift River to her feet.

"I feel dizzy," River said.

"I'll hold you," Christina promised.

But her poor abused hands weren't up to the task. Any movement or touch to fingers or wrists was excruciating, and she had no strength in her grip. She tried laying River's good arm over her shoulders, but River was supporting her injured arm and refused to let go.

So Christina picked up the box—*damned box*—and coaxed River to walk. River managed for a minute or two on her own. Then she swayed and sat down.

"I'm thirsty."

"I know, honey, but we have to keep going."

Christina tugged at River's good arm and gently pleaded with her, but it was no use. River lay back and closed her eyes.

That's it, Christina thought. It's up to me.

Chapter 73

With white knuckles, Ramirez squeezed the helicopter controls. His whole body was alert to shifts or sounds that might indicate a sudden change in the air pressure outside.

"Still locked on that signal, Mickey?"

"I've got it. The car is up this road somewhere," Mickey replied. He checked the computer. "That's funny. It hasn't moved at all."

"They're not moving?"

"No."

Ramirez digested this information. If their quarry had set off on foot, their job was going to get a lot harder.

"Let's hope the cure is still with the car," he said.

The helicopter followed the truck trail up, climbing steadily to match the elevation gain of the road. He took it easy, avoiding any sudden moves. Unfortunately, as the trail plunged deeper into the wilderness, the canyon narrowed.

"It's too damn dark in here," he said. He could see dawn light above, but it wasn't penetrating the canyon. "Should've asked that guy to show you how to use the searchlight."

He reduced their forward speed even more. "If it gets any tighter, we'll have to surface."

"The X-car is just ahead," Mickey said, taking his eyes off the computer and peering outside for a glimpse of the familiar lime green vehicle.

Suddenly the road made a sharp turn.

"Hang on!" Ramirez exclaimed.

The helicopter banked steeply; only the restraints kept the men from tumbling out of their seats. He heard the screech of the landing gear as it scraped the dusty rock wall of the canyon.

"That was close," Ramirez said. Beads of nervous sweat formed on his brow but he refused to spare a hand wiping it.

"There!" Mickey said, pointing.

The experimental car sat on the road just past the hairpin turn, a pile of rubble blocking its way forward. The car and surroundings were dark and lifeless.

"I think I have enough room to set down."

The helicopter landed with the lightest thump. Mickey gave the pilot an approving grin.

"Check it out," Ramirez said. He helped Mickey escape his seat belt harness. "Keep your head down."

Mickey lowered himself from the helicopter and ran to the car. Ramirez watched him circle around the outrageously colored vehicle. Mickey knelt down and examined something under the car; then he opened the doors and crawled inside. The tiny automobile rocked as he rooted through the front and back seat areas.

"Come on, be there," Ramirez said.

The youth emerged from the car shaking his head. The noise in the cockpit rose a few dozen decibels when Mickey opened the co-pilot's door and climbed back in.

"They're gone," Mickey said. "Looks like the car broke down and they kept going on foot."

"Chen's cure for the petroplague?"

"They must've taken it with them. The car's empty. They had a couple of backpacks, too, and they're gone."

"Shit," Ramirez said.

"Maybe we'll spot them up ahead," Mickey said. "I can't imagine they'd leave the road."

"We'll have to try."

He launched the helicopter into the air. It skipped effortlessly over the rock pile that had put an end to the wheeled vehicle's journey.

"You think they'll hide from us?" he asked.

"I don't know," Mickey replied. "I sure hope not. We'll have a hard enough time seeing them in the open."

But they both knew it was possible. Mickey had failed to make contact since he parted from the girls. As far as Christina and River knew, they were wanted women.

And of course they were completely ignorant of Neil's countdown to global disaster.

Ramirez blinked to clear his vision, then realized that a thin veil of smoke was draped around them. As they proceeded up the canyon, the veil thickened.

"There's a fire somewhere," he said. "Just what we need."

Within minutes, visibility became too poor to continue in the narrow confines of the canyon walls. They had seen no trace of Christina and River. Ramirez found a place to set down. The chopper blades churned through the smoke, producing chaotic patterns. He fought back a memory of similar patterns in black smoke mixed with light-colored sand, illuminated by exploding ordnance.

"I doubt they got any farther than this," Ramirez said. "I bet the smoke forced them off-road."

"Yeah. Into the wilderness."

CHAPTER 74

"I'm going to get help," Christina said. "You stay here."

"Right," River replied sleepily.

Using her feet, Christina tried to sweep the area around River clear of flammable forest debris. She realized it wouldn't make any difference if the fire raged through, but maybe it would provide some protection from a smaller blaze.

"I'm heading for that rise over there," she said, pointing toward an area uphill that looked clear on top. Apologetically she added, "I'll have to take the phone."

"Yeah."

With the sun up, Christina was able to establish a sense of direction. *North, I'm heading north.* She was terrified that she might not be able to find her cousin again and decided to leave a trail. As she walked, she picked up every rock she could find, and left them in small piles or stacked as cairns, always starting the next one in sight of the previous. Her progress was slow, and her hands hurt. Often instead of picking up a rock, she shuffled it with her feet like a soccer ball. But as a result of her work, she was confident she'd be able to find her way back.

The temperature rose with the sun. The warmth would be good for River, though it would hasten the risk of dehydration for both of them. The trees and shrubs were getting thinner; she could move much further before needing to build another cairn. As she gritted her teeth and took another stone in hand, Christina gasped in surprise and dropped the rock.

The cell phone was ringing. It was Mickey.

"Mickey!" she shrieked, then sobbed. She babbled into the handset like a crazy thing, panicked words and bits of stories spilling out.

"It's okay, Chrissy. It's okay. We're coming," he said, his voice barely discernable over background noise as loud as a nightclub at midnight. "We have a lock on your location from the cell phone. River's phone was being monitored, and as soon as you wandered into a covered area, we were alerted."

"We? Are you with the police?"

"Not exactly. But don't worry, they're on your side now. Do you still have Dr. Chen's stuff?"

"Yes."

"Thank God," Mickey said. Christina heard him repeat this news to someone, eliciting an ecstatic whoop. "We need it, like, yesterday. I'll tell you all about it in person in about a minute."

"What? How?" Christina said. Then she heard the rhythmic beating noise of a helicopter approaching.

"I see you," Mickey said. "We're going to land a little farther ahead, the pilot sees a spot where there's more room. Follow us."

Dizzy from, well, everything, Christina stumbled forward, keeping the chopper in view. Excited as she was, she didn't forget the most important thing: she paused to erect one more cairn.

The sound of the helicopter dropped in pitch and volume as the aircraft landed. Mickey leaped out of the passenger's side. Tears flowing, Christina ran to him and nearly fell at his feet. He rubbed her head with a soothing touch.

The pilot stepped out a moment later and removed his helmet. Christina saw the man and did a double-take.

"Mr. Mayor," she said, surprised and disproportionately pleased to see him.

"At your service, Miss González," he said, a fleeting smile crossing his face. He pointed at the box with orange biohazard symbols. "Is that Robert Chen's cure for the petroplague?"

"Such as it is," Christina said, handing it to him. Both Ramirez and Mickey gasped when they saw her hands.

"Chrissy, what the hell happened? Where's River?"

"I had to leave her behind. She's been shot."

"Shot? How? By whom?" Mickey said, balling his fists.

"No time to explain. We have to go get her now."

"Is it far?" Ramirez asked.

"About a mile and half, I'd say."

Ramirez looked at the smoke. The fire was moving fast.

"Better get a move on if we're going to beat those flames."

"Follow me," Christina said.

Mickey dug a tarp out of the emergency supplies box in the helicopter, and they raced toward the first cairn.

CHAPTER 75

The smoke thickened as they retraced Christina's steps back to River.

"The fire's coming this way. Hurry," Christina said, though in truth she was the one slowing them down. "It's not much farther."

Her prudent effort to leave a trail made all the difference. As she guided the men into the forest, she knew she'd never have found her way without the rocks.

Mickey and Ramirez covered their faces with their shirts to filter out some of the smoke. To do the same for herself was too painful on her hands, so she tried to take shallow breaths only through her nose. The forest was no longer quiet, but rumbled with the dull roar of fire.

"There!"

River's supine form came into view. Mickey sprinted to her, stirring up a thin layer of ash that covered the ground. An occasional glowing ember drifted through the air, threatening to ignite a parched shrub or dried-up leaf. The fire was definitely getting close.

Ramirez spread the tarp on the ground, then helped Mickey lift River onto it. They each grabbed two corners and hoisted the fabric over their shoulders. Christina didn't have to push herself as hard on the return trip; lugging River made it slow going. She tried to speak to her cousin, but River was hidden in the low-hanging tarp hammock and didn't respond.

The wildfire sprinted in their direction. Small pockets of flames appeared in the tree canopy, as well as here and there on the ground. Mickey and Ramirez grunted and coughed as they struggled to carry their burden with greater speed.

By the time they reached the clearing where the helicopter waited, the air was hot and crackling with the sound of burning wood. Christina's fingers stung from the heat. She couldn't help at all as Mickey and Ramirez loaded River into the passenger compartment.

When they finished, she put her elbows on the floor to drag herself into the helicopter. But Ramirez gently touched her arms to quell her effort; then he jumped down and lifted her in. Mickey fastened her seat belt.

"Mickey, I need you up front," Ramirez said as he closed the hatch.

Within seconds, pilot and assistant were in their seats, and before they even had their helmets and safety restraints secured, Ramirez fired up the engine and got the blades spinning. The helicopter lurched into the air, swirling the smoke like batter in a mixing bowl. Instinctively, Christina grabbed a strap but released it just as quickly when stabs of pain pierced her hand.

"Chrissy?"

River's plea was barely audible over the ear-splitting engine noise in the compartment. Christina struggled with a buckle but freed herself from her seat and sank to the floor. She pulled back the tarp from River's face. River's eyes were open.

"I'm here," she said but dared not stroke her cousin's cheek.

No fresh blood stained the tarp, which meant the tourniquet was working. She wondered how long River's arm could survive without blood, but she couldn't risk releasing the pressure. Rummaging around the chamber for something to drink, she found a bottle of water.

"Drink this," she said, dribbling it into River's mouth. The helicopter jerked and she spilled some on River's face. She found a small towel to wipe the ash from River's eyes and nose.

"Can you take them to a hospital outside of L.A.?" Mickey shouted over the noise in the cockpit.

"Can't break the quarantine," Ramirez said. "We'll be shot down. I'm taking them to UCLA Medical Center. They've been at the top of our priority list for supply shipments since the petroplague began."

Compared to how long it took River and Christina to travel in the opposite direction, the flight back to UCLA felt like teleporting. River groaned when they bumped on landing. The door opened and many hands swiftly transferred her to a stretcher. Christina watched with relief as her cousin was whisked away to surgery.

Ramirez appeared. "Let me help you," he said.

She swung her legs over the edge of the opening in the side of the helicopter. He put his hands on her waist and lifted her down, then dashed to fetch a wheelchair.

"I can walk," she said.

"Mickey, you'll see that she's taken care of?" he said.

"Of course," Mickey said, turning his attention to Christina now that River was gone.

"I'll relieve you of that box, Christina," Ramirez said. "I'll make sure Chen's work goes to people who will finish it right. We'll stop Neil and the Big One."

She gladly surrendered the box. *I'm only a student, with a dead mentor at that. I never wanted the responsibility.*

A glimmer of cheer momentarily broke the tension in Ramirez's face.

"I'll see you again."

The rotor started to turn, whipping a wind on the rooftop. Mickey guided her indoors as the mayor waved and lifted off.

Mickey stayed with her in the ER while her burns were treated. They filled each other in on all that had happened since Mickey tackled Trinley at the lab. She learned about the dual threats hounding them: Neil's plot to spread the plague worldwide, and the rising pressures in the San Andreas fault.

"Wait a sec," she said and sat up straight on the hospital bed. "You're saying the petroplague is in the ground outside the quarantine zone?"

"Yes."

"Then Dr. Chen's antibiotic won't work."

"What do you mean?" Mickey said.

When she and River fled in the X-car, she knew that the petroplague had contaminated the oil underground in the L.A.

basin, and was probably causing the earthquakes. Based on what Trinley told her, she also suspected the bacteria had escaped the quarantine. But she assumed they were in the fuel supply. The truth was much worse.

"The plague bacteria are in the big Kern County oil fields?" she said. "And they're affecting the San Andreas fault?"

"That's what the mayor said."

"Mickey, an antibiotic can't fix that."

"Why not? I thought it was a cure."

"It'll only work as a gasoline or diesel additive. If we put it in the fuel supply, it'll keep *Syntrophus* from growing there. Adding chemicals like this antibiotic to fuel is easy if you do it at the refinery. But you can't treat an underground oil reservoir. Oil fields are huge, and dispersed, and static. You might be able to pump some antibiotic in a pocket here or there, but you can't stir it. The plague bacteria, on the other hand, will multiply and move through the field on their own. They'll occupy every nook and cranny in the rock and eat and eat until all the oil in the field is gone."

Mickey digested this analysis and showed surprising insight. "Even with your antibiotic, the gas pressure on the San Andreas will keep rising."

"And if those crazy survivalists get the plague into more oil fields, Neil's global warming nightmare might come true, antibiotic or no."

"Chrissy, are you telling me that after all we've been through, we're no closer to a solution than before?"

She raised her bandaged wrists and nodded. "We're closer to catastrophe."

Chapter 76

When they finished dressing her burns, Christina checked out of the hospital against medical advice and returned to her lab. Remnants of police tape still hung around the door. She tore them down and with a heavy heart entered the once-welcoming space. There was no one to greet her. Piles of papers and broken equipment were strewn around the site of Mickey's struggle with Trinley. She did her best to clean up without soiling the bandages on her wrists.

While she worked, she thought things over. It was so unfair. Dr. Chen's antibiotic could prevent the plague from releasing greenhouse gases, but only in petroleum already pumped to the surface. The *E. coli* isobutanol could gradually replace petroleum as a transportation fuel, albeit at a high cost. But neither of these two brilliant technical accomplishments could save them from plague-infected oil fields, or from a sudden, nationwide sabotage of the fuel system.

There had to be another way.

What would Dr.Chen do?

In an attempt to channel her mentor's spirit, she went into Chen's office. She sat in his chair, something she'd never done before. His handwritten notes illustrated his unique script, a tidy fusion of Chinese character brush strokes and English block letters. Absently, she flipped through some stacks of journal articles, searching for inspiration. She found his lab book, where he recorded the details of the experiments he'd done on the mutant *Syntrophus* bacteria. Christina read these notes with interest, especially the sections where he summarized his thoughts. The sentences had a warm familiarity about them. As she read, it felt like he was speaking to her. Dr. Chen was gone, but maybe it wasn't so far-fetched to think she could consult him after all.

The lab notebook revealed the work of a meticulous, original thinker. Much of what was written Christina already knew from her collaboration with him. But some of it was new, such as his hypotheses on the natural composition of microbial communities in petroleum reservoirs. Chen speculated that the diversity of life in these extreme environments was far greater than many realized. Every possible niche ought to be filled by some microscopic organism perfectly adapted to the strange underground world in which it lived. Like the surface world, in the underground world there would be competition and evolution, predators and prey, scavengers and decomposers. The bacteria in that world would even be plagued by plagues.

Viruses.

Christina set the notebook down and let her thoughts wander. Dr. Chen believed the oil-eating bacteria had natural predators—viruses that could kill them. What if he was right? Antibiotics were merely chemicals that acted as poisons or growth inhibitors; they had to be manufactured, delivered, replenished. In contrast, viruses were living things—unimaginably small, but alive nevertheless—and when they killed, they reproduced. You didn't have to make them. They made themselves.

Eagerly, she flipped through Dr. Chen's lab book to find any references to viruses that infected *Syntrophus*. To her delight, she learned that he had done some experiments on this subject. She devoured his notes and plunged into some published research papers he referred to.

Three hours later, she burrowed into one of the lab's freezers and found the most precious three hundred microliters on the planet.

CHAPTER 77

The geologists were breathing down Ramirez's neck.

"You told me earthquake prediction isn't precise," Ramirez argued. "Now you're saying you're certain?"

The USGS scientist explained. "Weather forecasting is error-prone, too. But what we're seeing on the San Andreas and several other faults in the area is comparable to tracking a hurricane approach over the Gulf. I can't predict exactly where it will make landfall or how strong it will be, but I predict that a storm will strike. The pressures in the region are utterly unsustainable. Something has to give."

"What are you suggesting?"

"To minimize loss of life, an evacuation may be appropriate."

"Are you fucking kidding? Evacuate L.A.? On foot?"

"The northern parts of the city are at greatest risk," she said. "At the very least, perhaps people could be moved from older structures into new or retrofitted shelters."

"That would be a massive task even under the best circumstances. I doubt my government can handle it. We're immobilized and understaffed. Not to mention underfed."

Molton had a suggestion. "You could announce a voluntary evacuation. Give people a chance to weigh the risks and decide for themselves."

"Totally impractical. Can you imagine the pandemonium? Tens of thousands—or more—homeless people wandering around? Who'll provide security? What will those people drink and eat? And where should they go? We've got earthquake faults in every county."

"South," the geologist said. "Right now the plague gases seem to be concentrated in the north."

"All right, so we tell everybody in the San Fernando Valley to walk to San Diego. Most of them will take one look at the outside temperature and say, forget that. Some will panic and head out unprepared and collapse two miles from home. Then the rest will start looting," Ramirez said. "We need another option."

He drummed his fingers and tried to think creatively.

"Gas buildup is what got us into this situation, right? Is there some way to release the gas? Drill holes or something to bleed off the pressure?"

The geologist reflected on this suggestion. "The drilling process would be dangerous. And slow. Not to mention expensive. But in theory, it could be done. The oil companies have the technology."

Ramirez clapped his hands. "Let's make that theory a reality. Molton, get the CEO of CaliPetro on the phone."

CHAPTER 78

The high-pitched whir of a benchtop microcentrifuge rolled down the frequency scale as the rotor decelerated and finally stopped spinning. Christina looked up from her reading. The machine was programmed to spin for another five minutes; why had it quit?

Its digital readout was dark and the centrifuge refused to start again. She fought frustration. In her quest for a virus that would kill the petroplague, every minute counted. The unbearable time pressure amplified the ordinary aggravations of lab work into torture.

She unplugged the machine and tried a different power outlet. To her relief, that was all it took to solve the problem. Other difficulties she'd encountered in the last two days required more creative solutions. Some, like running out of certain perishable reagents, were impossible to overcome and she had to make do without.

Dr. Chen and all the saints, pray for us.

Less than forty-eight hours to go until Tequila Jack and his allies dispersed the plague. From what Christina had heard, only two suspects had been identified and found. The rest presumably had their contaminated gasoline in hand and were ready to use it.

By ear she could tell the centrifuge had reached its maximum rotational speed and she went back to reviewing protocols. The protocols described step by step how to genetically engineer a virus. That was her goal.

River's ring tone jingled from her phone.

"Need a hand, cousin?" River asked. "I've got one to spare."

"Did the hospital discharge you?" Christina asked.

"Me and every other patient they don't want to feed anymore. Seriously, I'm fine, but if you can walk out the door, they'll give you a shove to speed you along. The staff tried to cover it up, but they're stretched really thin. They're rationing pain meds and serving quarter-size meals. I don't want to know what corners they're cutting behind the scenes."

Twenty minutes later, River and Mickey appeared at the lab. They looked worn-out and hungry, but the three of them shared a moment of joy that they were all together again.

"I'm close," Christina said. "The crude sample that Dr. Chen had in the freezer contained a virus that infects *Syntrophus*, the petroplague bacteria. I've purified the virus."

"Have you told Ramirez?"

Her face felt warm at the mention of the mayor. They had, in fact, been in frequent contact.

"I'm keeping his office informed. The problem is, this virus isn't very good at killing. It gets inside the bacteria and then makes a decision. It can set up camp and quietly hang out inside the cell. Or, it can hijack the bacterium and force it to manufacture hundreds of copies of new virus. When the cell is exhausted and packed full of viruses, it dies and fresh viruses spill out to attack more bacteria. I'm trying to change the DNA of the virus so it can only choose the second option—a lytic cycle, as it's called."

"Is it safe, to make the virus a killer like that?"

"It is. I'm not giving it any new abilities, just taking away its power to choose. Plus, viruses are very finicky about what kind of cell they're willing to infect. This virus will only attack *Syntrophus*."

"Seems I've heard you make assurances like that before," River said.

Christina winced. "We don't have a choice."

CHAPTER 79

Christina bolted awake with dried drool at the corner of her mouth and the impression of a spiral notebook carved into her cheek. She'd fallen asleep, which was easy to understand considering she's allowed herself only naps for the past three days. Dismayed, she found the time: just after 5 AM Pacific Standard Time. It was Tequila Jack's D-Day. A mere four hours remained between the present and the disastrous post-oil future.

The antibiotic wasn't ready, she knew. Ramirez said the groups working on it had elucidated the chemical structure but couldn't produce significant quantities for weeks at least. They needed her virus. They needed it today.

But her virus wasn't ready either.

She hustled about the lab, juggling a half-dozen experiments at once when the beleaguered mayor called. His voice sounded frayed and compared to their other conversations the past few days, his manner was brusque.

"Time's up," Ramirez said. "We've got tremors in Kern County. The geologists say the activity on lesser faults is going to trigger the San Andreas within twenty-four hours if more isn't done to reduce the pressure."

"I thought CaliPetro stuck some holes in the ground to release the gas in the fault. Isn't that working?"

"Gas is spewing out but apparently the plague bacteria are replacing it just as fast. There's a hell of a lot of petroleum under that ground. We're going in with your virus."

"I'm not finished testing it."

"Then consider this your final test," Ramirez said. "I'll meet you at the hospital helipad in an hour."

"But—"

"No buts. I've made the decision. Be there."

He hung up, allowing no argument.

Don't take it personally. He's trying to lead through a terrible crisis.

She woke River and Mickey, who'd been assisting with her work and scavenging for food.

"Ramirez is making a big gamble," she said as she reluctantly prepared vials of virus for transport to Kern County.

"What gamble? Either it works or it doesn't," River said.

"It's not that simple. If I haven't fully flipped the genetic switch, then the virus will infect the plague bacteria but not kill them."

"How does that make us any worse off than we are already?"

"Only one virus particle can infect a cell at a time. *Syntrophus* carrying a dormant virus inside are immune to further infection. Once we treat this oil field, we don't get a second chance."

*   *   *

Christina stood on the helipad and ducked when the Aerospatiale ASTAR landed with Ramirez at the helm. He didn't waste time getting out and waved at her to get in.

"They're reporting engine failures around Bakersfield. The quarantine is officially broken," he said. "On the bright side, that means we won't be shot down when we fly in."

The helicopter lifted into the air and its nose dipped as Ramirez accelerated forward. The city rolled past until they reached the mountains, and the relentless development yielded to wilderness. Out-of-control wildfires pocked the Angeles National Forest; Christina smelled the smoke and wondered if the fire she started was still burning. Her stomach heaved as the flight went on and on, bouncing and weaving over the mountains. She wished Ramirez would say something, but tension rendered them both mute. Their mission would be decided by actions, not words.

Finally, they reached the flat emptiness of the Central Valley and the ride smoothed out. Though the day was young, she could feel it was already getting hot.

"Midway-Sunset oil field is below us," Ramirez said, breaking the long silence. "We'll put down near McKittrick."

Looking down, Christina noticed a column of faint blue color, reaching up from the ground like a spectral pillar. She spotted another flicker of blue a short distance away, then another, and another. As the helicopter flew lower, the blue phantoms quivered like candle fire. After a moment's reflection, she guessed what she was looking at.

"Are those relief wells for the gas?" she said.

"Yes. The CaliPetro crews lit the spouts to prevent explosions. What you see are burning jets of methane originating from the plague bacteria in the oil field."

The methane fires were a rare visible manifestation of the plague's awesome power. To think that something as tiny as her *Syntrophus* bacteria could have such a profound impact on the planet was astonishing.

They flew past the relief wells, and men with heavy equipment. Ramirez landed near the established part of the oil field and released his seat straps. He turned to reach into the back of the helicopter and their eyes met.

"Are you sure about this?" Christina said.

"They say it's better to try and to fail than to never try at all," Ramirez said and touched her cheek. "Have faith."

She blushed. The virus *had* to work.

She climbed out of the helicopter and choked on the hot, dry air. Ramirez had brought the aircraft down on the edge of a densely-packed area of oil wells, power lines, and utility poles that interrupted the monotony of the flat, dusty plain. Steam leaked from the parched ground. The pumpjacks' heads rocked up and down out of synch with each other, creating a confusing visual rhythm that distressed her uneasy stomach. Each pumpjack was enclosed by a rectangle of mesh fence. Pipelines snaked over the ground in an elaborate network connecting wells and cylindrical storage tanks. Clanging, grinding, and whistling noises emanated from equipment near and far.

"USGS gave me the location of a monitored pressure sensor that'll give us real-time information on what's happening down there," Ramirez said. "We'll drop your virus in the well closest to the sensor. But take this. You'll need it."

He then drew a most unlikely item from the helicopter bay and handed it to her: an ordinary household broom. He picked up a second broom for himself, along with a toolbox. As he walked into the oil field, he swept the broom in front of him, keeping the corn bristles just above the dirt.

"What are you doing?"

"They've had problems with hydrogen leaks," he said. "You know more about that than I do."

Of course, Christina thought and remembered Linda and the accident at La Brea. Hydrogen flames are invisible in daylight. The broom was a primitive but effective fire detector. If she or Ramirez approached a burning gas leak, the broom would ignite as a warning.

"A little trick my fire chief suggested. Keep it in front of you at all times."

Toolbox in one hand and broomstick in the other, Ramirez led her into the field, using the GPS in his cell phone to find their target. Christina carried a box with tubes of her virus inside. Mentally, she reviewed her work for errors, recalling the genetic modifications she'd chosen, the experimental design, and the preliminary data. She found no flaw except that the testing was incomplete.

Have faith.

The oil field was an obstacle course. Horizontal pipes as tall as her hips repeatedly blocked their path. At each pipe Ramirez would sweep the opposite side for flames and then offer a hand to help her clamber over.

He paused with his phone in the air, searching for the right pumpjack. "Almost there."

Advancing slowly with brooms extended, they finally reached the location of the USGS underground sensor. The nearest pumpjack was surrounded by a chain-link fence.

"This is it," he said, setting down his broom and unpacking a few tools. He shoved a wrench through the fence and climbed over.

While Ramirez tugged furiously on the wrench, Christina opened the box and imagined the appearance of her tiny viruses, a hundred times smaller than their bacterial prey.

Come on, little guys. Kill, kill, kill.

He grunted and strained until the bolt came loose, then moved to the next bolt and finished a minute later.

"I've got access to the drilling shaft," he said. "Hand me the virus."

No turning back.

He smiled, a smile that was neither arrogant nor fearful, but calm and assured. She passed the vials through the chain-link fence.

His fingers wrestled with the tiny caps. She heard the distinctive pop of an Eppendorf tube opening. Then he poured the contents down the shaft, tapping one tube after another to empty the last drop. The pumpjack's shaft rose and fell, mixing the virus into the subsurface petroleum.

Now we wait. And while they waited, Christina prayed for death, the death of the life form she'd created. If the virus worked, it would multiply underground in the oil reservoir and exterminate the petroplague. Would it avert an earthquake on the nearby San Andreas fault? The next few hours would tell.

His job done, Ramirez scaled the fence and dropped agilely next to her. "My people have direct access to the pressure data," he said as they retraced their steps toward the helicopter. "If the pressure starts to go down, we'll know."

"It may take a while—"

Christina screamed. Her jeans were on fire.

Chapter 80

In the excitement, Christina had forgotten her broom, and like a fool she'd walked straight into a jet of burning hydrogen.

Ramirez shoved her away from the invisible fire and wrestled her to the ground. Heat seared her legs and she felt his weight crushing her as he tried to smother the flames with his body. Through the panic, she mustered the gumption to roll, and the two of them thrashed about like beached fish. Ramirez extricated himself and scooped up handfuls of dust, slapping them on her legs until the fire went out, leaving a mess of charred cotton fabric partially fused to her scorched shins. She realized she was still screaming.

"Christina, look at me," Ramirez said, his hands on the sides of her head. She clung to him and fixed her eyes on his. "Stay calm. I'll call for help," he said.

She shivered. "Don't leave me."

He gathered her in his arms and stumbled out of the maze of pipes and pumpjacks. The background noise of the oil field became a lullaby as Christina's body slipped into shock: the clanging of the pumpjacks; the squeak of rusty gear; the whistle of wind blowing through man-made obstacles on the desolate plain.

Is this how River felt?

Her eyes were closed when Ramirez hoisted her into the helicopter.

*   *   *

Ramirez slammed the cockpit door and readied the helicopter for take-off. The nearest emergency room was in Bakersfield, about thirty-five miles. He could have Christina there in minutes.

It's my fault, he thought as he rushed through his checklist. I should have—

Something was wrong. The fuel gauge said he was low on fuel. *Not true. I should have plenty. Unless . . .*

He remembered what the air support tech had said about the police helicopters losing fuel while just sitting on the platform.

"Shit."

An ambulance would have to do, though it would take a long time to reach the remote oil field. Ramirez called for help.

"I don't care if you're the president or the pope," the dispatcher said. "The plague is in our fleet. We're down to two functioning ambulances in the entire county, and we're not sending either one all the way out there. You'll have to bring her in."

He cursed himself for failing to protect her. She had given all she had. Now he had to do the same.

He scrambled to Christina's side and grasped her hand. It felt cold.

"Trust me," he said as he used any straps he could find to create a makeshift harness around her body. Then he secured himself into the pilot's seat and started the engine.

"Just give me ten minutes, baby," he said to the aircraft. If the petroplague was in his fuel tank, every minute was costing him fuel. A high-speed flight, leaving right now, was their best chance of reaching Bakersfield before the fuel ran out.

The helicopter jerked into the air as he opened the throttle and pressed to maximum velocity. He followed the highway until Bakersfield came into view, and he spotted a large white cross on the roof of a hospital-shaped building. A landing pad. They were going to make it.

Then the telltale odor of vinegar drifted into the cockpit. Ramirez gritted his teeth and prayed. The fuel gauge dipped to zero. Moments later, the helicopter's engine sputtered and died, the intense noise of the cockpit yielding to agonizing silence. The rotor blades kept spinning from their own momentum, and the sound of their whooshing filled his ears as he gripped the controls.

Last time there was smoke.

He let déjà vu guide his hands. Last time, he survived.

"We're going down," he said. "Brace for impact!"

The helicopter skids caught the ground and the world went black.

CHAPTER 81

I never sleep on my back, Christina thought before she opened her eyes.

She was supine in a bed that was too firm, her body pinched under stiff, scratchy white sheets and a cheap polyester blanket. A thin pillow barely cushioned her head. Above, she saw an unfamiliar ceiling, illuminated by sunlight the color of early morning.

"What hap . . . ouch!" she said, quickly abandoning her effort to sit up. Her body hurt most everywhere she had nerves. Then she remembered the hydrogen fire. But why did her head hurt?

She lay still and assessed her injuries. In addition to the burns on her legs, she felt discomfort in her back and neck. Her head was bandaged, and a sling was draped over her shoulder. A broken collarbone? How?

"Good morning, Christina."

Joyfully, she recognized the voice. "Mr. Mayor!"

"Call me Felipe. I think after what I did to you yesterday, you've earned the right."

Yesterday? Had she been unconscious through a day and a night? If so, that meant 4 PM Greenwich Mean Time had come and gone.

"The petroplague—is it out? Did the pressures change? Did they find Neil's contacts?"

"Whoa, one question at a time, please."

She couldn't see him. Her fingers groped for the controls to adjust the bed, and she raised her head to bring him into view.

He sat in a vinyl-covered lounge chair, one leg raised on the footrest and bound in a cast. Rather than a properly mayoral business suit, he wore a hospital gown. His face was a panoply of bruises and stitches, but the expression was clearly one of contentment.

"The virus worked," she said.

He nodded.

She burst into tears. *Hallelujah! Dr. Chen, you were right. Wherever you are, I hope you know you got it right.*

Ramirez leaned as far as he could from the chair, trying to reach her. She stretched her good arm toward his, and their fingertips met. His touch made her fingers tingle.

"The pressure in the oil field showed a slight drop soon after we got the virus in the ground," he said. "Within twelve hours, the flames from the relief wells were at half height. There was a 5.4 quake on the San Andreas—a moderate shaker, no big problems in L.A. After that the underground pressures in Kern County fell dramatically. The geologists think tons of gas were released by the quake, and the gas isn't being replaced."

"My virus kills the petroplague," she said. The words gave sweet satisfaction; she repeated them over and over in her mind.

"That's not all. A lot happened during your eighteen-hour nap."

"They must have given me something to make me sleep," she said, embarrassed.

"Of course they did. But it's a pity you missed it."

"Don't tease, tell me!"

"Those survivalist crackpots carried out their plan. Mini plague outbreaks sprang up all over the place last night. But we're harvesting your virus from the Midway-Sunset field via the relief wells. By this afternoon, samples of your cure will be chasing down every one of those outbreaks, and preventing any new ones."

It was over, then. She sank into the mattress, an unbearable weight lifted from her shoulders.

"Thank you for believing in me," she said. "Dr. Chen always did."

"Obviously with good reason. I think it's safe to say you did it."

A nurse wearing rose-colored scrubs bustled into the room. She checked the IV drip hanging on a pole next to Christina's bed.

"Did the mayor tell you he's a hero?" the nurse said.

"I just heard," Christina said. "He conquered the petroplague."

The nurse opened the blinds to let in more sunlight. "Not that," she said. "He landed—if you can call it that—in the traffic circle not twenty yards from the emergency room here at Bakersfield Memorial. Quite a feat without an engine."

She breezed out of the room saying, "I'll have your breakfast sent up."

Christina gaped at Felipe. "What happened?"

He cast his gaze down at his hands. "I knew the petroplague had infected our helicopter, but I had to get you to a hospital. I'm sorry, I shouldn't have taken the risk. But we almost made it."

"You risked your life to bring me here?" she said gently.

He looked into her eyes and her heart fluttered.

"I'm becoming something of an expert at crash landings," he said.

CHAPTER 82

Tequila Jack heard them coming.

Federal agents weren't so stupid as to blare their sirens when they approached the hidden canyon, but like an animal in a familiar lair, Jack knew something was amiss. And he'd been expecting them. A surveillance helicopter flew over the cabin at dawn. They'd found him at last. The winding roads through the Angeles National Forest would slow them down. He had time to run, and with his skills and knowledge of the mountains, he could slip away. But since the petroplague plot failed, he was a diminished man. All his life he'd been impulsive, a person of action. Waiting and hiding were against his nature. This federal raid to arrest him was an opportunity. For glory and honor, Tequila Jack chose to stay and fight.

The rumble of engines on the fire road reached his ears. He trained his rifle scope on the path leading up to the cabin, but trees limited his view. The attackers would have a hard time of it. Because the back of his cabin was dug into the mountain, they could only get at him from the front or sides. If it weren't for his dog Manley, Jack would've set booby traps and brought the whole place down on them.

Booted feet cracked dry twigs and leaves closer and closer to the cabin, but still he saw no one. Finally a voice bellowed from a loudspeaker.

"Jonathon Sandler, this is the FBI. Please come out with your hands up."

Waco time.

He fired into the woods, randomly spraying bullets through the shattered window. The ferocious noise of his rifle sent Manley flying into the back room. The federal agents returned fire.

A pang of regret pierced him when the dog left. If he thought he could go on the lam with Manley, he might have chosen differently. But the fugitive life would put them both in danger. It was better this way. If he played it right, Manley would be unharmed. And even a federal agent wouldn't intentionally hurt a Lab.

Jack shifted to the window on the other side of the cabin and fired again. Then he stood behind the front door, one hand on his gun, the other on the knob.

"Good-bye, boy," he said, and opened the door.

CHAPTER 83

A jazzy little lime green car with the UCLA logo on it zipped into the parking lot at the La Brea Tar Pits. Mickey bounced out of the driver's seat.

"I love this car," he said as River and Christina climbed out the other side. "I'm so glad they're experimenting with the fuel again."

"I've got a soft spot for it, too," River said, patting the roof. "We've had some adventures, haven't we, old girl?"

"Girl? What do you mean, girl? This car is all boy," Mickey said.

"I don't know, when I hear X, I think female," Christina said. "As in X chromosomes."

"Don't get technical on me. I know what I know," Mickey said. "Shall we?"

He motioned for Christina to lead the way into Hancock Park. She obliged, carrying a purse-sized nylon pouch and a bouquet of freshly-cut white calla lilies. They followed the original path toward Pit 91 a short distance, until the path was swallowed by a puddle of liquid asphalt and they had to take a detour.

"Wow, this place has changed," River said.

"You haven't been here since before the petroplague, have you?" Christina said.

They reached what was left of Pit 91 and stood in silent respect by a memorial plaque posted in honor of Linda, who had perished there one year ago today. No one would dig at this site again; the pit had completely filled with tar. Christina tossed the lilies into the simmering muck and watched them slowly sink beneath the surface.

Rest in peace, Linda, she prayed and made the Sign of the Cross. She added a prayer for Dr. Chen, too.

They left Pit 91 and all its memories, and wandered to another corner of the park.

"Still smells as bad as ever," Mickey said.

Christina noted the odor of hydrogen sulfide, a foul but reassuring reminder that all was normal at La Brea.

"The disruption caused by the petroplague changed the locations of the tar seeps," she said. "The old Lake Pit doubled in size. We've also got several new pits, including the one that opened under the art museum. But the lawn has recovered pretty well. See? Lots of green grass again."

"So your boyfriend has his parks department working overtime. Great. Can we get this over with and go back to the car?" Mickey said while holding his nose.

"That's the sweet smell of my doctoral degree you're dissing," Christina said. She unzipped the nylon pouch and removed an assortment of test tubes and sampling equipment. "The microbial ecology of this place changed completely when the petroplague bacteria took over. After they were killed by my virus, new ecological niches opened for a variety of bacteria that are entirely new to science."

She dipped a sterile scoop into a bubbling black pool.

"I'm going to get a species named after me," she said.

THE END

Technical notes from Professor Rogers

Oil-eating bacteria and syntrophy

Hydrocarbons are a rich energy source that can be used as food by some types of bacteria. These oil-eating bacteria, especially certain species of *Pseudomonas*, are natural and common. Bacteria's ability to degrade hydrocarbons can be exploited by humans to help us clean up oil spills in a process called bioremediation. With bioremediation, oil-eating bacteria that naturally exist in the environment are encouraged to eat more oil faster by giving them oxygen and fertilizers (potassium and nitrogen). After the Exxon *Valdez* accident in 1989, bioremediation was used effectively to clean up rocks and shallow sands of the Alaskan shoreline, and natural bioremediation played a role in the warm waters of the Gulf of Mexico after the Deepwater Horizon blowout.

The biochemical pathways these oil-eating bacteria use to break down hydrocarbons are aerobic; that is, they require oxygen. Deep underground in oil fields, however, there is little or no oxygen. Completely different biochemical pathways are required to degrade oil in an anaerobic (oxygen-free) environment. The existence of such pathways in bacteria was discovered only recently, around the year 2000. The scientists in PETROPLAGUE use one particular genus of anaerobic oil-eating bacteria: *Syntrophus*. *Syntrophus* species are gram-negative rods which are killed by oxygen (in other words, they're obligate anaerobes). They have several other fascinating properties. *Syntrophus* species are thermophiles; that is, they're happiest when it's hot. Their optimal growth temperature is around 50°C (over 120°F). They also thrive under high pressures (50 to 150 atmospheres). Thus they are well-adapted to survive deep underground.

As described in the book, *Syntrophus* "eat" crude oil, breaking down the hydrocarbons into acetate, hydrogen gas, and carbon dioxide. Because of a negative energy yield, however, these reactions only occur if the products are converted into something else. This means *Syntrophus* cannot survive by itself. It must live in a syntrophic (mutually-dependent) community of several different species of bacteria. In such a community, *Syntrophus* waste (hydrogen, carbon dioxide) is used as food by another species. Typically the other species are methanogens (bacteria that make methane) from the domain *Archaea*. Like *Syntrophus*, these bacteria are obligate anaerobes that thrive at high temperatures and pressures. In this marvelous ecosystem, one organism's trash is another organism's meal, and the two cannot live without each other. (For more details see work by Dr. Michael McInerney of the University of Oklahoma, e.g. *Proc Natl Acad Sci USA* 2007 **104**: 7600-05.)

Working together, these two types of syntrophic bacteria convert crude oil into methane (natural gas). The existence of this process in nature encouraged to scientists (led by Dr. Steve Larter of the University of Calgary) to seek a way to access the energy of low-grade crude oil reserves (such as Canadian tar sands) without physically extracting the viscous petroleum. Larter's research on converting tar sands into natural gas is ongoing. See *Nature* 2008 **451**: 176-180.

Microbial biofuels

Other scientific research described in PETROPLAGUE is also real. Many, many people are trying to find ways to use microorganisms to produce renewable transportation fuels.

The most progress has been made using algae (single-celled plants) to produce biodiesel. (They sometimes call these specially-designed algae "oilgae".) However, real scientists at UCLA led by Dr. James Liao are also using *E. coli* bacteria to produce isobutanol (*Nature* 2008 **451**: 86-89). In PETROPLAGUE, the fictional scientists take on the even more ambitious task of joining this work with a separate effort to make photosynthetic *E. coli*. Real scientists (led by Dr. Jan Liphardt) at UC Berkeley and the Lawrence Berkeley National Lab are modifying *E. coli* to allow them to get their energy from sunlight (*Proc Natl Acad Sci USA* 2007; **104**: 2408-12).

Lateral gene transfers

In PETROPLAGUE, Christina and Dr. Chen use genetic engineering to make their *Syntrophus* bacteria more efficient at breaking down hydrocarbons. But later, when the bacteria are released into the environment around the gas station, they undergo additional genetic changes on their own.

The change from anaerobe (killed by oxygen) to aerobe (living with oxygen) is not trivial, and it takes more than a single random mutation. In fact it would require the transfer of entire genes from one bacterium to another. And believe it or not, this is not only possible, it's natural and common. Bacteria have sex. Yes, two bacteria can hook up via a "conjugation bridge" and exchange DNA with one another. This process is called lateral gene transfer.

Biology of temperate phages
(viruses that infect bacteria)

Bacteria, which are single-celled organisms, do indeed suffer from viral infections. Some of the viruses that infect them "choose" between a latent or *lysogenic* phase and a lytic (killer) phase. In the lysogenic phase, the virus hides inside the host bacterium by inserting its DNA into the bacterial DNA. Bacteria carrying a virus like this are called lysogens. In response to certain triggers (such as ultraviolet light), the virus DNA activates and instructs the bacterium to produce new, complete virus particles. When enough new virus has been made, the bacterium breaks open (lyses), and spills virus into the environment.

In PETROPLAGUE, storytelling trumps truth in the timing and efficiency of virus activity. The speed of the virus's effect is accelerated for dramatic reasons. In terms of efficiency, no real virus would ever kill 100% of its target population. No matter how deadly the virus (in humans or bacteria), some potential victims always survive. Those who survive often have some protective trait that they pass on to their offspring. Thus over time, "old" viruses that have been circulating through a population become less dangerous, as the most susceptible individuals are eliminated. This would be a major problem with the petroplague because bacteria reproduce quickly. Christina's virus might slow down the oil-eating activity, but it probably could not end the plague entirely.

Peak oil and Collapsitarians

According to *The Economist* (Dec. 10, 2009), the International Energy Agency believes that based on current discoveries and increasing demand, global conventional oil production will peak in 2020. Personally, that scares the heck out of me. We have a lot of work to do on alternative energy in the next decade if our civilization is going to survive the inevitable transition away from petroleum. But we can kill two birds with one stone: preparations for peak oil are pretty much the same as actions to fight global warming, as both involve a shift from carbon-emitting petroleum to renewable energy sources.

The "collapsitarian" movement is growing. (See the July/August 2009 issue of *Mother Jones* for a smart and snarky summary.) *The New York Times* has also reported on Americans preparing for the end (for example, June 5, 2010 article "Imagining Life Without Oil, and Being Ready").

Earthquakes and gas buildup

I made this stuff up. True, an important part of earthquake prediction is monitoring the pressure in known fault zones. Increases in pressure over time can indicate increased quake risk, and earthquakes often relieve built-up pressure. However, seismic pressures result from tectonic plates of the Earth's crust pressing against each other. It's unlikely that underground gas production—no matter how massive—would generate pressure of a magnitude large enough to affect quake activity. But I'm not a geologist—maybe it could!

Acknowledgments

Writers need information. Thank you, Ken Weeks, for teaching me about the oil industry and introducing me to "pigs".

Writers need critics. Thank you, Elisa Arostegui, Tina Bonilla, Christi Graham, Douglas Perry, Dr. William Pevec, and Michael White for helpful feedback on early *Petroplague* manuscripts.

Writers need other writers. Thank you, California Writers Club and International Thriller Writers, for education, friendship, and much-needed inspiration.

Writers need industry professionals. Thank you, Scott Waxman and Diversion Books, for making this book the best it can be and getting it into the hands of readers.

Writers need fans. Thank you to my first and forever fans: Jim & Sharon Malecki and Bill & Gloria Rogers.

Writers need love. Thank you, Jason. Yours makes all things possible.

If you enjoy this book, please tell your friends or post a review online. Wondering what to read next? Explore the book reviews at my website ScienceThrillers.com, where you can also subscribe to my mailing list and read my blog. Or, follow me on Twitter (@ScienceThriller), Facebook (Amy Rogers fan page), or at AmyRogers.com.

I welcome your comments at amy@amyrogers.com.